MARVEL-VERSE

VENOM

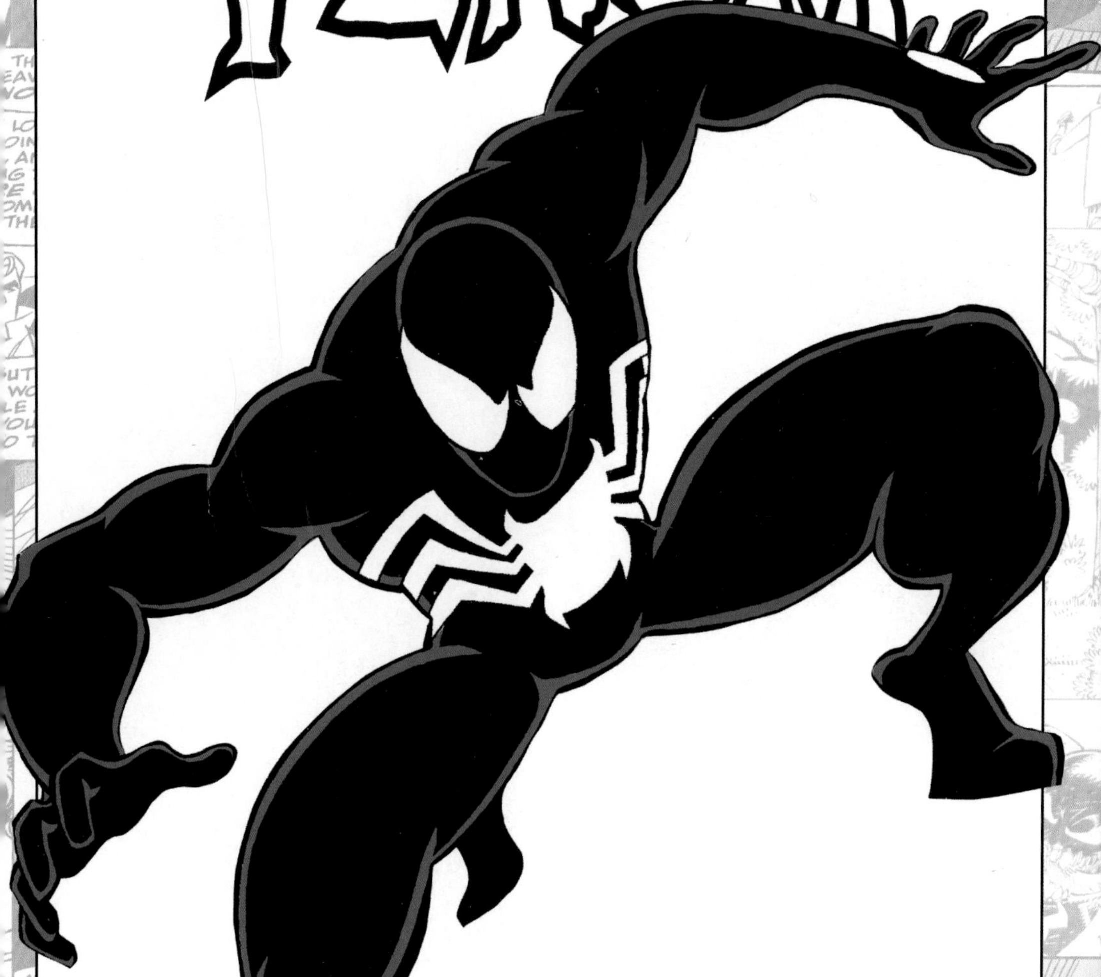

MARVEL-VERSE

VENOM

SPIDER-MAN ADVENTURES #8-10

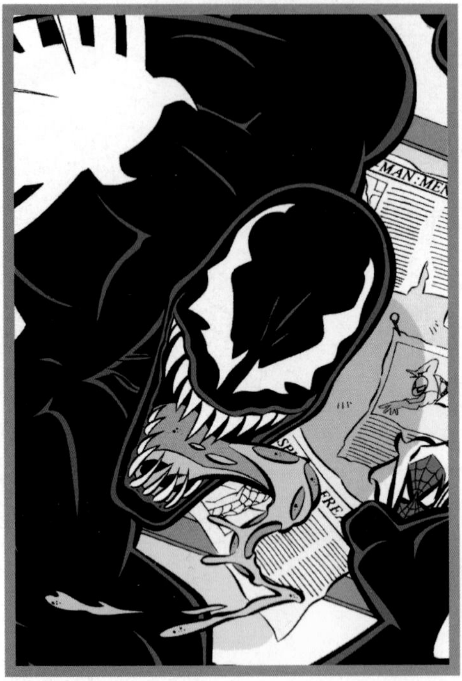

WRITER: NEL YOMTOV
PENCILER: ALEX SAVIUK
INKER: ROB STULL
COLORIST: KEVIN TINSLEY
LETTERER: STEVE DUTRO
EDITOR: SARRA MOSSOFF

FREELY ADAPTED FROM STORIES BY
AVI ARAD, STAN LEE,
BRYNNE STEPHENS, JOHN SEMPER &
MARK HOFFMEIER; AND TELEPLAYS BY
LEN WEIN, MEG MCLAUGHLIN,
STAN BERKOWITZ, JOHN SEMPER,
BRYNNE STEPHENS &
MARK HOFFMEIER

AMAZING SPIDER-MAN #317

WRITER: DAVID MICHELINIE
ARTIST: TODD McFARLANE
COLORIST: BOB SHAREN
LETTERER: RICK PARKER
ASSISTANT EDITOR: GLENN HERDLING
EDITOR: JIM SALICRUP

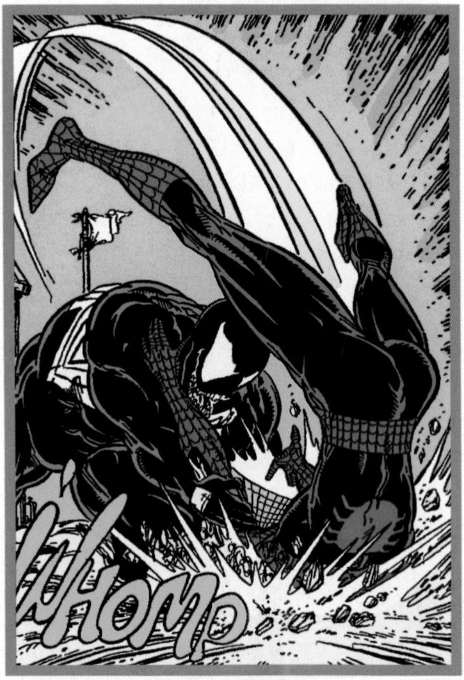
WHOMP

MARVEL ADVENTURES SPIDER-MAN #35

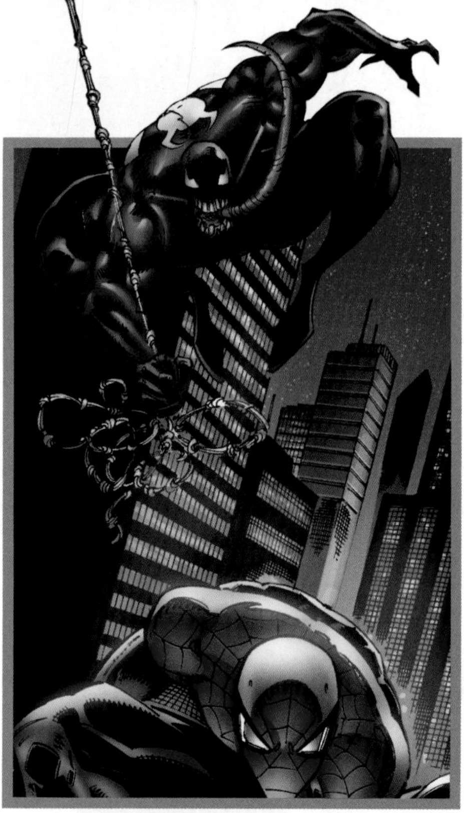

WRITER: **FRED VAN LENTE**

ARTISTS: **CORY HAMSCHER** WITH **TERRY PALLOT**

COLORIST: **GURU-eFX**

LETTERER: **DAVE SHARPE**

COVER ART: **FRANCIS TSAI**

ASSISTANT EDITOR: **NATHAN COSBY**

EDITOR: **MARK PANICCIA**

SNEAK PEEK! SPIDER-MAN & VENOM: DOUBLE TROUBLE GN-TPB

WRITER: **MARIKO TAMAKI**

ARTIST & COLORIST: **GURIHIRU**

LETTERER: **VC's TRAVIS LANHAM**

COVER ART: **GURIHIRU**

ASSISTANT EDITOR: **DANNY KHAZEM**

EDITOR: **DEVIN LEWIS**

EXECUTIVE EDITOR: **NICK LOWE**

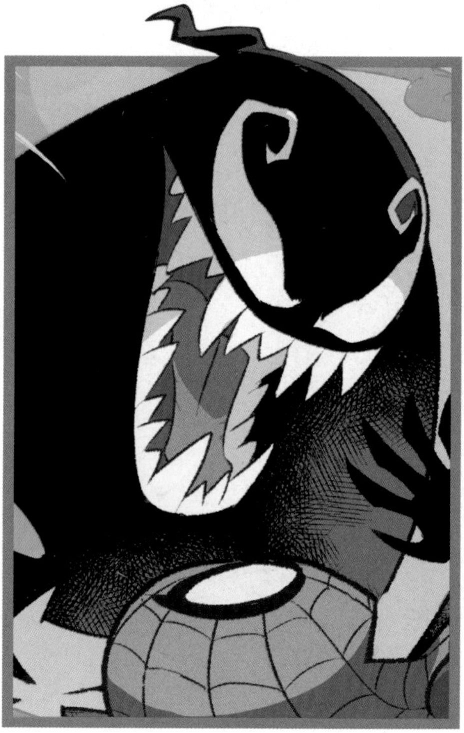

COLLECTION EDITOR: **JENNIFER GRÜNWALD** ASSISTANT EDITOR: **DANIEL KIRCHHOFFER**
ASSISTANT MANAGING EDITOR: **MAIA LOY** ASSOCIATE MANAGER, TALENT RELATIONS: **LISA MONTALBANO**
ASSOCIATE MANAGER, DIGITAL ASSETS: **JOE HOCHSTEIN** VP PRODUCTION & SPECIAL PROJECTS: **JEFF YOUNGQUIST**
RESEARCH: **JESS HARROLD & JEPH YORK** PRODUCTION: **JERRON QUALITY COLOR, COLORTEK & DAN KIRCHHOFFER**
BOOK DESIGNERS: **STACIE ZUCKER** AND **ADAM DEL RE** WITH **JAY BOWEN**

SVP PRINT, SALES & MARKETING: **DAVID GABRIEL** EDITOR IN CHIEF: **C.B. CEBULSKI**

MARVEL-VERSE: VENOM. MARVEL-VERSE: VENOM. Contains material originally published in magazine form as SPIDER-MAN ADVENTURES (1994) #8-10, AMAZING SPIDER-MAN (1963) #317, and MARVEL ADVENTURES SPIDER-MAN (2005) #35. Second printing 2021. ISBN 978-1-302-92535-2. Published by MARVEL WORLDWIDE, INC., a subsidiary of MARVEL ENTERTAINMENT, LLC. OFFICE OF PUBLICATION: 1290 Avenue of the Americas, New York, NY 10104. © 2020 MARVEL No similarity between any of the names, characters, persons, and/or institutions in this book with those of any living or dead person or institution is intended, and any such similarity which may exist is purely coincidental. **Printed in Canada.** KEVIN FEIGE, Chief Creative Officer; DAN BUCKLEY, President, Marvel Entertainment; JOE QUESADA, EVP & Creative Director; DAVID BOGART, Associate Publisher & SVP of Talent Affairs; TOM BREVOORT, VP, Executive Editor; NICK LOWE, Executive Editor, VP of Content, Digital Publishing; DAVID GABRIEL, VP of Print & Digital Publishing; JEFF YOUNGQUIST, VP of Production & Special Projects; ALEX MORALES, Director of Publishing Operations; DAN EDINGTON, Managing Editor; RICKEY PURDIN, Director of Talent Relations; JENNIFER GRÜNWALD, Senior Editor, Special Projects; SUSAN CRESPI, Production Manager; STAN LEE, Chairman Emeritus. For information regarding advertising in Marvel Comics or on Marvel.com, please contact Vit DeBellis, Custom Solutions & Integrated Advertising Manager, at vdebellis@marvel.com. For Marvel subscription inquiries, please call 888-511-5480. **Manufactured between 12/24/2021 and 1/25/2022 by SOLISCO PRINTERS, SCOTT, QC, CANADA.**

10 9 8 7 6 5 4 3 2

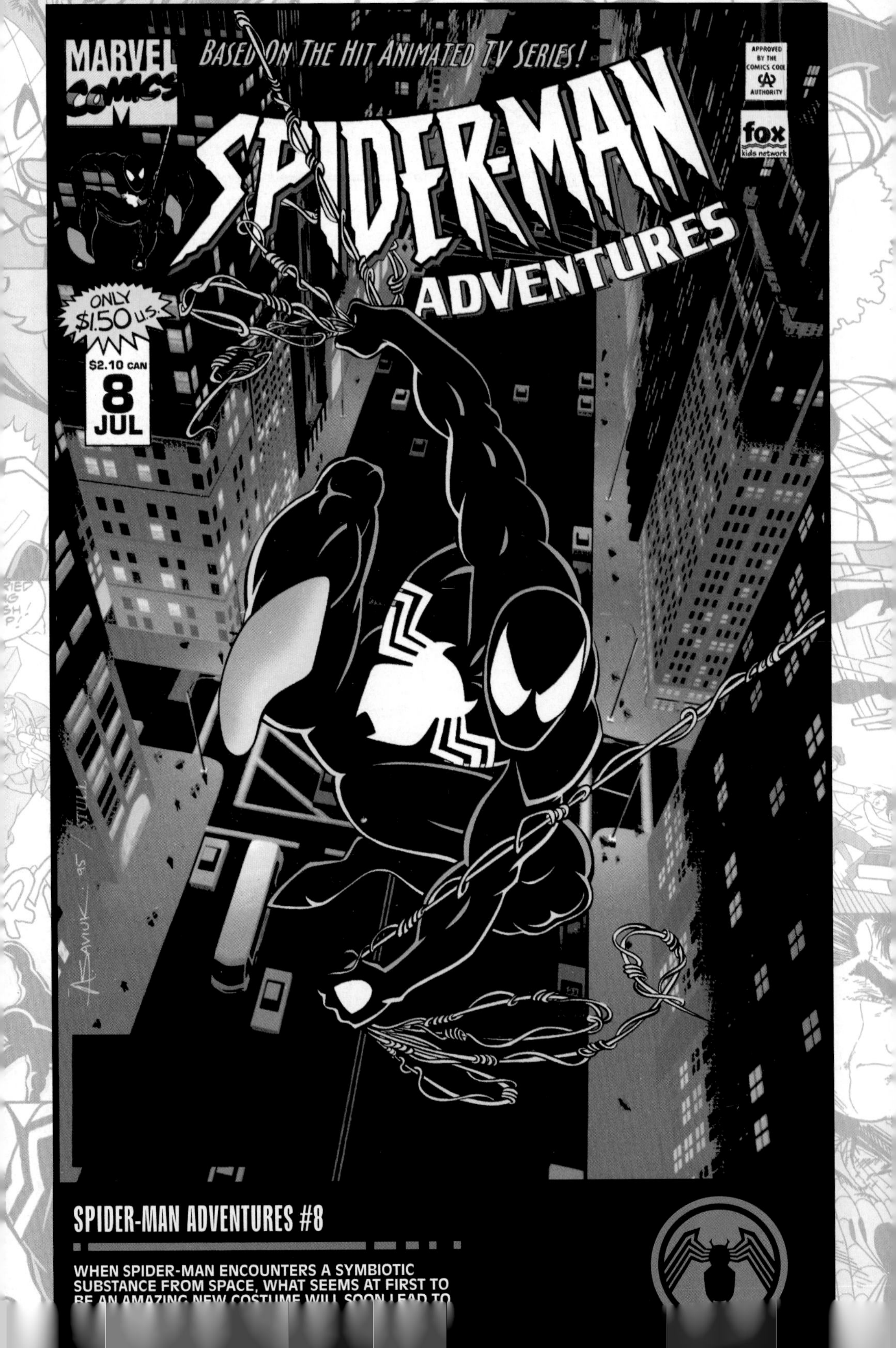
MARVEL COMICS
BASED ON THE HIT ANIMATED TV SERIES!
APPROVED BY THE COMICS CODE AUTHORITY
fox kids network
SPIDER-MAN
ADVENTURES
ONLY $1.50 U.S.
$2.10 CAN
8
JUL

SPIDER-MAN ADVENTURES #8

WHEN SPIDER-MAN ENCOUNTERS A SYMBIOTIC SUBSTANCE FROM SPACE, WHAT SEEMS AT FIRST TO BE AN AMAZING NEW COSTUME WILL SOON LEAD TO

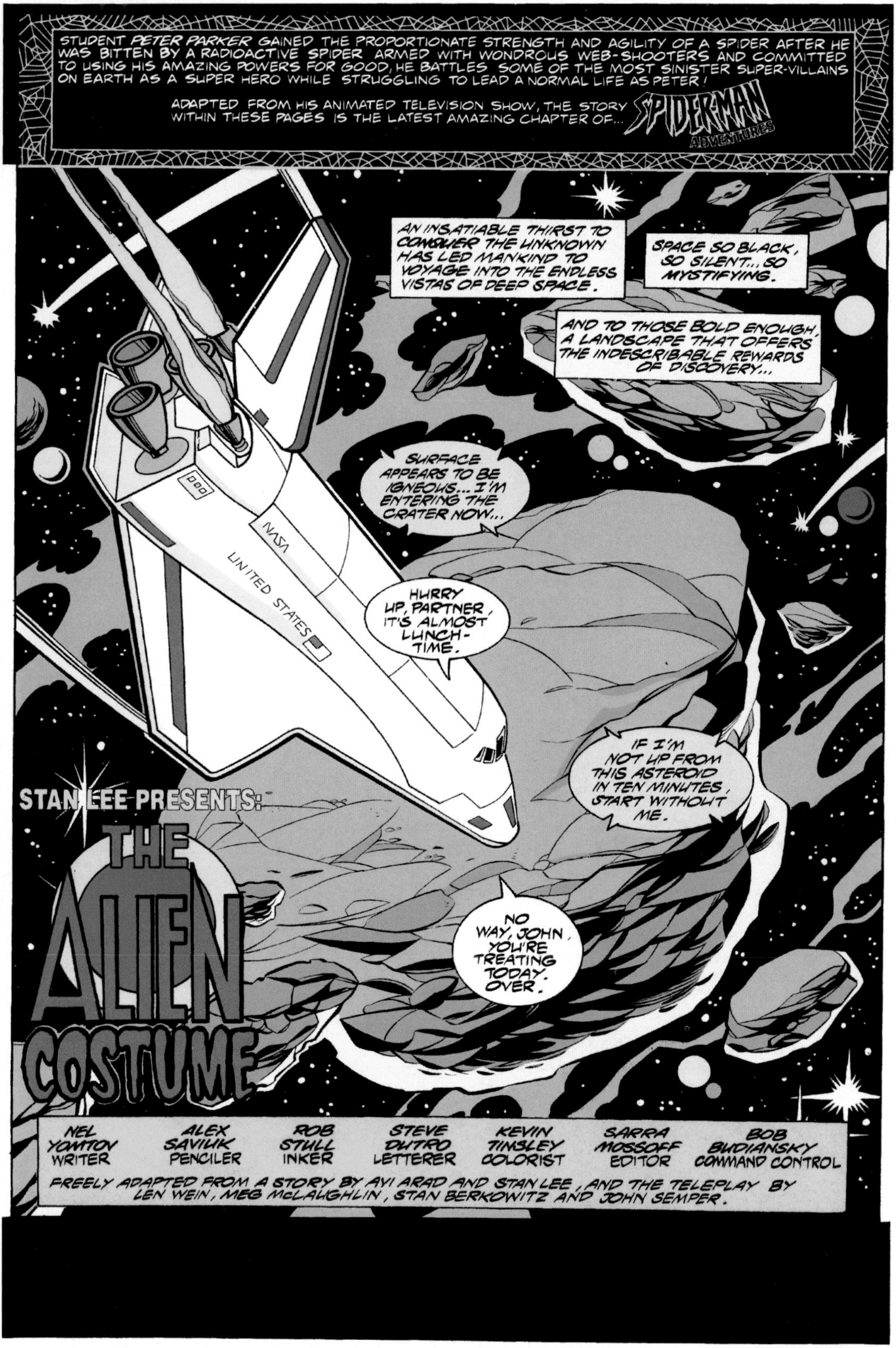
STUDENT PETER PARKER GAINED THE PROPORTIONATE STRENGTH AND AGILITY OF A SPIDER AFTER HE WAS BITTEN BY A RADIOACTIVE SPIDER. ARMED WITH WONDROUS WEB-SHOOTERS AND COMMITTED TO USING HIS AMAZING POWERS FOR GOOD, HE BATTLES SOME OF THE MOST SINISTER SUPER-VILLAINS ON EARTH AS A SUPER HERO WHILE STRUGGLING TO LEAD A NORMAL LIFE AS PETER!
ADAPTED FROM HIS ANIMATED TELEVISION SHOW, THE STORY WITHIN THESE PAGES IS THE LATEST AMAZING CHAPTER OF... SPIDER-MAN ADVENTURES
AN INSATIABLE THIRST TO CONQUER THE UNKNOWN HAS LED MANKIND TO VOYAGE INTO THE ENDLESS VISTAS OF DEEP SPACE.
SPACE SO BLACK, SO SILENT... SO MYSTIFYING.
AND TO THOSE BOLD ENOUGH, A LANDSCAPE THAT OFFERS THE INDESCRIBABLE REWARDS OF DISCOVERY...
SURFACE APPEARS TO BE IGNEOUS... I'M ENTERING THE CRATER NOW...
NASA
UNITED STATES
HURRY UP, PARTNER, IT'S ALMOST LUNCH-TIME.
IF I'M NOT UP FROM THIS ASTEROID IN TEN MINUTES, START WITHOUT ME.
NO WAY, JOHN, YOU'RE TREATING TODAY. OVER.
STAN LEE PRESENTS:
THE ALIEN COSTUME
NEL YOMTOV WRITER
ALEX SAVIUK PENCILER
ROB STULL INKER
STEVE DUTRO LETTERER
KEVIN TINSLEY COLORIST
SARRA MOSSOFF EDITOR
BOB BUDIANSKY COMMAND CONTROL
FREELY ADAPTED FROM A STORY BY AVI ARAD AND STAN LEE, AND THE TELEPLAY BY LEN WEIN, MEG McLAUGHLIN, STAN BERKOWITZ AND JOHN SEMPER.

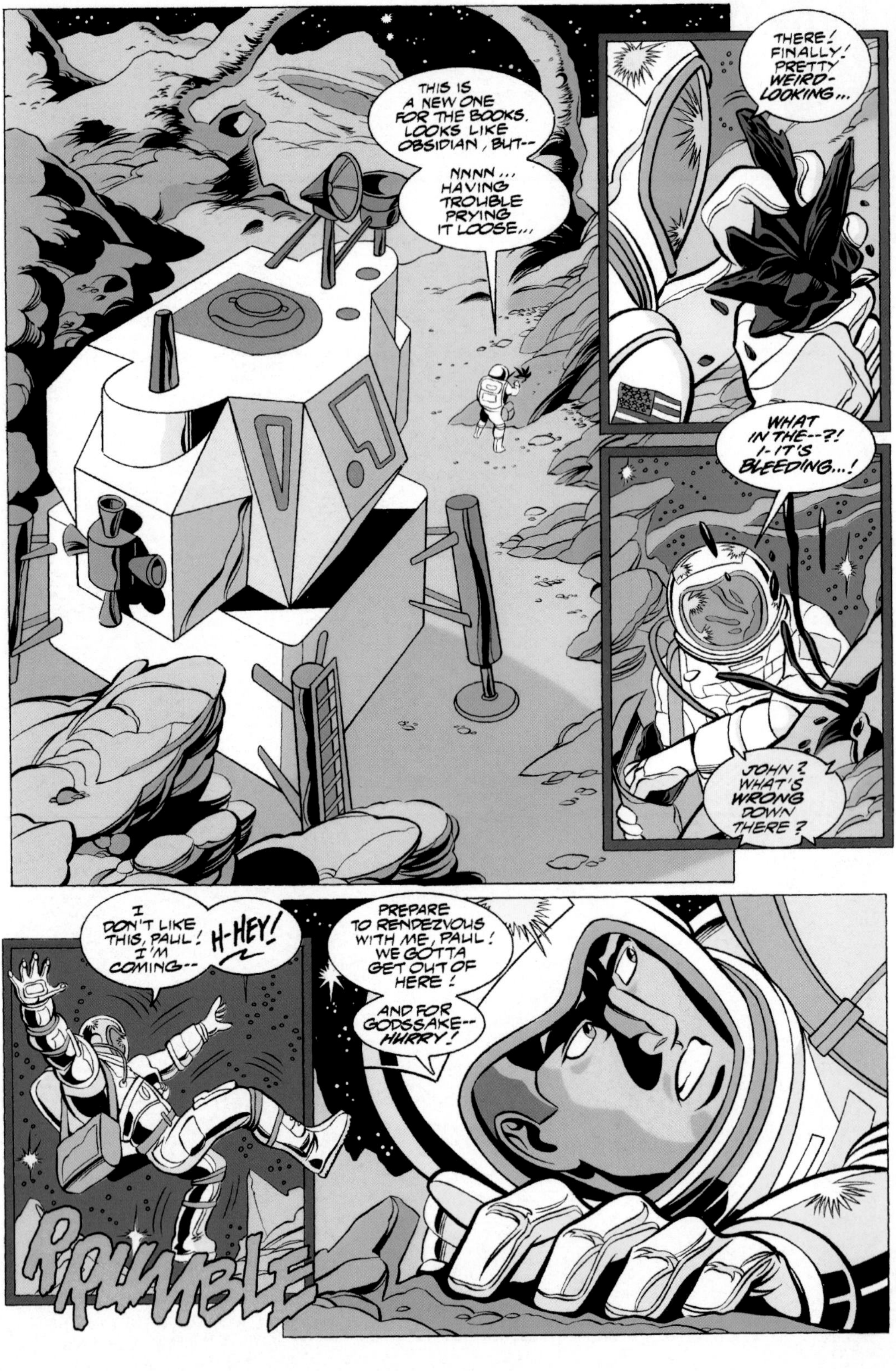
THIS IS A NEW ONE FOR THE BOOKS. LOOKS LIKE OBSIDIAN, BUT--
NNNN... HAVING TROUBLE PRYING IT LOOSE...
THERE! FINALLY! PRETTY WEIRD-LOOKING...
WHAT IN THE--?! I-IT'S BLEEDING...!
JOHN? WHAT'S WRONG DOWN THERE?
I DON'T LIKE THIS, PAUL! I'M COMING--
H-HEY!
PREPARE TO RENDEZVOUS WITH ME, PAUL! WE GOTTA GET OUT OF HERE!
AND FOR GODSSAKE-- HURRY!
RRUMBLE

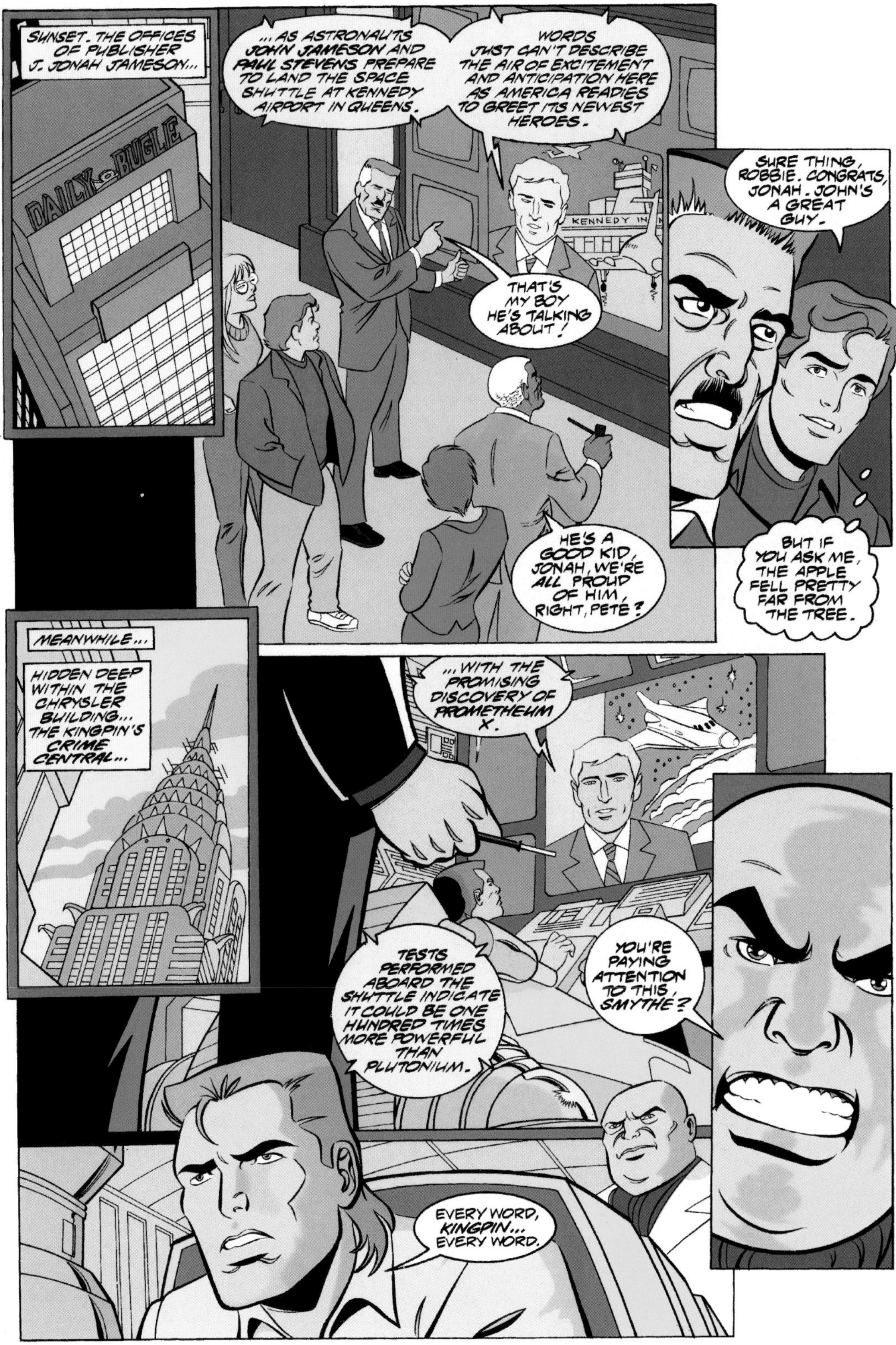

SUNSET. THE OFFICES OF PUBLISHER J. JONAH JAMESON...
DAILY BUGLE
...AS ASTRONAUTS JOHN JAMESON AND PAUL STEVENS PREPARE TO LAND THE SPACE SHUTTLE AT KENNEDY AIRPORT IN QUEENS.
WORDS JUST CAN'T DESCRIBE THE AIR OF EXCITEMENT AND ANTICIPATION HERE AS AMERICA READIES TO GREET ITS NEWEST HEROES.
THAT'S MY BOY HE'S TALKING ABOUT!
HE'S A GOOD KID, JONAH. WE'RE ALL PROUD OF HIM. RIGHT, PETE?
SURE THING, ROBBIE. CONGRATS, JONAH. JOHN'S A GREAT GUY.
BUT IF YOU ASK ME, THE APPLE FELL PRETTY FAR FROM THE TREE.
MEANWHILE...
HIDDEN DEEP WITHIN THE CHRYSLER BUILDING... THE KINGPIN'S CRIME CENTRAL...
...WITH THE PROMISING DISCOVERY OF PROMETHEUM X.
TESTS PERFORMED ABOARD THE SHUTTLE INDICATE IT COULD BE ONE HUNDRED TIMES MORE POWERFUL THAN PLUTONIUM.
YOU'RE PAYING ATTENTION TO THIS, SMYTHE?
EVERY WORD, KINGPIN... EVERY WORD.

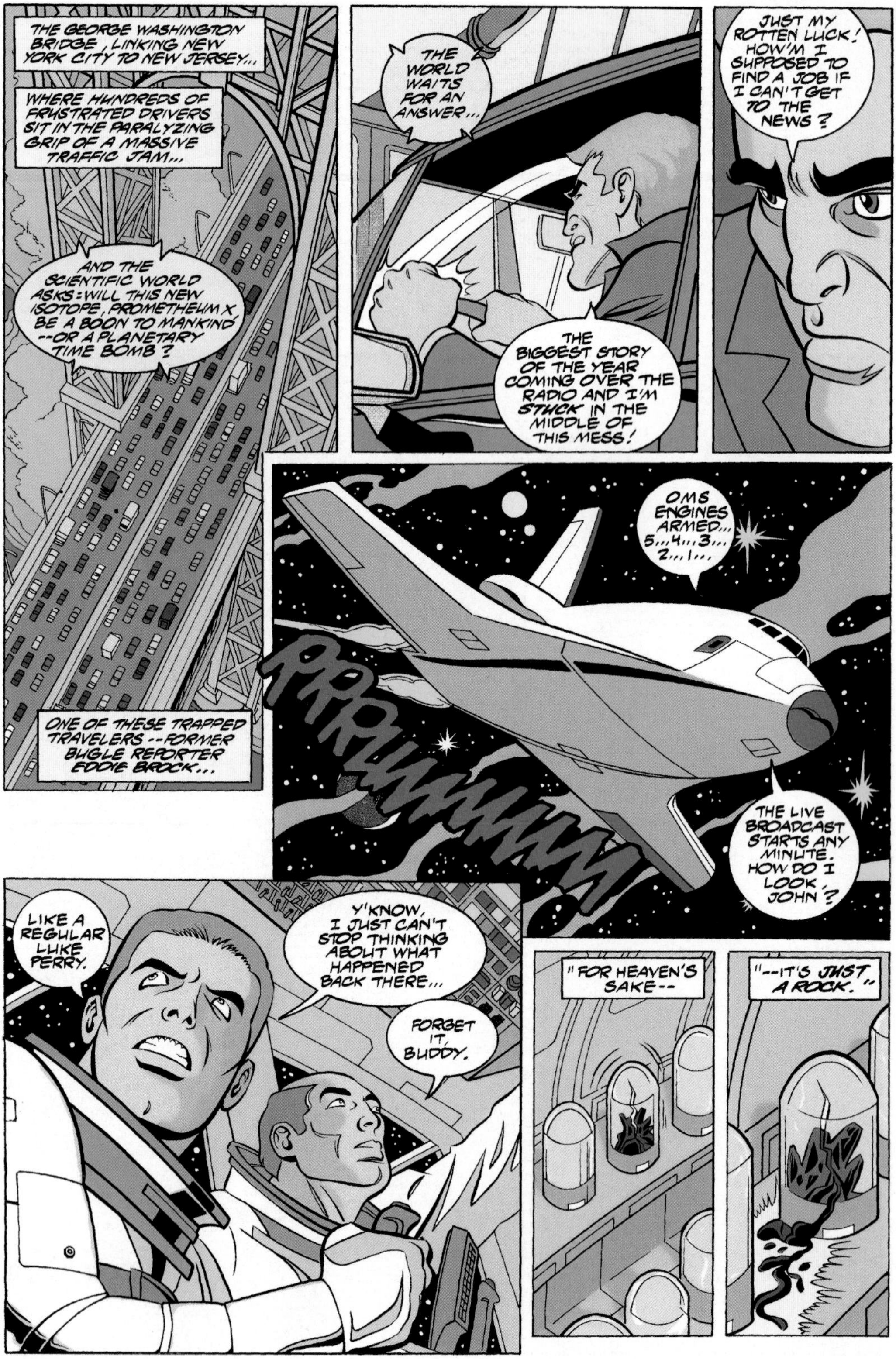
THE GEORGE WASHINGTON BRIDGE, LINKING NEW YORK CITY TO NEW JERSEY...
WHERE HUNDREDS OF FRUSTRATED DRIVERS SIT IN THE PARALYZING GRIP OF A MASSIVE TRAFFIC JAM...
AND THE SCIENTIFIC WORLD ASKS: WILL THIS NEW ISOTOPE, PROMETHEUM X BE A BOON TO MANKIND --OR A PLANETARY TIME BOMB?
ONE OF THESE TRAPPED TRAVELERS --FORMER BUGLE REPORTER EDDIE BROCK...
THE WORLD WAITS FOR AN ANSWER...
THE BIGGEST STORY OF THE YEAR COMING OVER THE RADIO AND I'M STUCK IN THE MIDDLE OF THIS MESS!
JUST MY ROTTEN LUCK! HOW'M I SUPPOSED TO FIND A JOB IF I CAN'T GET TO THE NEWS?
OMS ENGINES ARMED... 5...4...3... 2...1...
PRRUMMMMM
THE LIVE BROADCAST STARTS ANY MINUTE. HOW DO I LOOK, JOHN?
LIKE A REGULAR LUKE PERRY.
Y'KNOW, I JUST CAN'T STOP THINKING ABOUT WHAT HAPPENED BACK THERE...
FORGET IT, BUDDY.
"FOR HEAVEN'S SAKE--
"--IT'S JUST A ROCK."

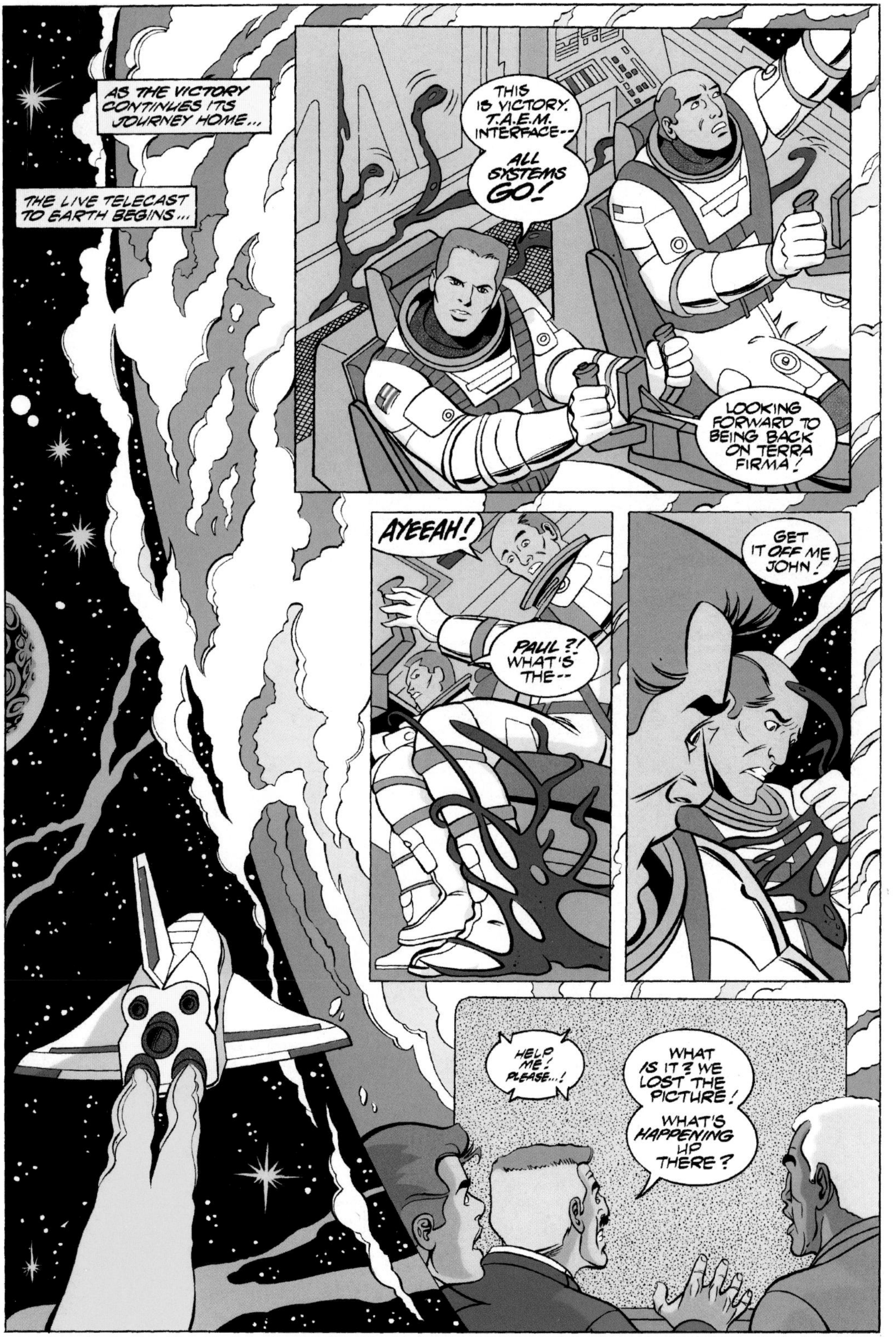
AS THE VICTORY CONTINUES ITS JOURNEY HOME...
THE LIVE TELECAST TO EARTH BEGINS...
THIS IS VICTORY. T.A.E.M. INTERFACE--
ALL SYSTEMS GO!
LOOKING FORWARD TO BEING BACK ON TERRA FIRMA!
AYEEAH!
PAUL?! WHAT'S THE--
GET IT OFF ME JOHN!
HELP ME! PLEASE...!
WHAT IS IT? WE LOST THE PICTURE!
WHAT'S HAPPENING UP THERE?

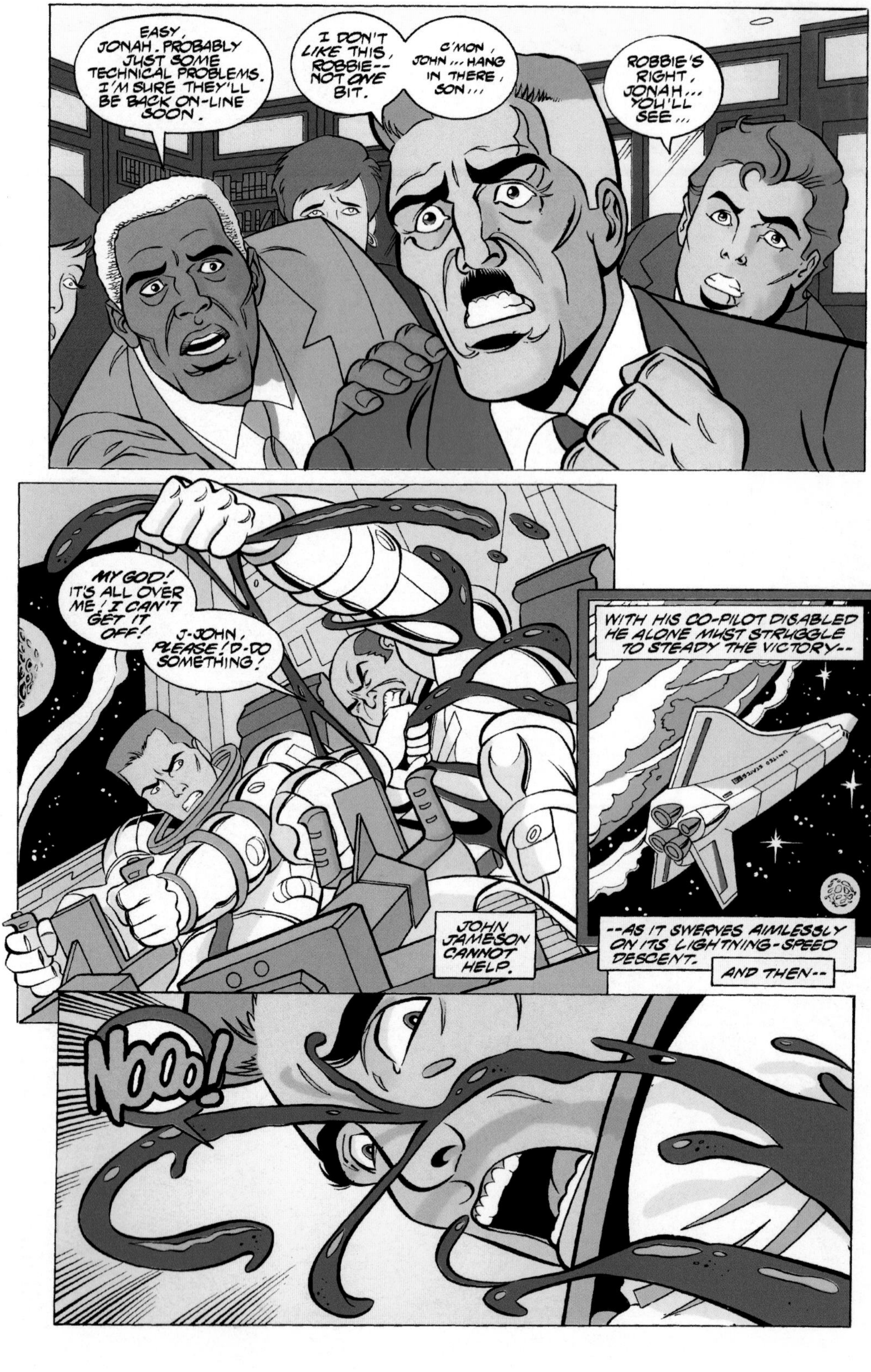

EASY, JONAH. PROBABLY JUST SOME TECHNICAL PROBLEMS. I'M SURE THEY'LL BE BACK ON-LINE SOON.
I DON'T LIKE THIS, ROBBIE-- NOT ONE BIT.
C'MON, JOHN... HANG IN THERE, SON...
ROBBIE'S RIGHT, JONAH... YOU'LL SEE...
MY GOD! IT'S ALL OVER ME! I CAN'T GET IT OFF!
J-JOHN, PLEASE! D-DO SOMETHING!
JOHN JAMESON CANNOT HELP.
WITH HIS CO-PILOT DISABLED HE ALONE MUST STRUGGLE TO STEADY THE VICTORY--
--AS IT SWERVES AIMLESSLY ON ITS LIGHTNING-SPEED DESCENT.
AND THEN--
NOOO!

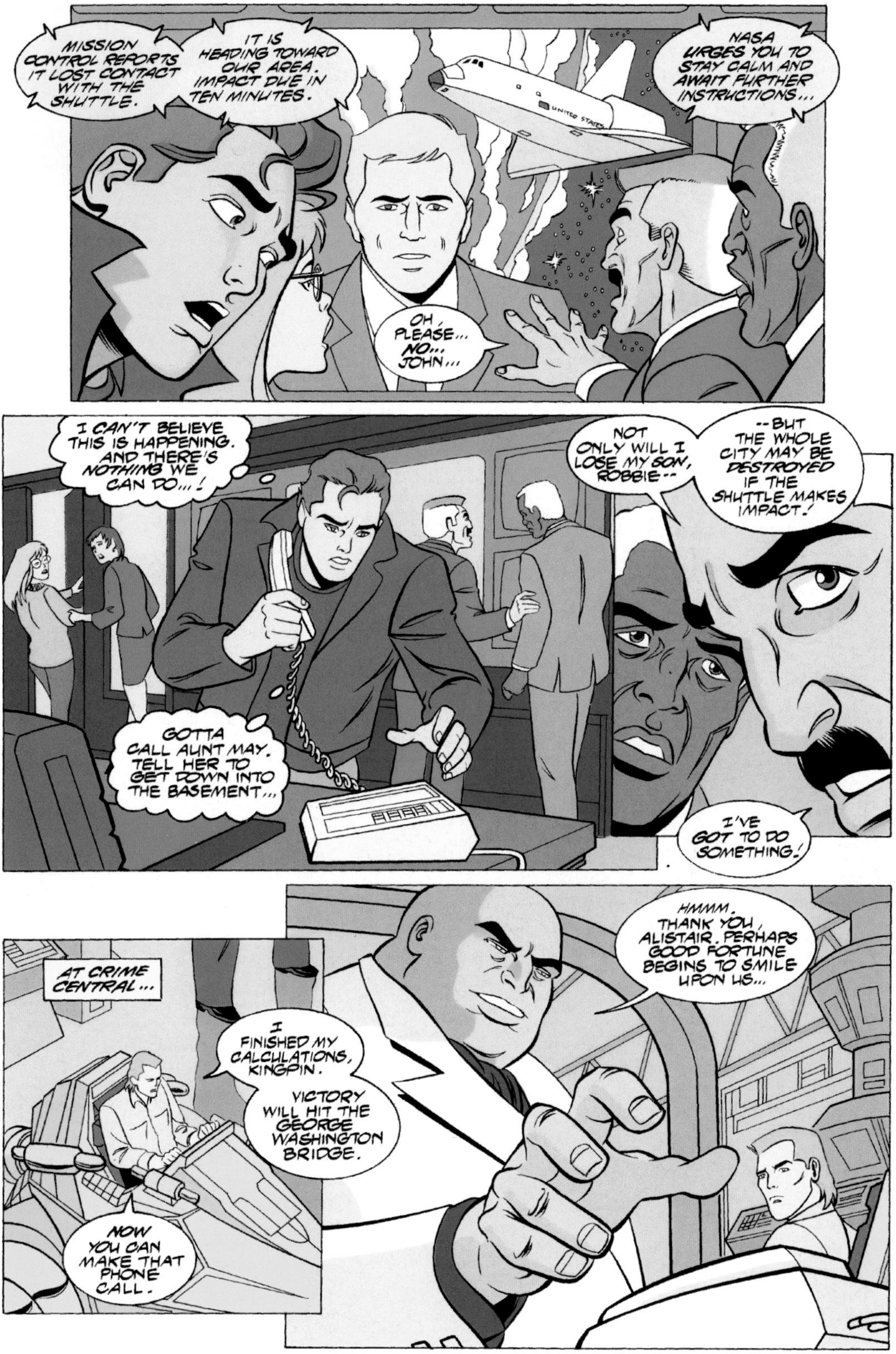
MISSION CONTROL REPORTS IT LOST CONTACT WITH THE SHUTTLE.
IT IS HEADING TOWARD OUR AREA. IMPACT DUE IN TEN MINUTES.
NASA URGES YOU TO STAY CALM AND AWAIT FURTHER INSTRUCTIONS...
OH, PLEASE... NO... JOHN...
I CAN'T BELIEVE THIS IS HAPPENING. AND THERE'S NOTHING WE CAN DO...!
GOTTA CALL AUNT MAY. TELL HER TO GET DOWN INTO THE BASEMENT...
NOT ONLY WILL I LOSE MY SON, ROBBIE--
--BUT THE WHOLE CITY MAY BE DESTROYED IF THE SHUTTLE MAKES IMPACT!
I'VE GOT TO DO SOMETHING!
AT CRIME CENTRAL...
I FINISHED MY CALCULATIONS, KINGPIN.
VICTORY WILL HIT THE GEORGE WASHINGTON BRIDGE.
HMMM. THANK YOU, ALISTAIR. PERHAPS GOOD FORTUNE BEGINS TO SMILE UPON US...
NOW YOU CAN MAKE THAT PHONE CALL.

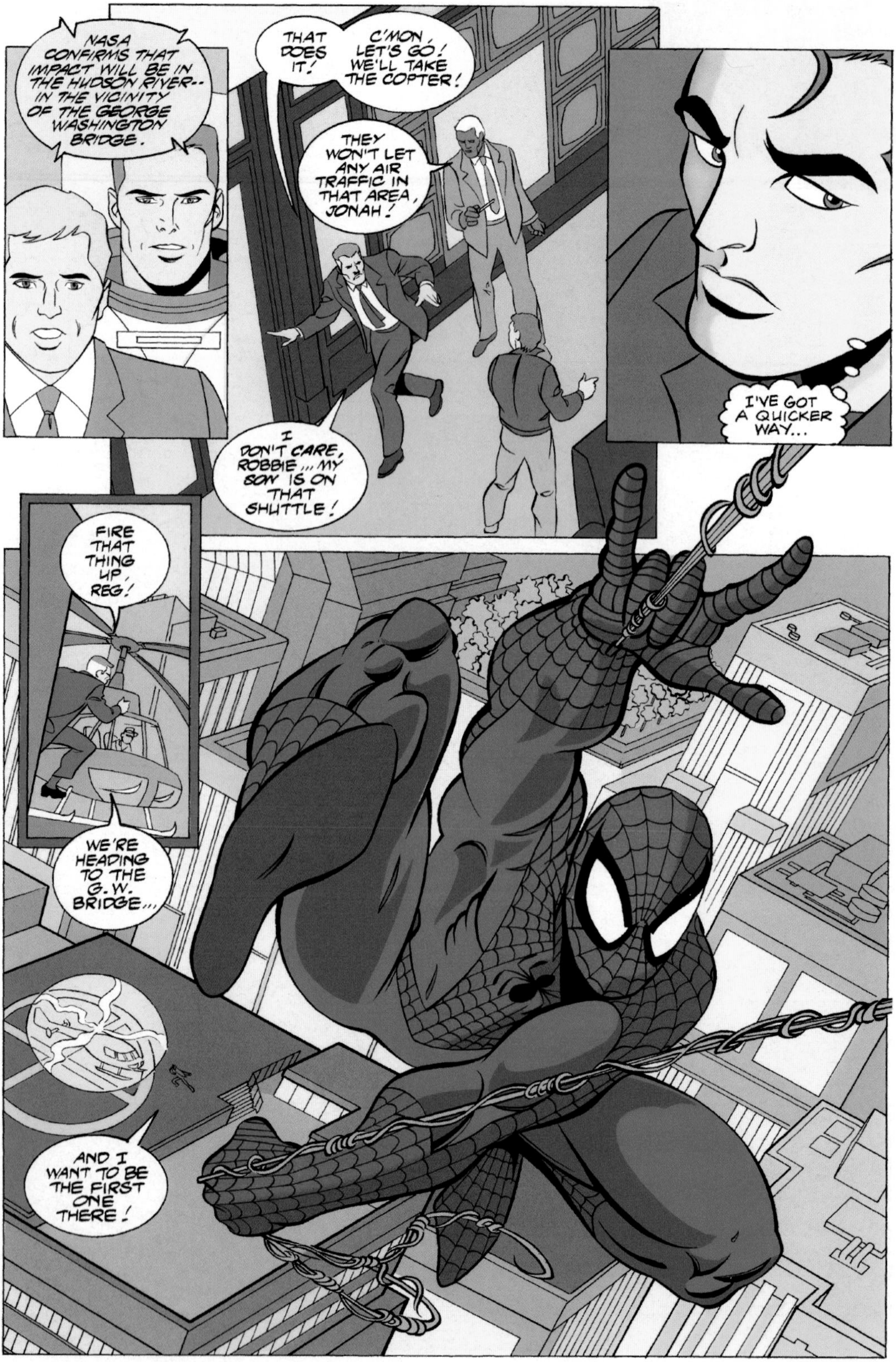
NASA CONFIRMS THAT IMPACT WILL BE IN THE HUDSON RIVER-- IN THE VICINITY OF THE GEORGE WASHINGTON BRIDGE.
THAT DOES IT!
C'MON, LET'S GO! WE'LL TAKE THE COPTER!
THEY WON'T LET ANY AIR TRAFFIC IN THAT AREA, JONAH!
I DON'T CARE, ROBBIE... MY SON IS ON THAT SHUTTLE!
I'VE GOT A QUICKER WAY...
FIRE THAT THING UP, REG!
WE'RE HEADING TO THE G.W. BRIDGE...
AND I WANT TO BE THE FIRST ONE THERE!

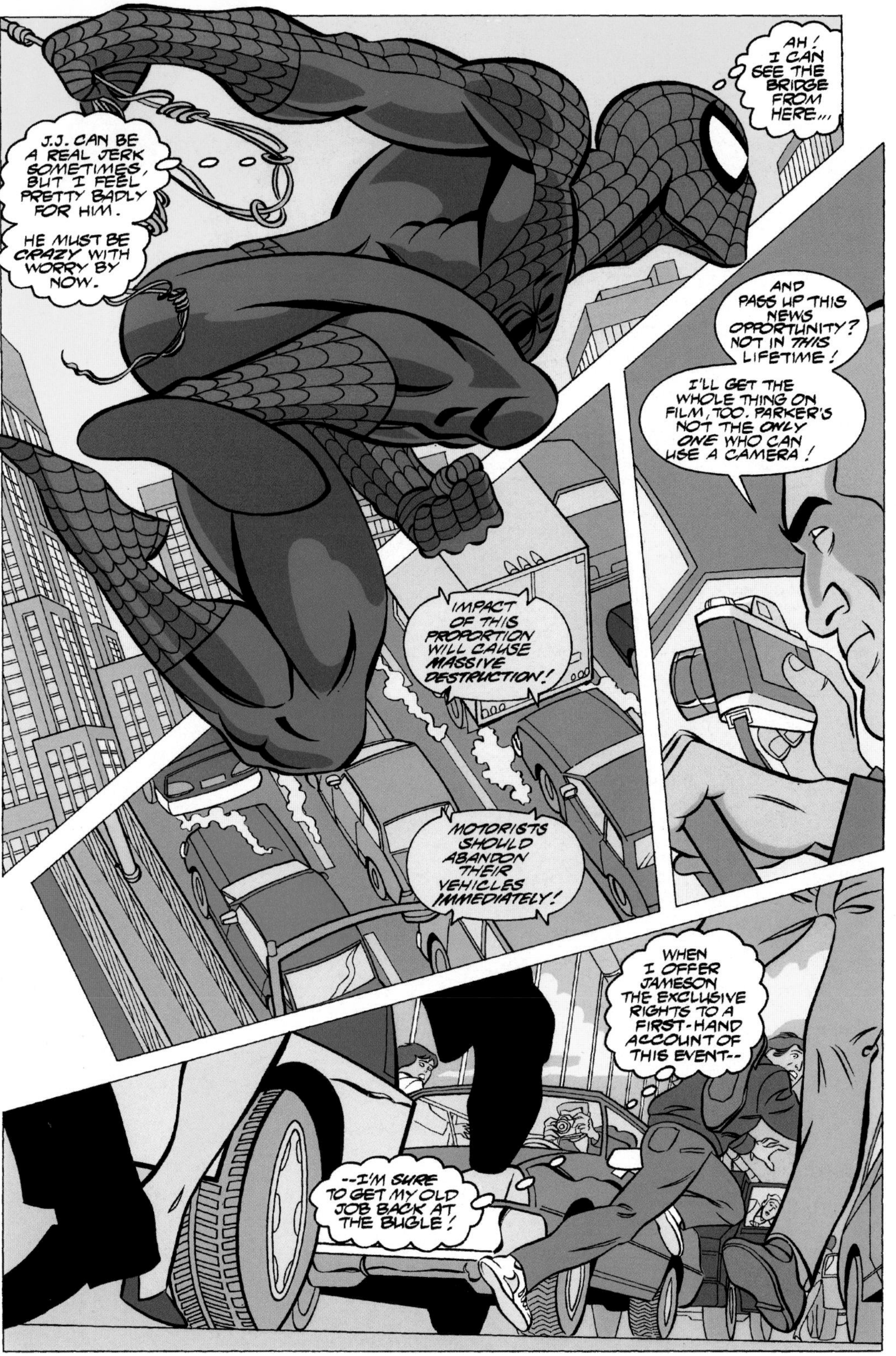
AH! I CAN SEE THE BRIDGE FROM HERE....
J.J. CAN BE A REAL JERK SOMETIMES, BUT I FEEL PRETTY BADLY FOR HIM.
HE MUST BE CRAZY WITH WORRY BY NOW.
AND PASS UP THIS NEWS OPPORTUNITY? NOT IN THIS LIFETIME!
I'LL GET THE WHOLE THING ON FILM, TOO. PARKER'S NOT THE ONLY ONE WHO CAN USE A CAMERA!
IMPACT OF THIS PROPORTION WILL CAUSE MASSIVE DESTRUCTION!
MOTORISTS SHOULD ABANDON THEIR VEHICLES IMMEDIATELY!
WHEN I OFFER JAMESON THE EXCLUSIVE RIGHTS TO A FIRST-HAND ACCOUNT OF THIS EVENT--
--I'M SURE TO GET MY OLD JOB BACK AT THE BUGLE!

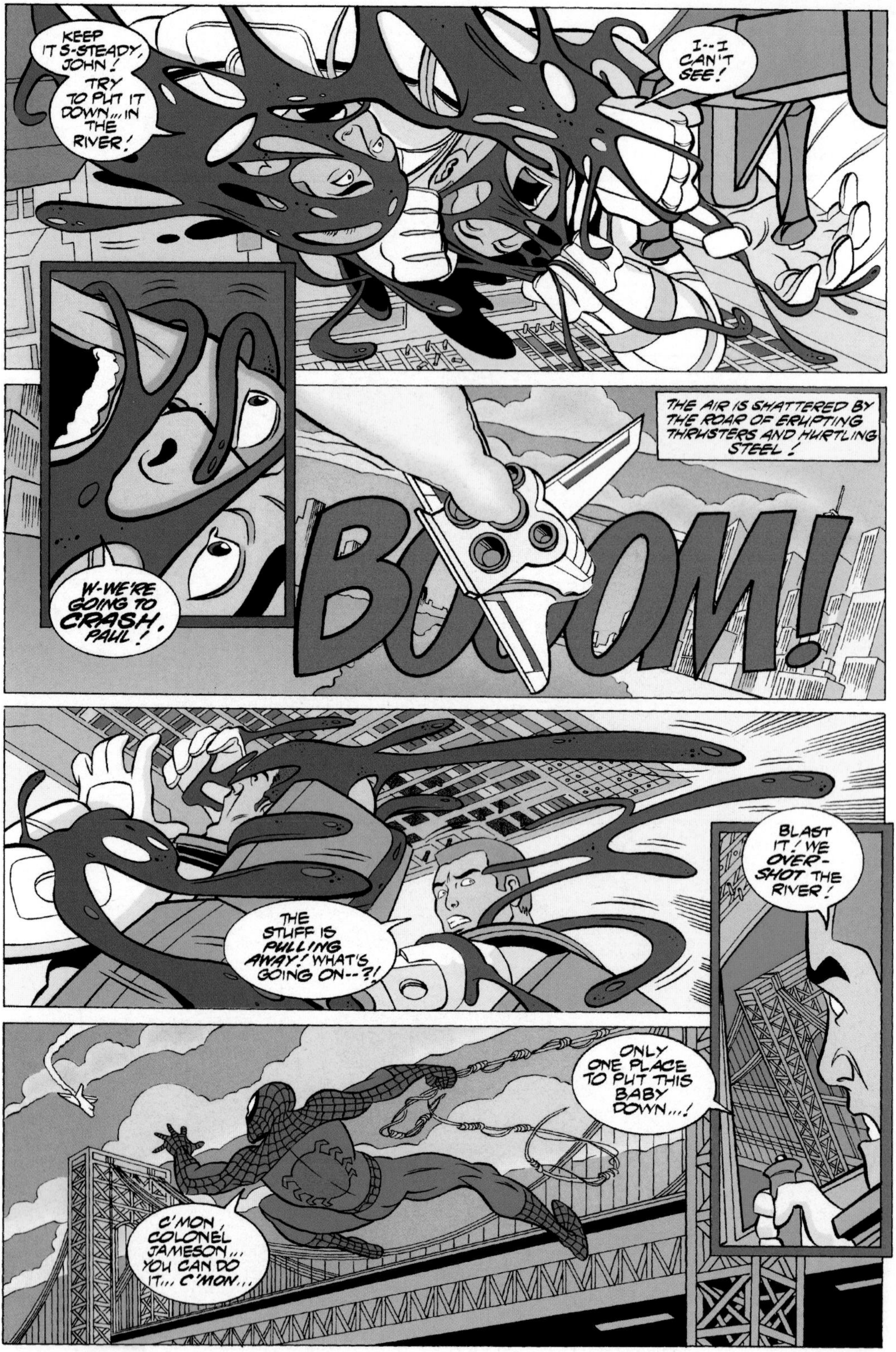
KEEP IT S-STEADY, JOHN! TRY TO PUT IT DOWN... IN THE RIVER!
I--I CAN'T SEE!
THE AIR IS SHATTERED BY THE ROAR OF ERUPTING THRUSTERS AND HURTLING STEEL!
W-WE'RE GOING TO CRASH, PAUL!
BOOOM!
THE STUFF IS PULLING AWAY! WHAT'S GOING ON--?!
BLAST IT! WE OVER-SHOT THE RIVER!
ONLY ONE PLACE TO PUT THIS BABY DOWN...!
C'MON, COLONEL JAMESON... YOU CAN DO IT... C'MON...

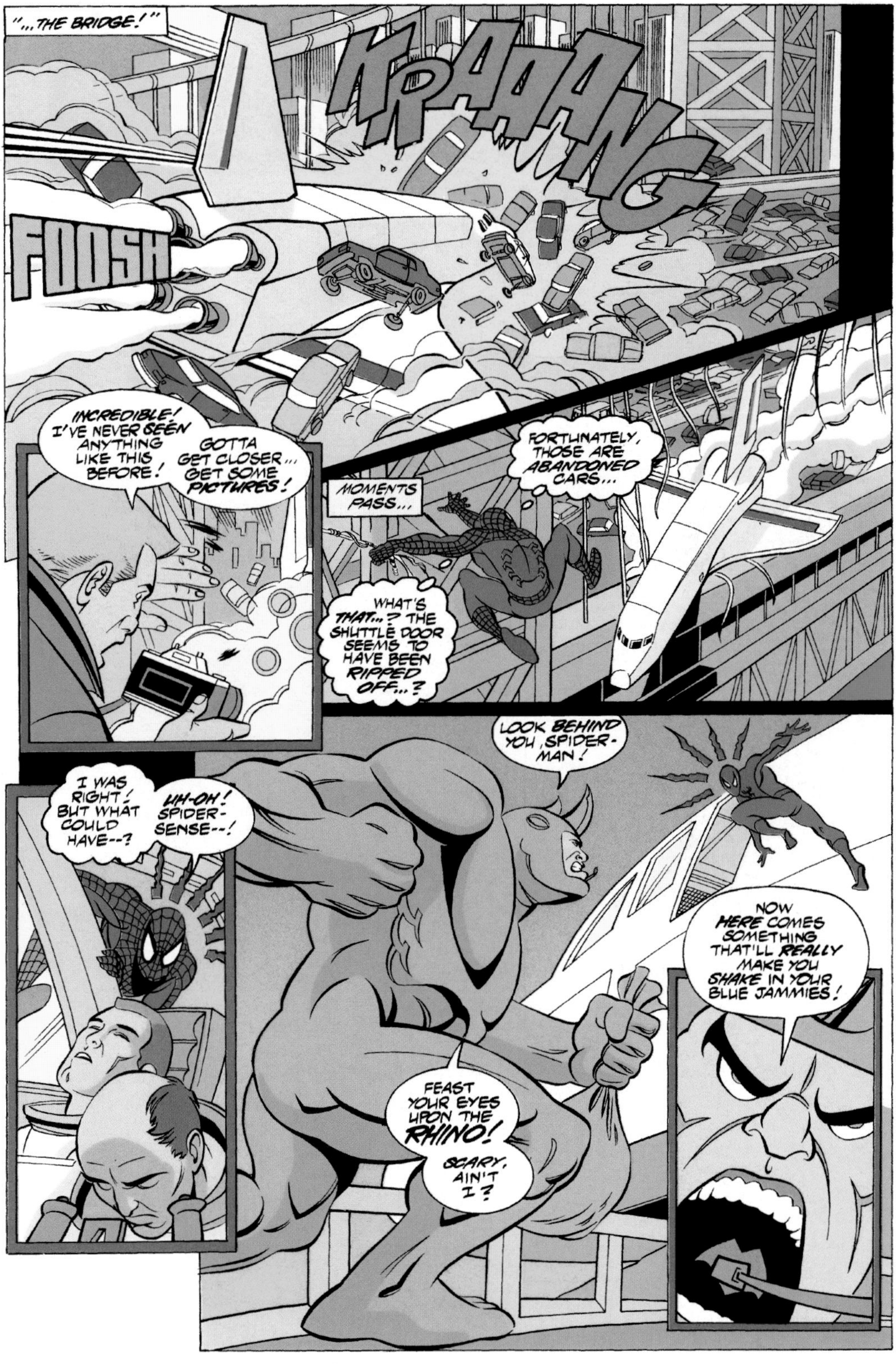

"...THE BRIDGE!"
KRAAAANG
FOOSH
INCREDIBLE! I'VE NEVER SEEN ANYTHING LIKE THIS BEFORE!
GOTTA GET CLOSER... GET SOME PICTURES!
MOMENTS PASS...
FORTUNATELY, THOSE ARE ABANDONED CARS...
WHAT'S THAT...? THE SHUTTLE DOOR SEEMS TO HAVE BEEN RIPPED OFF...?
I WAS RIGHT! BUT WHAT COULD HAVE--?
UH-OH! SPIDER-SENSE--!
LOOK BEHIND YOU, SPIDER-MAN!
FEAST YOUR EYES UPON THE RHINO!
SCARY, AIN'T I?
NOW HERE COMES SOMETHING THAT'LL REALLY MAKE YOU SHAKE IN YOUR BLUE JAMMIES!

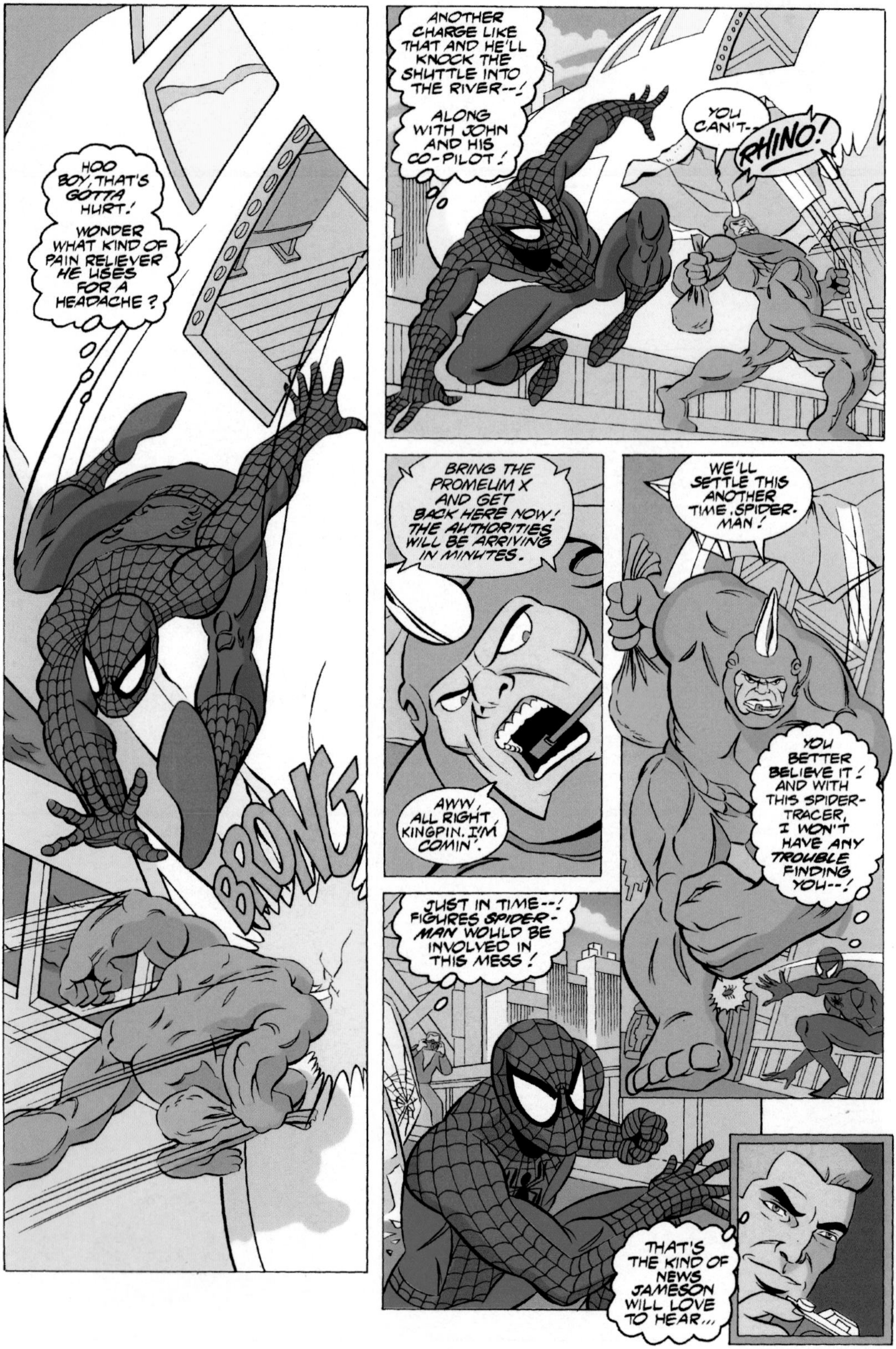
HOO BOY, THAT'S GOTTA HURT! WONDER WHAT KIND OF PAIN RELIEVER HE USES FOR A HEADACHE?
BRONG
ANOTHER CHARGE LIKE THAT AND HE'LL KNOCK THE SHUTTLE INTO THE RIVER--! ALONG WITH JOHN AND HIS CO-PILOT!
YOU CAN'T--
RHINO!
BRING THE PROMEUM X AND GET BACK HERE NOW! THE AUTHORITIES WILL BE ARRIVING IN MINUTES.
AWW, ALL RIGHT, KINGPIN. I'M COMIN'.
WE'LL SETTLE THIS ANOTHER TIME, SPIDER-MAN!
YOU BETTER BELIEVE IT! AND WITH THIS SPIDER-TRACER, I WON'T HAVE ANY TROUBLE FINDING YOU--!
JUST IN TIME--! FIGURES SPIDER-MAN WOULD BE INVOLVED IN THIS MESS!
THAT'S THE KIND OF NEWS JAMESON WILL LOVE TO HEAR...

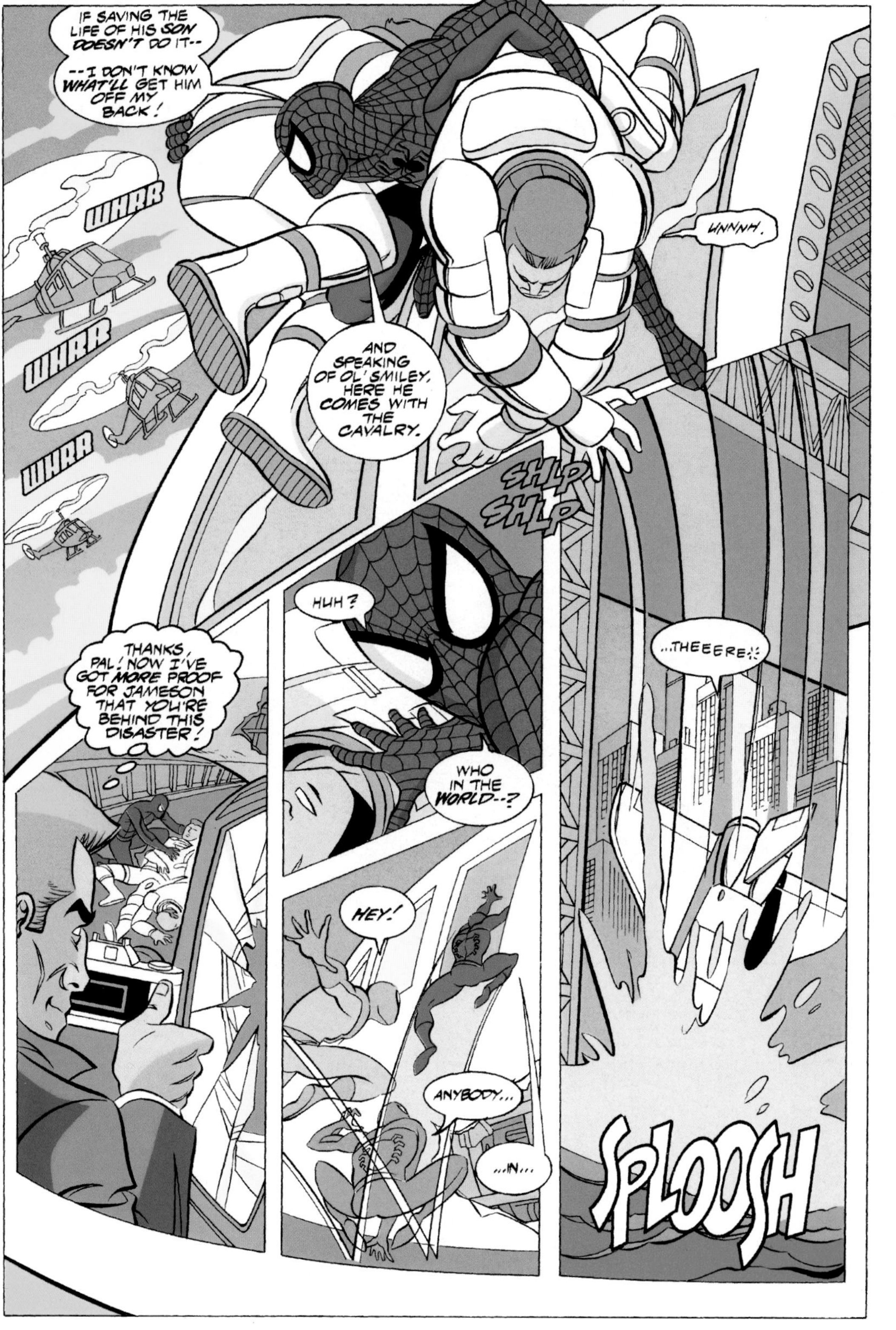
IF SAVING THE LIFE OF HIS SON DOESN'T DO IT--
--I DON'T KNOW WHAT'LL GET HIM OFF MY BACK!
WHRR
WHRR
WHRR
UNNNH.
AND SPEAKING OF OL' SMILEY, HERE HE COMES WITH THE CAVALRY.
SHLP SHLP
THANKS, PAL! NOW I'VE GOT MORE PROOF FOR JAMESON THAT YOU'RE BEHIND THIS DISASTER!
HUH?
WHO IN THE WORLD--?
HEY!
ANYBODY...
...IN...
...THEEERE!
SPLOOSH

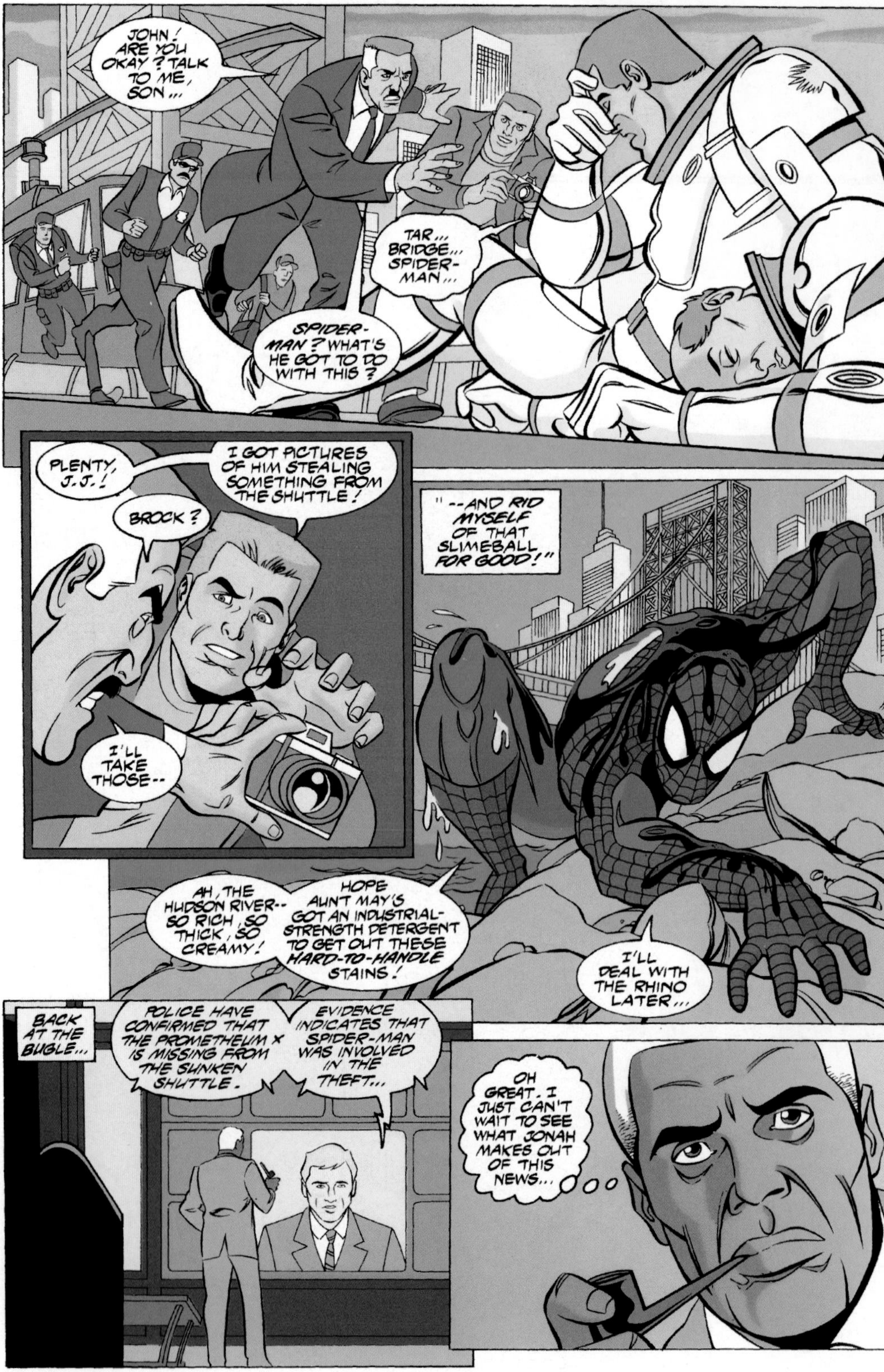
JOHN! ARE YOU OKAY? TALK TO ME, SON...
TAR... BRIDGE... SPIDER-MAN...
SPIDER-MAN? WHAT'S HE GOT TO DO WITH THIS?
PLENTY, J.J.!
I GOT PICTURES OF HIM STEALING SOMETHING FROM THE SHUTTLE!
BROCK?
I'LL TAKE THOSE--
"--AND RID MYSELF OF THAT SLIMEBALL FOR GOOD!"
AH, THE HUDSON RIVER-- SO RICH, SO THICK, SO CREAMY!
HOPE AUNT MAY'S GOT AN INDUSTRIAL-STRENGTH DETERGENT TO GET OUT THESE HARD-TO-HANDLE STAINS!
I'LL DEAL WITH THE RHINO LATER...
BACK AT THE BUGLE...
POLICE HAVE CONFIRMED THAT THE PROMETHEUM X IS MISSING FROM THE SUNKEN SHUTTLE.
EVIDENCE INDICATES THAT SPIDER-MAN WAS INVOLVED IN THE THEFT...
OH GREAT. I JUST CAN'T WAIT TO SEE WHAT JONAH MAKES OUT OF THIS NEWS...

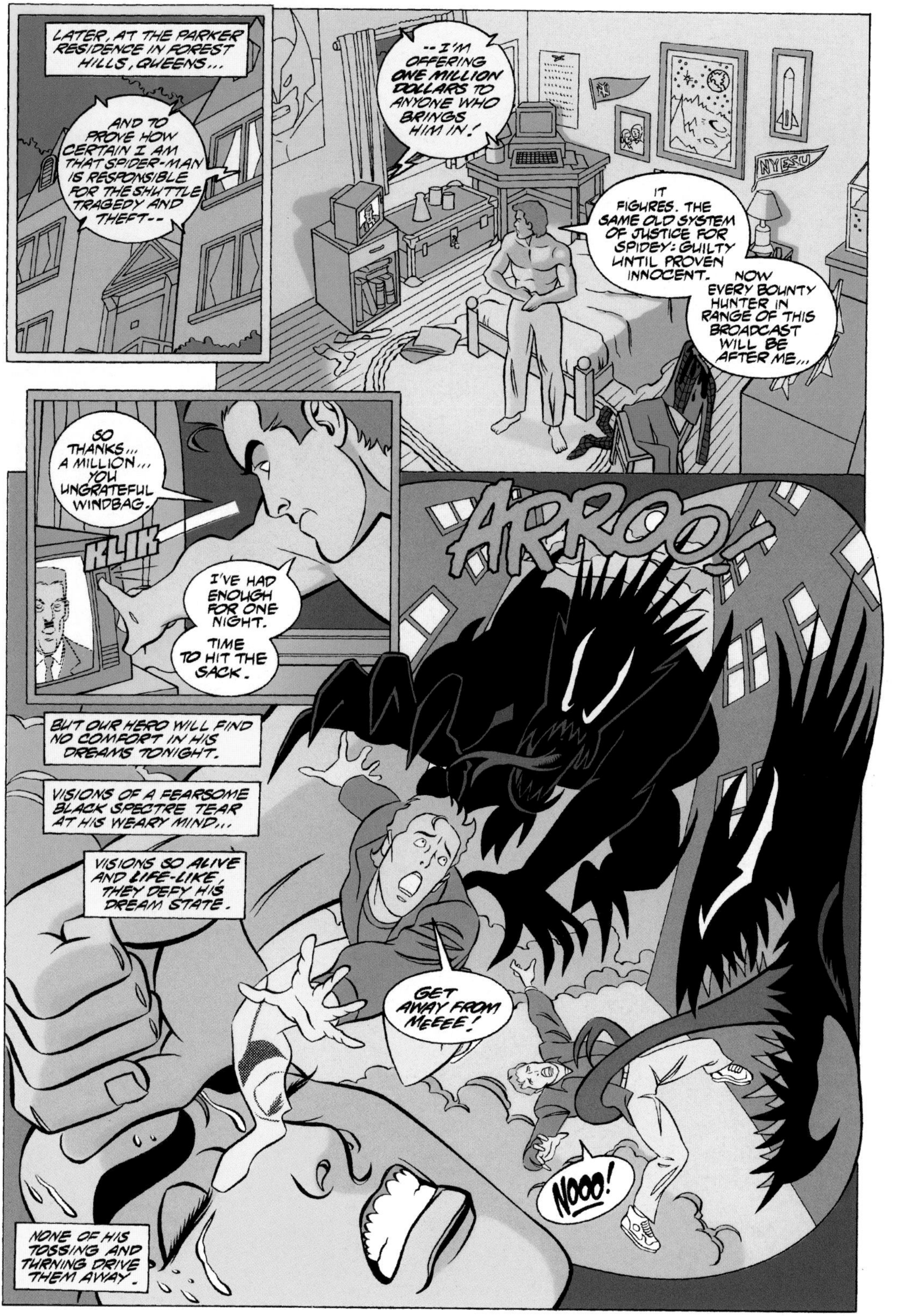
LATER, AT THE PARKER RESIDENCE IN FOREST HILLS, QUEENS...
AND TO PROVE HOW CERTAIN I AM THAT SPIDER-MAN IS RESPONSIBLE FOR THE SHUTTLE TRAGEDY AND THEFT--
--I'M OFFERING ONE MILLION DOLLARS TO ANYONE WHO BRINGS HIM IN!
IT FIGURES. THE SAME OLD SYSTEM OF JUSTICE FOR SPIDEY: GUILTY UNTIL PROVEN INNOCENT.
NOW EVERY BOUNTY HUNTER IN RANGE OF THIS BROADCAST WILL BE AFTER ME...
NYESU
SO THANKS... A MILLION... YOU UNGRATEFUL WINDBAG.
KLIK
I'VE HAD ENOUGH FOR ONE NIGHT.
TIME TO HIT THE SACK.
ARROO!
BUT OUR HERO WILL FIND NO COMFORT IN HIS DREAMS TONIGHT.
VISIONS OF A FEARSOME BLACK SPECTRE TEAR AT HIS WEARY MIND...
VISIONS SO ALIVE AND LIFE-LIKE, THEY DEFY HIS DREAM STATE.
GET AWAY FROM MEEEE!
NOOO!
NONE OF HIS TOSSING AND TURNING DRIVE THEM AWAY.

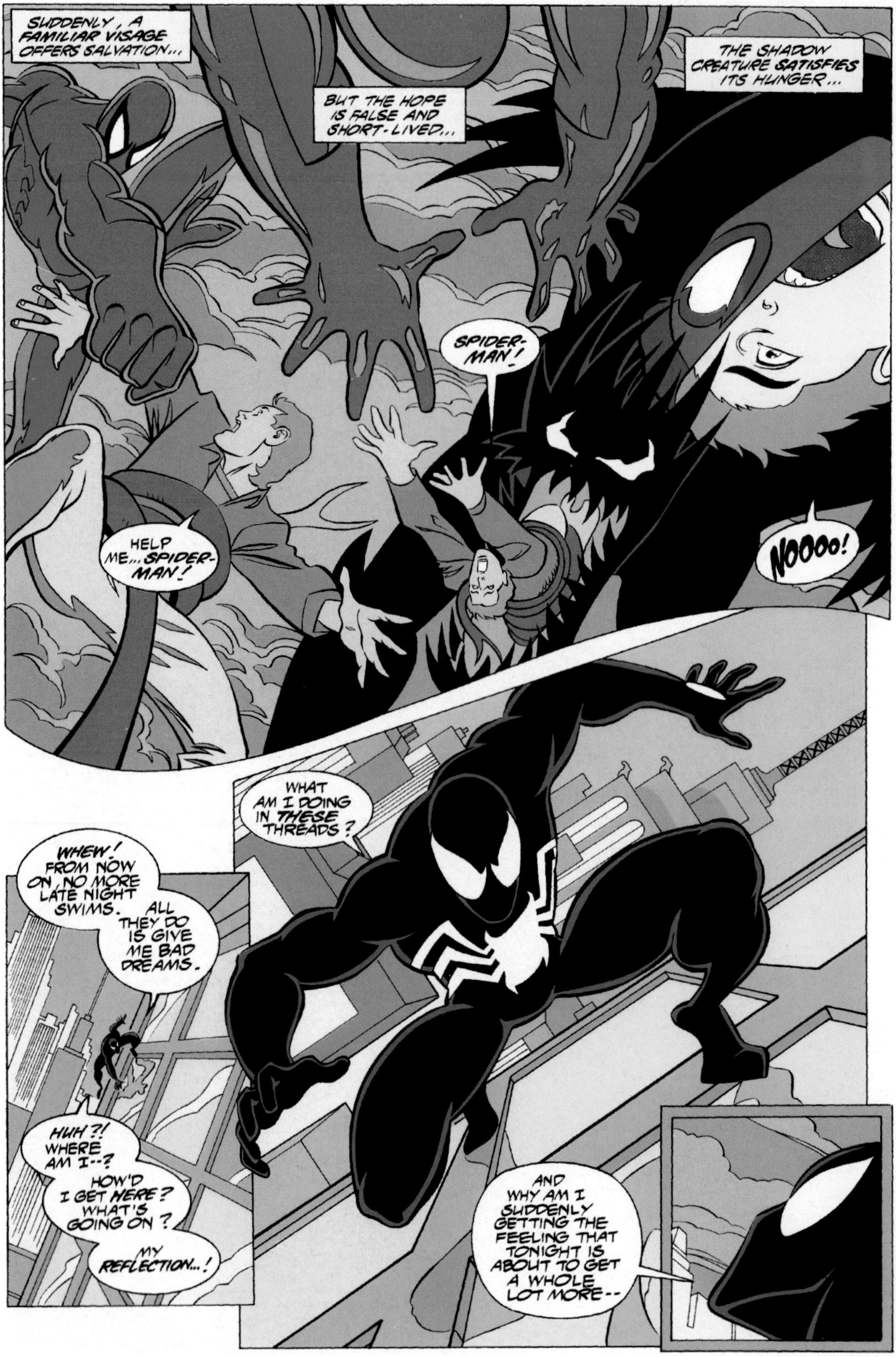
SUDDENLY, A FAMILIAR VISAGE OFFERS SALVATION...
BUT THE HOPE IS FALSE AND SHORT-LIVED...
THE SHADOW CREATURE SATISFIES ITS HUNGER...
SPIDER-MAN!
HELP ME... SPIDER-MAN!
NOOOO!
WHAT AM I DOING IN THESE THREADS?
WHEW! FROM NOW ON, NO MORE LATE NIGHT SWIMS.
ALL THEY DO IS GIVE ME BAD DREAMS.
HUH?! WHERE AM I--?
HOW'D I GET HERE? WHAT'S GOING ON?
MY REFLECTION...!
AND WHY AM I SUDDENLY GETTING THE FEELING THAT TONIGHT IS ABOUT TO GET A WHOLE LOT MORE--

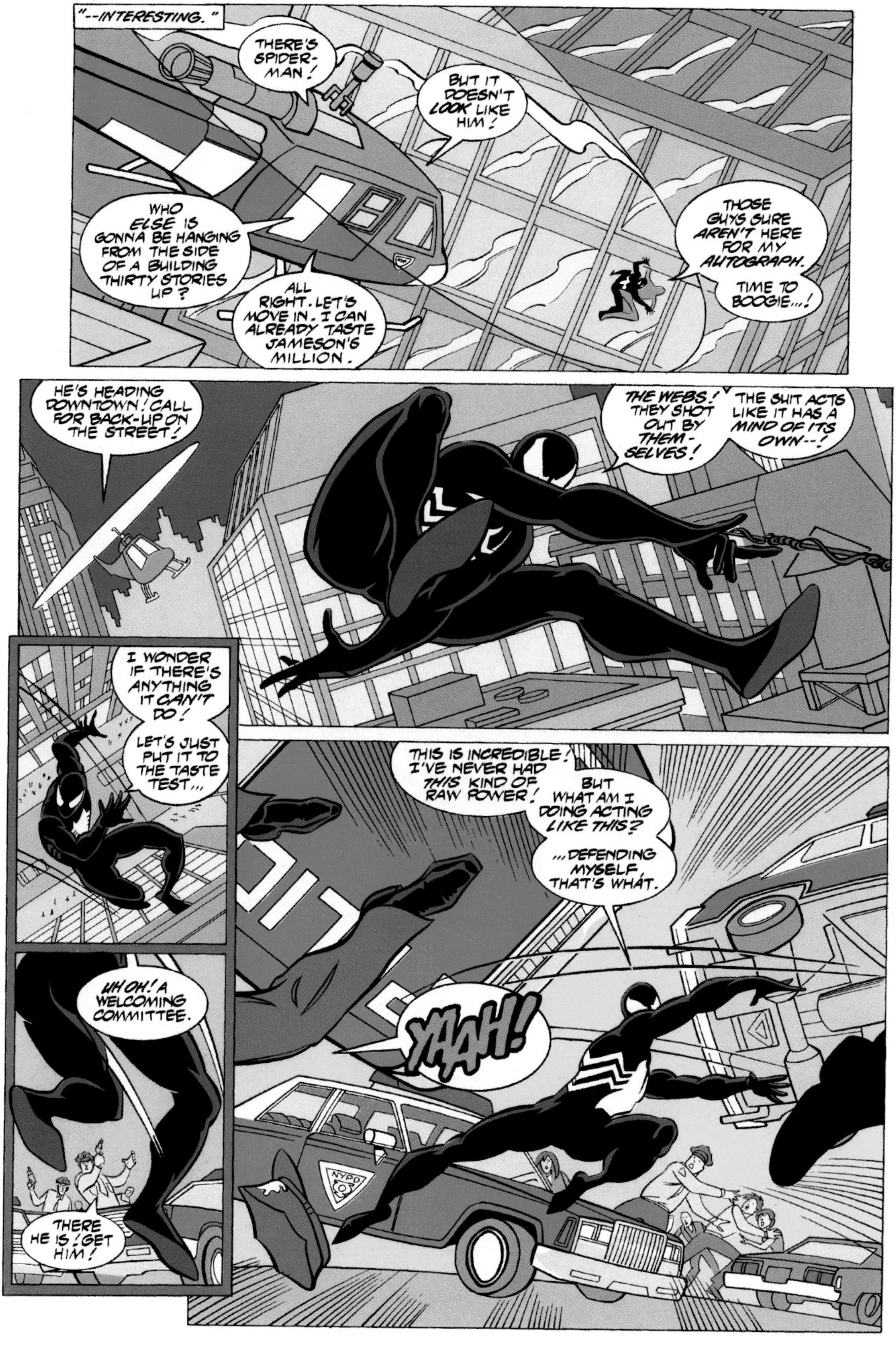
"--INTERESTING."
THERE'S SPIDER-MAN!
BUT IT DOESN'T LOOK LIKE HIM!
WHO ELSE IS GONNA BE HANGING FROM THE SIDE OF A BUILDING THIRTY STORIES UP?
ALL RIGHT. LET'S MOVE IN. I CAN ALREADY TASTE JAMESON'S MILLION.
THOSE GUYS SURE AREN'T HERE FOR MY AUTOGRAPH.
TIME TO BOOGIE...!
HE'S HEADING DOWNTOWN! CALL FOR BACK-UP ON THE STREET!
THE WEBS! THEY SHOT OUT BY THEMSELVES!
THE SUIT ACTS LIKE IT HAS A MIND OF ITS OWN--!
I WONDER IF THERE'S ANYTHING IT CAN'T DO!
LET'S JUST PUT IT TO THE TASTE TEST...
UH OH! A WELCOMING COMMITTEE.
THERE HE IS! GET HIM!
THIS IS INCREDIBLE! I'VE NEVER HAD THIS KIND OF RAW POWER!
BUT WHAT AM I DOING ACTING LIKE THIS?
...DEFENDING MYSELF, THAT'S WHAT.
YAAH!
NYPD

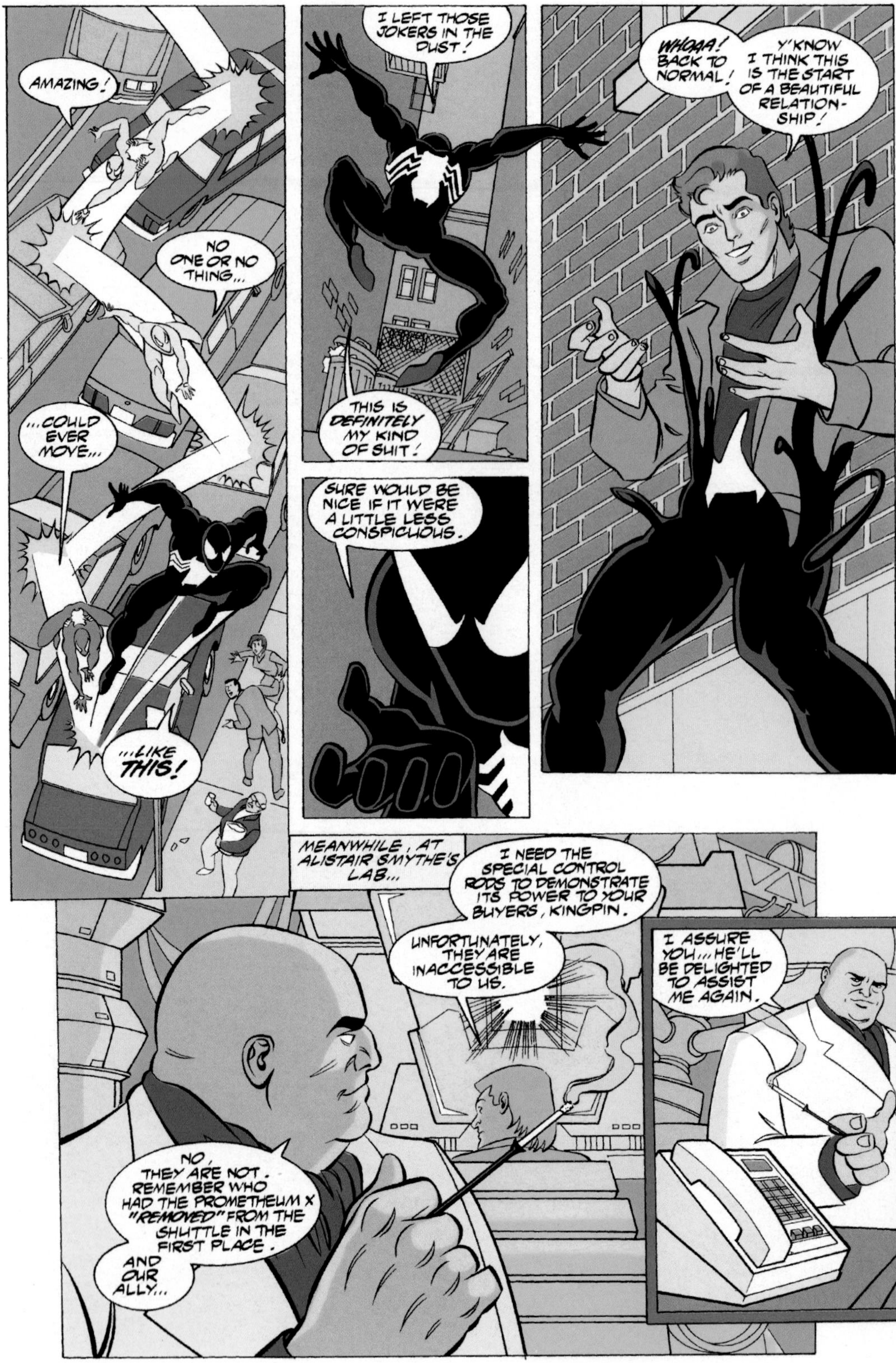
AMAZING!
NO ONE OR NO THING...
...COULD EVER MOVE...
...LIKE THIS!
I LEFT THOSE JOKERS IN THE DUST!
THIS IS DEFINITELY MY KIND OF SUIT!
SURE WOULD BE NICE IF IT WERE A LITTLE LESS CONSPICUOUS.
WHOAA! BACK TO NORMAL!
Y'KNOW I THINK THIS IS THE START OF A BEAUTIFUL RELATION-SHIP!
MEANWHILE, AT ALISTAIR SMYTHE'S LAB...
I NEED THE SPECIAL CONTROL RODS TO DEMONSTRATE ITS POWER TO YOUR BUYERS, KINGPIN.
UNFORTUNATELY, THEY ARE INACCESSIBLE TO US.
NO, THEY ARE NOT. REMEMBER WHO HAD THE PROMETHEUM X "REMOVED" FROM THE SHUTTLE IN THE FIRST PLACE.
AND OUR ALLY...
I ASSURE YOU... HE'LL BE DELIGHTED TO ASSIST ME AGAIN.

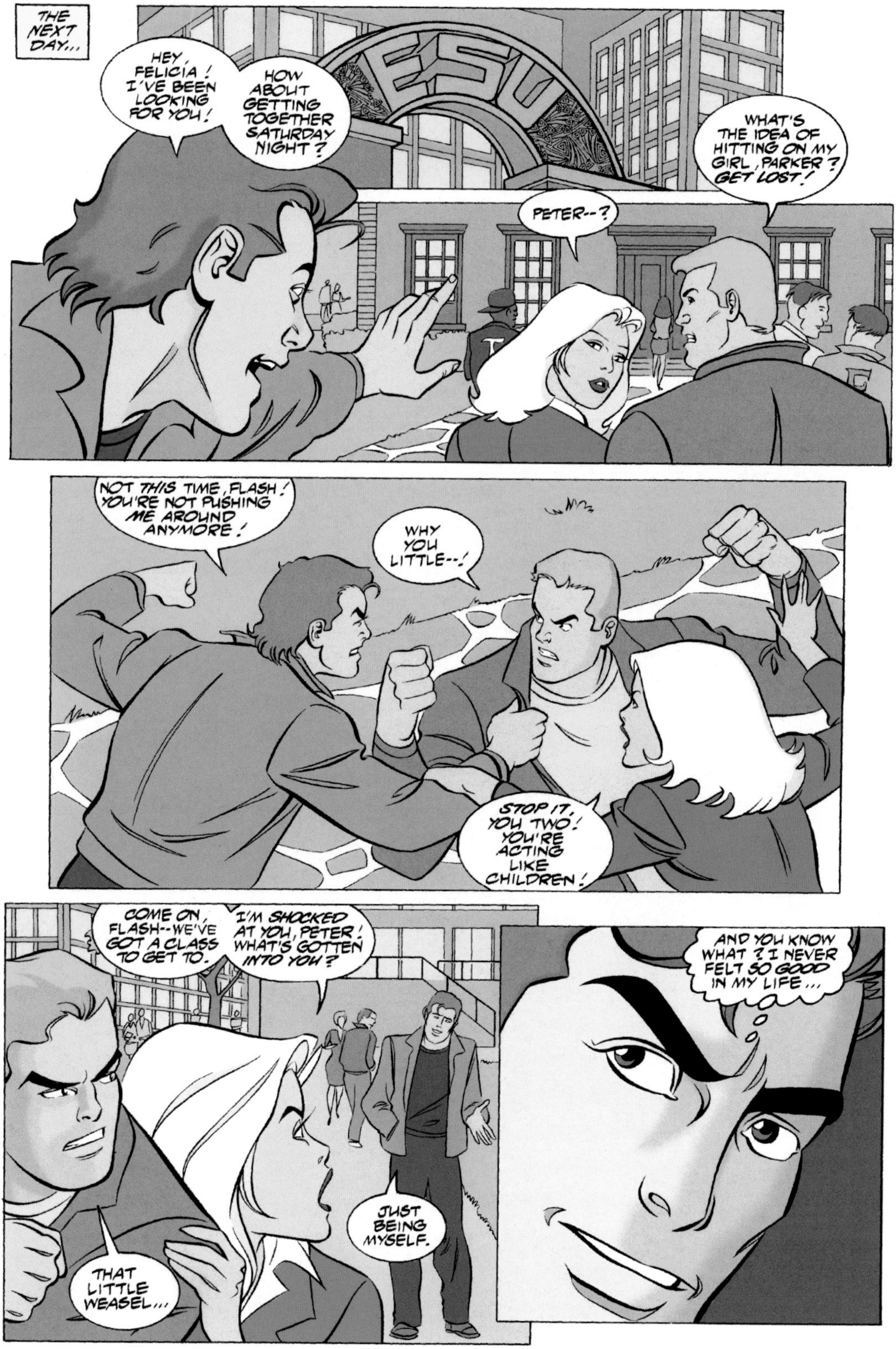
THE NEXT DAY...
HEY, FELICIA! I'VE BEEN LOOKING FOR YOU!
HOW ABOUT GETTING TOGETHER SATURDAY NIGHT?
ESU
PETER--?
WHAT'S THE IDEA OF HITTING ON MY GIRL, PARKER? GET LOST!
NOT THIS TIME, FLASH! YOU'RE NOT PUSHING ME AROUND ANYMORE!
WHY YOU LITTLE--!
STOP IT, YOU TWO! YOU'RE ACTING LIKE CHILDREN!
COME ON, FLASH--WE'VE GOT A CLASS TO GET TO.
I'M SHOCKED AT YOU, PETER! WHAT'S GOTTEN INTO YOU?
JUST BEING MYSELF.
THAT LITTLE WEASEL...
AND YOU KNOW WHAT? I NEVER FELT SO GOOD IN MY LIFE...

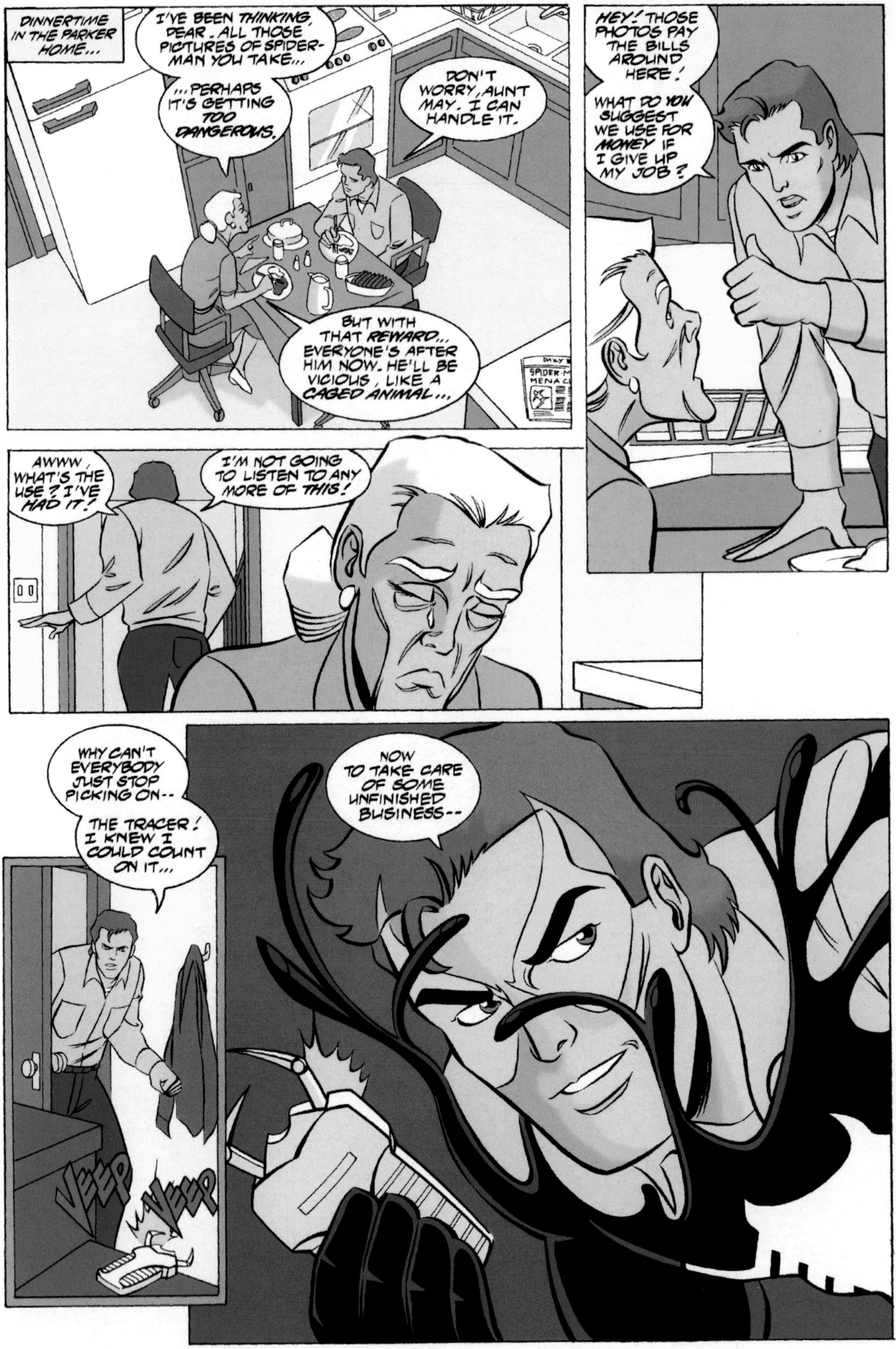
DINNERTIME IN THE PARKER HOME...
I'VE BEEN THINKING, DEAR. ALL THOSE PICTURES OF SPIDER-MAN YOU TAKE...
...PERHAPS IT'S GETTING TOO DANGEROUS.
DON'T WORRY, AUNT MAY. I CAN HANDLE IT.
BUT WITH THAT REWARD... EVERYONE'S AFTER HIM NOW. HE'LL BE VICIOUS, LIKE A CAGED ANIMAL...
SPIDER-M MENAC
HEY! THOSE PHOTOS PAY THE BILLS AROUND HERE!
WHAT DO YOU SUGGEST WE USE FOR MONEY IF I GIVE UP MY JOB?
AWWW, WHAT'S THE USE? I'VE HAD IT!
I'M NOT GOING TO LISTEN TO ANY MORE OF THIS!
WHY CAN'T EVERYBODY JUST STOP PICKING ON--
THE TRACER! I KNEW I COULD COUNT ON IT...
VEEP VEEP
NOW TO TAKE CARE OF SOME UNFINISHED BUSINESS--

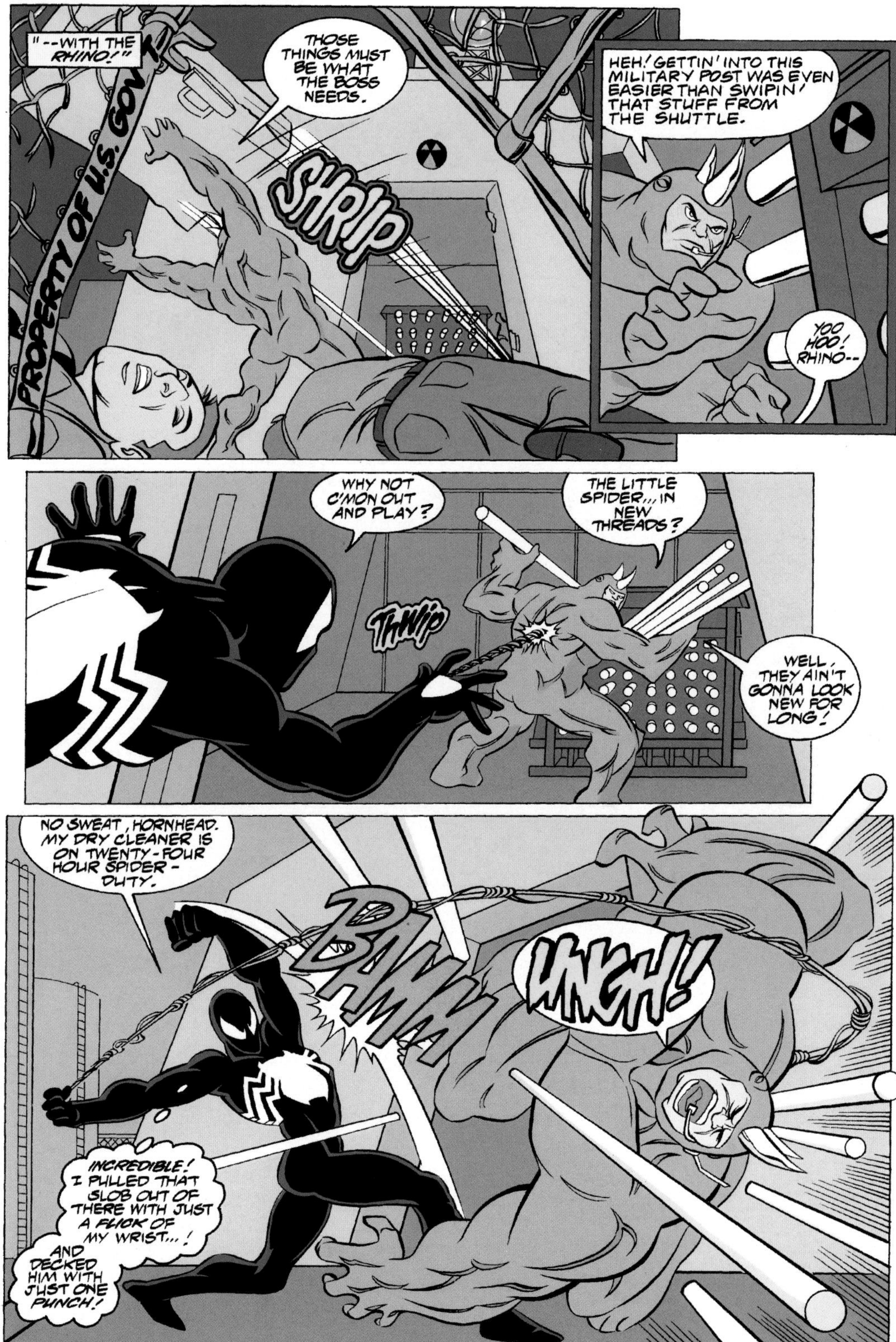
"--WITH THE RHINO!"
PROPERTY OF U.S. GOV'T
THOSE THINGS MUST BE WHAT THE BOSS NEEDS.
SHRIP
HEH! GETTIN' INTO THIS MILITARY POST WAS EVEN EASIER THAN SWIPIN' THAT STUFF FROM THE SHUTTLE.
YOO HOO! RHINO--
WHY NOT C'MON OUT AND PLAY?
THE LITTLE SPIDER... IN NEW THREADS?
THWIP
WELL, THEY AIN'T GONNA LOOK NEW FOR LONG!
NO SWEAT, HORNHEAD. MY DRY CLEANER IS ON TWENTY-FOUR HOUR SPIDER-DUTY.
BAMM
UNCH!
INCREDIBLE! I PULLED THAT SLOB OUT OF THERE WITH JUST A FLICK OF MY WRIST...!
AND DECKED HIM WITH JUST ONE PUNCH!

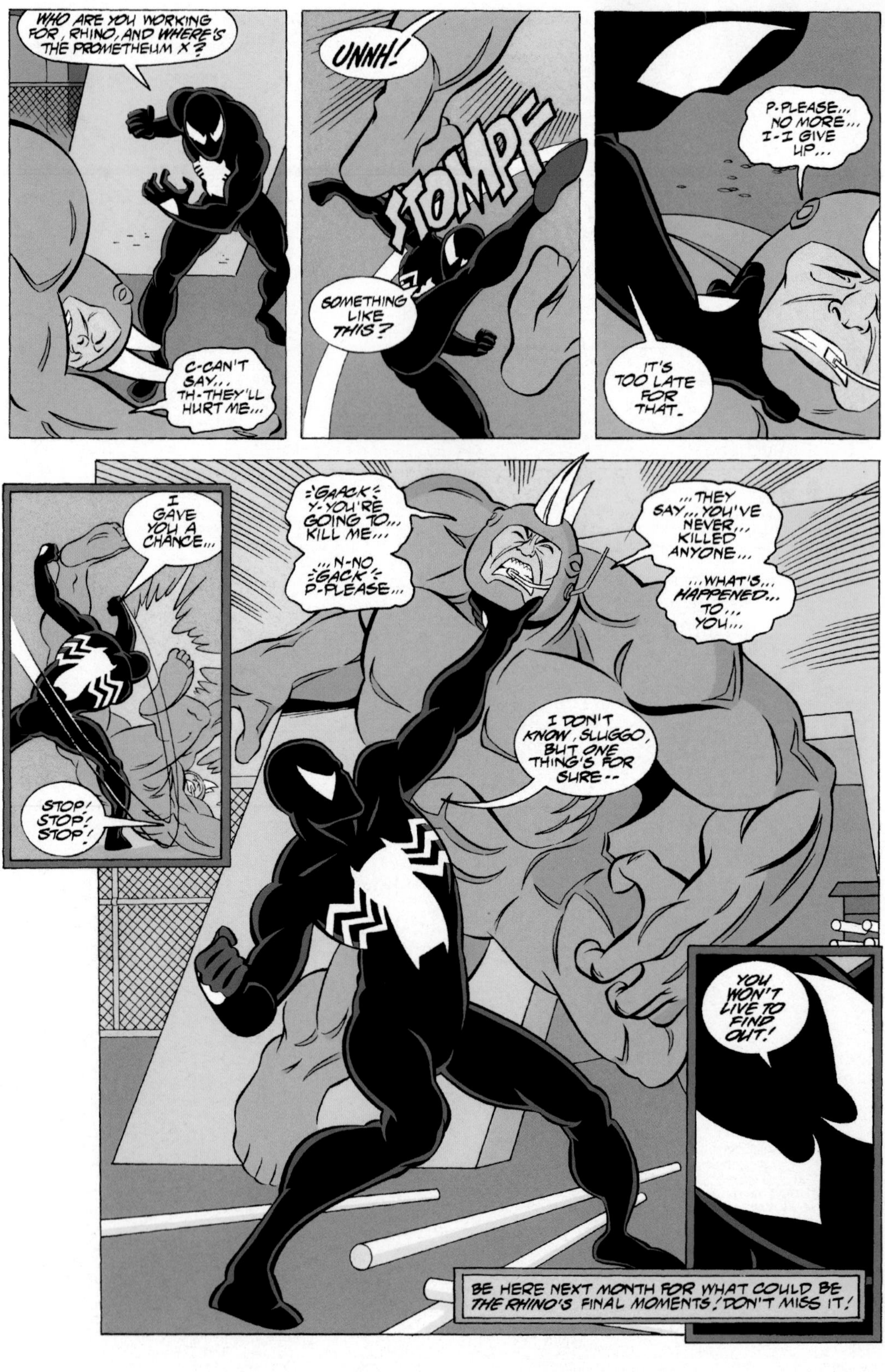
WHO ARE YOU WORKING FOR, RHINO, AND WHERE'S THE PROMETHEUM X?
C-CAN'T SAY... TH-THEY'LL HURT ME...
UNNH!
STOMPF
SOMETHING LIKE THIS?
P-PLEASE... NO MORE... I-I GIVE UP...
IT'S TOO LATE FOR THAT.
I GAVE YOU A CHANCE...
STOP! STOP! STOP!
GAACK Y-YOU'RE GOING TO... KILL ME...
N-NO GACK P-PLEASE...
...THEY SAY... YOU'VE NEVER... KILLED ANYONE...
...WHAT'S... HAPPENED... TO... YOU...
I DON'T KNOW, SLUGGO, BUT ONE THING'S FOR SURE--
YOU WON'T LIVE TO FIND OUT!
BE HERE NEXT MONTH FOR WHAT COULD BE THE RHINO'S FINAL MOMENTS! DON'T MISS IT!

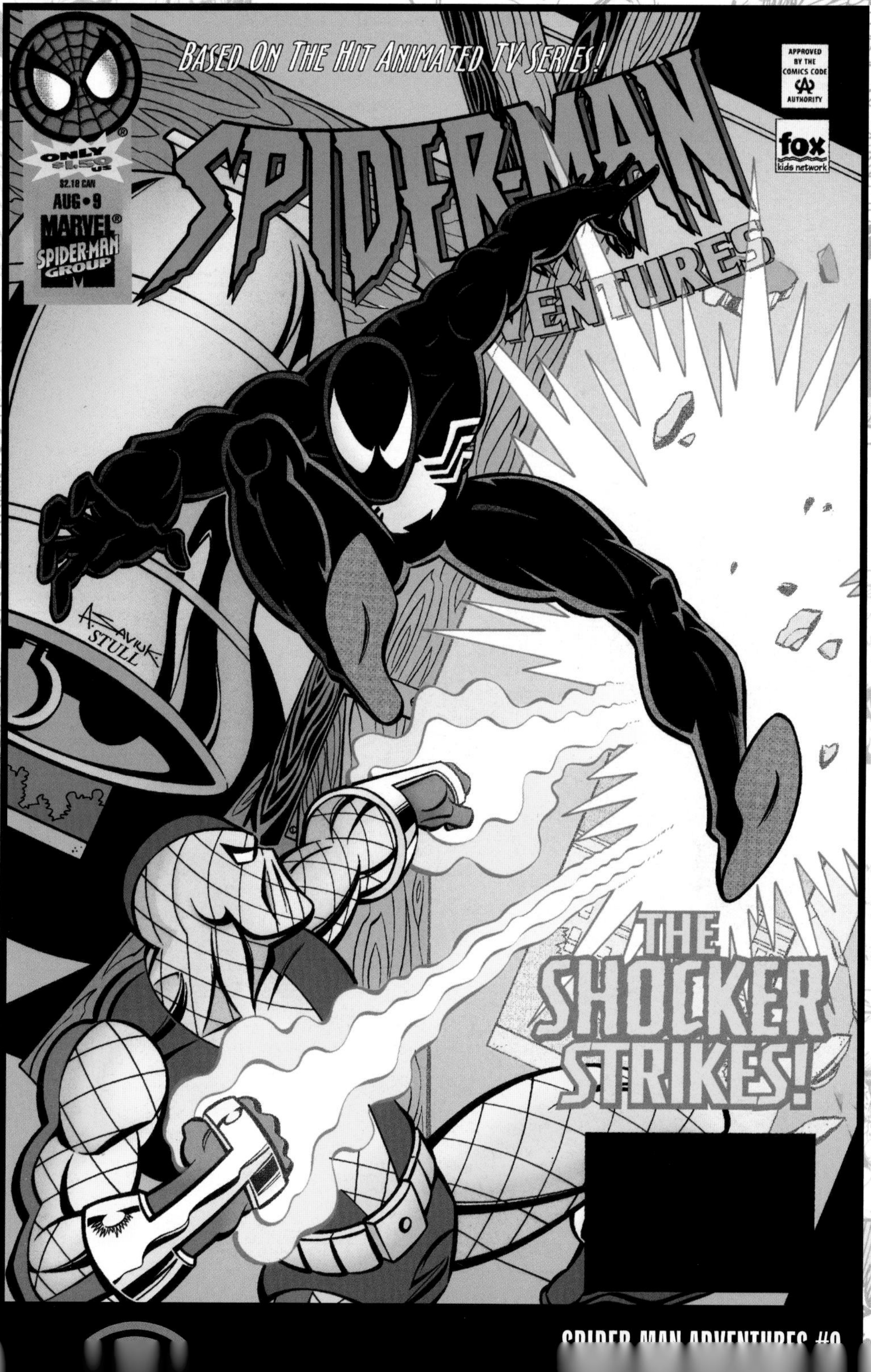

BASED ON THE HIT ANIMATED TV SERIES!
APPROVED BY THE COMICS CODE AUTHORITY
SPIDER-MAN
ADVENTURES
fox kids network
ONLY $1.50 US
$2.18 CAN
AUG • 9
MARVEL
SPIDER-MAN GROUP
A. SAVIUK
STULL
THE SHOCKER STRIKES!

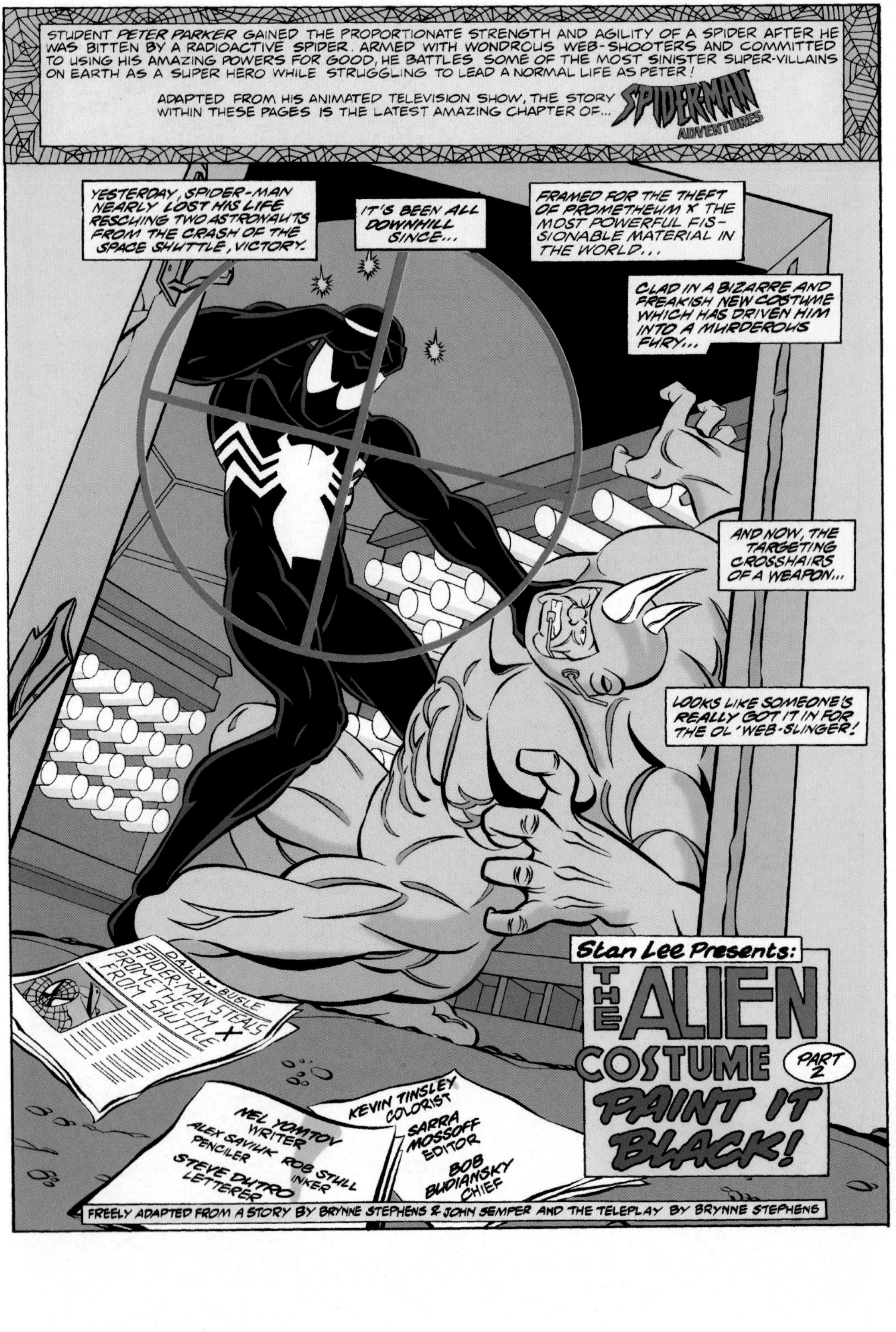
STUDENT PETER PARKER GAINED THE PROPORTIONATE STRENGTH AND AGILITY OF A SPIDER AFTER HE WAS BITTEN BY A RADIOACTIVE SPIDER. ARMED WITH WONDROUS WEB-SHOOTERS AND COMMITTED TO USING HIS AMAZING POWERS FOR GOOD, HE BATTLES SOME OF THE MOST SINISTER SUPER-VILLAINS ON EARTH AS A SUPER HERO WHILE STRUGGLING TO LEAD A NORMAL LIFE AS PETER!
ADAPTED FROM HIS ANIMATED TELEVISION SHOW, THE STORY WITHIN THESE PAGES IS THE LATEST AMAZING CHAPTER OF... SPIDER-MAN ADVENTURES
YESTERDAY, SPIDER-MAN NEARLY LOST HIS LIFE RESCUING TWO ASTRONAUTS FROM THE CRASH OF THE SPACE SHUTTLE, VICTORY.
IT'S BEEN ALL DOWNHILL SINCE...
FRAMED FOR THE THEFT OF PROMETHEUM X THE MOST POWERFUL FISSIONABLE MATERIAL IN THE WORLD...
CLAD IN A BIZARRE AND FREAKISH NEW COSTUME WHICH HAS DRIVEN HIM INTO A MURDEROUS FURY...
AND NOW, THE TARGETING CROSSHAIRS OF A WEAPON...
LOOKS LIKE SOMEONE'S REALLY GOT IT IN FOR THE OL' WEB-SLINGER!
DAILY BUGLE
SPIDER-MAN STEALS PROMETHEUM X FROM SHUTTLE
Stan Lee Presents:
THE ALIEN COSTUME PART 2
PAINT IT BLACK!
NEL YOMTOV WRITER
ALEX SAVIUK PENCILER
ROB STULL INKER
STEVE DUTRO LETTERER
KEVIN TINSLEY COLORIST
SARRA MOSSOFF EDITOR
BOB BUDIANSKY CHIEF
FREELY ADAPTED FROM A STORY BY BRYNNE STEPHENS & JOHN SEMPER AND THE TELEPLAY BY BRYNNE STEPHENS

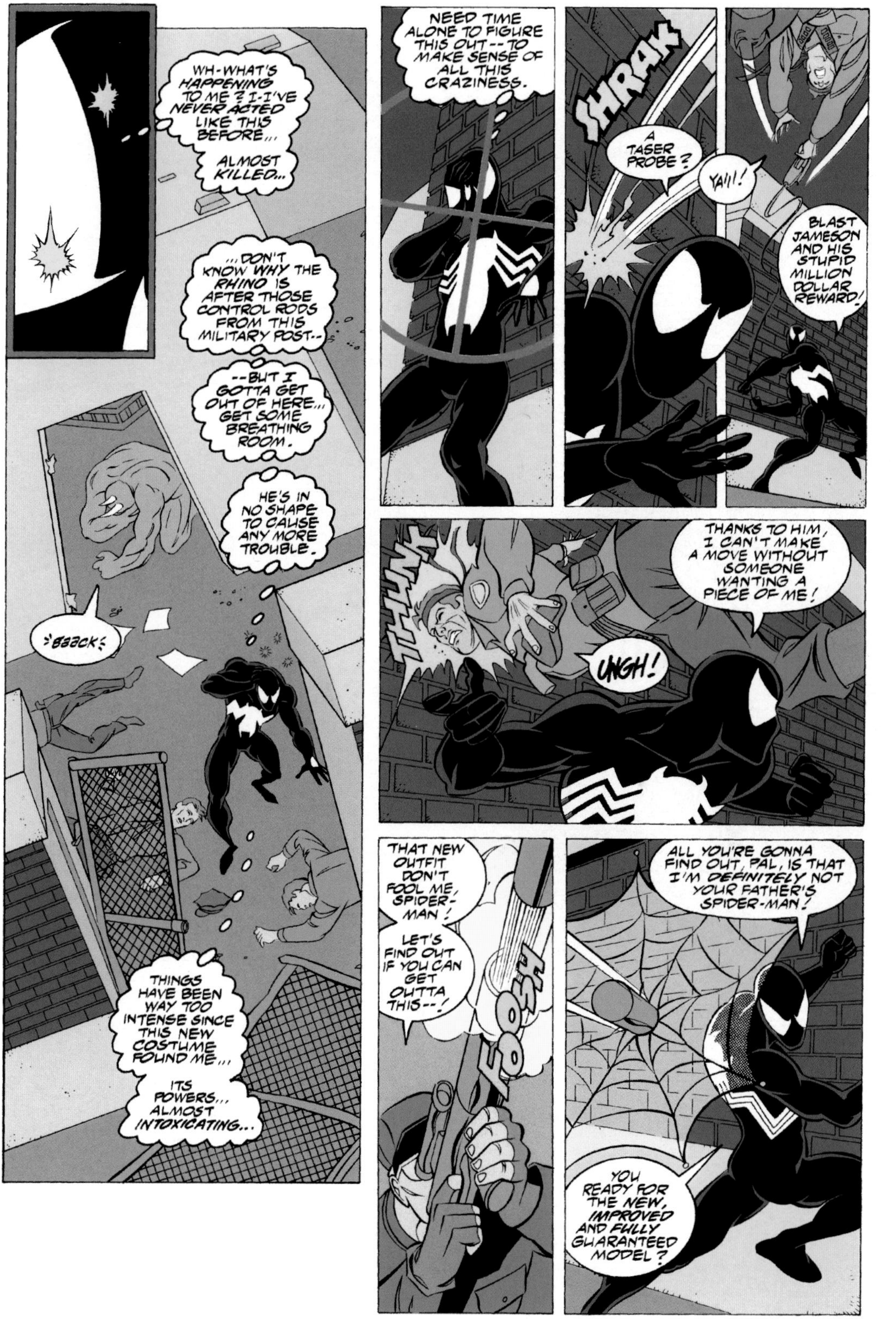
WH-WHAT'S HAPPENING TO ME? I-I'VE NEVER ACTED LIKE THIS BEFORE...
ALMOST KILLED...
...DON'T KNOW WHY THE RHINO IS AFTER THOSE CONTROL RODS FROM THIS MILITARY POST--
--BUT I GOTTA GET OUT OF HERE... GET SOME BREATHING ROOM.
HE'S IN NO SHAPE TO CAUSE ANY MORE TROUBLE.
BRACK
THINGS HAVE BEEN WAY TOO INTENSE SINCE THIS NEW COSTUME FOUND ME...
ITS POWERS... ALMOST INTOXICATING...
NEED TIME ALONE TO FIGURE THIS OUT -- TO MAKE SENSE OF ALL THIS CRAZINESS.
SHRAK
A TASER PROBE?
YAII!
BLAST JAMESON AND HIS STUPID MILLION DOLLAR REWARD!
THANKS TO HIM, I CAN'T MAKE A MOVE WITHOUT SOMEONE WANTING A PIECE OF ME!
THUNK
UNGH!
THAT NEW OUTFIT DON'T FOOL ME, SPIDER-MAN!
LET'S FIND OUT IF YOU CAN GET OUTTA THIS--!
FOOSH
ALL YOU'RE GONNA FIND OUT, PAL, IS THAT I'M DEFINITELY NOT YOUR FATHER'S SPIDER-MAN!
YOU READY FOR THE NEW, IMPROVED AND FULLY GUARANTEED MODEL?

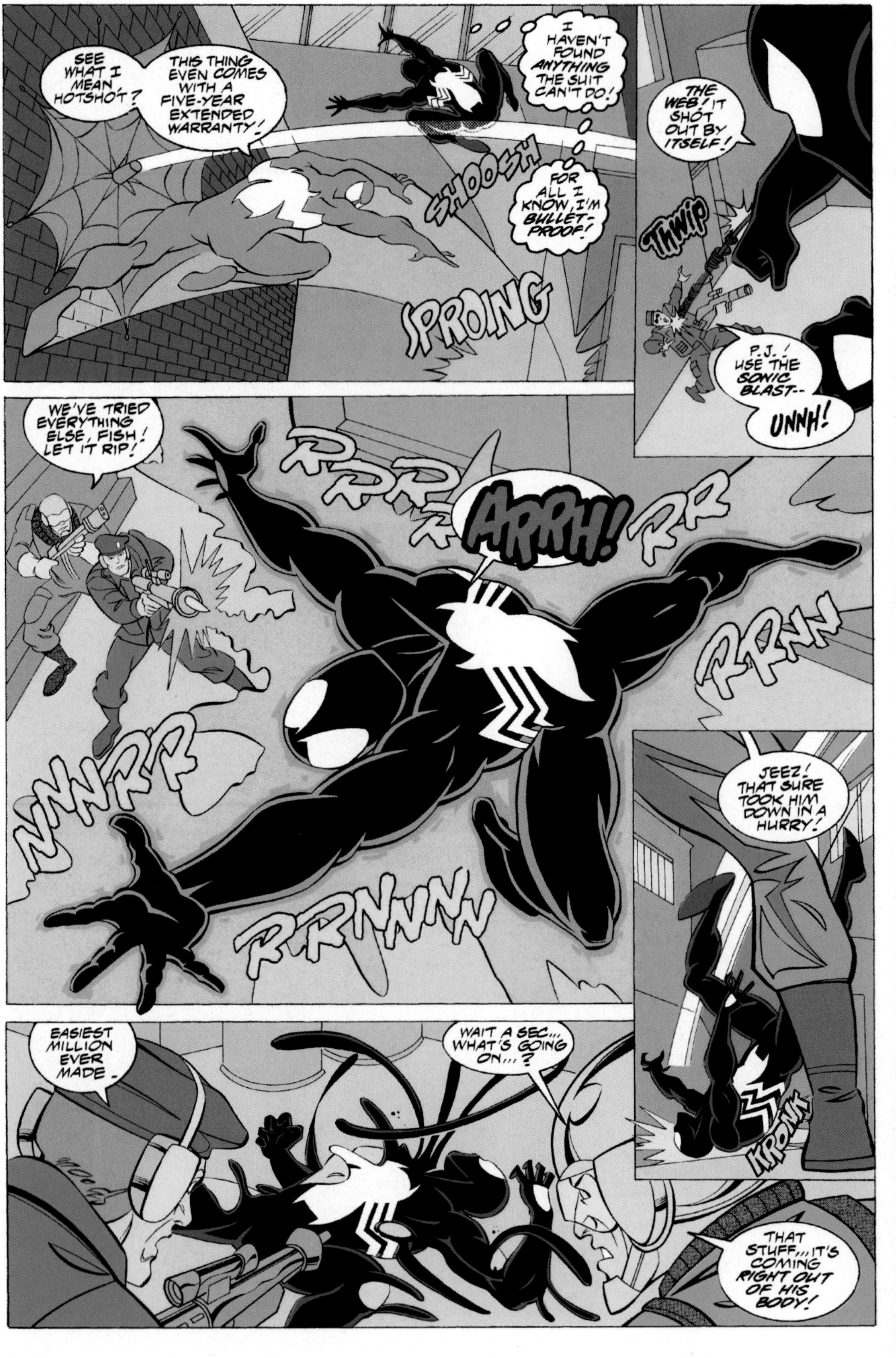
SEE WHAT I MEAN HOTSHOT?
THIS THING EVEN COMES WITH A FIVE-YEAR EXTENDED WARRANTY!
I HAVEN'T FOUND ANYTHING THE SUIT CAN'T DO!
FOR ALL I KNOW, I'M BULLET-PROOF!
SHOOSH
SPROING
THE WEB! IT SHOT OUT BY ITSELF!
THWIP
P.J.! USE THE SONIC BLAST-- UNNH!
WE'VE TRIED EVERYTHING ELSE, FISH! LET IT RIP!
RRRRR
ARRH!
RR
RRNN
NNNRR
RRNNNN
JEEZ! THAT SURE TOOK HIM DOWN IN A HURRY!
KRONK
EASIEST MILLION EVER MADE.
WAIT A SEC... WHAT'S GOING ON...?
THAT STUFF... IT'S COMING RIGHT OUT OF HIS BODY!

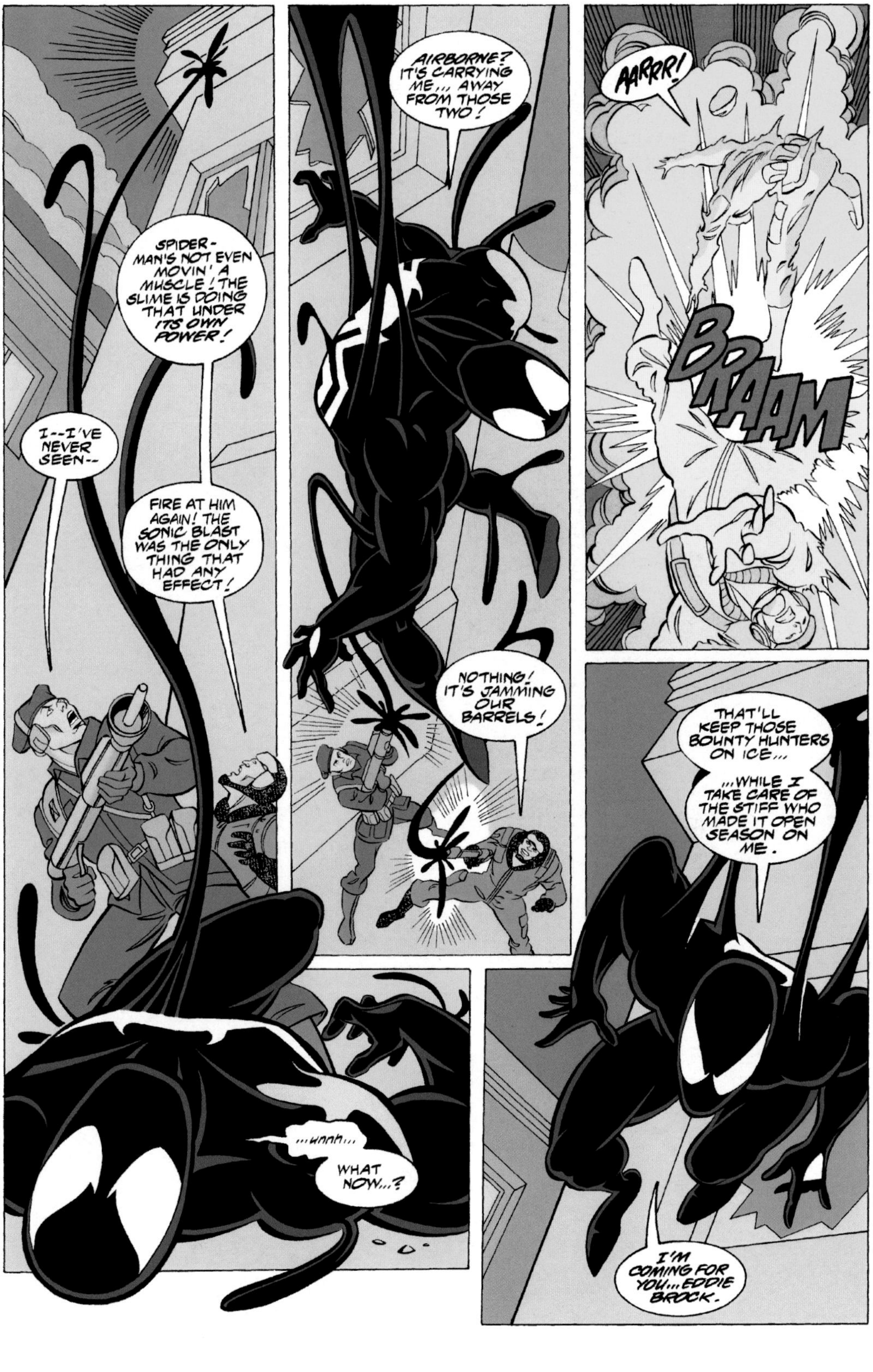
SPIDER-MAN'S NOT EVEN MOVIN' A MUSCLE! THE SLIME IS DOING THAT UNDER ITS OWN POWER!
I--I'VE NEVER SEEN--
FIRE AT HIM AGAIN! THE SONIC BLAST WAS THE ONLY THING THAT HAD ANY EFFECT!
AIRBORNE? IT'S CARRYING ME... AWAY FROM THOSE TWO!
NOTHING! IT'S JAMMING OUR BARRELS!
AARRR!
BRAAAM
...unnh...
WHAT NOW...?
THAT'LL KEEP THOSE BOUNTY HUNTERS ON ICE...
...WHILE I TAKE CARE OF THE STIFF WHO MADE IT OPEN SEASON ON ME.
I'M COMING FOR YOU...EDDIE BROCK.

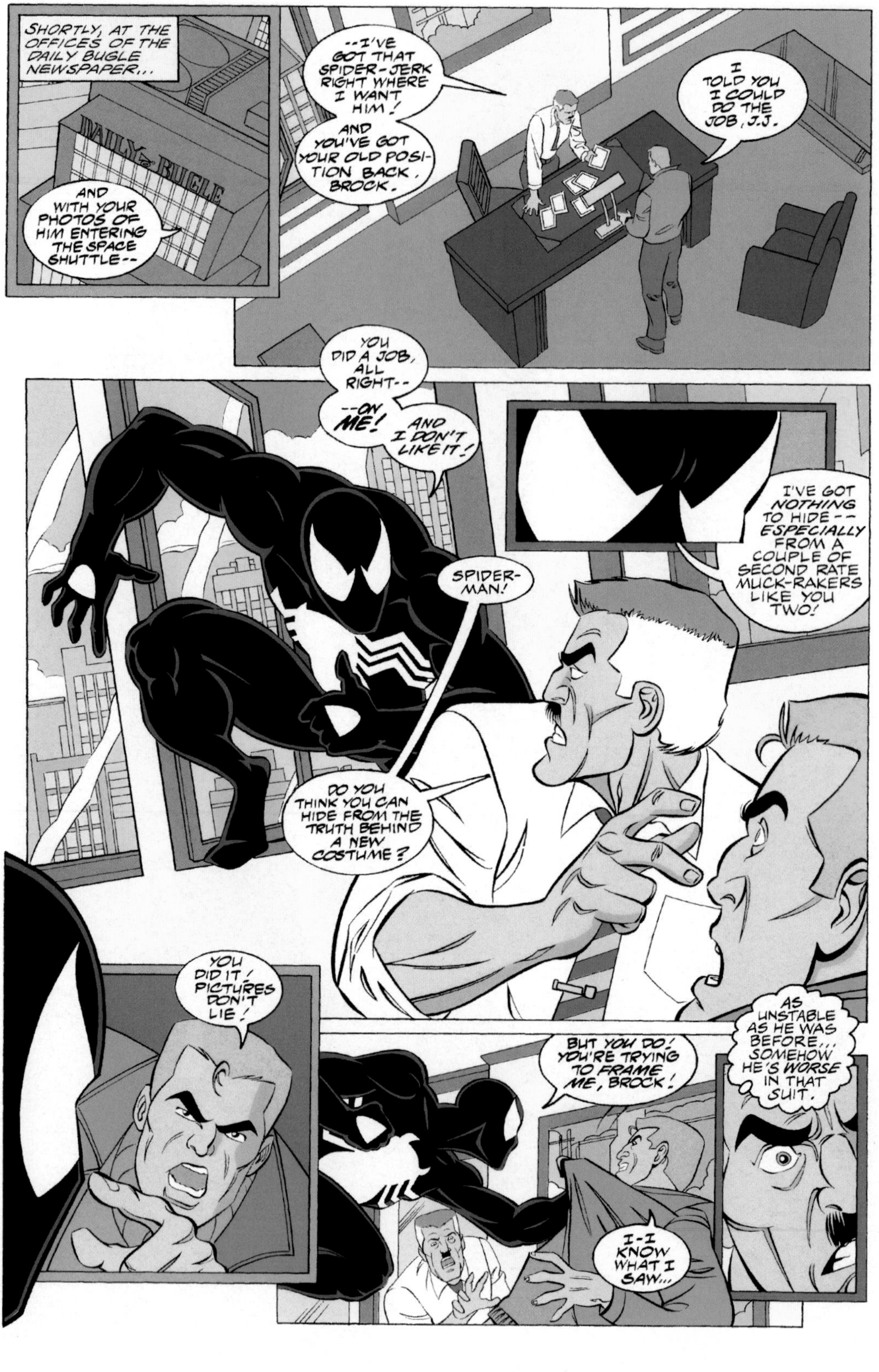
SHORTLY, AT THE OFFICES OF THE DAILY BUGLE NEWSPAPER...
DAILY BUGLE
AND WITH YOUR PHOTOS OF HIM ENTERING THE SPACE SHUTTLE--
--I'VE GOT THAT SPIDER-JERK RIGHT WHERE I WANT HIM!
AND YOU'VE GOT YOUR OLD POSITION BACK, BROCK.
I TOLD YOU I COULD DO THE JOB, J.J.
YOU DID A JOB, ALL RIGHT--
--ON ME!
AND I DON'T LIKE IT!
I'VE GOT NOTHING TO HIDE--ESPECIALLY FROM A COUPLE OF SECOND RATE MUCK-RAKERS LIKE YOU TWO!
SPIDER-MAN!
DO YOU THINK YOU CAN HIDE FROM THE TRUTH BEHIND A NEW COSTUME?
YOU DID IT! PICTURES DON'T LIE!
BUT YOU DO! YOU'RE TRYING TO FRAME ME, BROCK!
AS UNSTABLE AS HE WAS BEFORE... SOMEHOW HE'S WORSE IN THAT SUIT.
I-I KNOW WHAT I SAW...

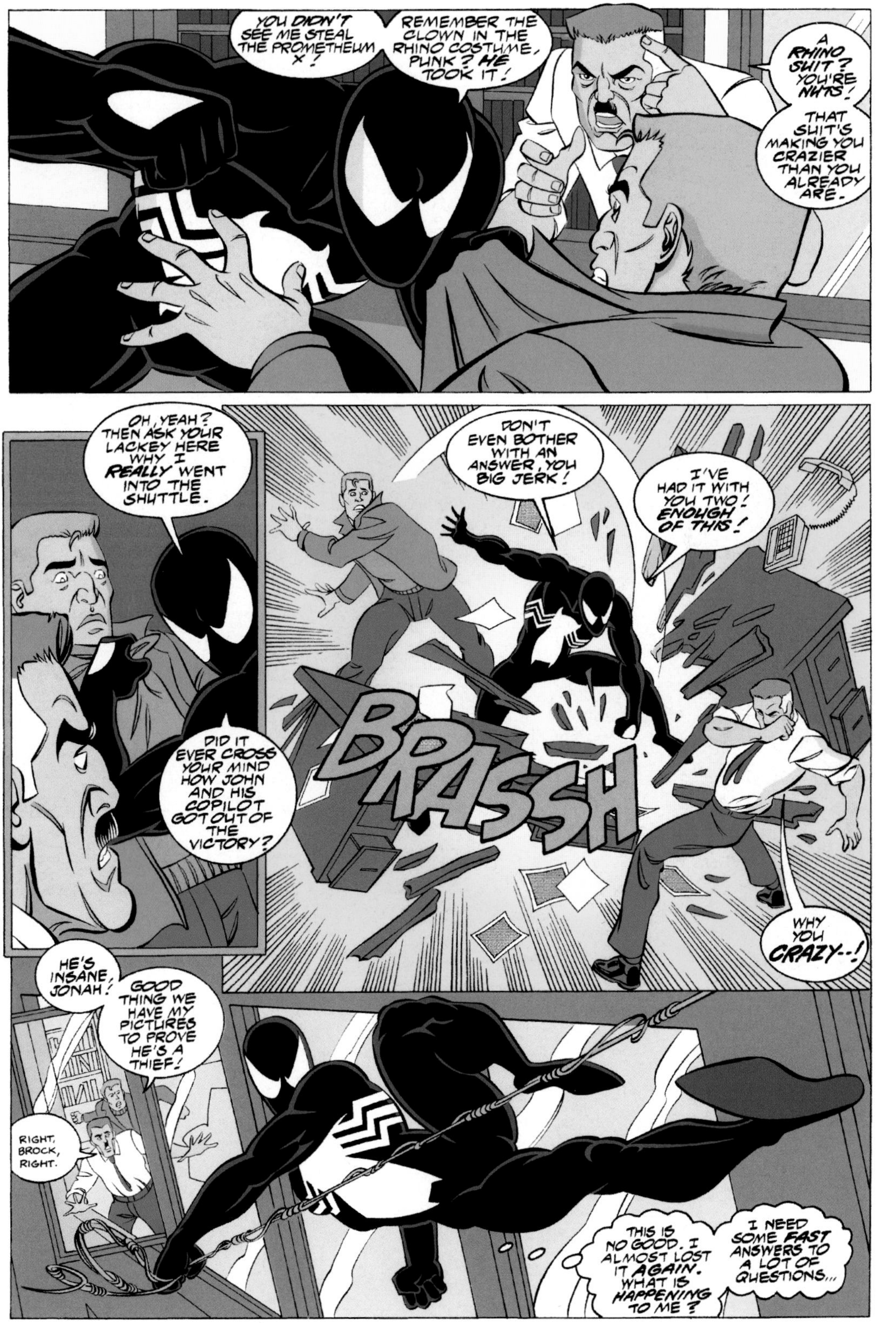
YOU DIDN'T SEE ME STEAL THE PROMETHEUM X!
REMEMBER THE CLOWN IN THE RHINO COSTUME, PUNK? HE TOOK IT!
A RHINO SUIT? YOU'RE NUTS!
THAT SUIT'S MAKING YOU CRAZIER THAN YOU ALREADY ARE.
OH, YEAH? THEN ASK YOUR LACKEY HERE WHY I REALLY WENT INTO THE SHUTTLE.
DID IT EVER CROSS YOUR MIND HOW JOHN AND HIS COPILOT GOT OUT OF THE VICTORY?
DON'T EVEN BOTHER WITH AN ANSWER, YOU BIG JERK!
I'VE HAD IT WITH YOU TWO! ENOUGH OF THIS!
BRASSH
WHY YOU CRAZY--!
HE'S INSANE, JONAH!
GOOD THING WE HAVE MY PICTURES TO PROVE HE'S A THIEF!
RIGHT, BROCK, RIGHT.
THIS IS NO GOOD. I ALMOST LOST IT AGAIN. WHAT IS HAPPENING TO ME?
I NEED SOME FAST ANSWERS TO A LOT OF QUESTIONS...

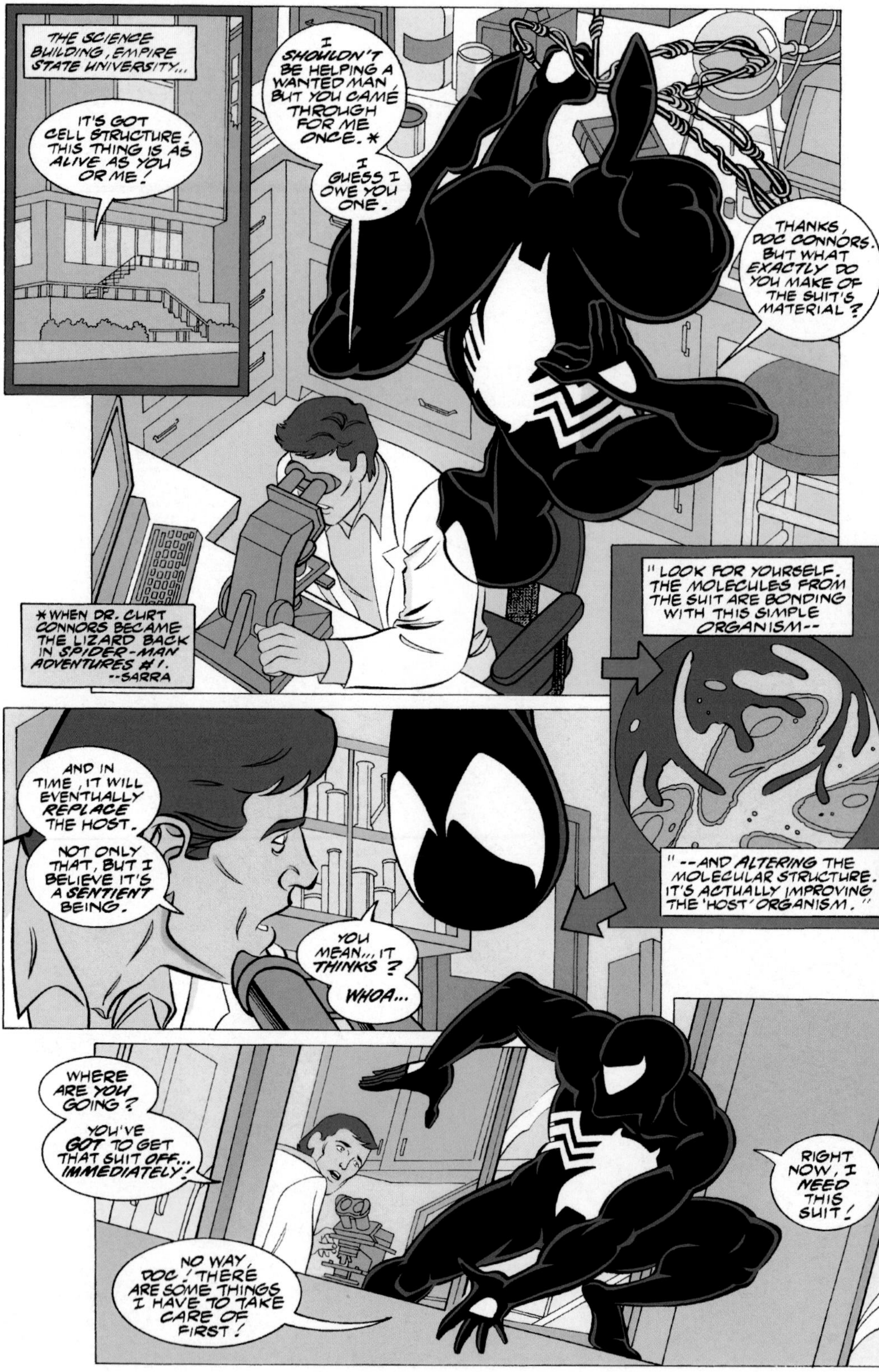
THE SCIENCE BUILDING, EMPIRE STATE UNIVERSITY...
IT'S GOT CELL STRUCTURE! THIS THING IS AS ALIVE AS YOU OR ME!
I SHOULDN'T BE HELPING A WANTED MAN, BUT YOU CAME THROUGH FOR ME ONCE.*
I GUESS I OWE YOU ONE.
THANKS, DOC CONNORS. BUT WHAT EXACTLY DO YOU MAKE OF THE SUIT'S MATERIAL?
*WHEN DR. CURT CONNORS BECAME THE LIZARD BACK IN SPIDER-MAN ADVENTURES #1. --SARRA
"LOOK FOR YOURSELF. THE MOLECULES FROM THE SUIT ARE BONDING WITH THIS SIMPLE ORGANISM--
"--AND ALTERING THE MOLECULAR STRUCTURE. IT'S ACTUALLY IMPROVING THE 'HOST' ORGANISM."
AND IN TIME, IT WILL EVENTUALLY REPLACE THE HOST.
NOT ONLY THAT, BUT I BELIEVE IT'S A SENTIENT BEING.
YOU MEAN... IT THINKS?
WHOA...
WHERE ARE YOU GOING?
YOU'VE GOT TO GET THAT SUIT OFF... IMMEDIATELY!
RIGHT NOW, I NEED THIS SUIT!
NO WAY, DOC! THERE ARE SOME THINGS I HAVE TO TAKE CARE OF FIRST!

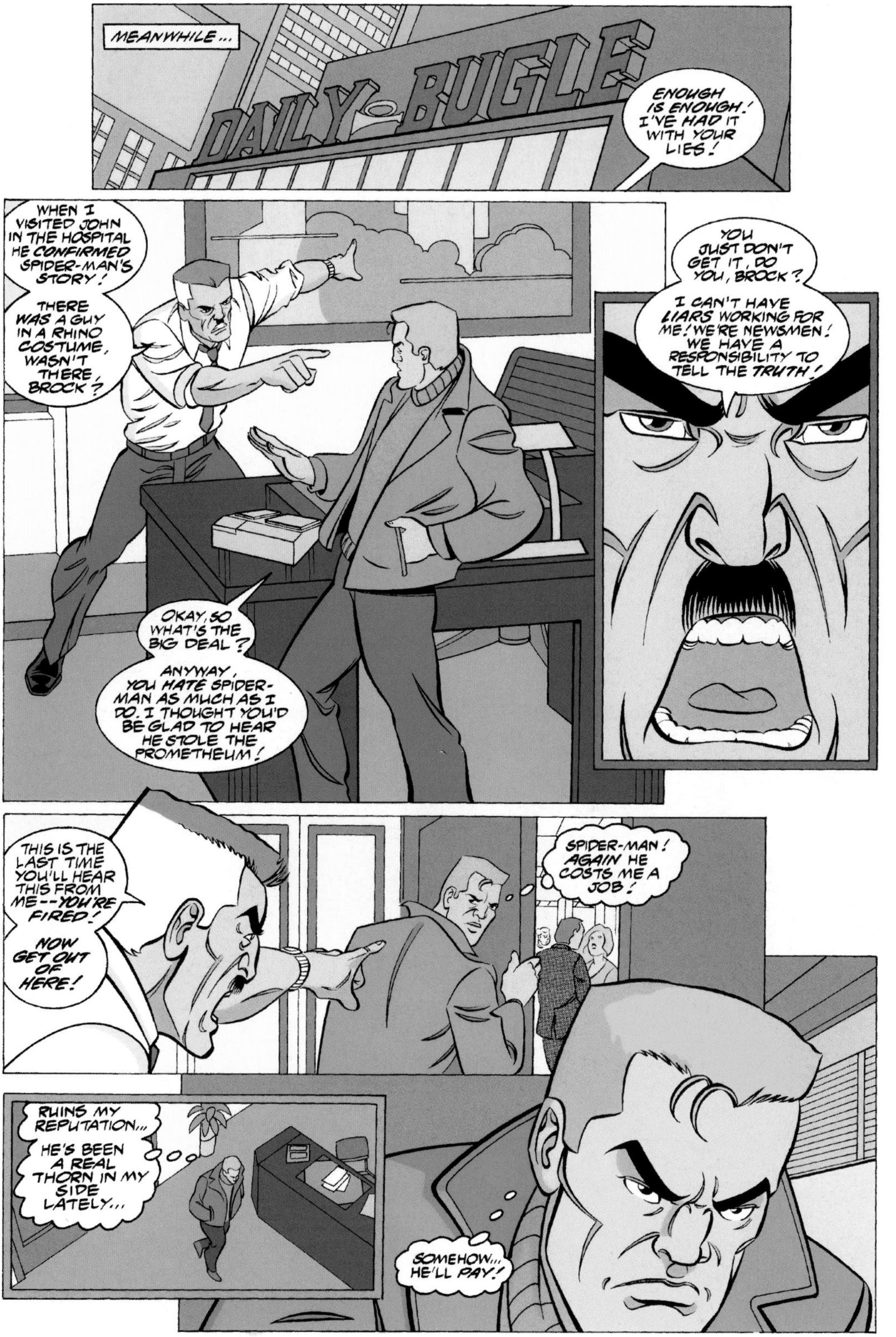
MEANWHILE...
DAILY BUGLE
ENOUGH IS ENOUGH! I'VE HAD IT WITH YOUR LIES!
WHEN I VISITED JOHN IN THE HOSPITAL HE CONFIRMED SPIDER-MAN'S STORY!
THERE WAS A GUY IN A RHINO COSTUME, WASN'T THERE, BROCK?
OKAY, SO WHAT'S THE BIG DEAL?
ANYWAY, YOU HATE SPIDER-MAN AS MUCH AS I DO. I THOUGHT YOU'D BE GLAD TO HEAR HE STOLE THE PROMETHEUM!
YOU JUST DON'T GET IT, DO YOU, BROCK?
I CAN'T HAVE LIARS WORKING FOR ME! WE'RE NEWSMEN! WE HAVE A RESPONSIBILITY TO TELL THE TRUTH!
THIS IS THE LAST TIME YOU'LL HEAR THIS FROM ME--YOU'RE FIRED!
NOW GET OUT OF HERE!
SPIDER-MAN! AGAIN HE COSTS ME A JOB!
RUINS MY REPUTATION...
HE'S BEEN A REAL THORN IN MY SIDE LATELY...
SOMEHOW... HE'LL PAY!

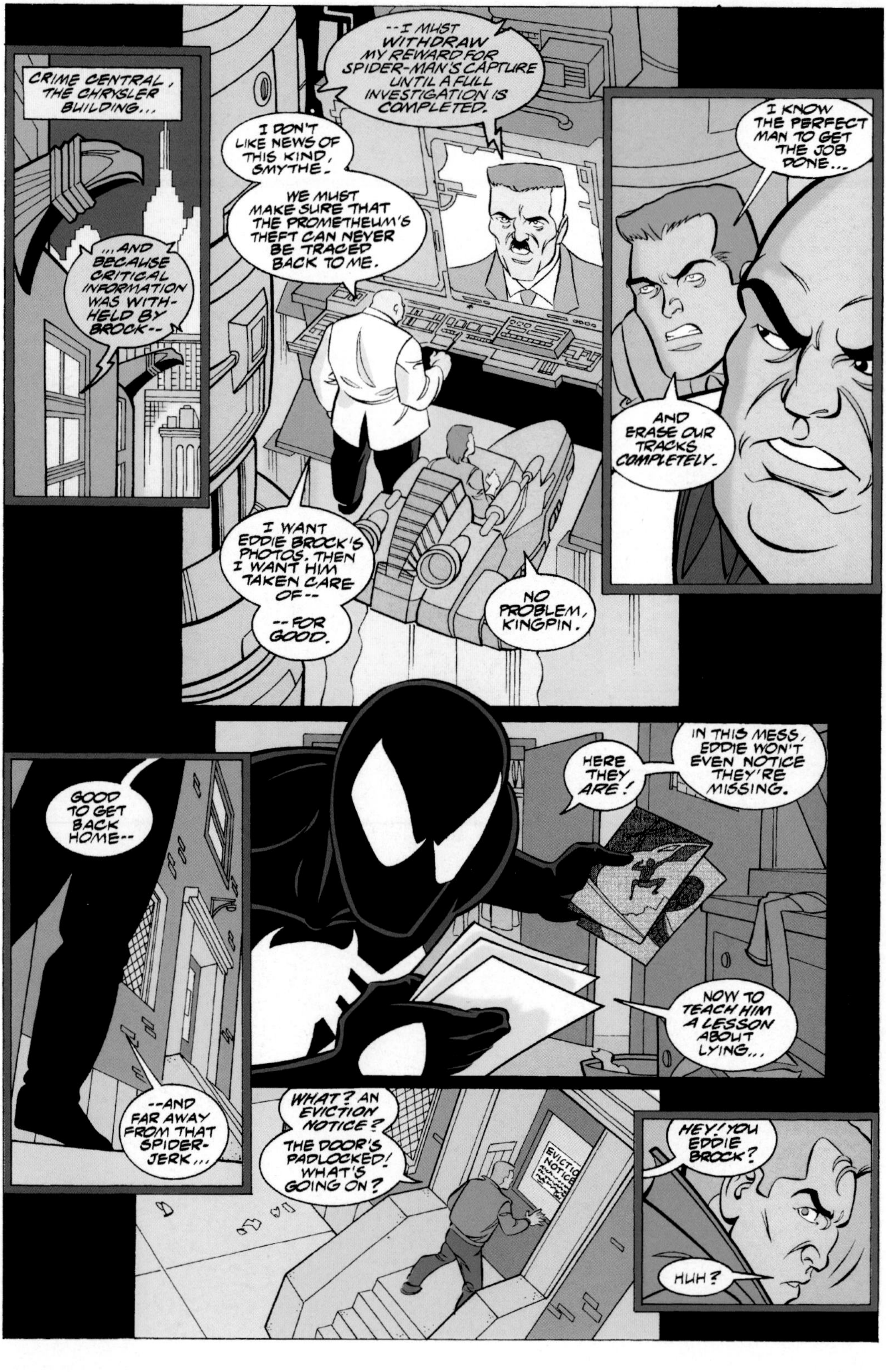
CRIME CENTRAL, THE CHRYSLER BUILDING...
...AND BECAUSE CRITICAL INFORMATION WAS WITHHELD BY BROCK--
--I MUST WITHDRAW MY REWARD FOR SPIDER-MAN'S CAPTURE UNTIL A FULL INVESTIGATION IS COMPLETED.
I DON'T LIKE NEWS OF THIS KIND, SMYTHE.
WE MUST MAKE SURE THAT THE PROMETHEUM'S THEFT CAN NEVER BE TRACED BACK TO ME.
I WANT EDDIE BROCK'S PHOTOS. THEN I WANT HIM TAKEN CARE OF--
--FOR GOOD.
NO PROBLEM, KINGPIN.
I KNOW THE PERFECT MAN TO GET THE JOB DONE...
AND ERASE OUR TRACKS COMPLETELY.
GOOD TO GET BACK HOME--
--AND FAR AWAY FROM THAT SPIDER-JERK...
HERE THEY ARE!
IN THIS MESS, EDDIE WON'T EVEN NOTICE THEY'RE MISSING.
NOW TO TEACH HIM A LESSON ABOUT LYING...
WHAT? AN EVICTION NOTICE?
THE DOOR'S PADLOCKED! WHAT'S GOING ON?
HEY! YOU EDDIE BROCK?
HUH?

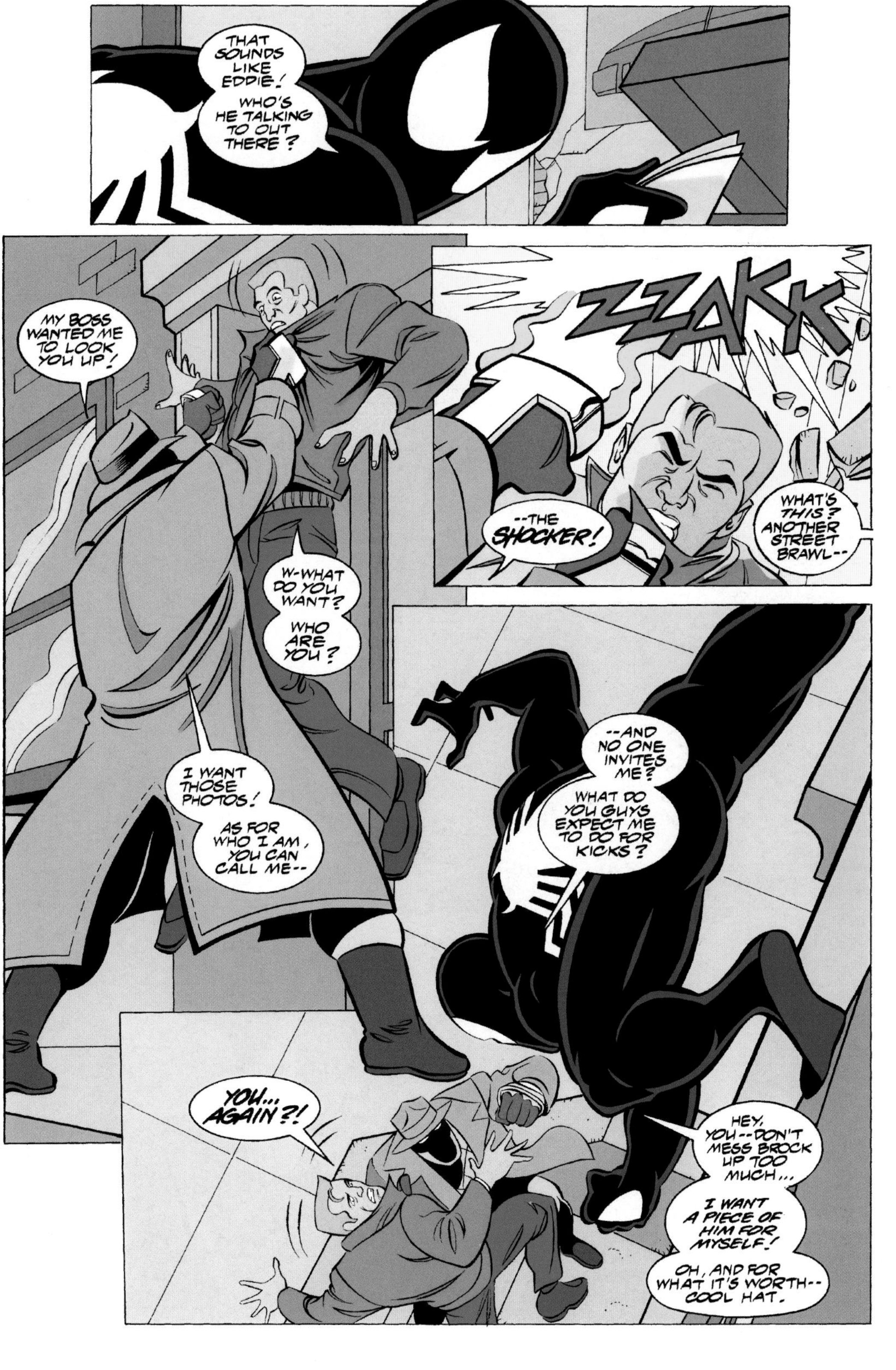
THAT SOUNDS LIKE EDDIE!
WHO'S HE TALKING TO OUT THERE?
MY BOSS WANTED ME TO LOOK YOU UP!
W-WHAT DO YOU WANT?
WHO ARE YOU?
I WANT THOSE PHOTOS!
AS FOR WHO I AM, YOU CAN CALL ME--
--THE SHOCKER!
ZZAKK
WHAT'S THIS? ANOTHER STREET BRAWL--
--AND NO ONE INVITES ME?
WHAT DO YOU GUYS EXPECT ME TO DO FOR KICKS?
YOU... AGAIN?!
HEY, YOU--DON'T MESS BROCK UP TOO MUCH...
I WANT A PIECE OF HIM FOR MYSELF!
OH, AND FOR WHAT IT'S WORTH--COOL HAT.

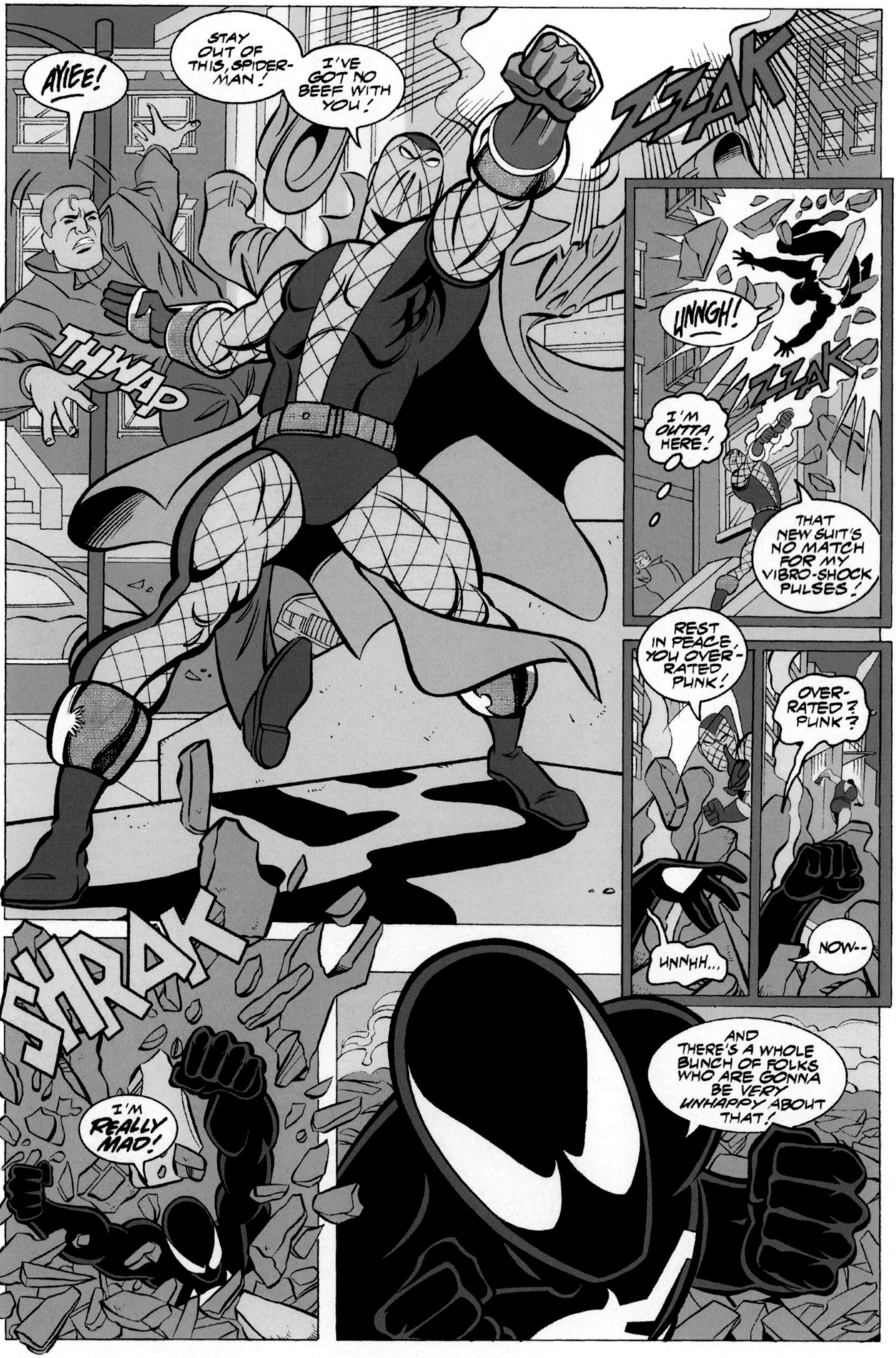
AYIEE!
STAY OUT OF THIS, SPIDER-MAN!
I'VE GOT NO BEEF WITH YOU!
ZZAK
THWAP
UNNGH!
ZZAK
I'M OUTTA HERE!
THAT NEW SUIT'S NO MATCH FOR MY VIBRO-SHOCK PULSES!
REST IN PEACE, YOU OVER-RATED PUNK!
UNNHH...
OVER-RATED? PUNK?
NOW--
SHRAK
I'M REALLY MAD!
AND THERE'S A WHOLE BUNCH OF FOLKS WHO ARE GONNA BE VERY UNHAPPY ABOUT THAT!

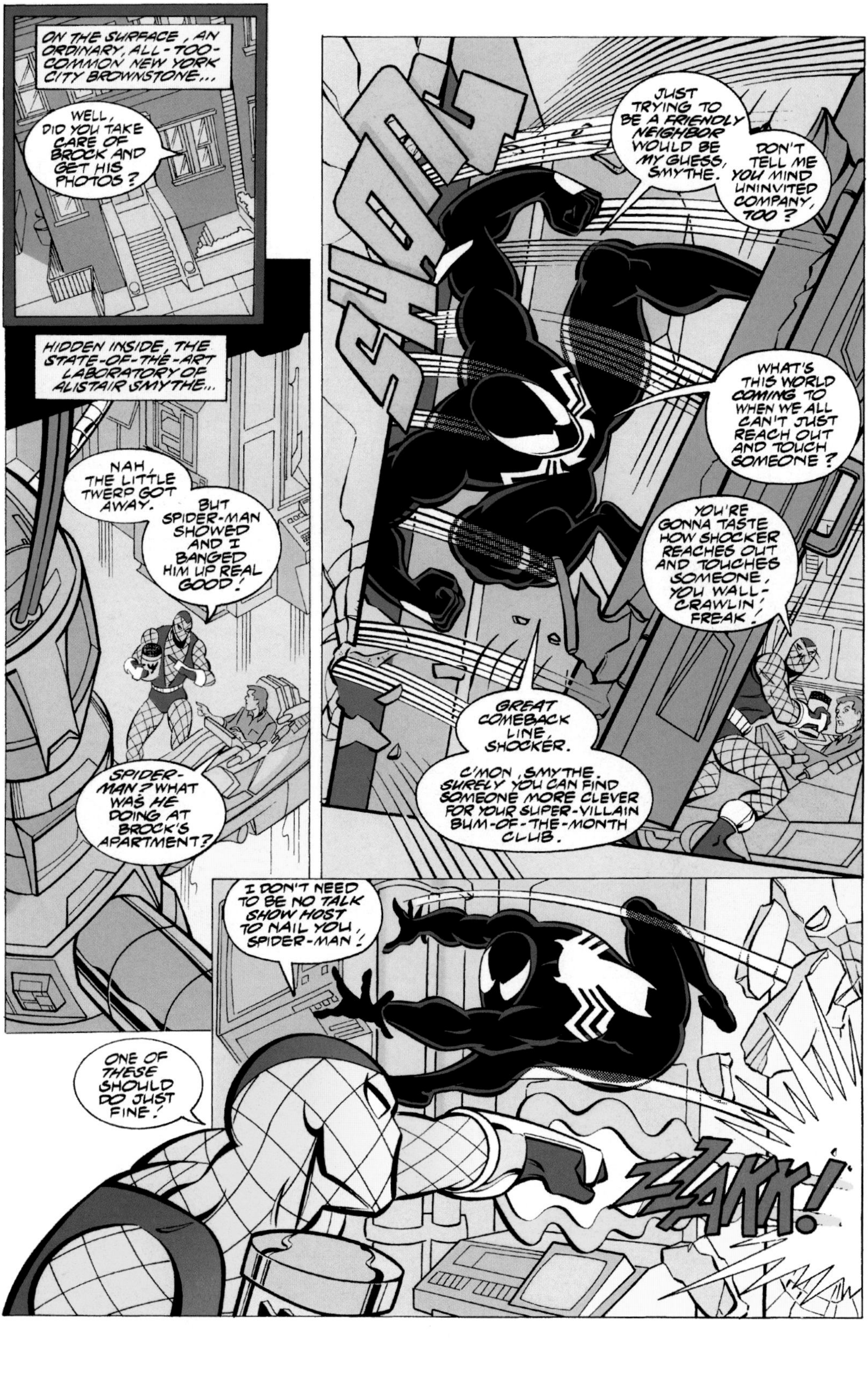

ON THE SURFACE, AN ORDINARY, ALL-TOO-COMMON NEW YORK CITY BROWNSTONE...
WELL, DID YOU TAKE CARE OF BROCK AND GET HIS PHOTOS?
HIDDEN INSIDE, THE STATE-OF-THE-ART LABORATORY OF ALISTAIR SMYTHE...
NAH, THE LITTLE TWERP GOT AWAY.
BUT SPIDER-MAN SHOWED AND I BANGED HIM UP REAL GOOD!
SPIDER-MAN? WHAT WAS HE DOING AT BROCK'S APARTMENT?
SHOOM
JUST TRYING TO BE A FRIENDLY NEIGHBOR WOULD BE MY GUESS, SMYTHE.
DON'T TELL ME YOU MIND UNINVITED COMPANY, TOO?
WHAT'S THIS WORLD COMING TO WHEN WE ALL CAN'T JUST REACH OUT AND TOUCH SOMEONE?
YOU'RE GONNA TASTE HOW SHOCKER REACHES OUT AND TOUCHES SOMEONE, YOU WALL-CRAWLIN' FREAK!
GREAT COMEBACK LINE, SHOCKER.
C'MON, SMYTHE. SURELY YOU CAN FIND SOMEONE MORE CLEVER FOR YOUR SUPER-VILLAIN BUM-OF-THE-MONTH CLUB.
I DON'T NEED TO BE NO TALK SHOW HOST TO NAIL YOU, SPIDER-MAN!
ONE OF THESE SHOULD DO JUST FINE!
ZAKK!

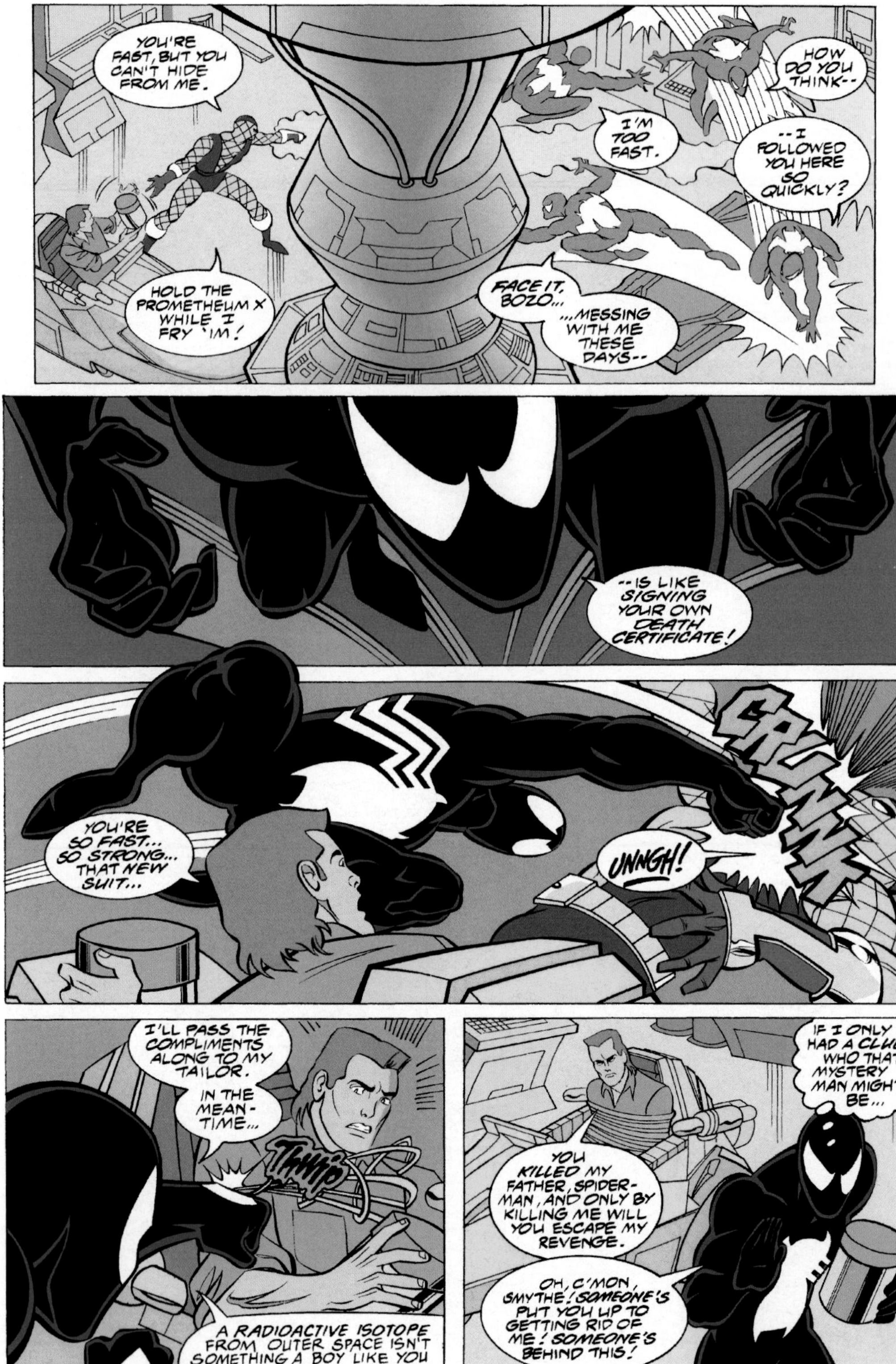
YOU'RE FAST, BUT YOU CAN'T HIDE FROM ME.
HOW DO YOU THINK--
I'M TOO FAST.
--I FOLLOWED YOU HERE SO QUICKLY?
HOLD THE PROMETHEUM X WHILE I FRY 'IM!
FACE IT, BOZO...
...MESSING WITH ME THESE DAYS--
--IS LIKE SIGNING YOUR OWN DEATH CERTIFICATE!
CRUNNK
YOU'RE... SO FAST... SO STRONG... THAT NEW SUIT...
UNNGH!
I'LL PASS THE COMPLIMENTS ALONG TO MY TAILOR.
IN THE MEAN-TIME...
THWIP
A RADIOACTIVE ISOTOPE FROM OUTER SPACE ISN'T SOMETHING A BOY LIKE YOU SHOULD BE PLAYING WITH.
IF I ONLY HAD A CLUE WHO THAT MYSTERY MAN MIGHT BE...
YOU KILLED MY FATHER, SPIDER-MAN, AND ONLY BY KILLING ME WILL YOU ESCAPE MY REVENGE.
OH, C'MON, SMYTHE! SOMEONE'S PUT YOU UP TO GETTING RID OF ME! SOMEONE'S BEHIND THIS!

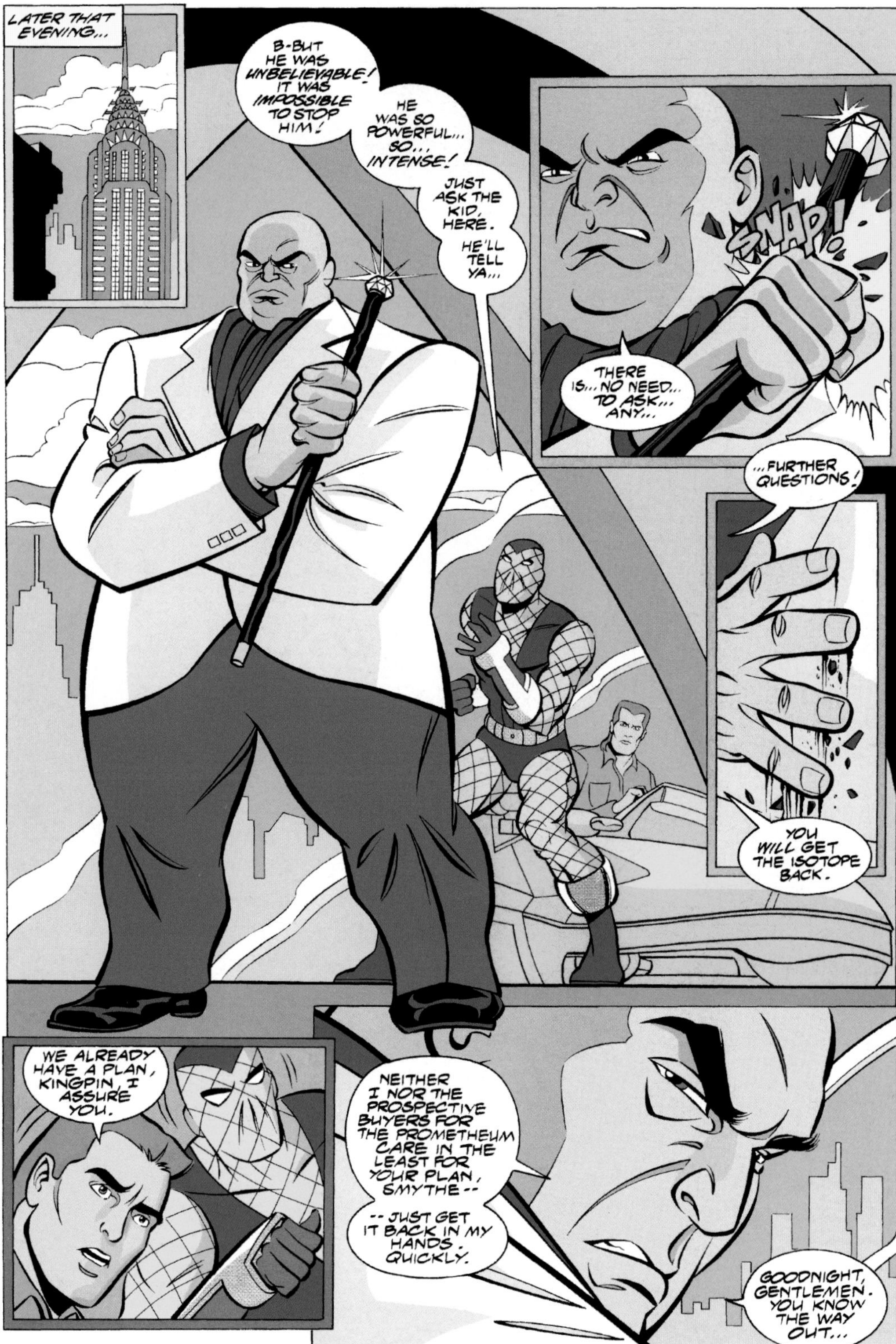
LATER THAT EVENING...
B-BUT HE WAS UNBELIEVABLE! IT WAS IMPOSSIBLE TO STOP HIM!
HE WAS SO POWERFUL... SO... INTENSE!
JUST ASK THE KID, HERE.
HE'LL TELL YA...
SNAP!
THERE IS... NO NEED... TO ASK... ANY...
...FURTHER QUESTIONS!
YOU WILL GET THE ISOTOPE BACK.
WE ALREADY HAVE A PLAN, KINGPIN, I ASSURE YOU.
NEITHER I NOR THE PROSPECTIVE BUYERS FOR THE PROMETHEUM CARE IN THE LEAST FOR YOUR PLAN, SMYTHE--
-- JUST GET IT BACK IN MY HANDS. QUICKLY.
GOODNIGHT, GENTLEMEN. YOU KNOW THE WAY OUT...

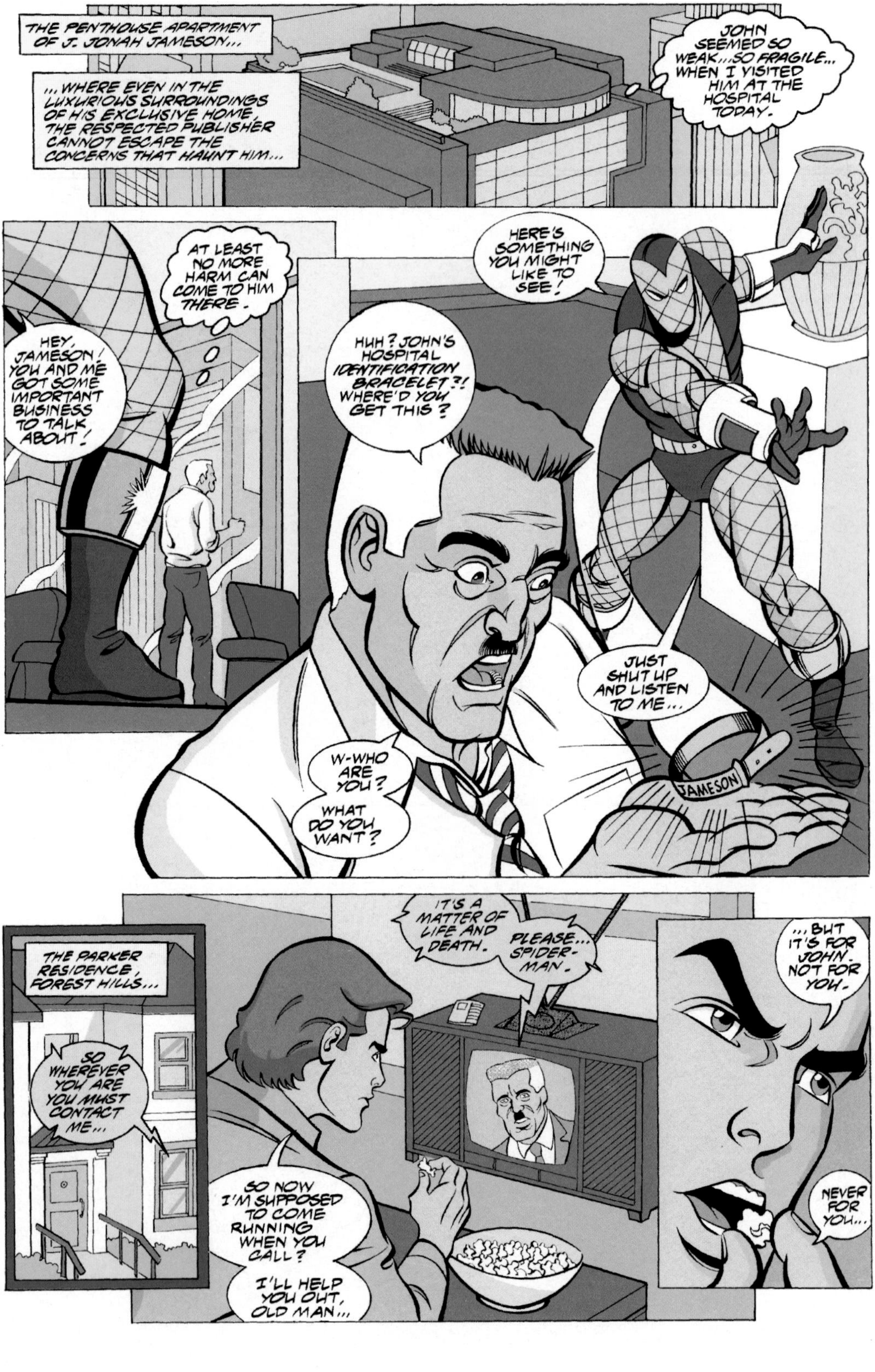
THE PENTHOUSE APARTMENT OF J. JONAH JAMESON...
...WHERE EVEN IN THE LUXURIOUS SURROUNDINGS OF HIS EXCLUSIVE HOME, THE RESPECTED PUBLISHER CANNOT ESCAPE THE CONCERNS THAT HAUNT HIM...
JOHN SEEMED SO WEAK...SO FRAGILE... WHEN I VISITED HIM AT THE HOSPITAL TODAY.
AT LEAST NO MORE HARM CAN COME TO HIM THERE.
HEY, JAMESON! YOU AND ME GOT SOME IMPORTANT BUSINESS TO TALK ABOUT!
HERE'S SOMETHING YOU MIGHT LIKE TO SEE!
HUH? JOHN'S HOSPITAL IDENTIFICATION BRACELET?! WHERE'D YOU GET THIS?
JUST SHUT UP AND LISTEN TO ME...
JAMESON
W-WHO ARE YOU?
WHAT DO YOU WANT?
THE PARKER RESIDENCE, FOREST HILLS...
SO WHEREVER YOU ARE YOU MUST CONTACT ME...
IT'S A MATTER OF LIFE AND DEATH.
PLEASE... SPIDER-MAN.
SO NOW I'M SUPPOSED TO COME RUNNING WHEN YOU CALL?
I'LL HELP YOU OUT, OLD MAN...
...BUT IT'S FOR JOHN. NOT FOR YOU.
NEVER FOR YOU...

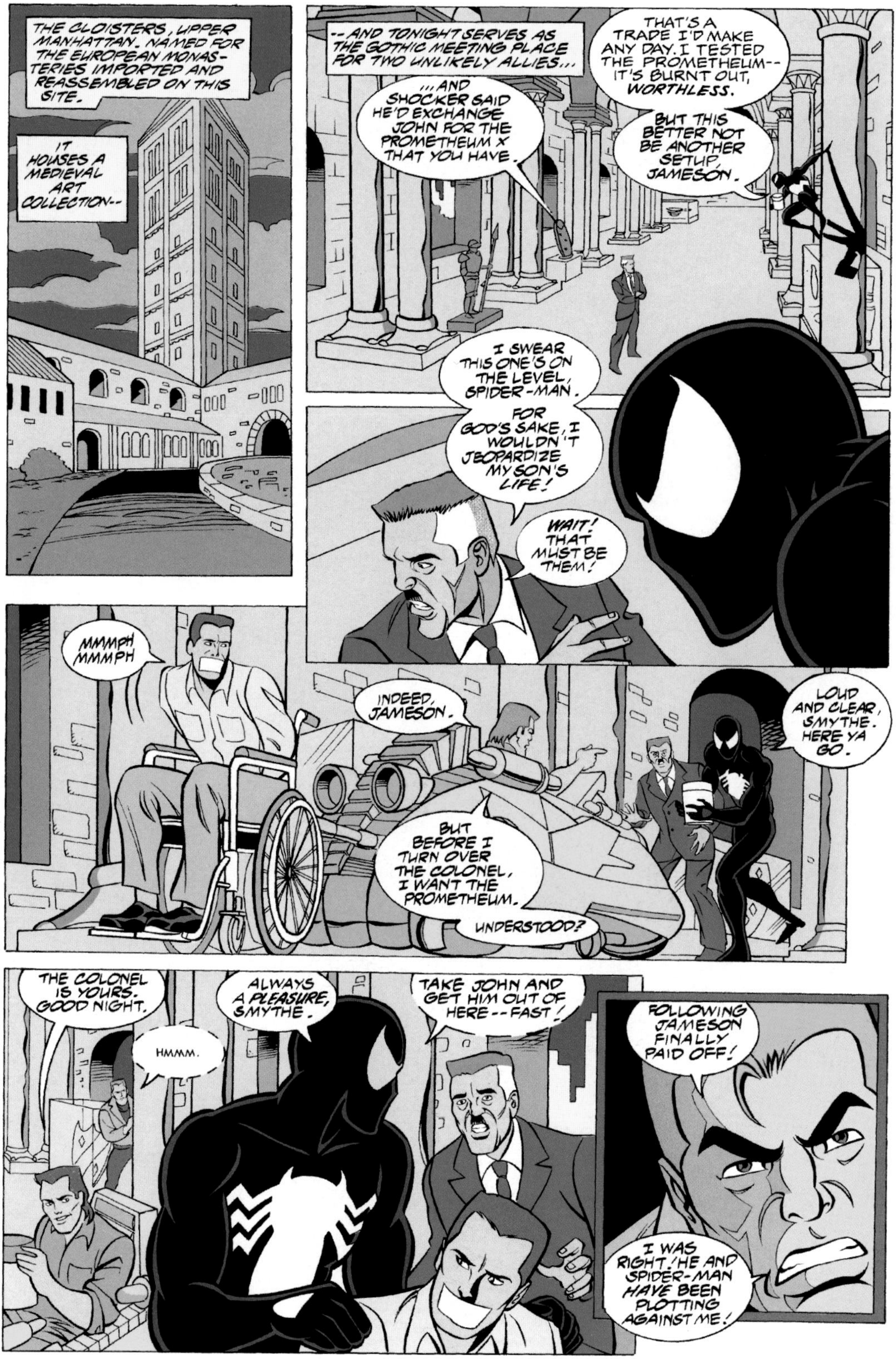
THE CLOISTERS, UPPER MANHATTAN. NAMED FOR THE EUROPEAN MONASTERIES IMPORTED AND REASSEMBLED ON THIS SITE.
IT HOUSES A MEDIEVAL ART COLLECTION--
--AND TONIGHT SERVES AS THE GOTHIC MEETING PLACE FOR TWO UNLIKELY ALLIES...
...AND SHOCKER SAID HE'D EXCHANGE JOHN FOR THE PROMETHEUM X THAT YOU HAVE.
THAT'S A TRADE I'D MAKE ANY DAY. I TESTED THE PROMETHEUM--IT'S BURNT OUT, WORTHLESS.
BUT THIS BETTER NOT BE ANOTHER SETUP, JAMESON.
I SWEAR THIS ONE'S ON THE LEVEL, SPIDER-MAN.
FOR GOD'S SAKE, I WOULDN'T JEOPARDIZE MY SON'S LIFE!
WAIT! THAT MUST BE THEM!
MMMPH MMMPH
INDEED, JAMESON.
LOUD AND CLEAR, SMYTHE. HERE YA GO.
BUT BEFORE I TURN OVER THE COLONEL, I WANT THE PROMETHEUM.
UNDERSTOOD?
THE COLONEL IS YOURS. GOOD NIGHT.
HMMM.
ALWAYS A PLEASURE, SMYTHE.
TAKE JOHN AND GET HIM OUT OF HERE--FAST!
FOLLOWING JAMESON FINALLY PAID OFF!
I WAS RIGHT! HE AND SPIDER-MAN HAVE BEEN PLOTTING AGAINST ME!

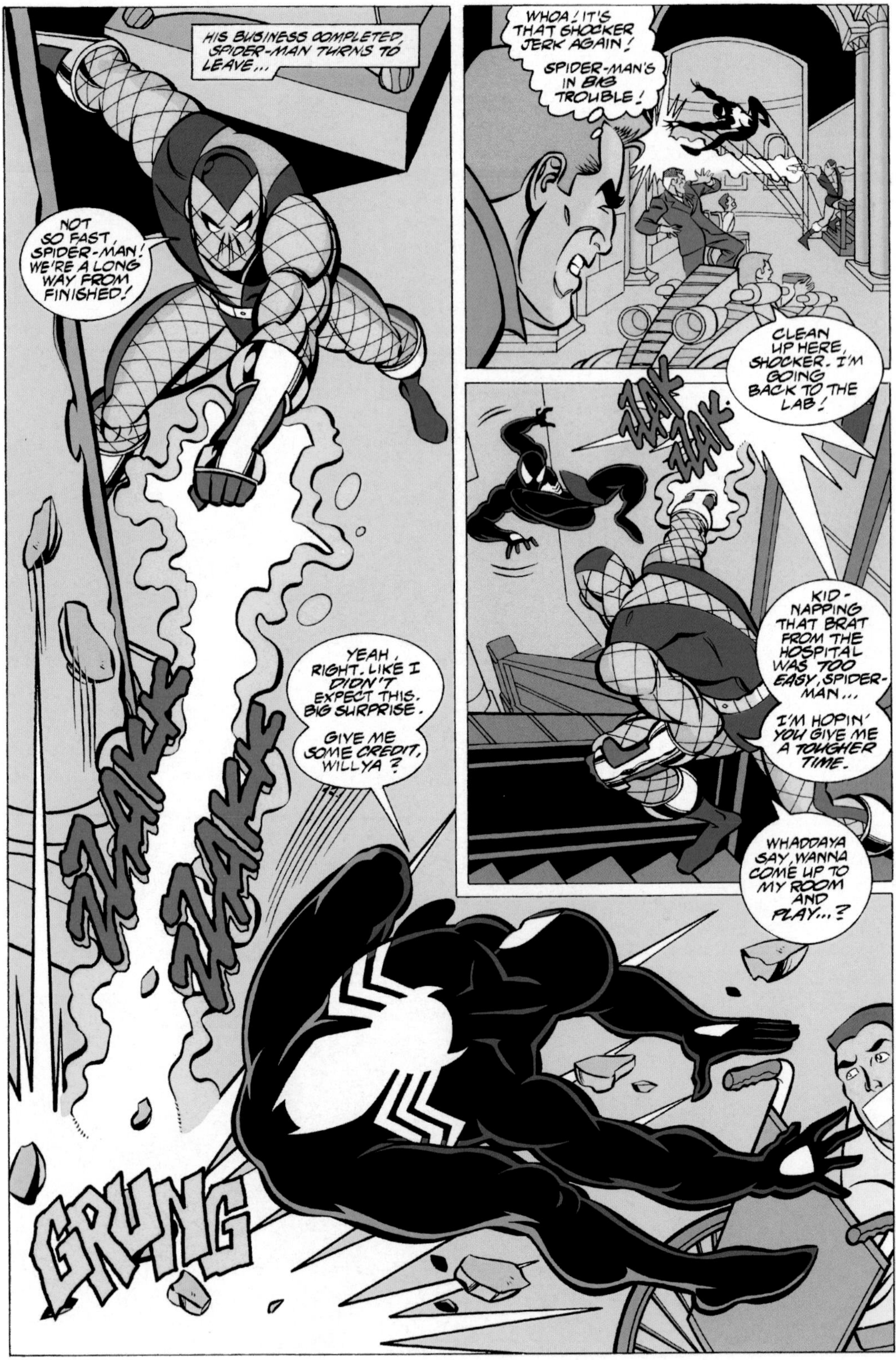
HIS BUSINESS COMPLETED, SPIDER-MAN TURNS TO LEAVE...
NOT SO FAST, SPIDER-MAN! WE'RE A LONG WAY FROM FINISHED!
ZAKK
ZAKK
YEAH, RIGHT. LIKE I DIDN'T EXPECT THIS. BIG SURPRISE.
GIVE ME SOME CREDIT, WILLYA?
GRUNG
WHOA! IT'S THAT SHOCKER JERK AGAIN!
SPIDER-MAN'S IN BIG TROUBLE!
CLEAN UP HERE, SHOCKER. I'M GOING BACK TO THE LAB!
ZAK
ZAK
KID-NAPPING THAT BRAT FROM THE HOSPITAL WAS TOO EASY, SPIDER-MAN...
I'M HOPIN' YOU GIVE ME A TOUGHER TIME.
WHADDAYA SAY, WANNA COME UP TO MY ROOM AND PLAY...?

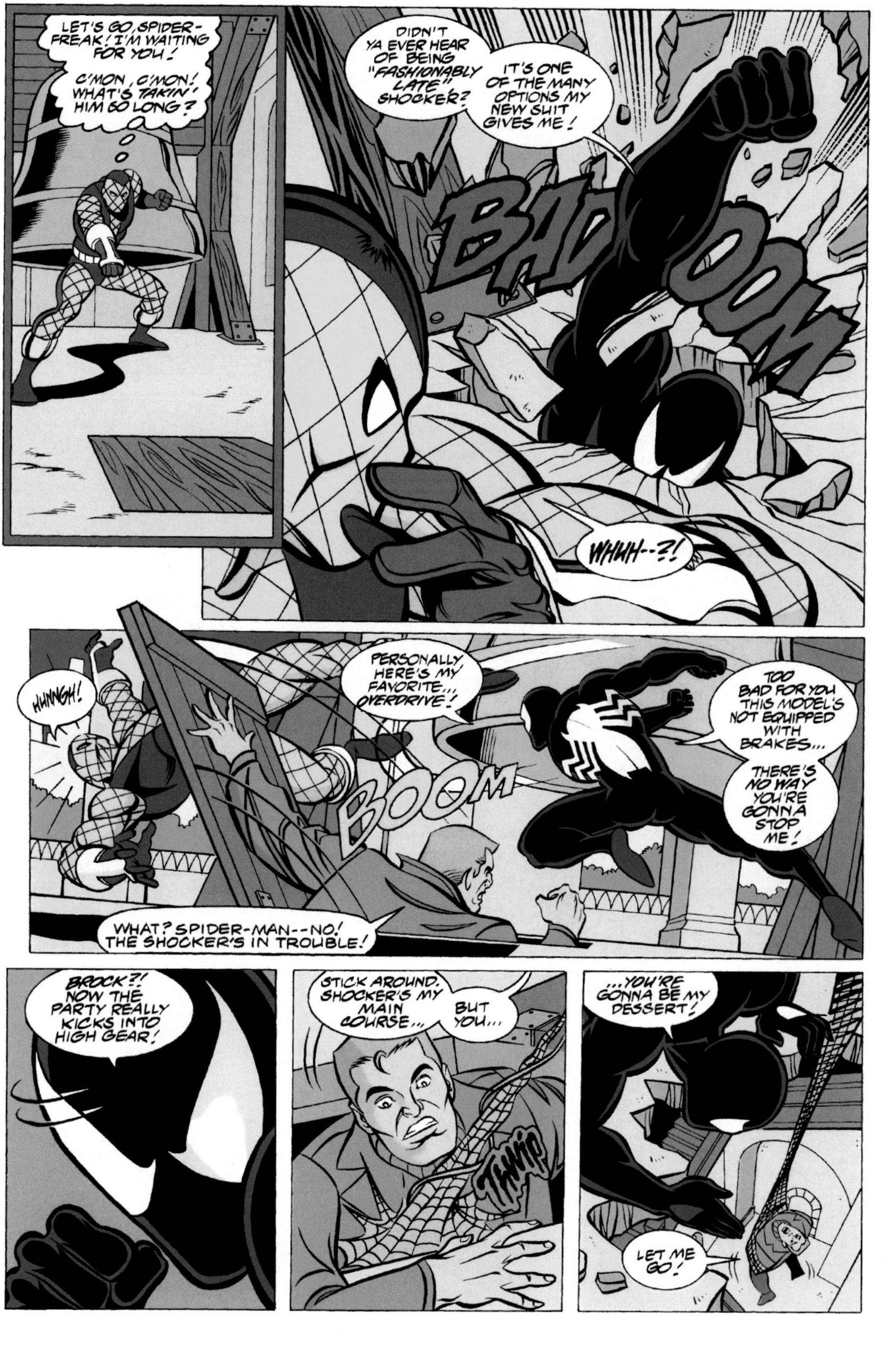
LET'S GO, SPIDER-FREAK! I'M WAITING FOR YOU!
C'MON, C'MON! WHAT'S TAKIN' HIM SO LONG?
DIDN'T YA EVER HEAR OF BEING "FASHIONABLY LATE" SHOCKER?
IT'S ONE OF THE MANY OPTIONS MY NEW SUIT GIVES ME!
BADOOOM
WHUH--?!
HUNNGH!
PERSONALLY HERE'S MY FAVORITE... OVERDRIVE!
BOOOM
TOO BAD FOR YOU THIS MODEL'S NOT EQUIPPED WITH BRAKES...
THERE'S NO WAY YOU'RE GONNA STOP ME!
WHAT? SPIDER-MAN--NO! THE SHOCKER'S IN TROUBLE!
BROCK?! NOW THE PARTY REALLY KICKS INTO HIGH GEAR!
STICK AROUND. SHOCKER'S MY MAIN COURSE...
BUT YOU...
THWIP
...YOU'RE GONNA BE MY DESSERT!
LET ME GO!

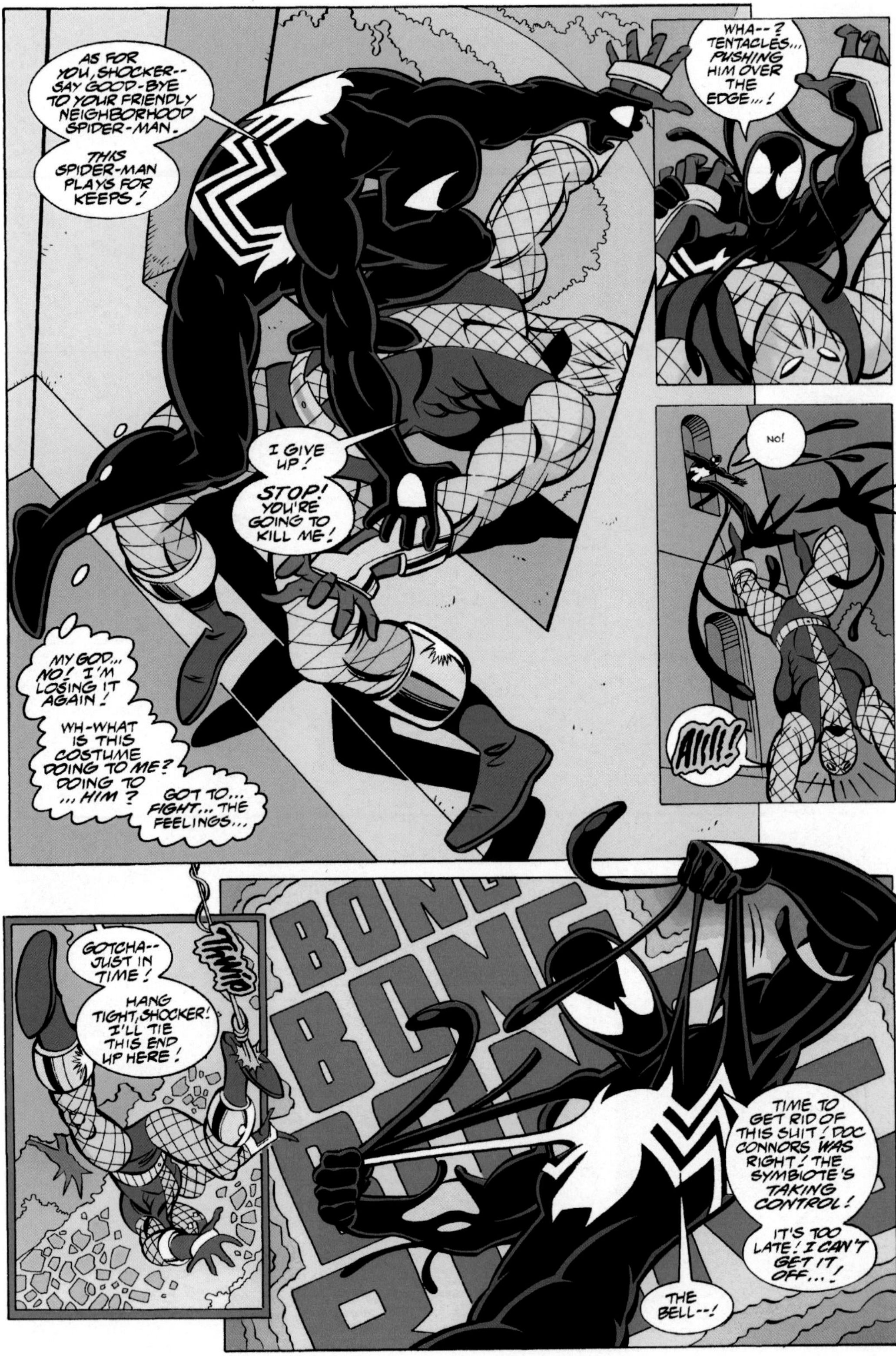
AS FOR YOU, SHOCKER-- SAY GOOD-BYE TO YOUR FRIENDLY NEIGHBORHOOD SPIDER-MAN.
THIS SPIDER-MAN PLAYS FOR KEEPS!
I GIVE UP!
STOP! YOU'RE GOING TO KILL ME!
MY GOD... NO! I'M LOSING IT AGAIN!
WH-WHAT IS THIS COSTUME DOING TO ME? DOING TO ...HIM?
GOT TO... FIGHT... THE FEELINGS...
WHA--? TENTACLES... PUSHING HIM OVER THE EDGE...!
NO!
AIII!
GOTCHA-- JUST IN TIME!
HANG TIGHT, SHOCKER! I'LL TIE THIS END UP HERE!
THWIP
BONG
BONG
TIME TO GET RID OF THIS SUIT! DOC CONNORS WAS RIGHT! THE SYMBIOTE'S TAKING CONTROL!
IT'S TOO LATE! I CAN'T GET IT OFF...!
THE BELL--!

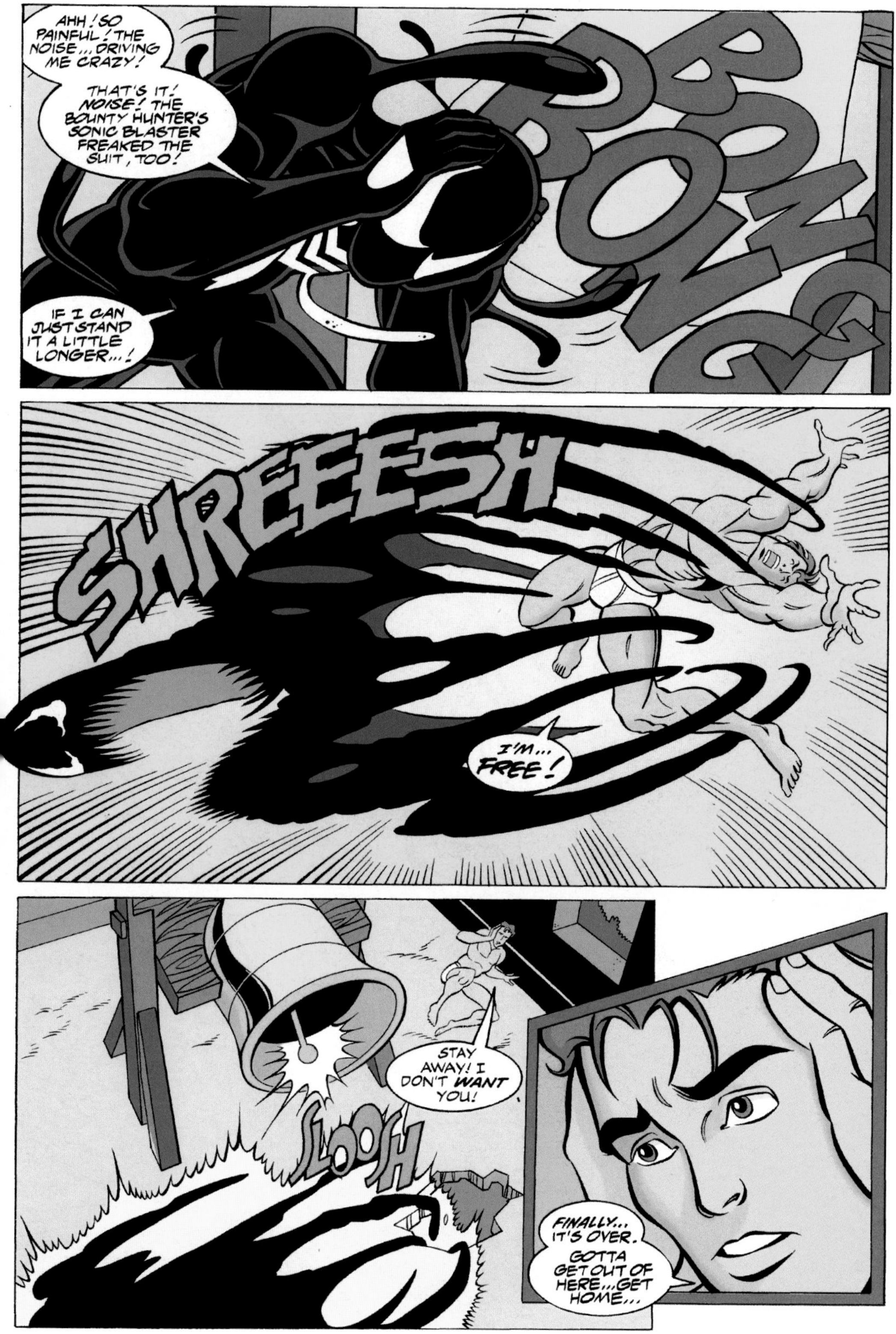
AHH! SO PAINFUL! THE NOISE... DRIVING ME CRAZY!
THAT'S IT! NOISE! THE BOUNTY HUNTER'S SONIC BLASTER FREAKED THE SUIT, TOO!
BBONNG
IF I CAN JUST STAND IT A LITTLE LONGER...!
SHREEESH
I'M... FREE!
STAY AWAY! I DON'T WANT YOU!
SLOOH
FINALLY... IT'S OVER.
GOTTA GET OUT OF HERE...GET HOME...

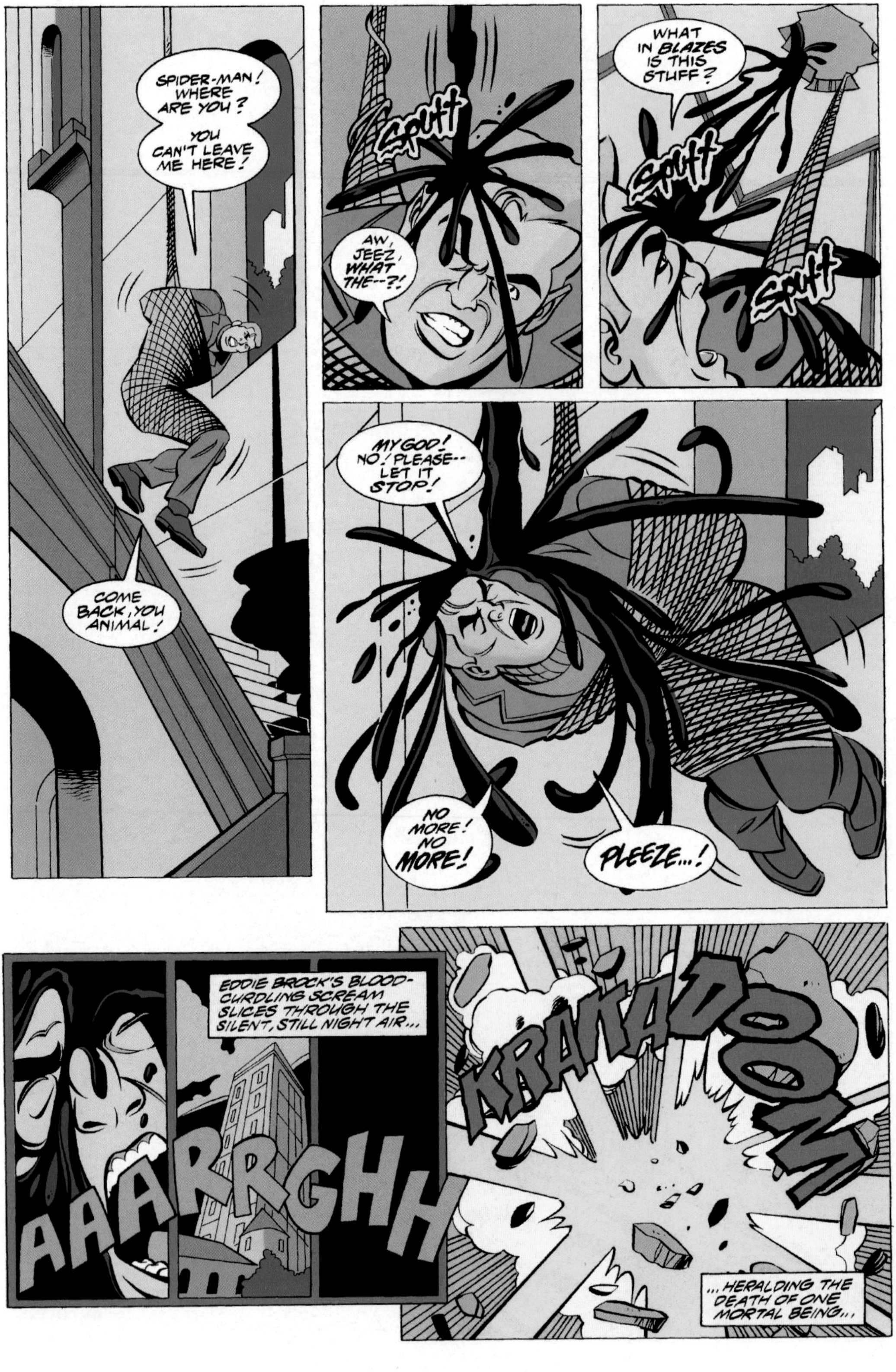
SPIDER-MAN! WHERE ARE YOU?
YOU CAN'T LEAVE ME HERE!
COME BACK, YOU ANIMAL!
SPUTT
AW, JEEZ, WHAT THE--?!
WHAT IN BLAZES IS THIS STUFF?
SPUTT
SPUTT
MY GOD! NO! PLEASE-- LET IT STOP!
NO MORE! NO MORE!
PLEEZE...!
EDDIE BROCK'S BLOOD-CURDLING SCREAM SLICES THROUGH THE SILENT, STILL NIGHT AIR...
AAARRGHH
KRAKADOOM
...HERALDING THE DEATH OF ONE MORTAL BEING...

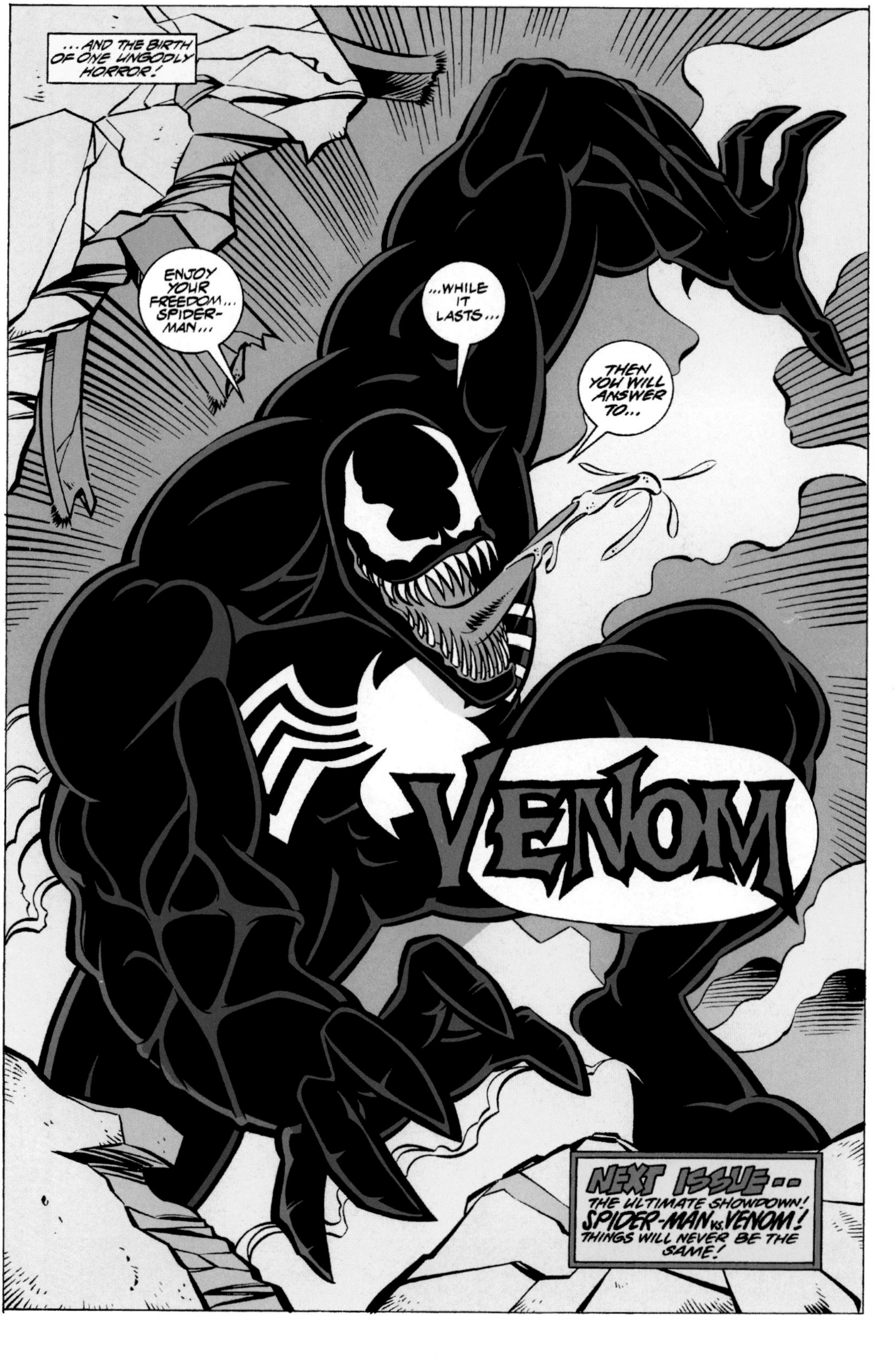
...AND THE BIRTH OF ONE UNGODLY HORROR!
ENJOY YOUR FREEDOM... SPIDER-MAN...
...WHILE IT LASTS...
THEN YOU WILL ANSWER TO...
VENOM
NEXT ISSUE.. THE ULTIMATE SHOWDOWN! SPIDER-MAN vs. VENOM! THINGS WILL NEVER BE THE SAME!

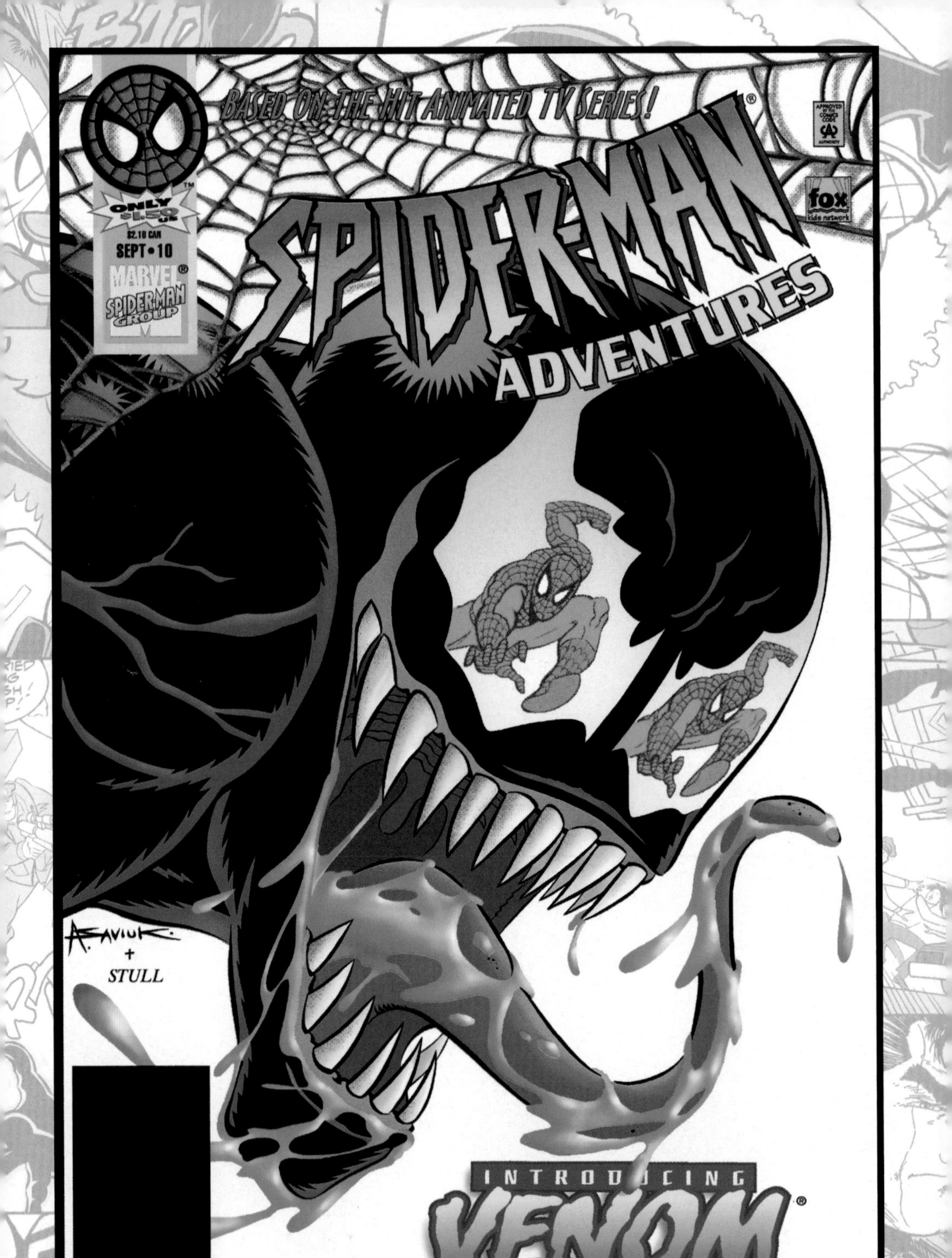
BASED ON THE HIT ANIMATED TV SERIES!
SPIDER-MAN®
ADVENTURES
ONLY $1.50 US
$2.10 CAN
SEPT • 10
MARVEL®
SPIDER-MAN GROUP
fox kids network
A. SAVIUK + STULL
INTRODUCING
VENOM®

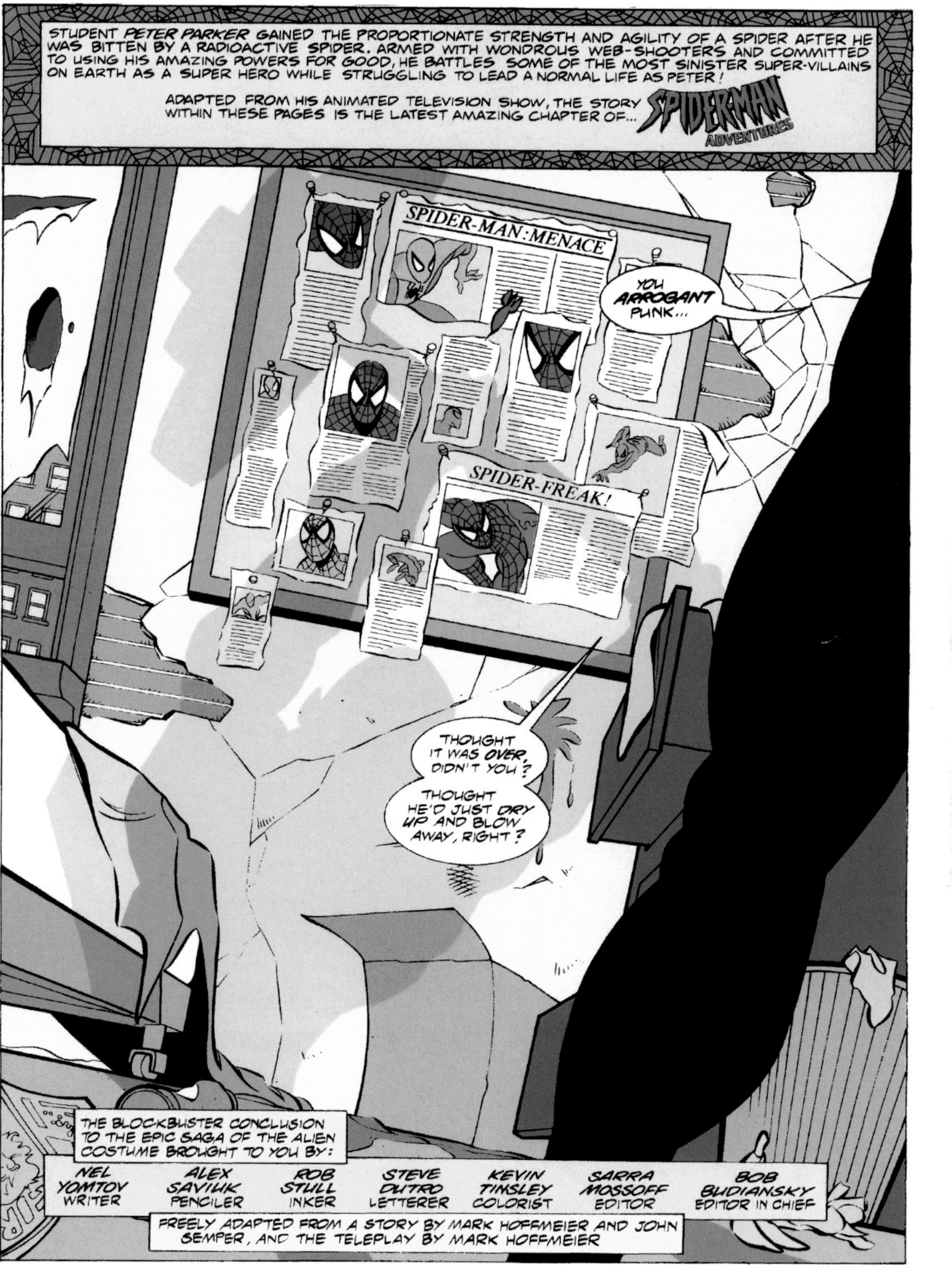

STUDENT PETER PARKER GAINED THE PROPORTIONATE STRENGTH AND AGILITY OF A SPIDER AFTER HE WAS BITTEN BY A RADIOACTIVE SPIDER. ARMED WITH WONDROUS WEB-SHOOTERS AND COMMITTED TO USING HIS AMAZING POWERS FOR GOOD, HE BATTLES SOME OF THE MOST SINISTER SUPER-VILLAINS ON EARTH AS A SUPER HERO WHILE STRUGGLING TO LEAD A NORMAL LIFE AS PETER!
ADAPTED FROM HIS ANIMATED TELEVISION SHOW, THE STORY WITHIN THESE PAGES IS THE LATEST AMAZING CHAPTER OF... SPIDER-MAN ADVENTURES
SPIDER-MAN: MENACE
SPIDER-FREAK!
YOU ARROGANT PUNK...
THOUGHT IT WAS OVER, DIDN'T YOU?
THOUGHT HE'D JUST DRY UP AND BLOW AWAY, RIGHT?
THE BLOCKBUSTER CONCLUSION TO THE EPIC SAGA OF THE ALIEN COSTUME BROUGHT TO YOU BY:
NEL YOMTOV WRITER
ALEX SAVIUK PENCILER
ROB STULL INKER
STEVE DUTRO LETTERER
KEVIN TINSLEY COLORIST
SARRA MOSSOFF EDITOR
BOB BUDIANSKY EDITOR IN CHIEF
FREELY ADAPTED FROM A STORY BY MARK HOFFMEIER AND JOHN SEMPER, AND THE TELEPLAY BY MARK HOFFMEIER

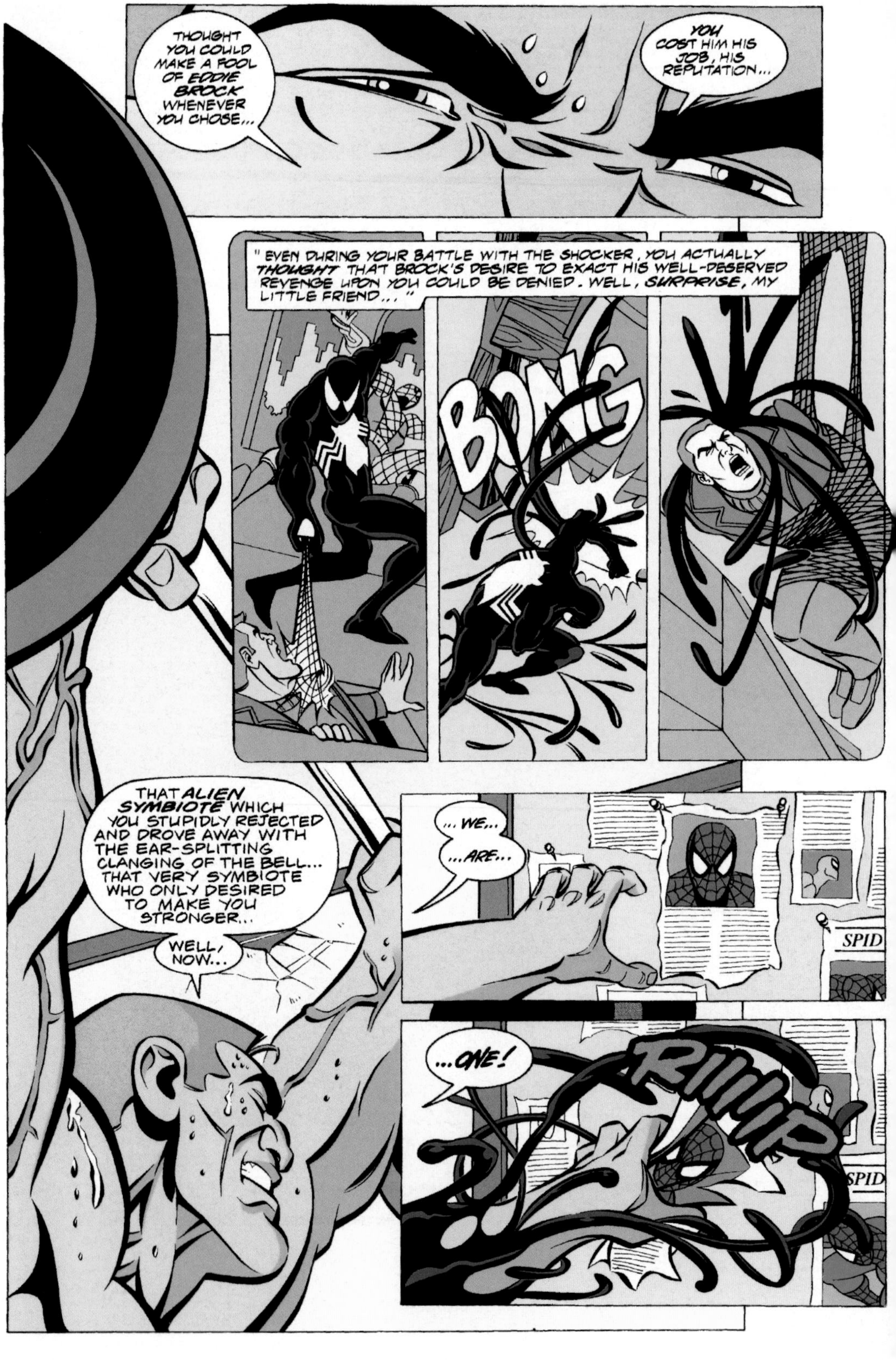
THOUGHT YOU COULD MAKE A FOOL OF EDDIE BROCK WHENEVER YOU CHOSE...
YOU COST HIM HIS JOB, HIS REPUTATION...
" EVEN DURING YOUR BATTLE WITH THE SHOCKER, YOU ACTUALLY THOUGHT THAT BROCK'S DESIRE TO EXACT HIS WELL-DESERVED REVENGE UPON YOU COULD BE DENIED. WELL, SURPRISE, MY LITTLE FRIEND... "
BONG
THAT ALIEN SYMBIOTE WHICH YOU STUPIDLY REJECTED AND DROVE AWAY WITH THE EAR-SPLITTING CLANGING OF THE BELL... THAT VERY SYMBIOTE WHO ONLY DESIRED TO MAKE YOU STRONGER...
WELL, NOW...
...WE...
...ARE...
SPID
...ONE!
RIIIIP
SPID

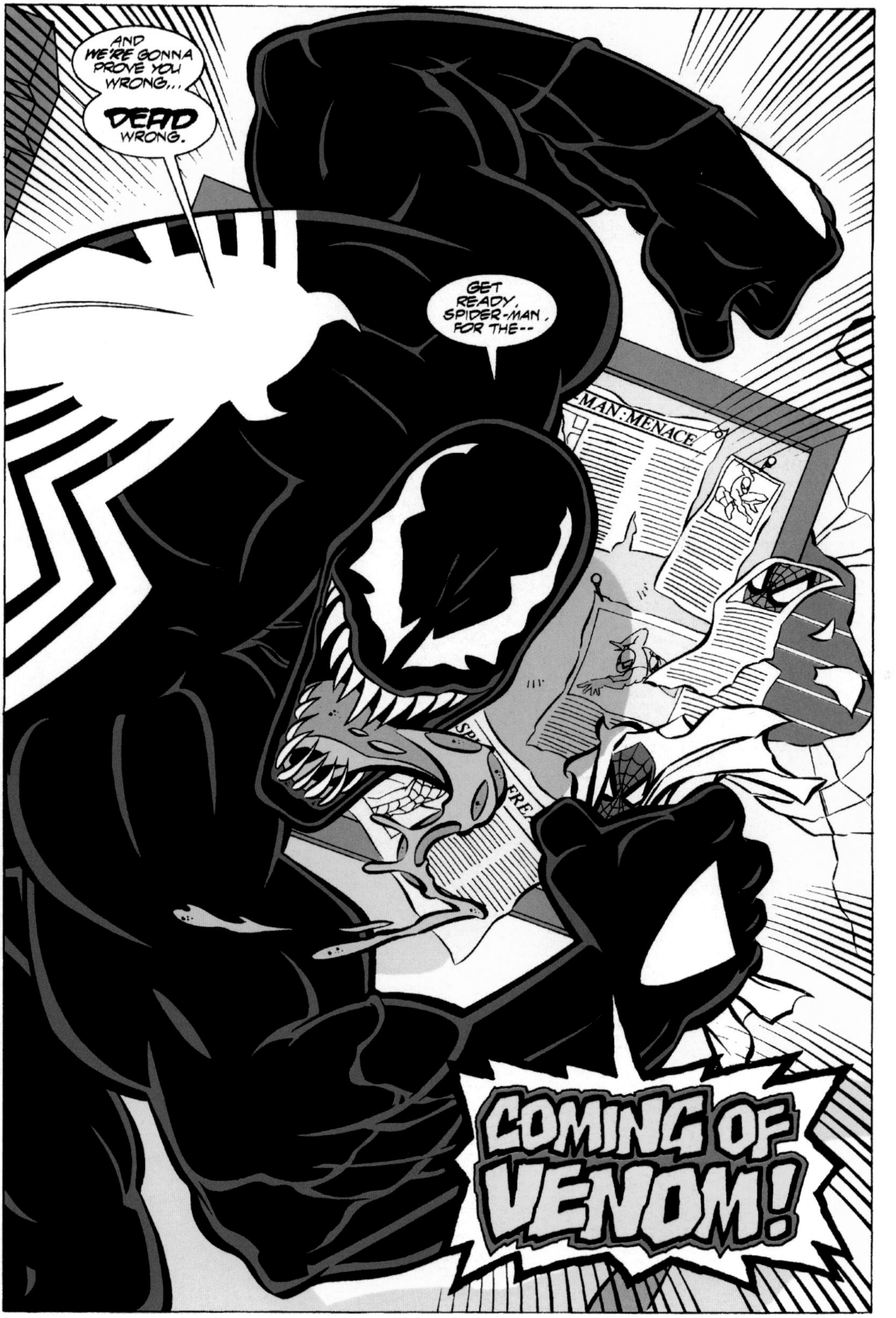
AND WE'RE GONNA PROVE YOU WRONG...
DEAD WRONG.
GET READY, SPIDER-MAN, FOR THE--
COMING OF VENOM!

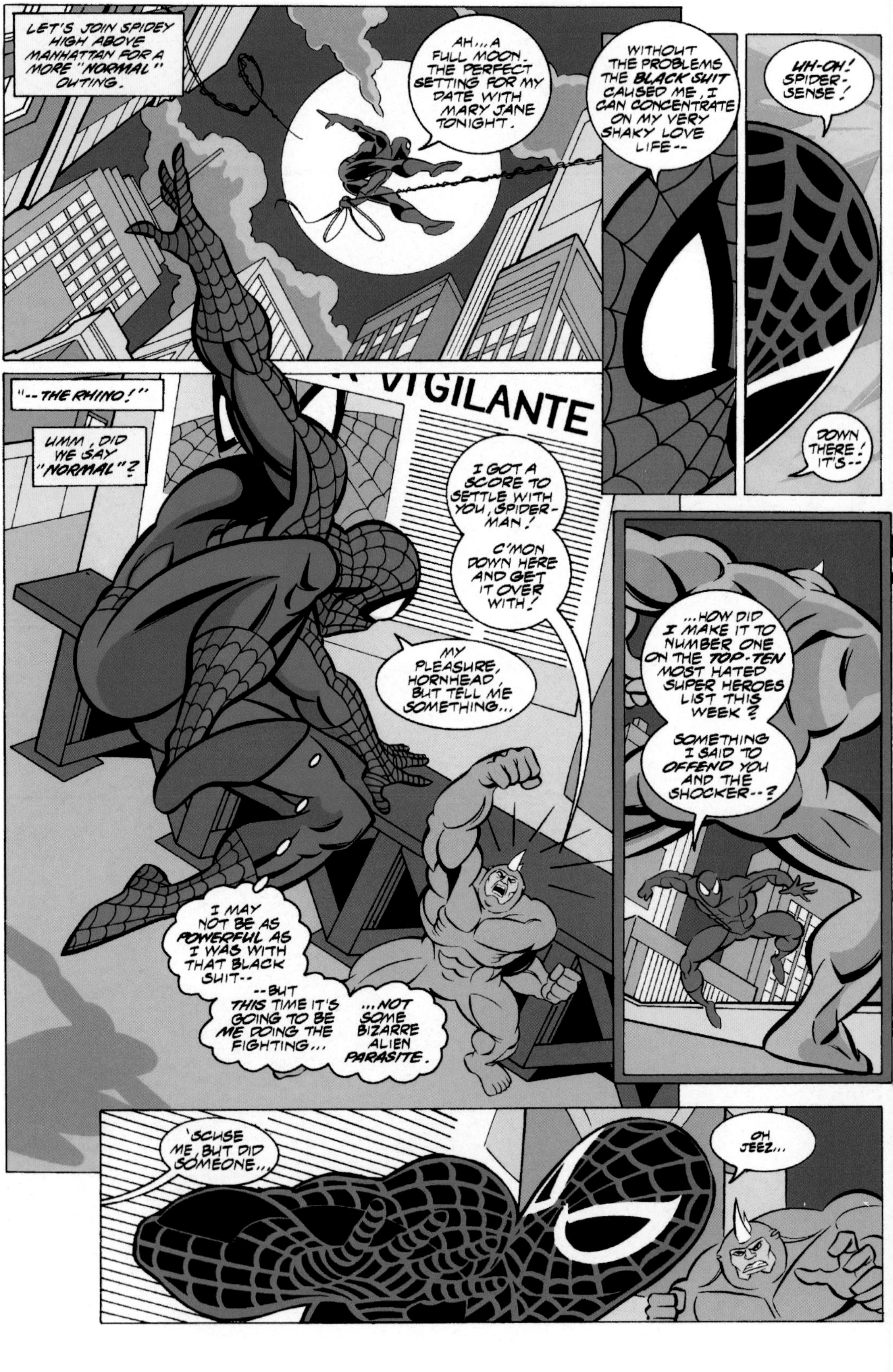
LET'S JOIN SPIDEY HIGH ABOVE MANHATTAN FOR A MORE "NORMAL" OUTING.
AH... A FULL MOON. THE PERFECT SETTING FOR MY DATE WITH MARY JANE TONIGHT.
WITHOUT THE PROBLEMS THE BLACK SUIT CAUSED ME, I CAN CONCENTRATE ON MY VERY SHAKY LOVE LIFE--
UH-OH! SPIDER-SENSE!
DOWN THERE! IT'S--
"--THE RHINO!"
UMM, DID WE SAY "NORMAL"?
VIGILANTE
I GOT A SCORE TO SETTLE WITH YOU, SPIDER-MAN!
C'MON DOWN HERE AND GET IT OVER WITH!
MY PLEASURE, HORNHEAD, BUT TELL ME SOMETHING...
...HOW DID I MAKE IT TO NUMBER ONE ON THE TOP-TEN MOST HATED SUPER HEROES LIST THIS WEEK?
SOMETHING I SAID TO OFFEND YOU AND THE SHOCKER--?
I MAY NOT BE AS POWERFUL AS I WAS WITH THAT BLACK SUIT--
--BUT THIS TIME IT'S GOING TO BE ME DOING THE FIGHTING...
...NOT SOME BIZARRE ALIEN PARASITE.
'SCUSE ME, BUT DID SOMEONE...
OH JEEZ...

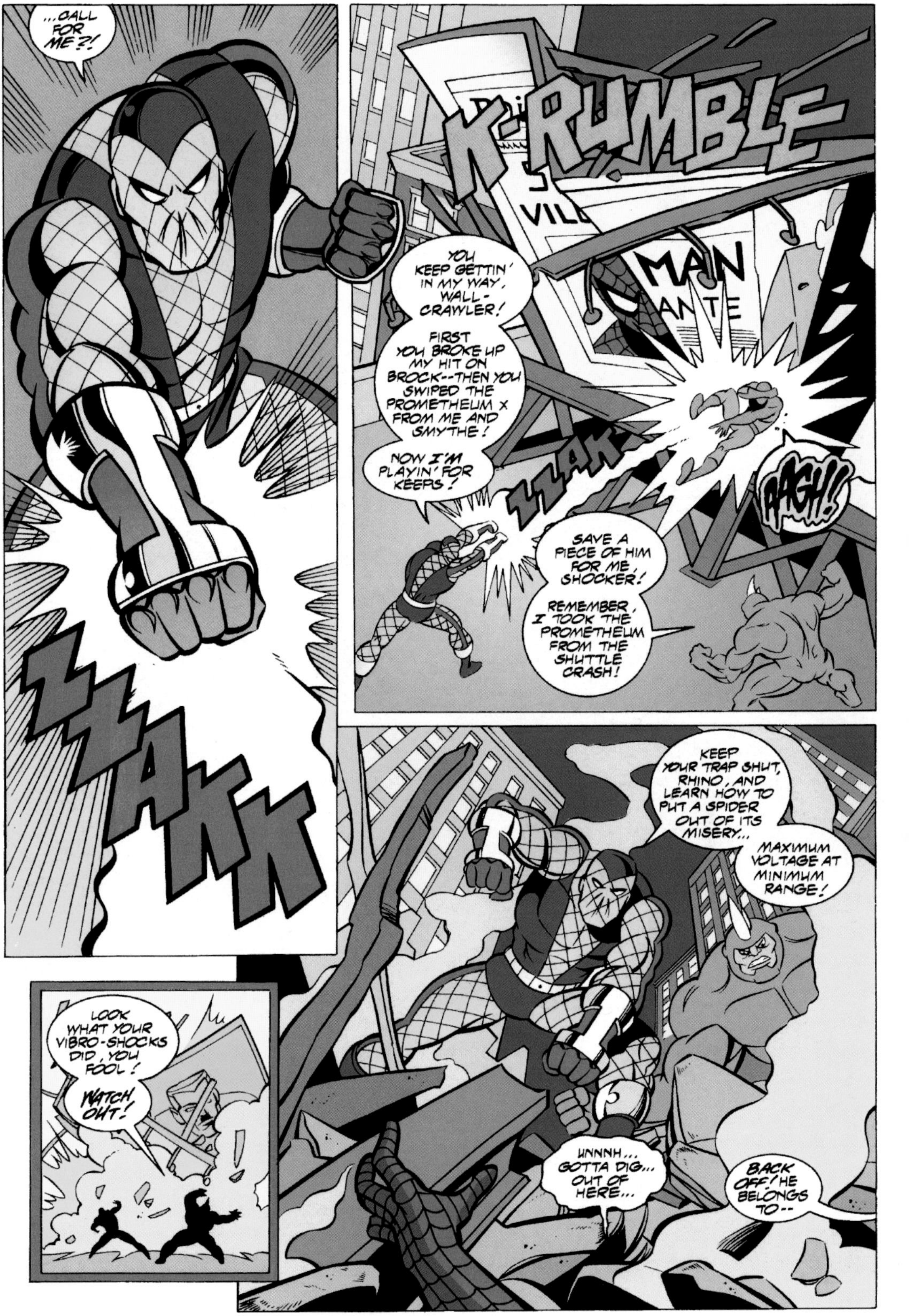

...CALL FOR ME?!
ZZAKK
K-RUMBLE
YOU KEEP GETTIN' IN MY WAY, WALL-CRAWLER!
FIRST YOU BROKE UP MY HIT ON BROCK--THEN YOU SWIPED THE PROMETHEUM X FROM ME AND SMYTHE!
NOW I'M PLAYIN' FOR KEEPS!
ZZAK
AAGH!!
SAVE A PIECE OF HIM FOR ME, SHOCKER!
REMEMBER, I TOOK THE PROMETHEUM FROM THE SHUTTLE CRASH!
KEEP YOUR TRAP SHUT, RHINO, AND LEARN HOW TO PUT A SPIDER OUT OF ITS MISERY...
MAXIMUM VOLTAGE AT MINIMUM RANGE!
LOOK WHAT YOUR VIBRO-SHOCKS DID, YOU FOOL!
WATCH OUT!
UNNNH... GOTTA DIG... OUT OF HERE...
BACK OFF! HE BELONGS TO--

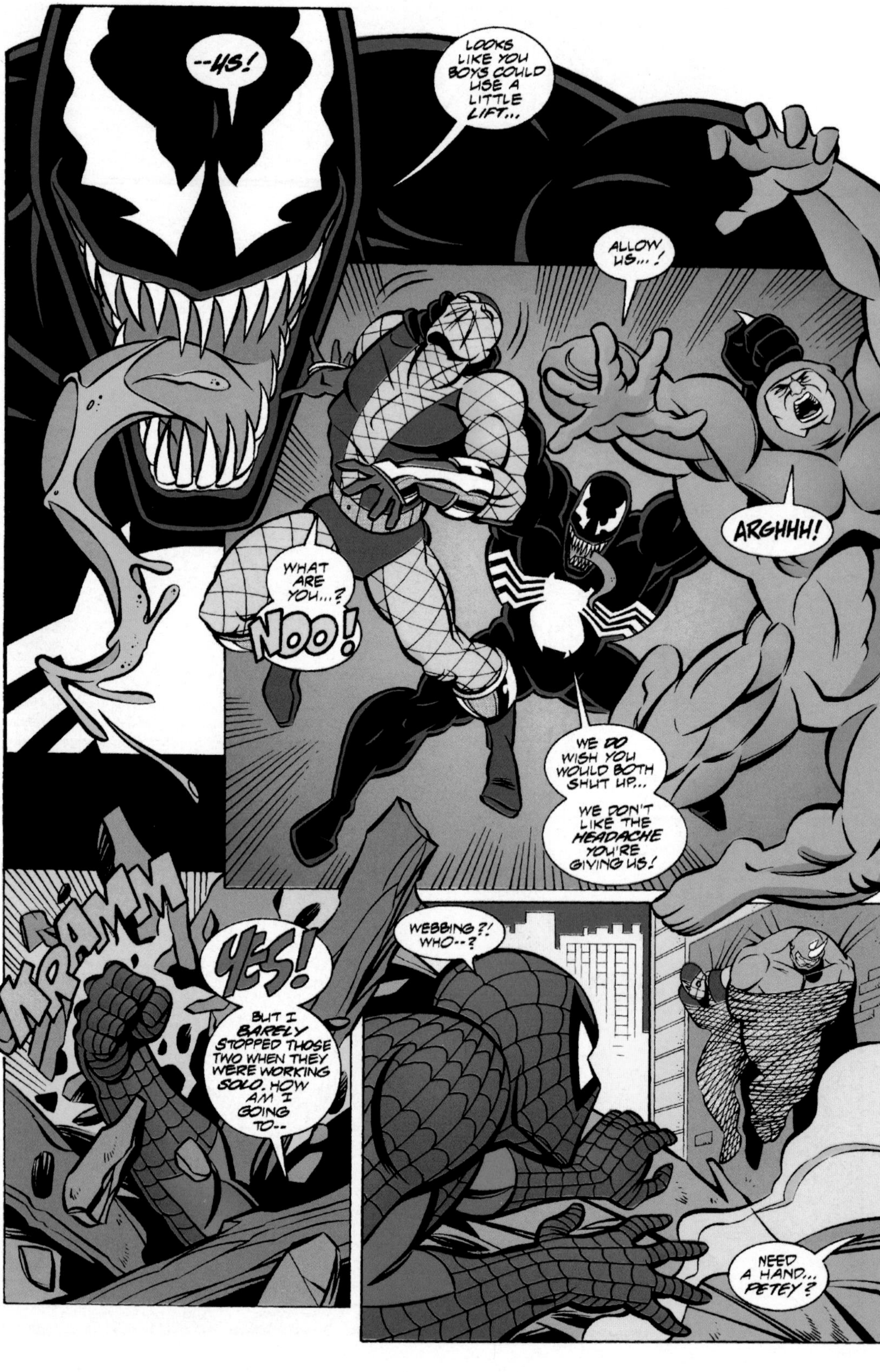
--US!
LOOKS LIKE YOU BOYS COULD USE A LITTLE LIFT...
ALLOW US...!
ARGHHH!
WHAT ARE YOU...?
NOO!
WE DO WISH YOU WOULD BOTH SHUT UP...
WE DON'T LIKE THE HEADACHE YOU'RE GIVING US!
YES!
BUT I BARELY STOPPED THOSE TWO WHEN THEY WERE WORKING SOLO. HOW AM I GOING TO--
WEBBING?! WHO--?
NEED A HAND... PETEY?

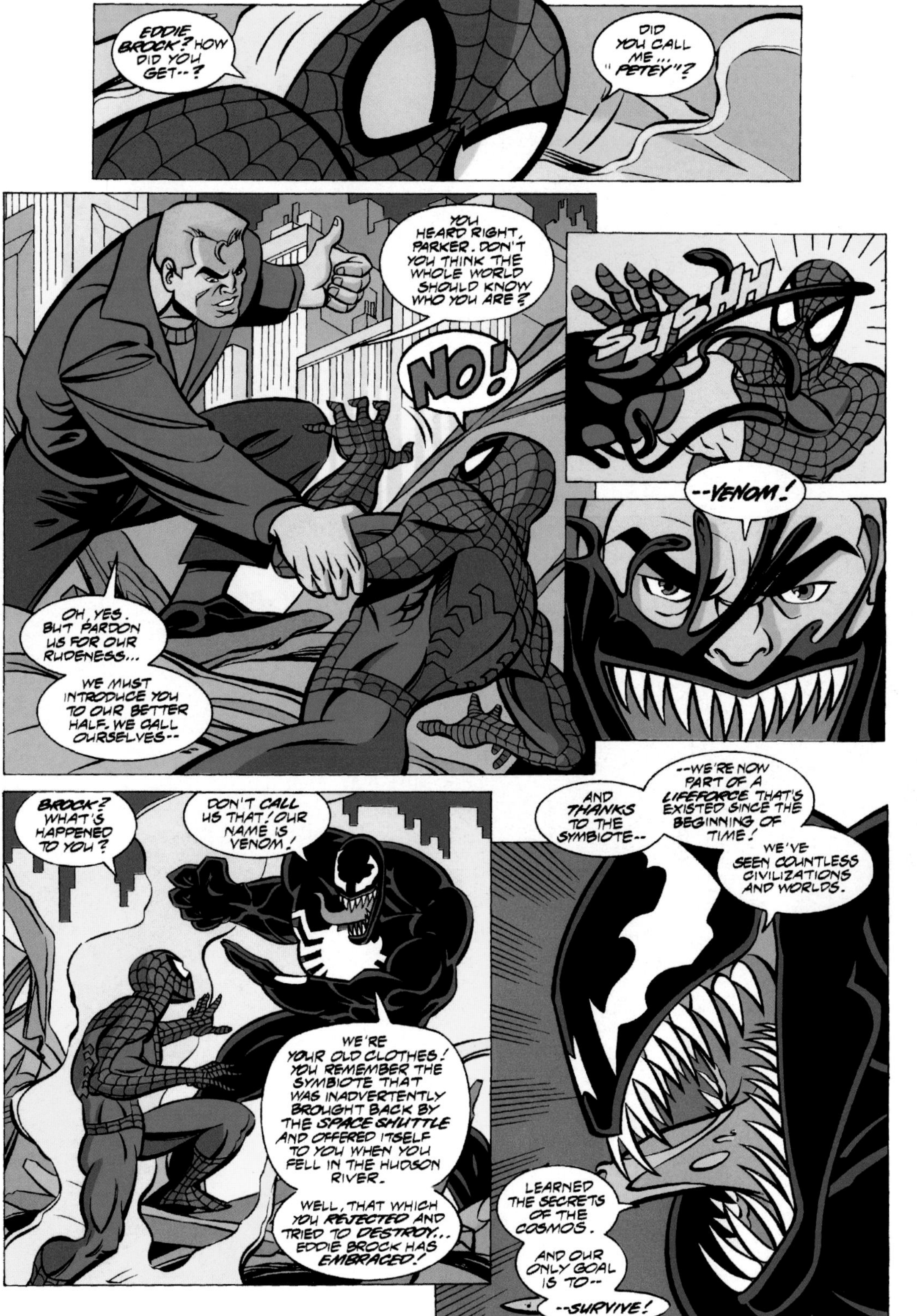
EDDIE BROCK? HOW DID YOU GET--?
DID YOU CALL ME... "PETEY"?
YOU HEARD RIGHT, PARKER. DON'T YOU THINK THE WHOLE WORLD SHOULD KNOW WHO YOU ARE?
NO!
OH, YES. BUT PARDON US FOR OUR RUDENESS...
WE MUST INTRODUCE YOU TO OUR BETTER HALF. WE CALL OURSELVES--
SLISHH
--VENOM!
BROCK? WHAT'S HAPPENED TO YOU?
DON'T CALL US THAT! OUR NAME IS VENOM!
WE'RE YOUR OLD CLOTHES! YOU REMEMBER THE SYMBIOTE THAT WAS INADVERTENTLY BROUGHT BACK BY THE SPACE SHUTTLE AND OFFERED ITSELF TO YOU WHEN YOU FELL IN THE HUDSON RIVER.
WELL, THAT WHICH YOU REJECTED AND TRIED TO DESTROY... EDDIE BROCK HAS EMBRACED!
AND THANKS TO THE SYMBIOTE--
--WE'RE NOW PART OF A LIFEFORCE THAT'S EXISTED SINCE THE BEGINNING OF TIME!
WE'VE SEEN COUNTLESS CIVILIZATIONS AND WORLDS.
LEARNED THE SECRETS OF THE COSMOS.
AND OUR ONLY GOAL IS TO--
--SURVIVE!

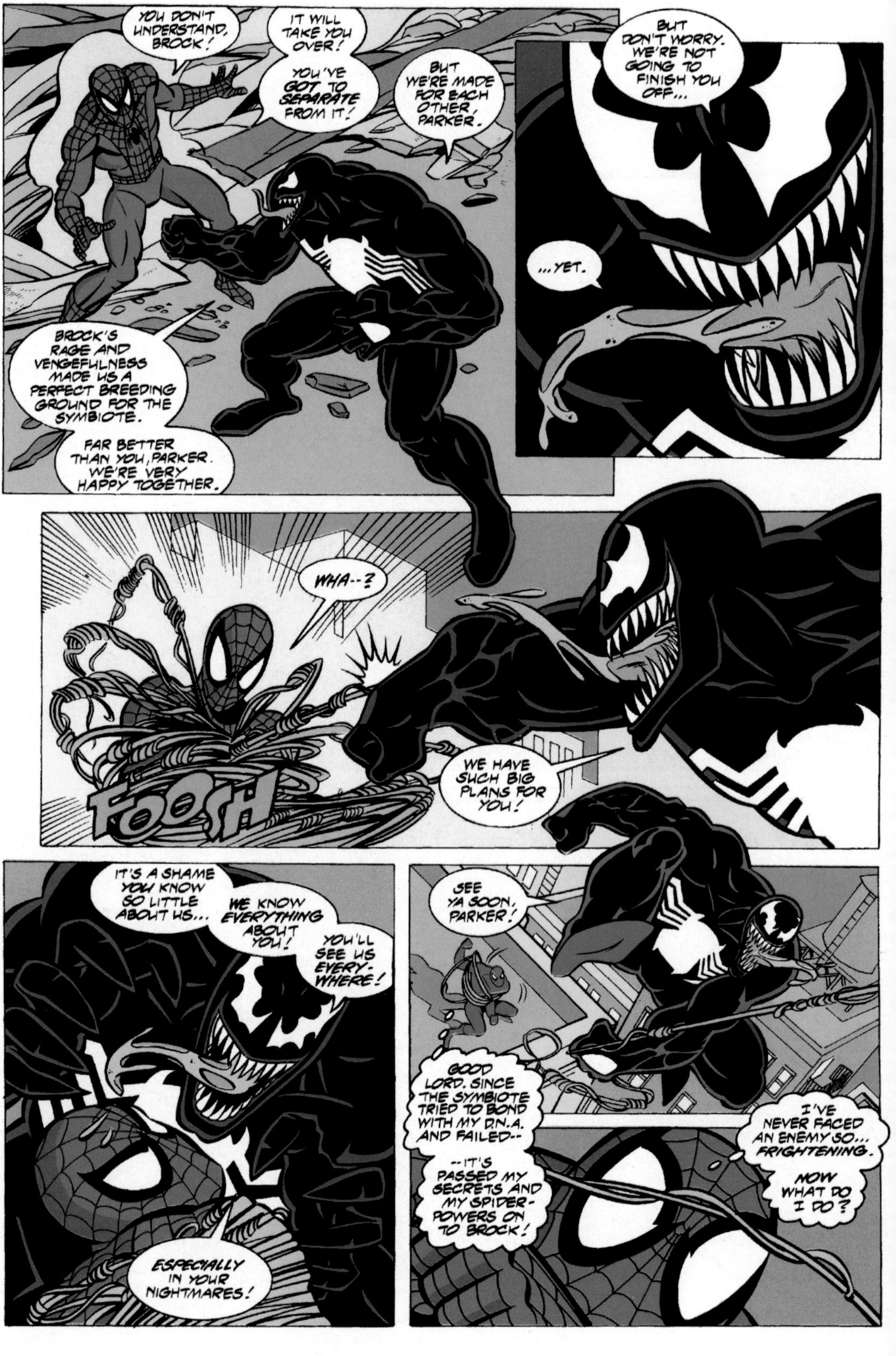
YOU DON'T UNDERSTAND, BROCK!
IT WILL TAKE YOU OVER!
YOU'VE GOT TO SEPARATE FROM IT!
BUT WE'RE MADE FOR EACH OTHER, PARKER.
BROCK'S RAGE AND VENGEFULNESS MADE US A PERFECT BREEDING GROUND FOR THE SYMBIOTE.
FAR BETTER THAN YOU, PARKER. WE'RE VERY HAPPY TOGETHER.
BUT DON'T WORRY. WE'RE NOT GOING TO FINISH YOU OFF...
...YET.
WHA--?
FOOSH
WE HAVE SUCH BIG PLANS FOR YOU!
IT'S A SHAME YOU KNOW SO LITTLE ABOUT US...
WE KNOW EVERYTHING ABOUT YOU!
YOU'LL SEE US EVERY-WHERE!
ESPECIALLY IN YOUR NIGHTMARES!
SEE YA SOON, PARKER!
GOOD LORD. SINCE THE SYMBIOTE TRIED TO BOND WITH MY D.N.A. AND FAILED--
--IT'S PASSED MY SECRETS AND MY SPIDER-POWERS ON TO BROCK!
I'VE NEVER FACED AN ENEMY SO... FRIGHTENING.
NOW WHAT DO I DO?

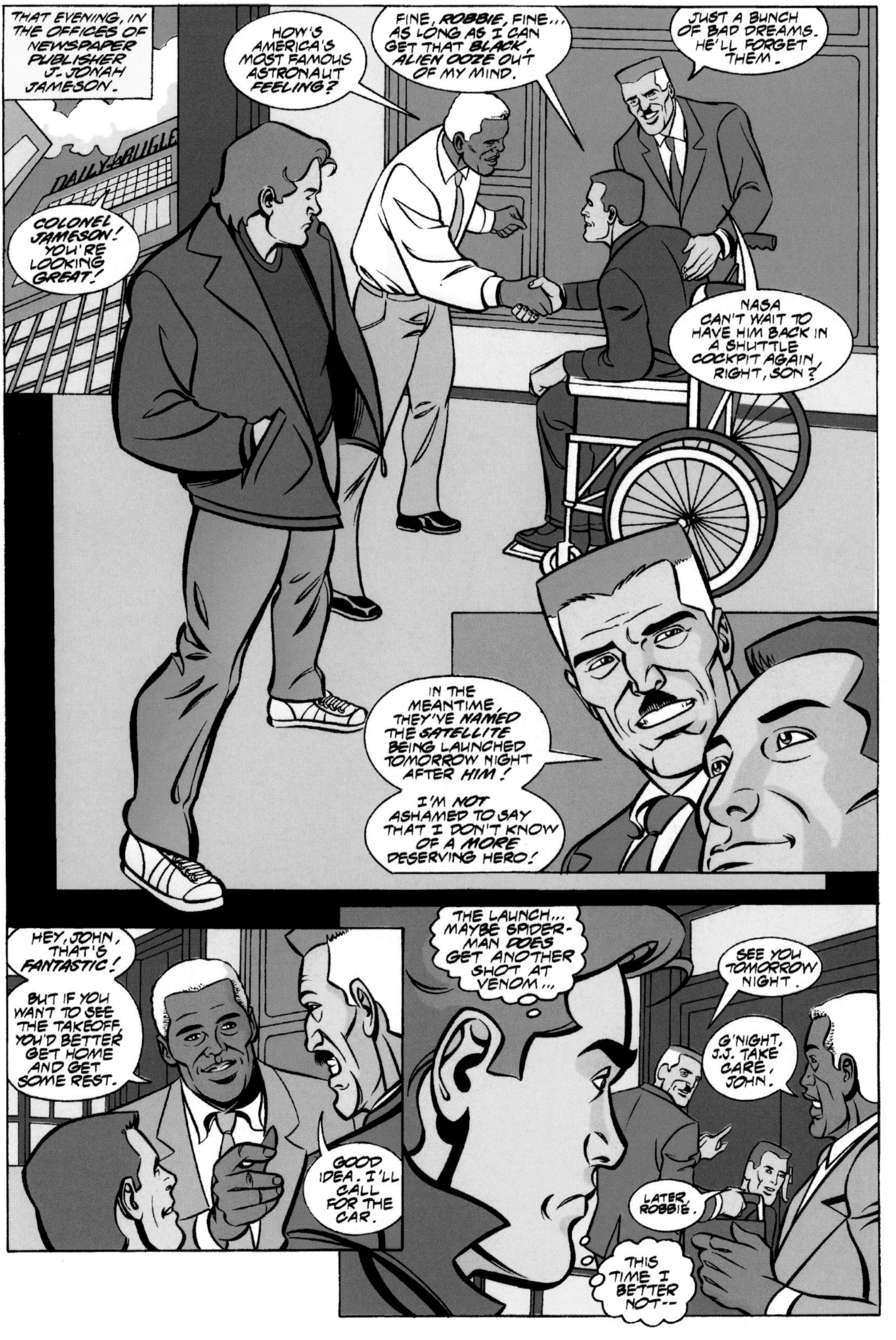
THAT EVENING, IN THE OFFICES OF NEWSPAPER PUBLISHER J. JONAH JAMESON.
DAILY BUGLE
COLONEL JAMESON! YOU'RE LOOKING GREAT!
HOW'S AMERICA'S MOST FAMOUS ASTRONAUT FEELING?
FINE, ROBBIE, FINE... AS LONG AS I CAN GET THAT BLACK, ALIEN OOZE OUT OF MY MIND.
JUST A BUNCH OF BAD DREAMS. HE'LL FORGET THEM.
NASA CAN'T WAIT TO HAVE HIM BACK IN A SHUTTLE COCKPIT AGAIN, RIGHT, SON?
IN THE MEANTIME, THEY'VE NAMED THE SATELLITE BEING LAUNCHED TOMORROW NIGHT AFTER HIM!
I'M NOT ASHAMED TO SAY THAT I DON'T KNOW OF A MORE DESERVING HERO!
HEY, JOHN, THAT'S FANTASTIC!
BUT IF YOU WANT TO SEE THE TAKEOFF, YOU'D BETTER GET HOME AND GET SOME REST.
GOOD IDEA. I'LL CALL FOR THE CAR.
THE LAUNCH... MAYBE SPIDER-MAN DOES GET ANOTHER SHOT AT VENOM...
SEE YOU TOMORROW NIGHT.
G'NIGHT, J.J. TAKE CARE, JOHN.
LATER, ROBBIE.
THIS TIME I BETTER NOT--

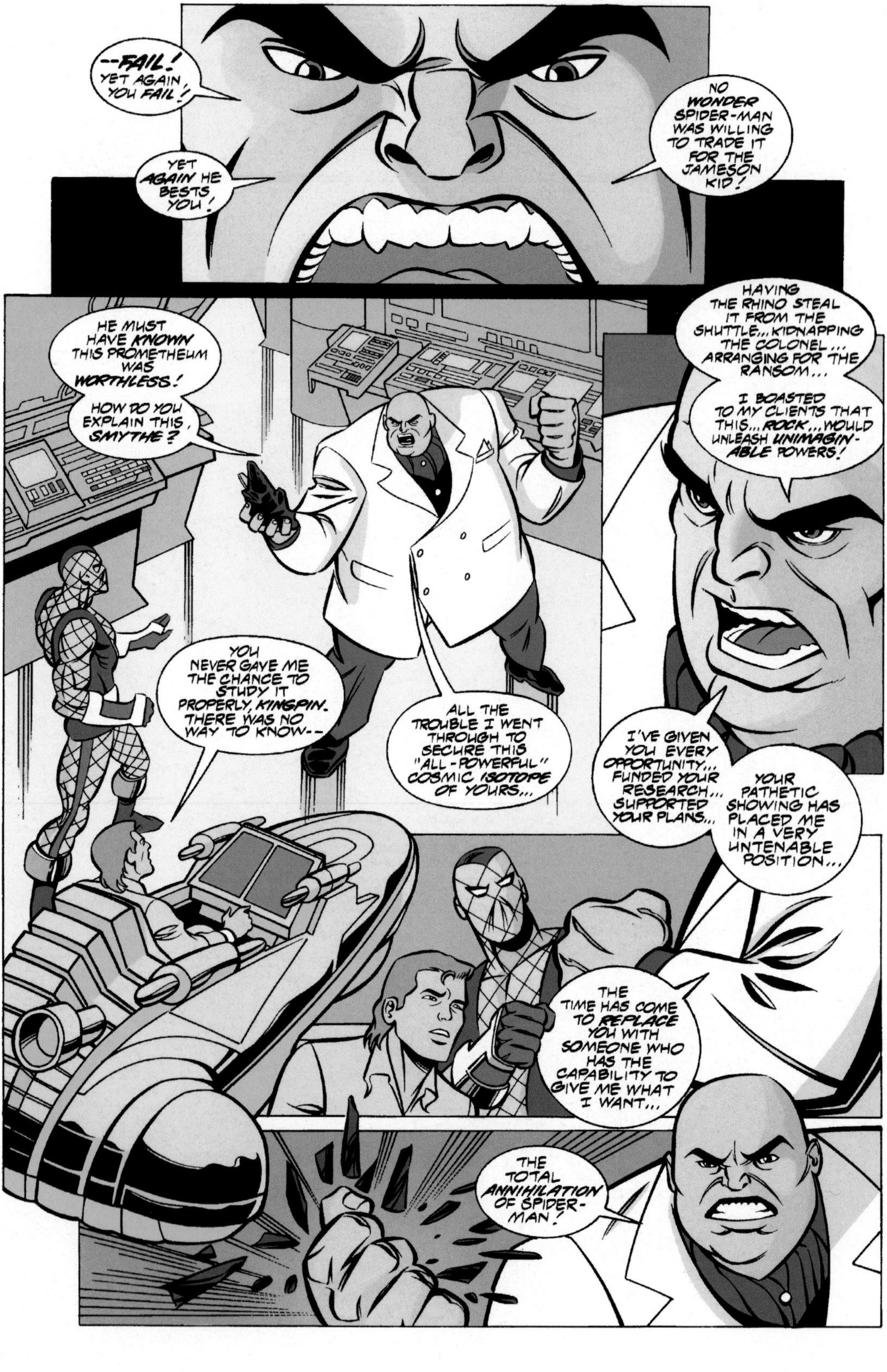
--FAIL! YET AGAIN, YOU FAIL!
YET AGAIN HE BESTS YOU!
NO WONDER SPIDER-MAN WAS WILLING TO TRADE IT FOR THE JAMESON KID!
HE MUST HAVE KNOWN THIS PROMETHEUM WAS WORTHLESS!
HOW DO YOU EXPLAIN THIS, SMYTHE?
HAVING THE RHINO STEAL IT FROM THE SHUTTLE... KIDNAPPING THE COLONEL... ARRANGING FOR THE RANSOM...
I BOASTED TO MY CLIENTS THAT THIS... ROCK... WOULD UNLEASH UNIMAGIN-ABLE POWERS!
YOU NEVER GAVE ME THE CHANCE TO STUDY IT PROPERLY, KINGPIN. THERE WAS NO WAY TO KNOW--
ALL THE TROUBLE I WENT THROUGH TO SECURE THIS "ALL-POWERFUL" COSMIC ISOTOPE OF YOURS...
I'VE GIVEN YOU EVERY OPPORTUNITY... FUNDED YOUR RESEARCH... SUPPORTED YOUR PLANS...
YOUR PATHETIC SHOWING HAS PLACED ME IN A VERY UNTENABLE POSITION...
THE TIME HAS COME TO REPLACE YOU WITH SOMEONE WHO HAS THE CAPABILITY TO GIVE ME WHAT I WANT...
THE TOTAL ANNIHILATION OF SPIDER-MAN!

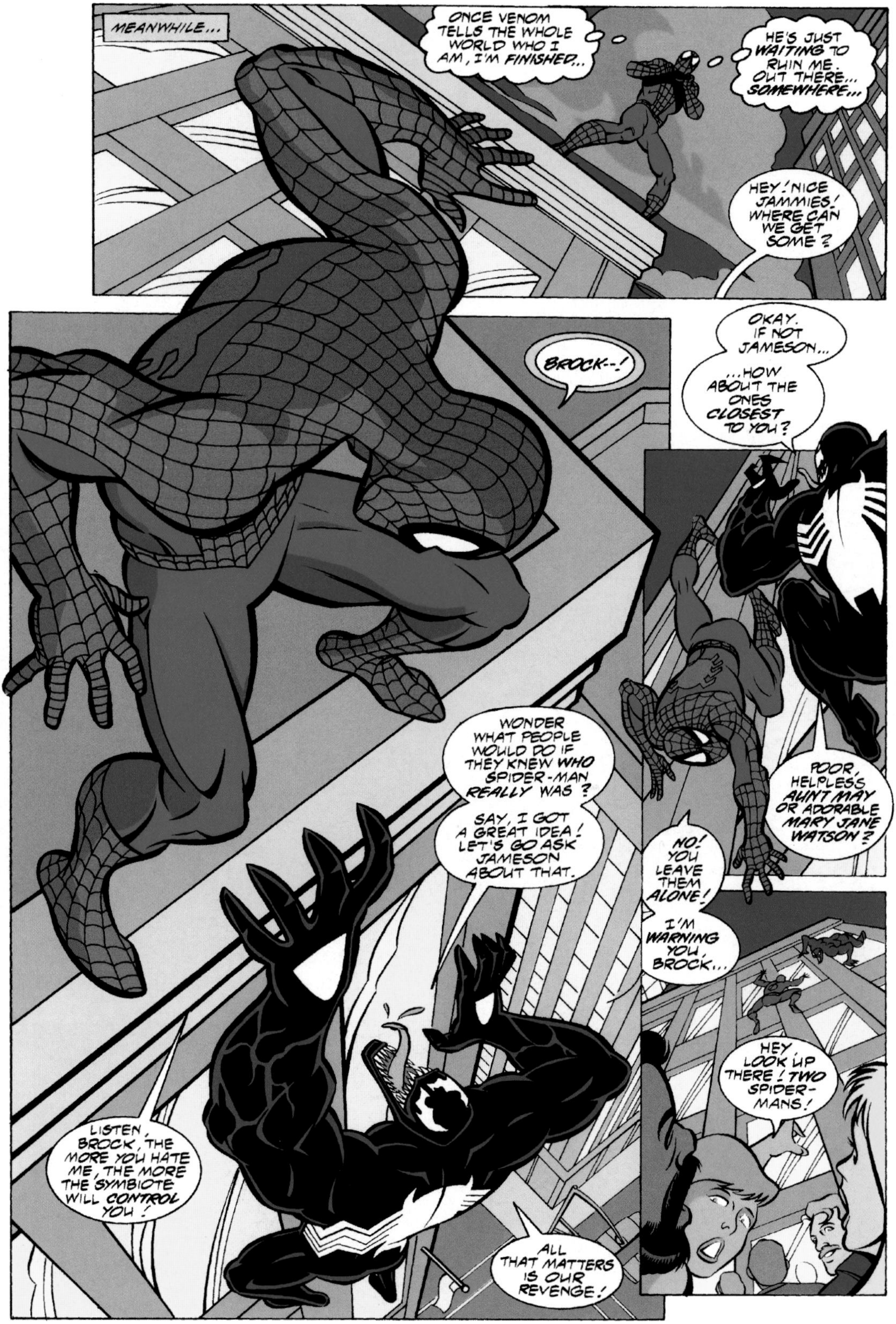
MEANWHILE...
ONCE VENOM TELLS THE WHOLE WORLD WHO I AM, I'M FINISHED...
HE'S JUST WAITING TO RUIN ME. OUT THERE... SOMEWHERE...
HEY! NICE JAMMIES! WHERE CAN WE GET SOME?
BROCK--!
WONDER WHAT PEOPLE WOULD DO IF THEY KNEW WHO SPIDER-MAN REALLY WAS?
SAY, I GOT A GREAT IDEA! LET'S GO ASK JAMESON ABOUT THAT.
LISTEN, BROCK, THE MORE YOU HATE ME, THE MORE THE SYMBIOTE WILL CONTROL YOU!
ALL THAT MATTERS IS OUR REVENGE!
OKAY. IF NOT JAMESON...
...HOW ABOUT THE ONES CLOSEST TO YOU?
POOR, HELPLESS AUNT MAY OR ADORABLE MARY JANE WATSON?
NO! YOU LEAVE THEM ALONE!
I'M WARNING YOU, BROCK...
HEY, LOOK UP THERE! TWO SPIDER-MANS!

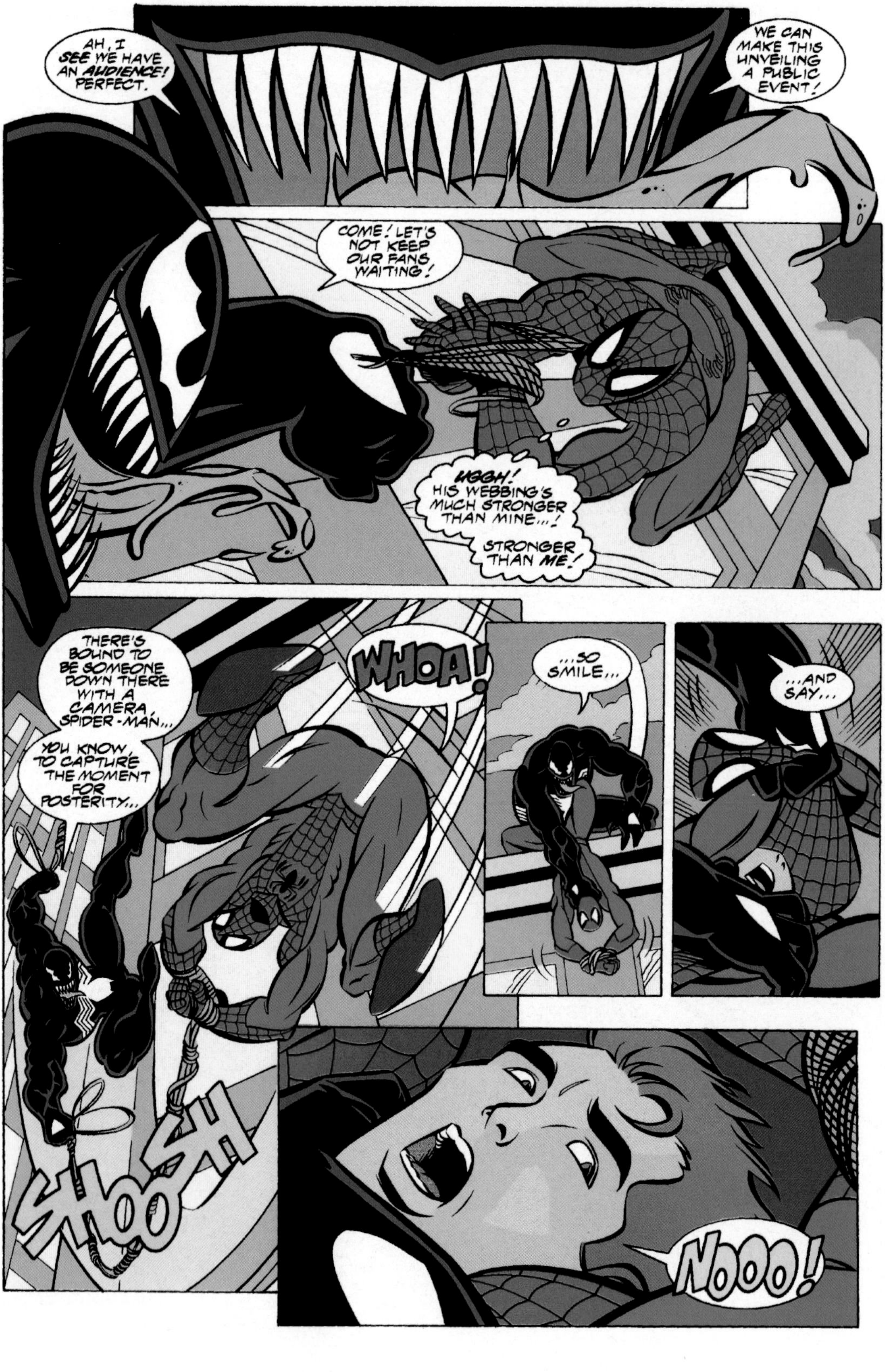
AH, I SEE WE HAVE AN AUDIENCE! PERFECT.
WE CAN MAKE THIS UNVEILING A PUBLIC EVENT!
COME! LET'S NOT KEEP OUR FANS WAITING!
UGGH! HIS WEBBING'S MUCH STRONGER THAN MINE...!
STRONGER THAN ME!
THERE'S BOUND TO BE SOMEONE DOWN THERE WITH A CAMERA, SPIDER-MAN...
YOU KNOW, TO CAPTURE THE MOMENT FOR POSTERITY...
WHOA!
SHOOSH
...SO SMILE...
...AND SAY...
NOOO!

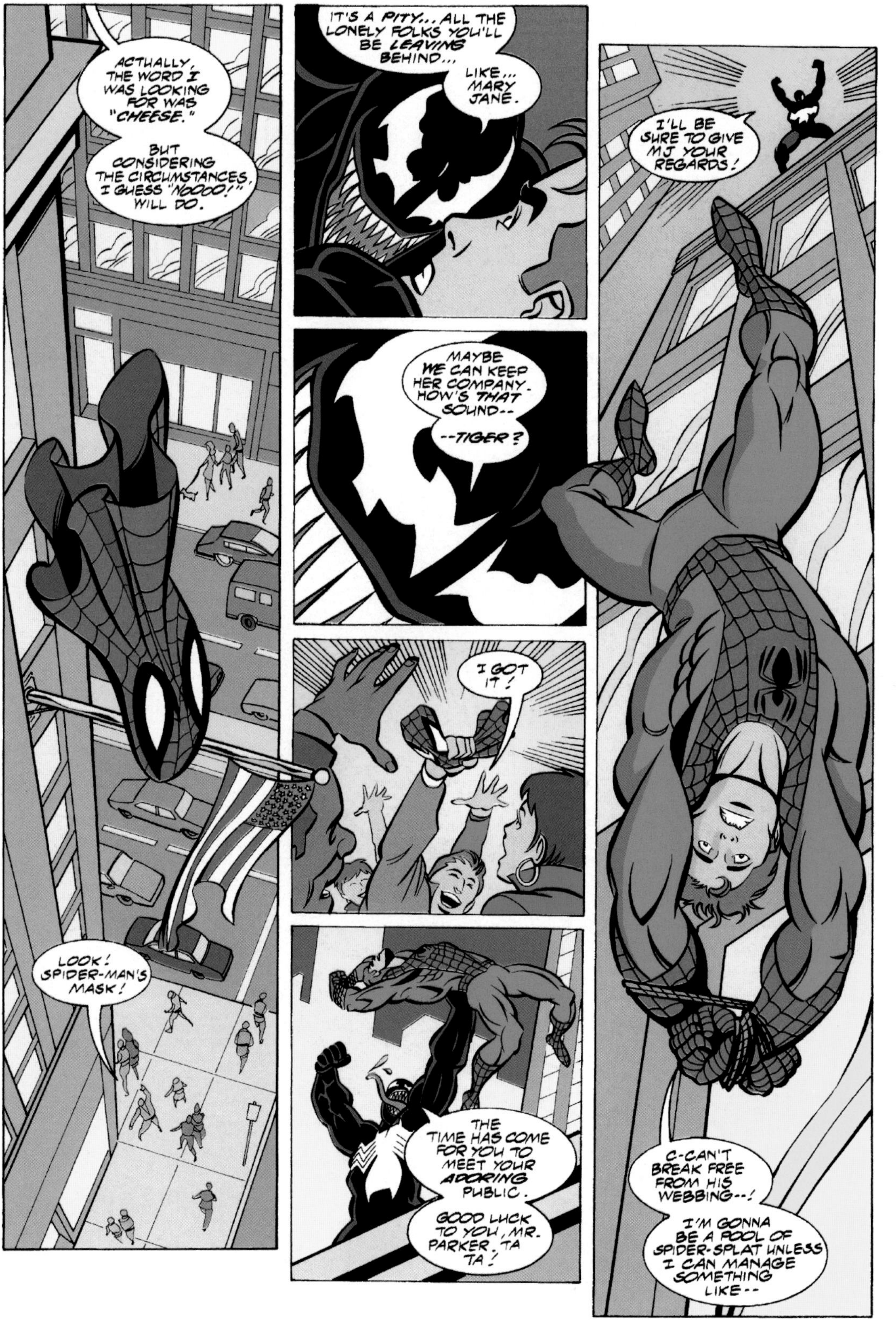
ACTUALLY, THE WORD I WAS LOOKING FOR WAS "CHEESE."
BUT CONSIDERING THE CIRCUMSTANCES, I GUESS "NOOOO!" WILL DO.
LOOK! SPIDER-MAN'S MASK!
IT'S A PITY... ALL THE LONELY FOLKS YOU'LL BE LEAVING BEHIND...
LIKE... MARY JANE.
MAYBE WE CAN KEEP HER COMPANY. HOW'S THAT SOUND--
--TIGER?
I GOT IT!
THE TIME HAS COME FOR YOU TO MEET YOUR ADORING PUBLIC.
GOOD LUCK TO YOU, MR. PARKER. TA TA!
I'LL BE SURE TO GIVE MJ YOUR REGARDS!
C-CAN'T BREAK FREE FROM HIS WEBBING--!
I'M GONNA BE A POOL OF SPIDER-SPLAT UNLESS I CAN MANAGE SOMETHING LIKE--

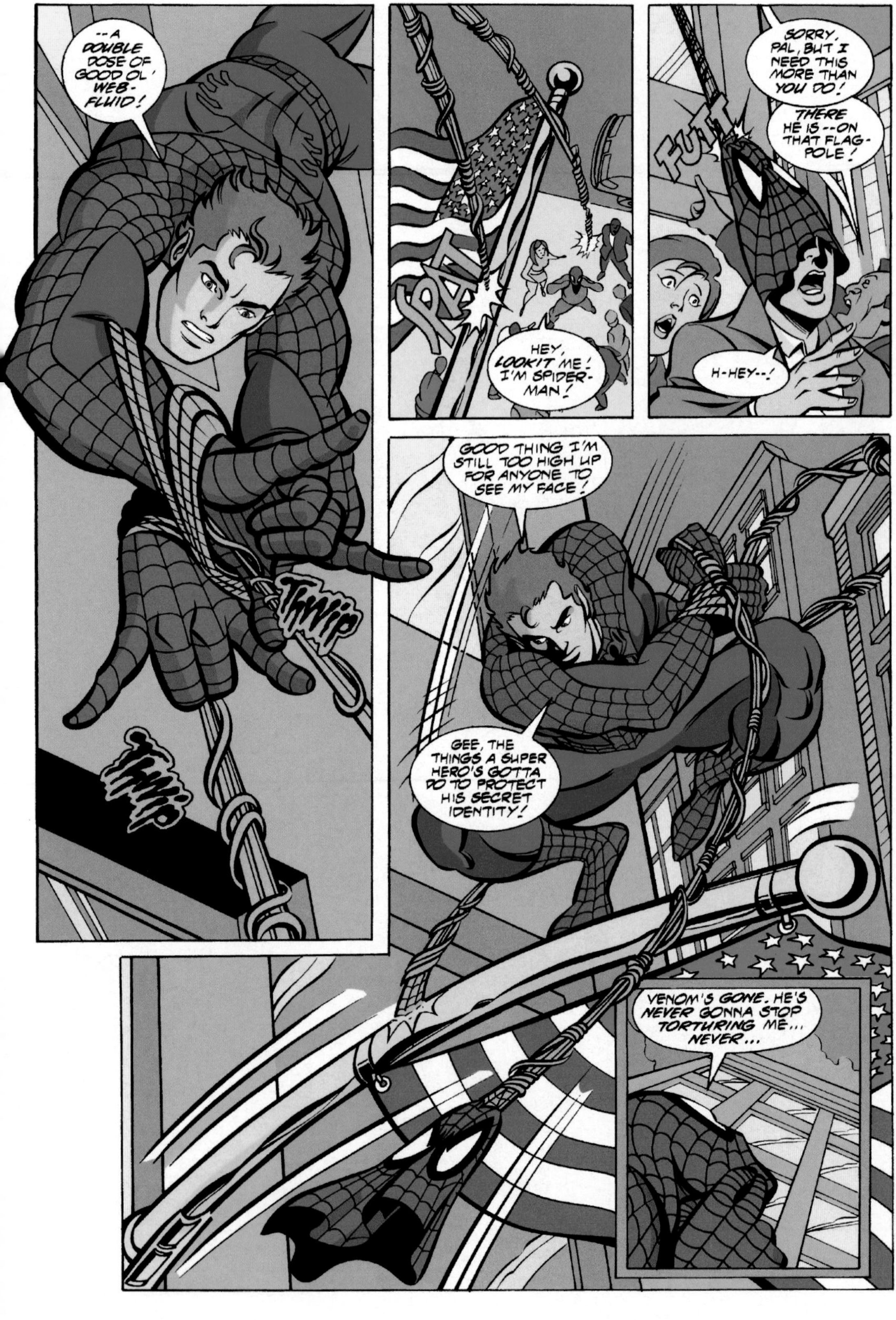
--A DOUBLE DOSE OF GOOD OL' WEB-FLUID!
THWIP
THWIP
PAT
HEY, LOOKIT ME! I'M SPIDER-MAN!
SORRY, PAL, BUT I NEED THIS MORE THAN YOU DO!
FUT
THERE HE IS--ON THAT FLAG-POLE!
H-HEY--!
GOOD THING I'M STILL TOO HIGH UP FOR ANYONE TO SEE MY FACE!
GEE, THE THINGS A SUPER HERO'S GOTTA DO TO PROTECT HIS SECRET IDENTITY!
VENOM'S GONE. HE'S NEVER GONNA STOP TORTURING ME... NEVER...

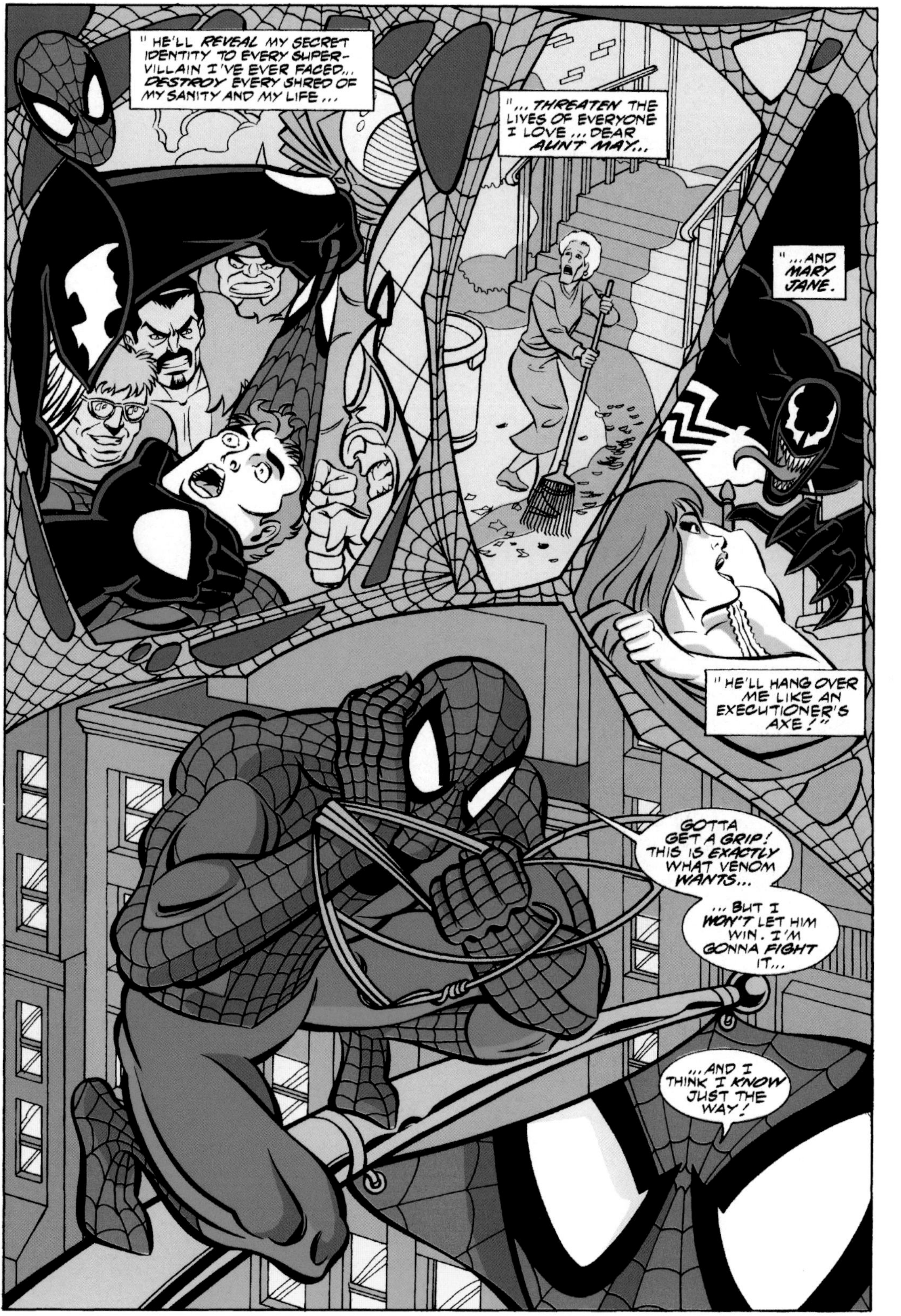
"HE'LL REVEAL MY SECRET IDENTITY TO EVERY SUPER-VILLAIN I'VE EVER FACED... DESTROY EVERY SHRED OF MY SANITY AND MY LIFE...
"...THREATEN THE LIVES OF EVERYONE I LOVE... DEAR AUNT MAY...
"...AND MARY JANE.
"HE'LL HANG OVER ME LIKE AN EXECUTIONER'S AXE!"
GOTTA GET A GRIP! THIS IS EXACTLY WHAT VENOM WANTS...
...BUT I WON'T LET HIM WIN. I'M GONNA FIGHT IT...
...AND I THINK I KNOW JUST THE WAY!

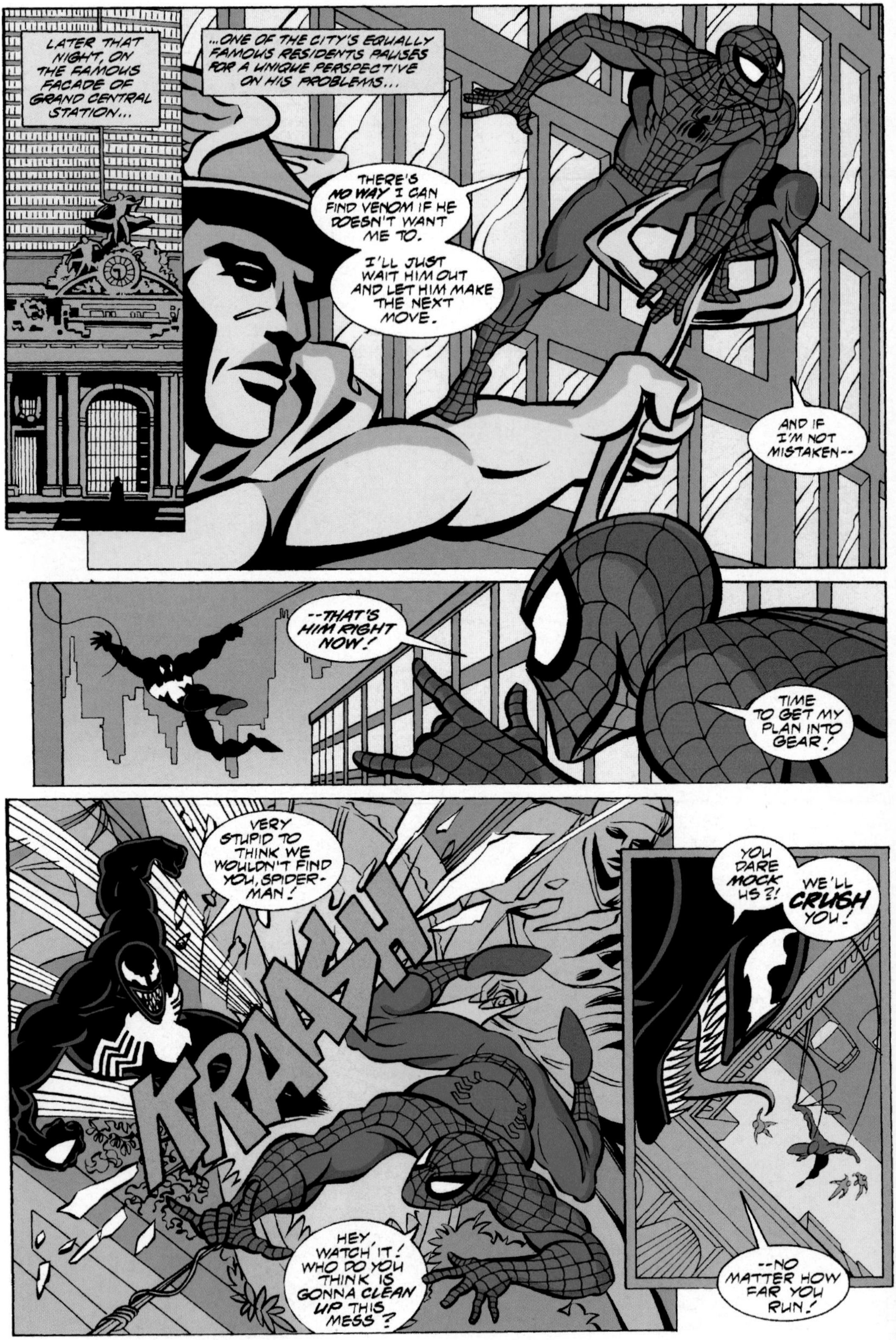
LATER THAT NIGHT, ON THE FAMOUS FACADE OF GRAND CENTRAL STATION...
...ONE OF THE CITY'S EQUALLY FAMOUS RESIDENTS PAUSES FOR A UNIQUE PERSPECTIVE ON HIS PROBLEMS...
THERE'S NO WAY I CAN FIND VENOM IF HE DOESN'T WANT ME TO.
I'LL JUST WAIT HIM OUT AND LET HIM MAKE THE NEXT MOVE.
AND IF I'M NOT MISTAKEN--
--THAT'S HIM RIGHT NOW!
TIME TO GET MY PLAN INTO GEAR!
VERY STUPID TO THINK WE WOULDN'T FIND YOU, SPIDER-MAN!
KRAASH
HEY WATCH IT! WHO DO YOU THINK IS GONNA CLEAN UP THIS MESS?
YOU DARE MOCK US?!
WE'LL CRUSH YOU!
--NO MATTER HOW FAR YOU RUN!

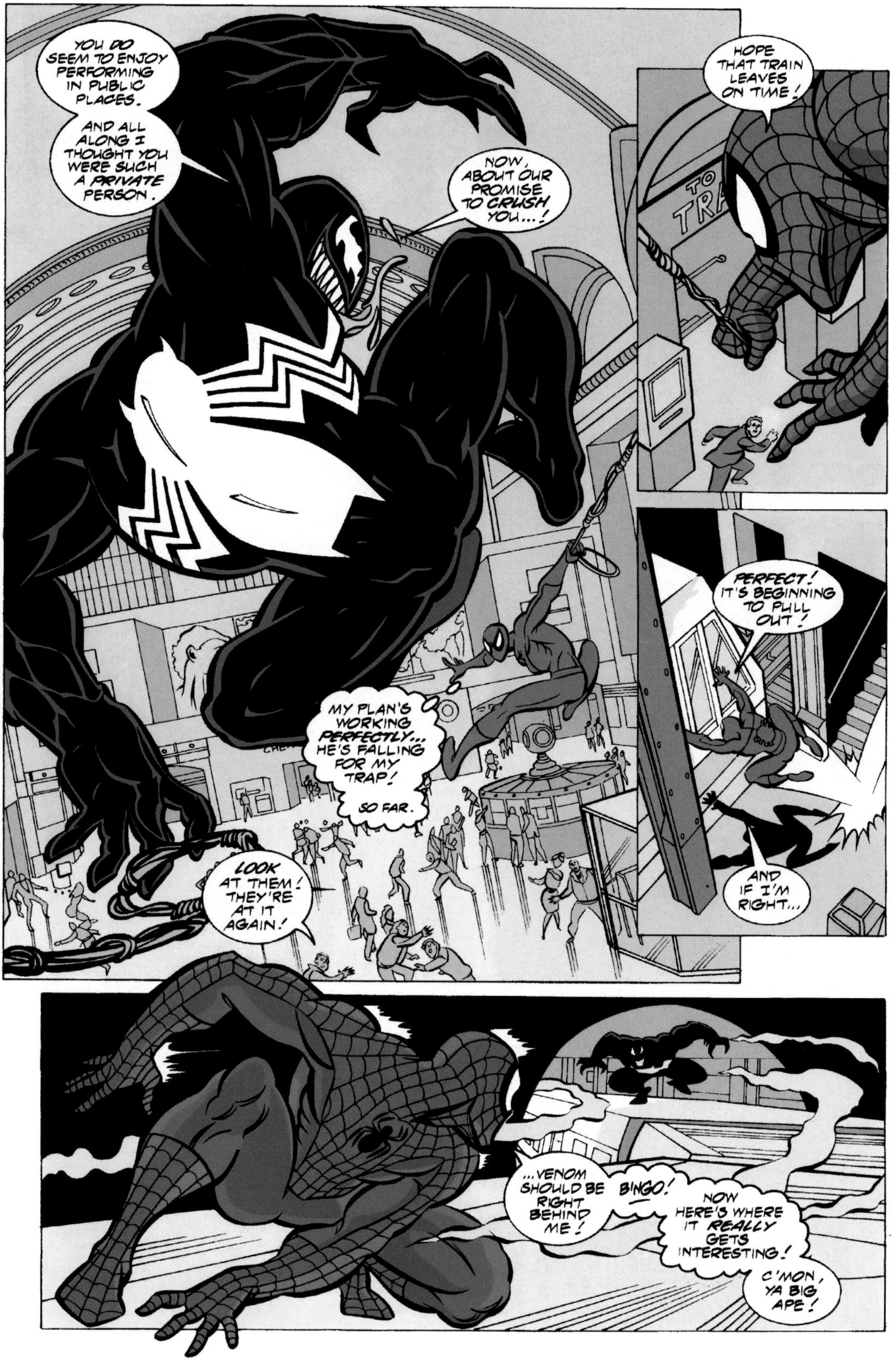
YOU DO SEEM TO ENJOY PERFORMING IN PUBLIC PLACES.
AND ALL ALONG I THOUGHT YOU WERE SUCH A PRIVATE PERSON.
NOW, ABOUT OUR PROMISE TO CRUSH YOU...!
MY PLAN'S WORKING PERFECTLY... HE'S FALLING FOR MY TRAP!
SO FAR.
LOOK AT THEM! THEY'RE AT IT AGAIN!
HOPE THAT TRAIN LEAVES ON TIME!
PERFECT! IT'S BEGINNING TO PULL OUT!
AND IF I'M RIGHT...
...VENOM SHOULD BE RIGHT BEHIND ME!
BINGO!
NOW HERE'S WHERE IT REALLY GETS INTERESTING!
C'MON, YA BIG APE!

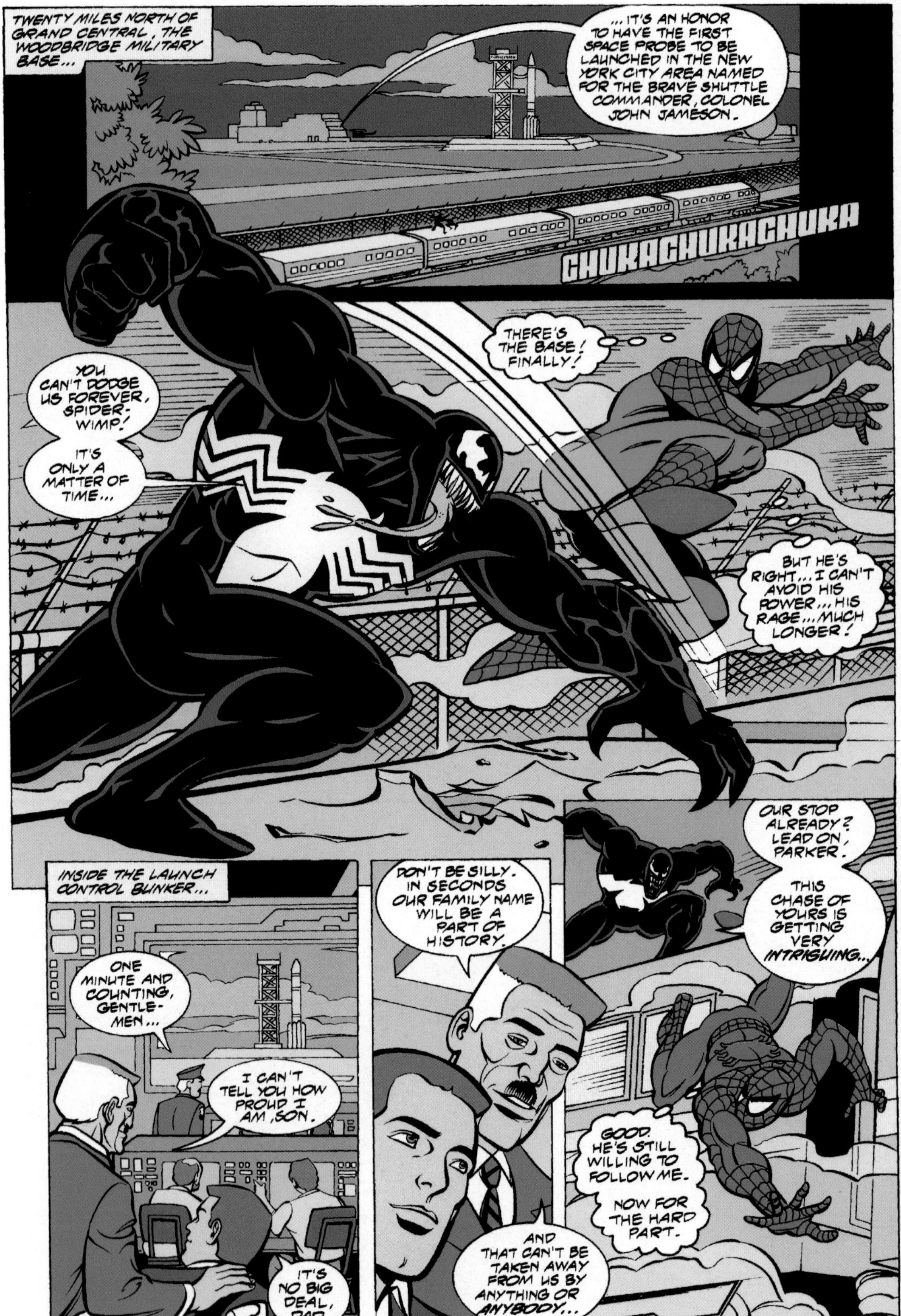
TWENTY MILES NORTH OF GRAND CENTRAL, THE WOODBRIDGE MILITARY BASE...
... IT'S AN HONOR TO HAVE THE FIRST SPACE PROBE TO BE LAUNCHED IN THE NEW YORK CITY AREA NAMED FOR THE BRAVE SHUTTLE COMMANDER, COLONEL JOHN JAMESON.
CHUKACHUKACHUKA
YOU CAN'T DODGE US FOREVER, SPIDER-WIMP!
IT'S ONLY A MATTER OF TIME...
THERE'S THE BASE! FINALLY!
BUT HE'S RIGHT... I CAN'T AVOID HIS POWER... HIS RAGE... MUCH LONGER!
INSIDE THE LAUNCH CONTROL BUNKER...
ONE MINUTE AND COUNTING, GENTLEMEN...
I CAN'T TELL YOU HOW PROUD I AM, SON.
IT'S NO BIG DEAL, DAD.
DON'T BE SILLY. IN SECONDS OUR FAMILY NAME WILL BE A PART OF HISTORY.
AND THAT CAN'T BE TAKEN AWAY FROM US BY ANYTHING OR ANYBODY...
OUR STOP ALREADY? LEAD ON, PARKER.
THIS CHASE OF YOURS IS GETTING VERY INTRIGUING...
GOOD. HE'S STILL WILLING TO FOLLOW ME.
NOW FOR THE HARD PART.

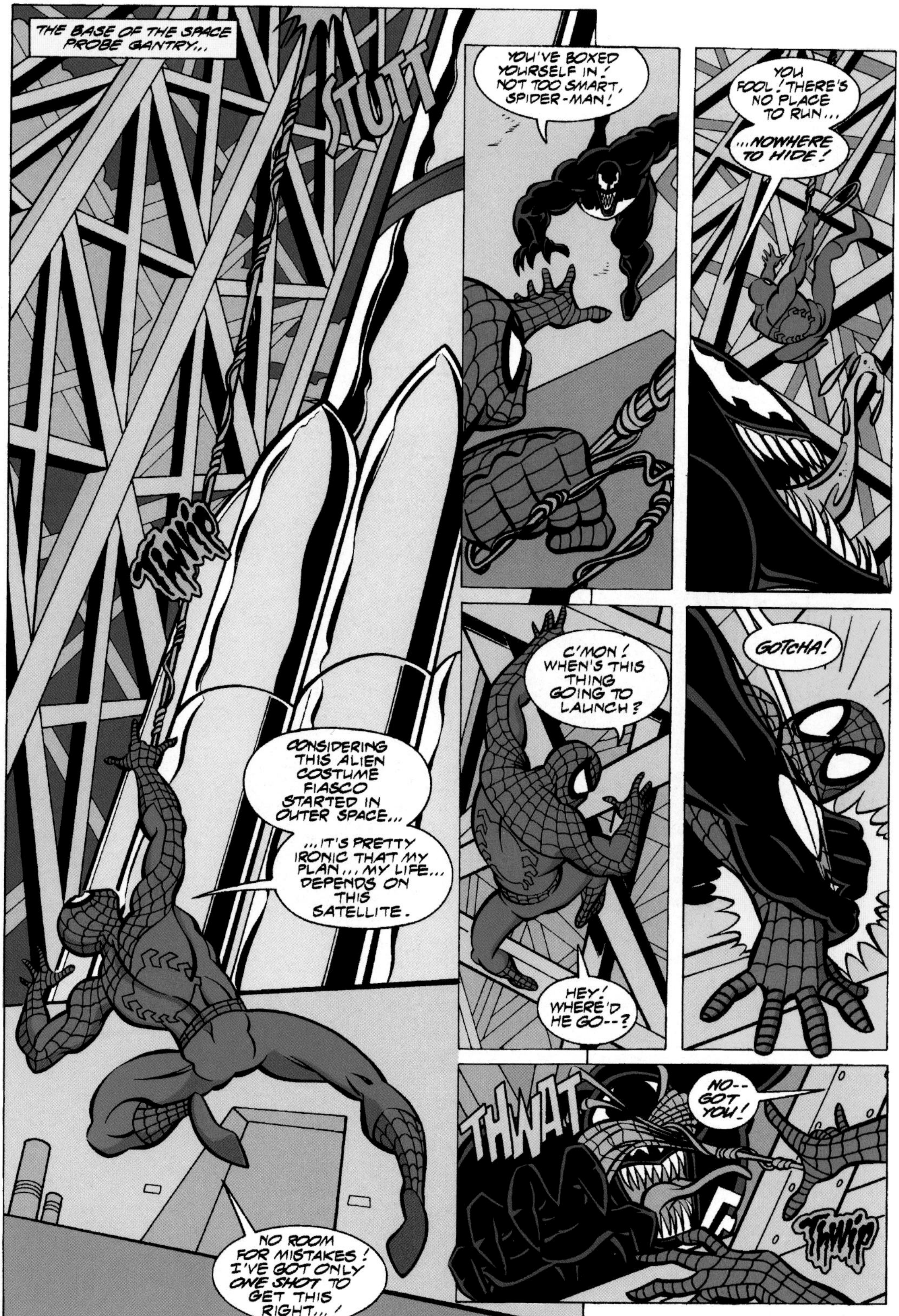

THE BASE OF THE SPACE PROBE GANTRY...
STUTT
THWIP
CONSIDERING THIS ALIEN COSTUME FIASCO STARTED IN OUTER SPACE...
...IT'S PRETTY IRONIC THAT MY PLAN... MY LIFE... DEPENDS ON THIS SATELLITE.
NO ROOM FOR MISTAKES! I'VE GOT ONLY ONE SHOT TO GET THIS RIGHT...!
YOU'VE BOXED YOURSELF IN! NOT TOO SMART, SPIDER-MAN!
YOU FOOL! THERE'S NO PLACE TO RUN...
...NOWHERE TO HIDE!
C'MON! WHEN'S THIS THING GOING TO LAUNCH?
HEY! WHERE'D HE GO--?
GOTCHA!
THWAT
NO-- GOT YOU!
THWIP

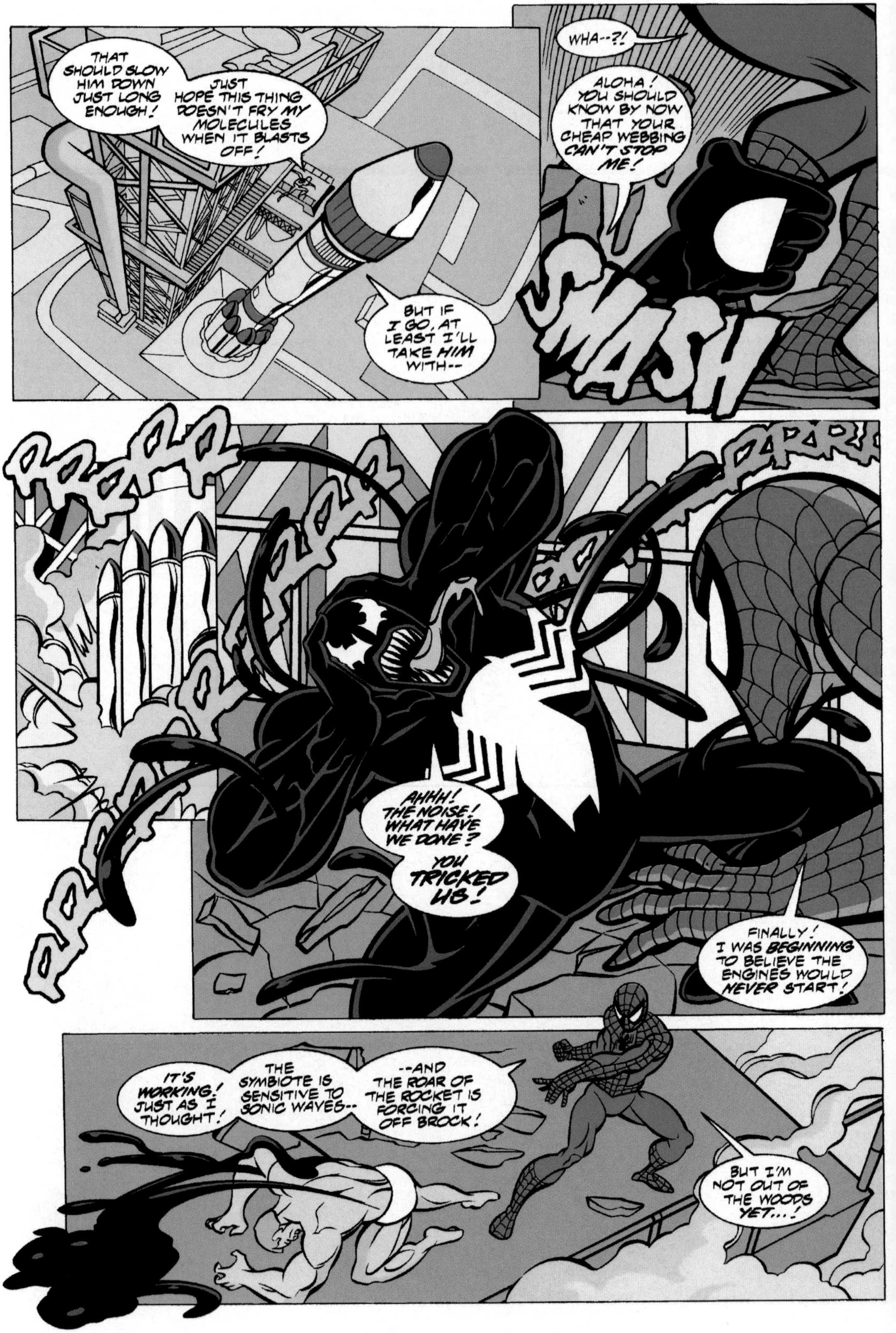
THAT SHOULD SLOW HIM DOWN JUST LONG ENOUGH!
JUST HOPE THIS THING DOESN'T FRY MY MOLECULES WHEN IT BLASTS OFF!
BUT IF I GO, AT LEAST I'LL TAKE HIM WITH--
WHA--?!
ALOHA! YOU SHOULD KNOW BY NOW THAT YOUR CHEAP WEBBING CAN'T STOP ME!
SMASH
RRRRR
RRRRRRRRR
RRRRR
AHHH! THE NOISE! WHAT HAVE WE DONE?
YOU TRICKED US!
FINALLY! I WAS BEGINNING TO BELIEVE THE ENGINES WOULD NEVER START!
IT'S WORKING! JUST AS I THOUGHT!
THE SYMBIOTE IS SENSITIVE TO SONIC WAVES--
--AND THE ROAR OF THE ROCKET IS FORCING IT OFF BROCK!
BUT I'M NOT OUT OF THE WOODS YET...!

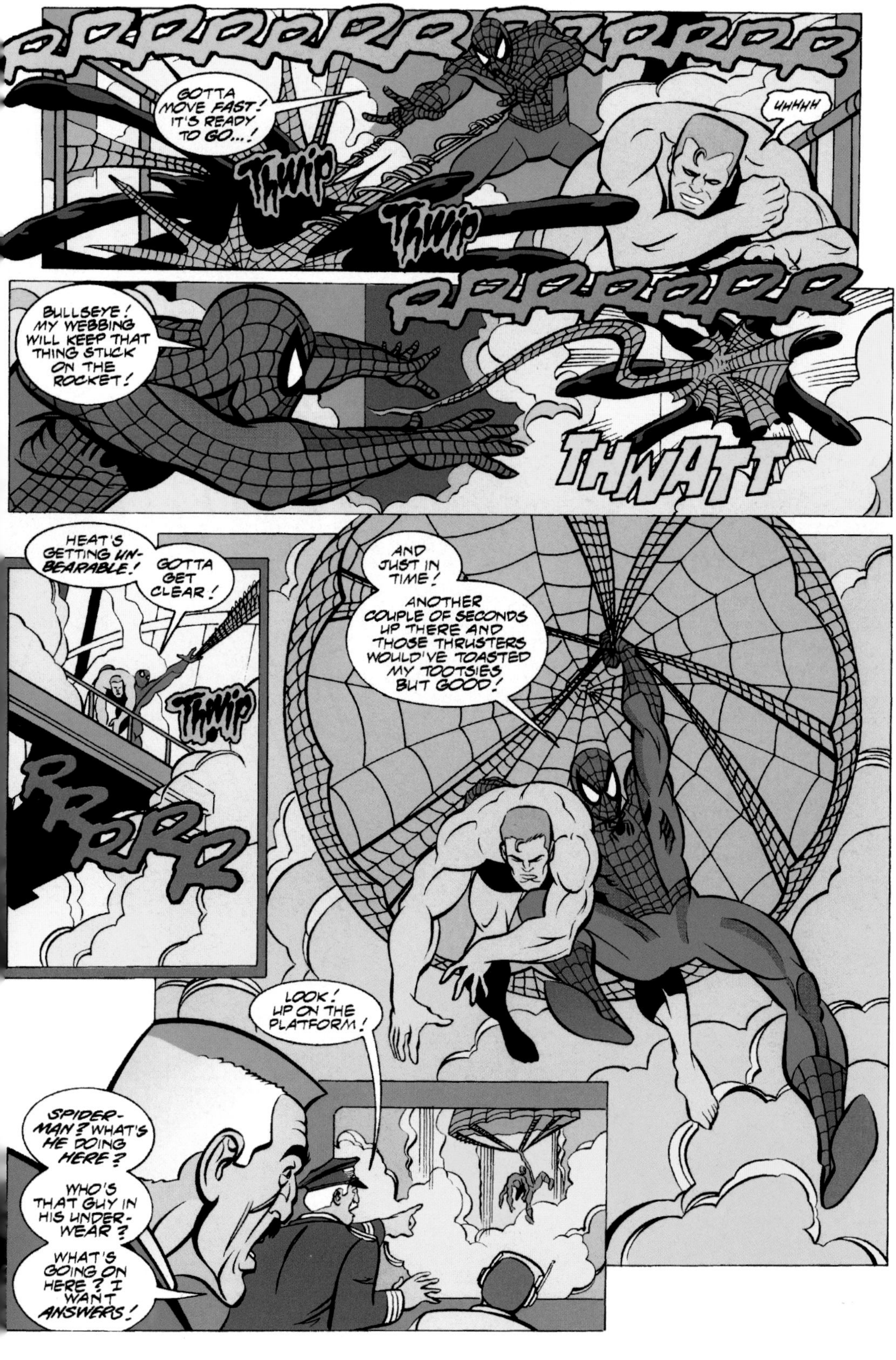
RRRRRRRRRRRRRRRR
GOTTA MOVE FAST! IT'S READY TO GO...!
UHHHH
THWIP
THWIP
RRRRRRRRR
BULLSEYE! MY WEBBING WILL KEEP THAT THING STUCK ON THE ROCKET!
THWATT
HEAT'S GETTING UNBEARABLE!
GOTTA GET CLEAR!
THWIP
RRRRR
AND JUST IN TIME!
ANOTHER COUPLE OF SECONDS UP THERE AND THOSE THRUSTERS WOULD'VE TOASTED MY TOOTSIES BUT GOOD!
LOOK! UP ON THE PLATFORM!
SPIDER-MAN? WHAT'S HE DOING HERE?
WHO'S THAT GUY IN HIS UNDERWEAR?
WHAT'S GOING ON HERE? I WANT ANSWERS!

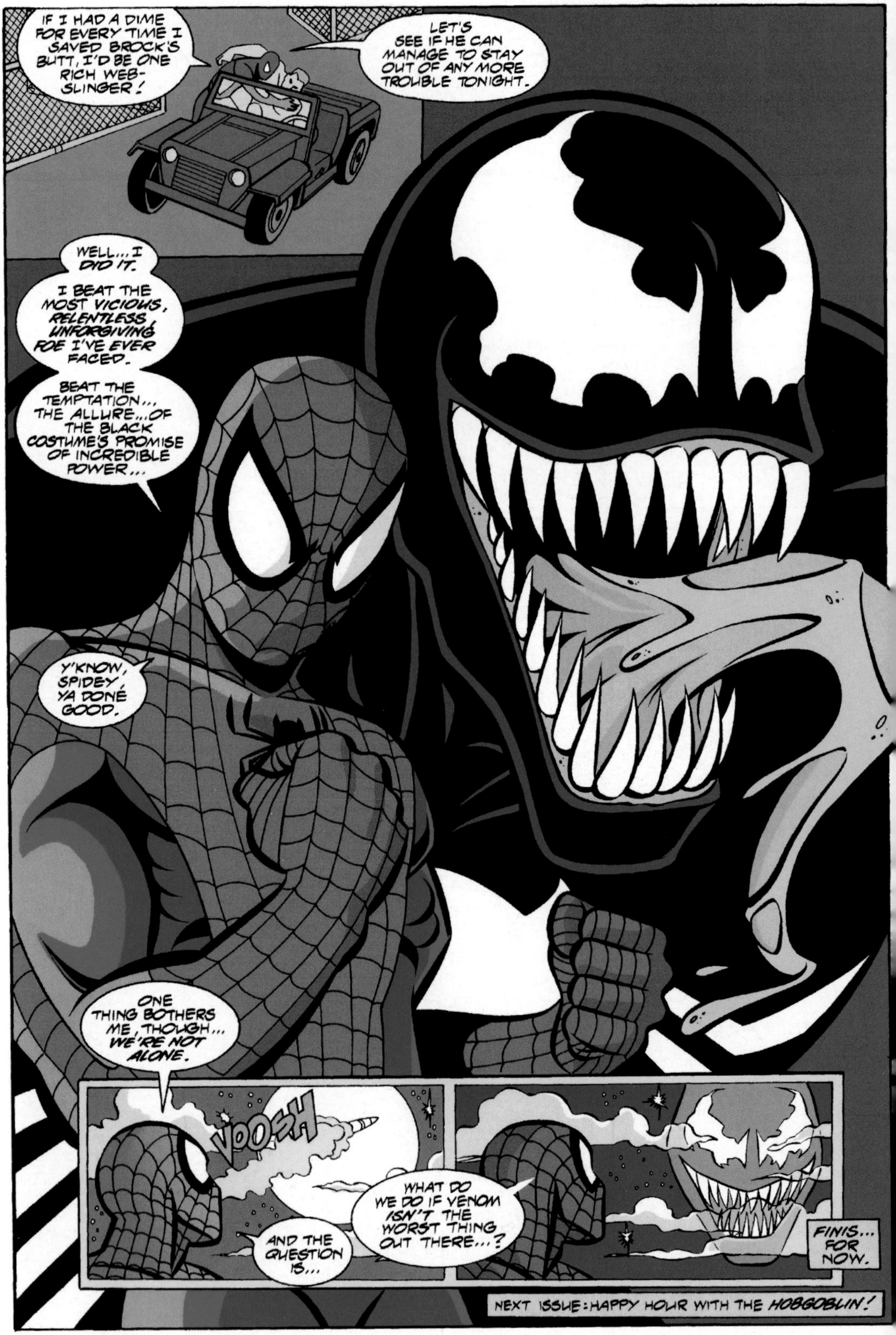
IF I HAD A DIME FOR EVERY TIME I SAVED BROCK'S BUTT, I'D BE ONE RICH WEB-SLINGER!
LET'S SEE IF HE CAN MANAGE TO STAY OUT OF ANY MORE TROUBLE TONIGHT.
WELL... I DID IT.
I BEAT THE MOST VICIOUS, RELENTLESS, UNFORGIVING FOE I'VE EVER FACED.
BEAT THE TEMPTATION... THE ALLURE... OF THE BLACK COSTUME'S PROMISE OF INCREDIBLE POWER...
Y'KNOW, SPIDEY, YA DONE GOOD.
ONE THING BOTHERS ME, THOUGH... WE'RE NOT ALONE.
VOOSH
AND THE QUESTION IS...
WHAT DO WE DO IF VENOM ISN'T THE WORST THING OUT THERE...?
FINIS... FOR NOW.
NEXT ISSUE: HAPPY HOUR WITH THE HOBGOBLIN!

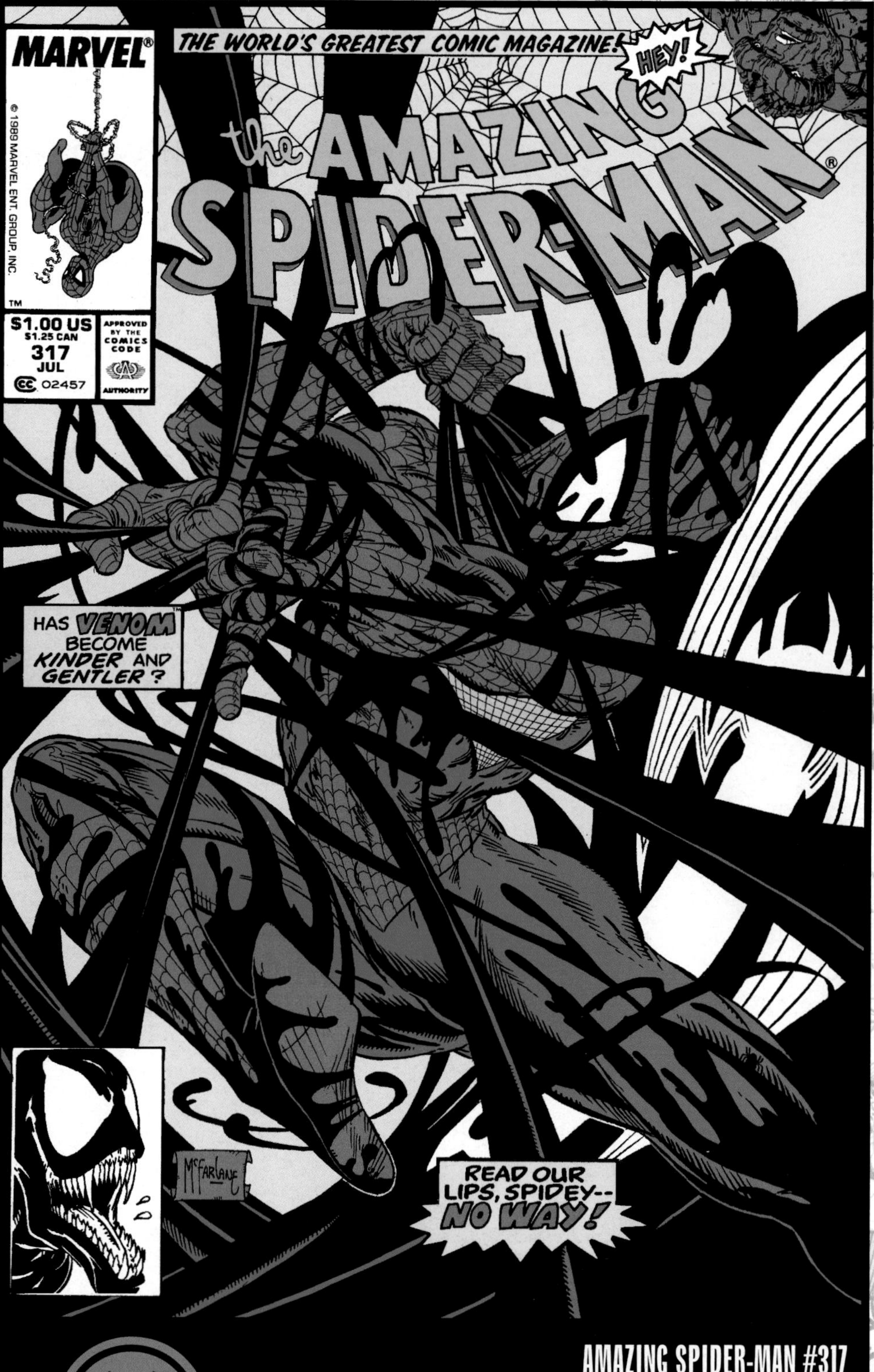
MARVEL
© 1989 MARVEL ENT. GROUP, INC.
THE WORLD'S GREATEST COMIC MAGAZINE!
HEY!
the AMAZING SPIDER-MAN
$1.00 US
$1.25 CAN
317
JUL
02457
APPROVED BY THE COMICS CODE AUTHORITY
HAS VENOM BECOME KINDER AND GENTLER?
McFARLANE
READ OUR LIPS, SPIDEY-- NO WAY!

AMAZING SPIDER-MAN #317

EDDIE BROCK AND THE ALIEN SYMBIOTE RETURNED TO MENACE SPIDER-MAN AGAIN AND AGAIN — BUT WHEN VENOM LEARNS WHERE SPIDER-MAN LIVES, HE PLANS TO MAKE THEIR FEUD PERSONAL! AND THIS TIME HE MAY BEST THE WEB-SLINGER!

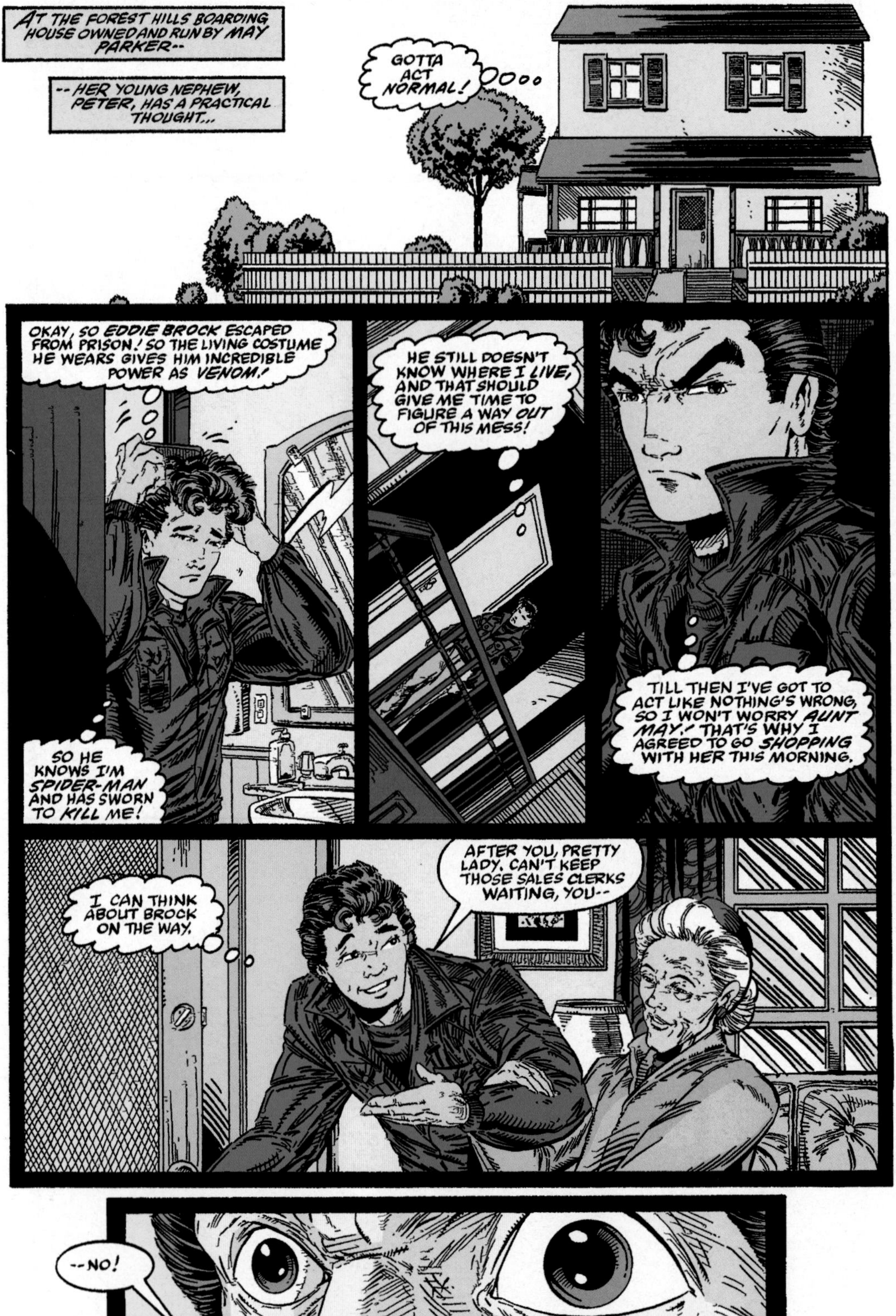
AT THE FOREST HILLS BOARDING HOUSE OWNED AND RUN BY MAY PARKER--
--HER YOUNG NEPHEW, PETER, HAS A PRACTICAL THOUGHT...
GOTTA ACT NORMAL!
OKAY, SO EDDIE BROCK ESCAPED FROM PRISON! SO THE LIVING COSTUME HE WEARS GIVES HIM INCREDIBLE POWER AS VENOM!
SO HE KNOWS I'M SPIDER-MAN AND HAS SWORN TO KILL ME!
HE STILL DOESN'T KNOW WHERE I LIVE, AND THAT SHOULD GIVE ME TIME TO FIGURE A WAY OUT OF THIS MESS!
TILL THEN I'VE GOT TO ACT LIKE NOTHING'S WRONG, SO I WON'T WORRY AUNT MAY! THAT'S WHY I AGREED TO GO SHOPPING WITH HER THIS MORNING.
I CAN THINK ABOUT BROCK ON THE WAY.
AFTER YOU, PRETTY LADY. CAN'T KEEP THOSE SALES CLERKS WAITING, YOU--
--NO!

Stan Lee PRESENTS: THE AMAZING SPIDER-MAN®

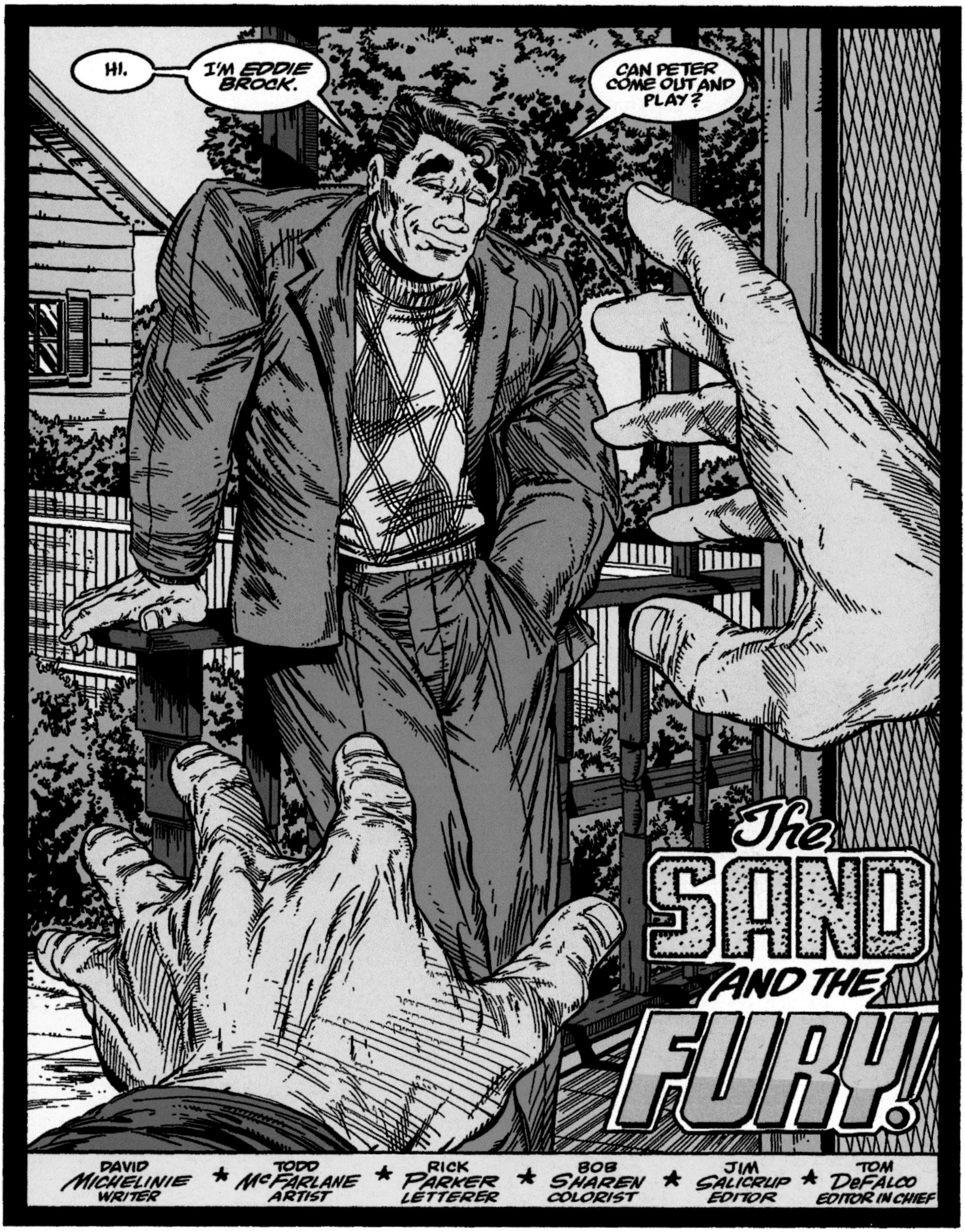

HI.
I'M EDDIE BROCK.
CAN PETER COME OUT AND PLAY?
The SAND AND THE FURY!
DAVID MICHELINIE WRITER ★ TODD McFARLANE ARTIST ★ RICK PARKER LETTERER ★ BOB SHAREN COLORIST ★ JIM SALICRUP EDITOR ★ TOM DeFALCO EDITOR IN CHIEF

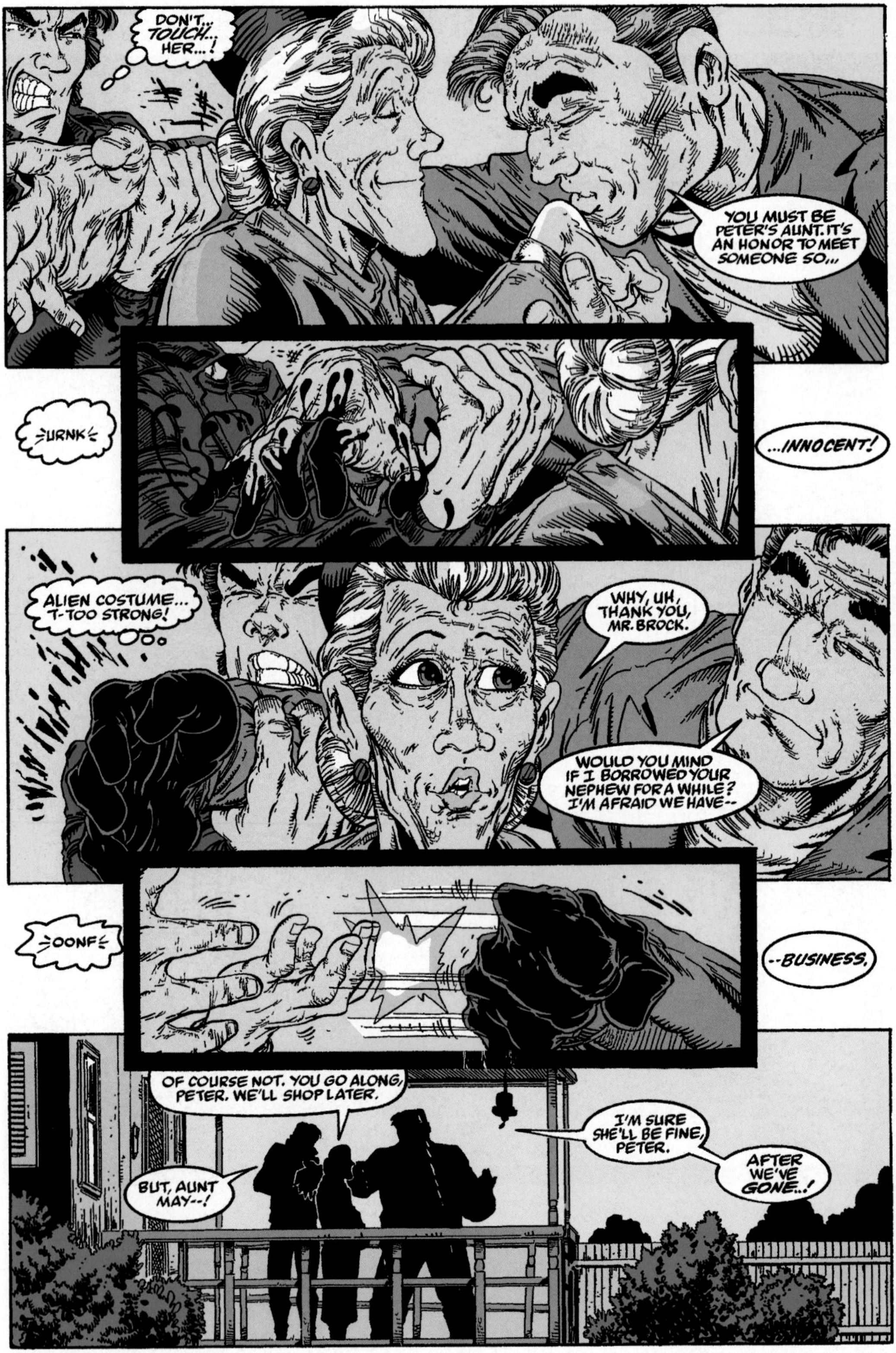
DON'T... TOUCH... HER...!
YOU MUST BE PETER'S AUNT. IT'S AN HONOR TO MEET SOMEONE SO...
URNK
...INNOCENT!
ALIEN COSTUME... T-TOO STRONG!
WHY, UH, THANK YOU, MR. BROCK.
WOULD YOU MIND IF I BORROWED YOUR NEPHEW FOR A WHILE? I'M AFRAID WE HAVE--
OONF
--BUSINESS.
OF COURSE NOT. YOU GO ALONG, PETER. WE'LL SHOP LATER.
BUT, AUNT MAY--!
I'M SURE SHE'LL BE FINE, PETER.
AFTER WE'VE GONE..!

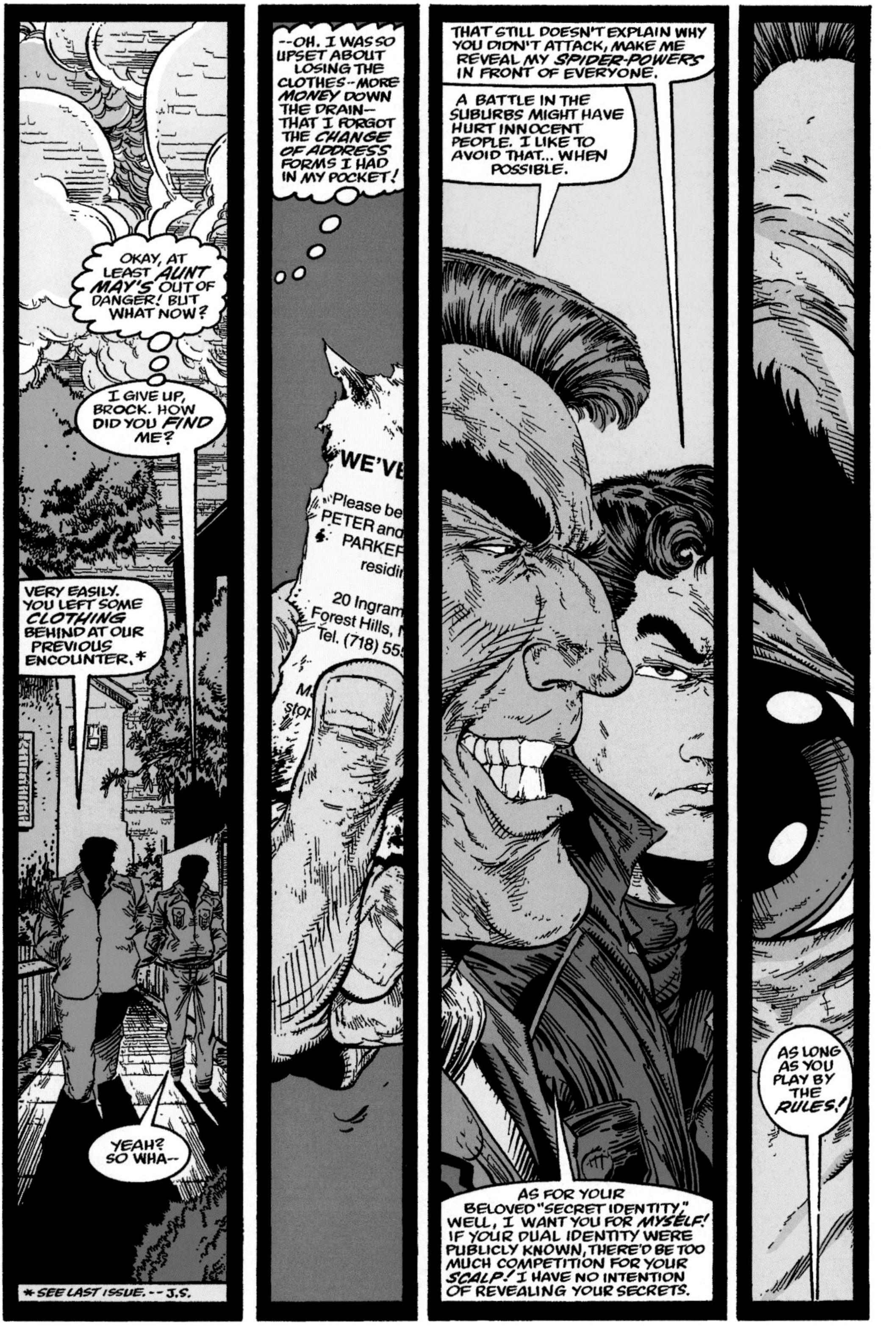
OKAY, AT LEAST AUNT MAY'S OUT OF DANGER! BUT WHAT NOW?
I GIVE UP, BROCK. HOW DID YOU FIND ME?
VERY EASILY. YOU LEFT SOME CLOTHING BEHIND AT OUR PREVIOUS ENCOUNTER.*
YEAH? SO WHA--
*SEE LAST ISSUE. --J.S.
--OH. I WAS SO UPSET ABOUT LOSING THE CLOTHES--MORE MONEY DOWN THE DRAIN-- THAT I FORGOT THE CHANGE OF ADDRESS FORMS I HAD IN MY POCKET!
WE'VE
Please be
PETER and
PARKER
residi
20 Ingram
Forest Hills,
Tel. (718) 55
THAT STILL DOESN'T EXPLAIN WHY YOU DIDN'T ATTACK, MAKE ME REVEAL MY SPIDER-POWERS IN FRONT OF EVERYONE.
A BATTLE IN THE SUBURBS MIGHT HAVE HURT INNOCENT PEOPLE. I LIKE TO AVOID THAT... WHEN POSSIBLE.
AS FOR YOUR BELOVED "SECRET IDENTITY," WELL, I WANT YOU FOR MYSELF! IF YOUR DUAL IDENTITY WERE PUBLICLY KNOWN, THERE'D BE TOO MUCH COMPETITION FOR YOUR SCALP! I HAVE NO INTENTION OF REVEALING YOUR SECRETS.
AS LONG AS YOU PLAY BY THE RULES!

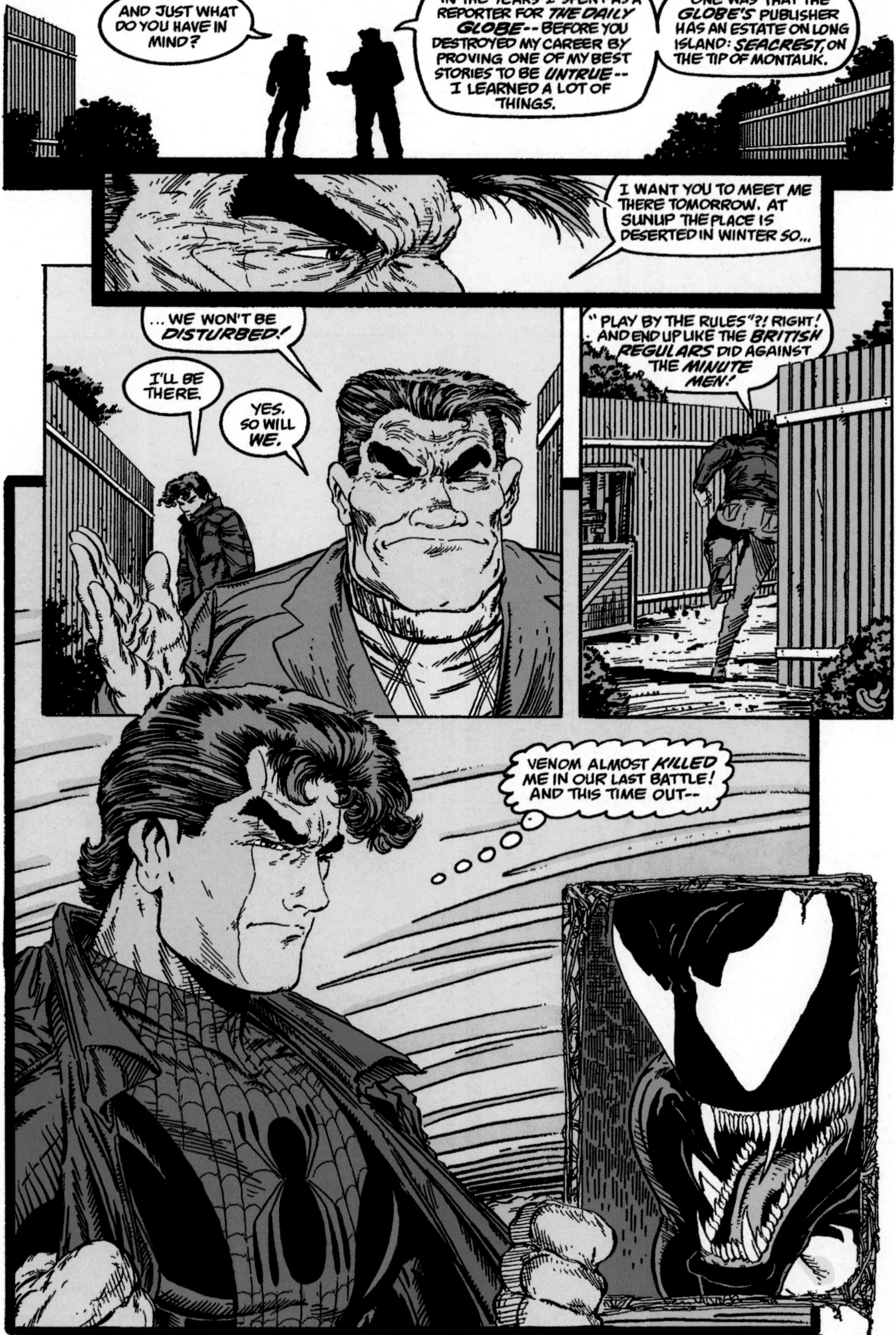
AND JUST WHAT DO YOU HAVE IN MIND?
IN THE YEARS I SPENT AS A REPORTER FOR THE DAILY GLOBE--BEFORE YOU DESTROYED MY CAREER BY PROVING ONE OF MY BEST STORIES TO BE UNTRUE--I LEARNED A LOT OF THINGS.
ONE WAS THAT THE GLOBE'S PUBLISHER HAS AN ESTATE ON LONG ISLAND: SEACREST, ON THE TIP OF MONTAUK.
I WANT YOU TO MEET ME THERE TOMORROW. AT SUNUP THE PLACE IS DESERTED IN WINTER SO...
...WE WON'T BE DISTURBED!
I'LL BE THERE.
YES. SO WILL WE.
"PLAY BY THE RULES"?! RIGHT! AND END UP LIKE THE BRITISH REGULARS DID AGAINST THE MINUTE MEN!
VENOM ALMOST KILLED ME IN OUR LAST BATTLE! AND THIS TIME OUT--

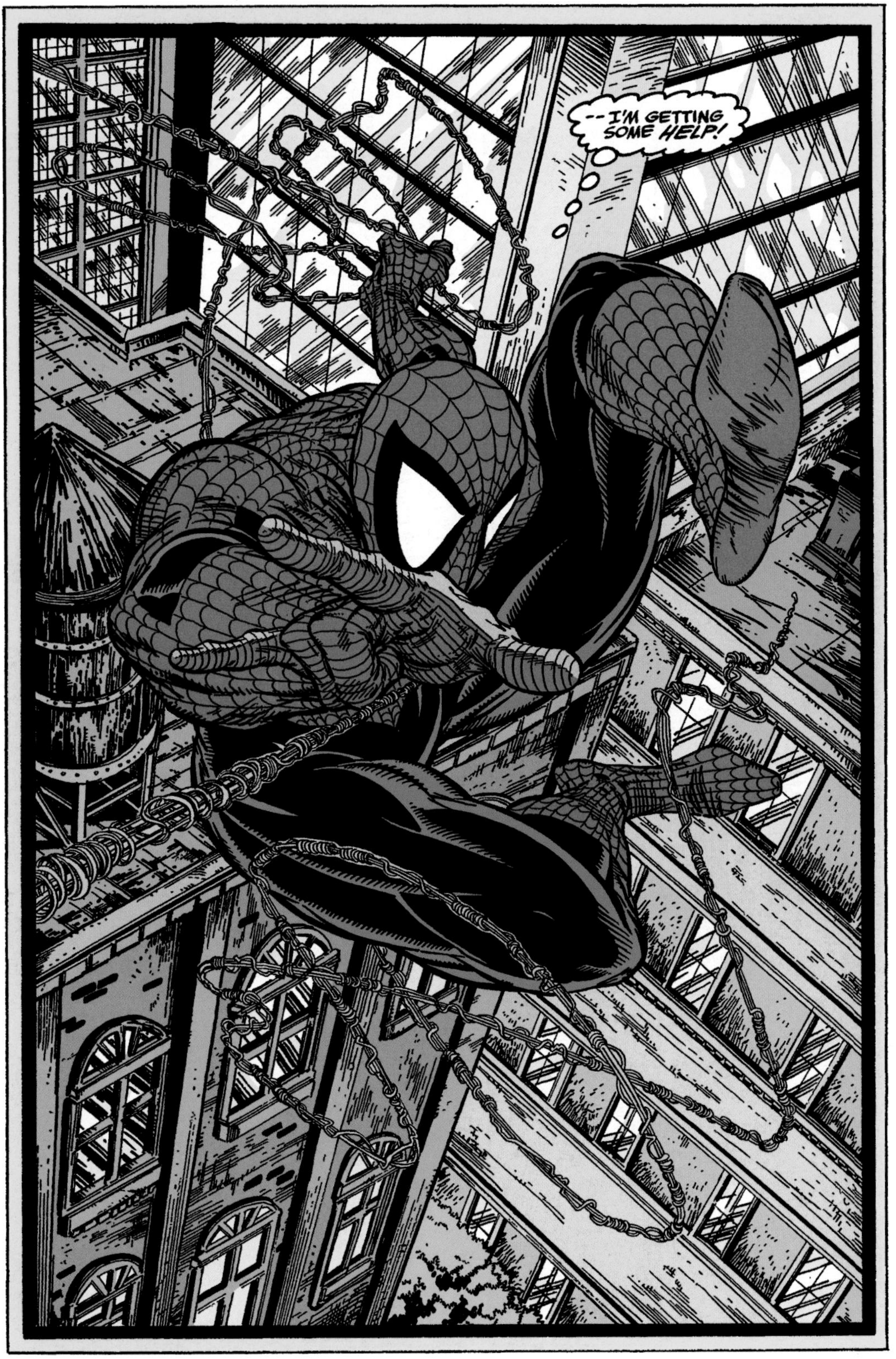
--I'M GETTING SOME HELP!

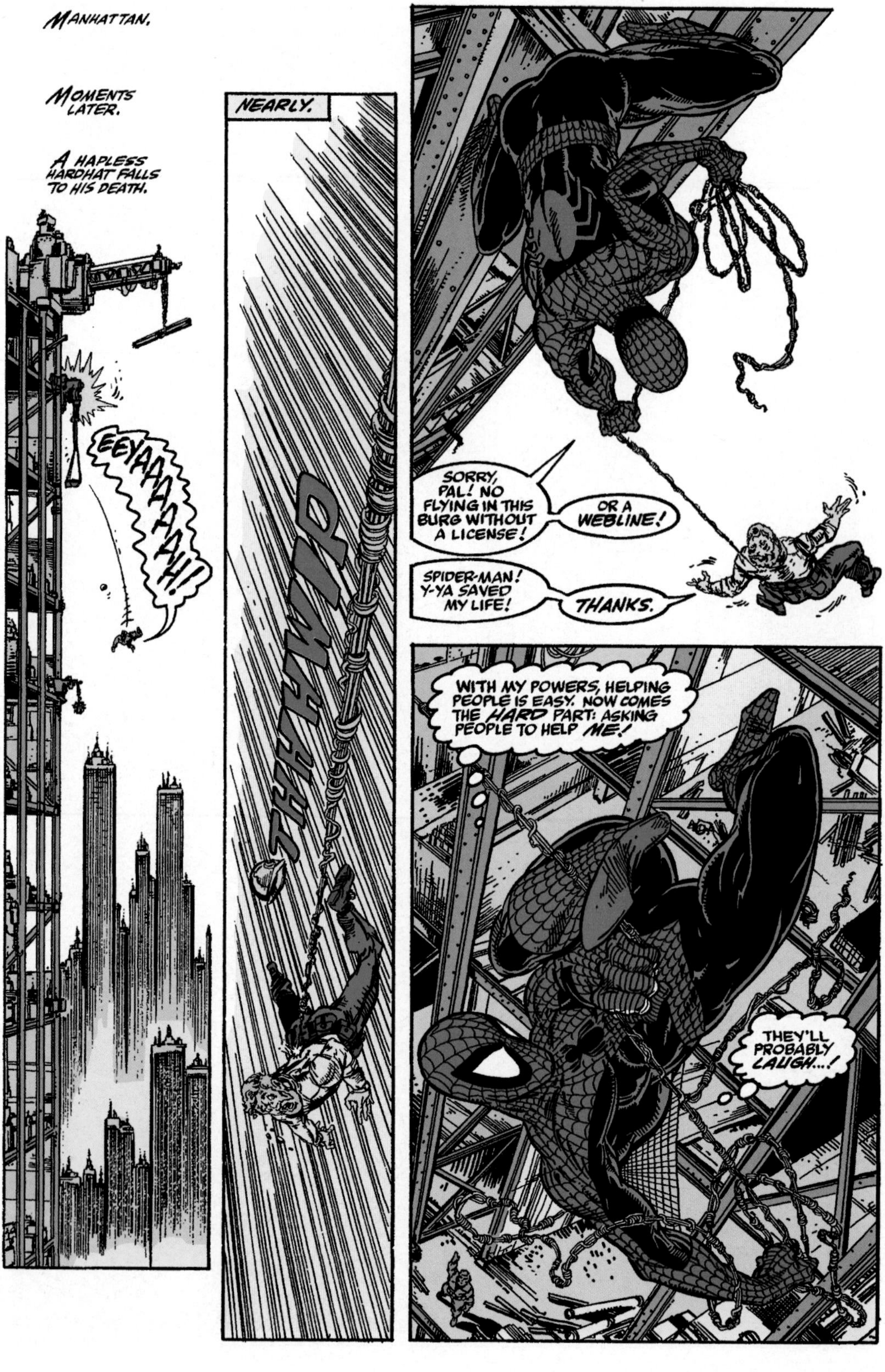
MANHATTAN.
MOMENTS LATER.
A HAPLESS HARDHAT FALLS TO HIS DEATH.
EEYAAAAAAAH!!
NEARLY.
THHWIP
SORRY, PAL! NO FLYING IN THIS BURG WITHOUT A LICENSE!
OR A WEBLINE!
SPIDER-MAN! Y-YA SAVED MY LIFE!
THANKS.
WITH MY POWERS, HELPING PEOPLE IS EASY. NOW COMES THE HARD PART: ASKING PEOPLE TO HELP ME!
THEY'LL PROBABLY LAUGH...!

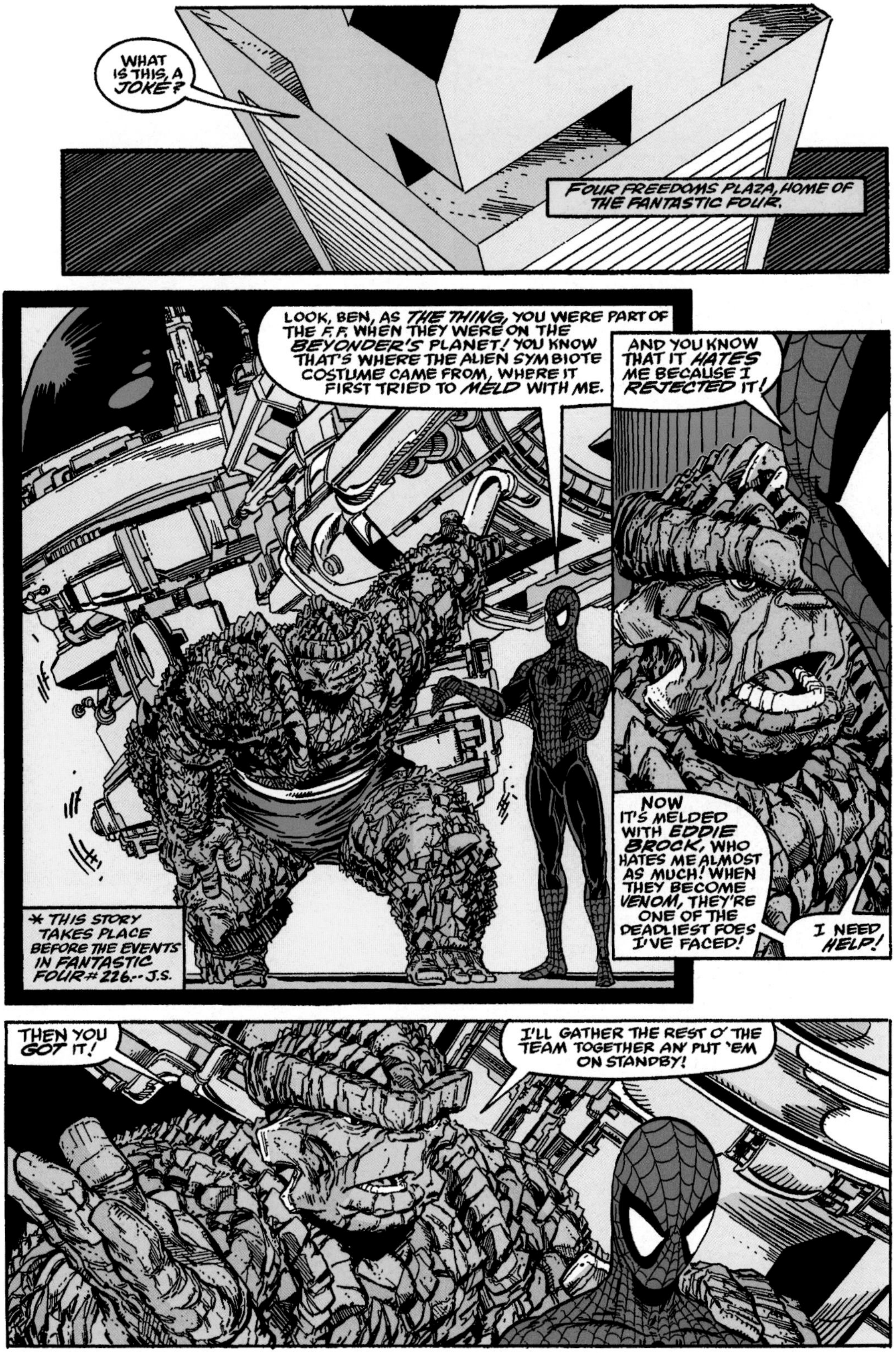
WHAT IS THIS, A JOKE?
FOUR FREEDOMS PLAZA, HOME OF THE FANTASTIC FOUR.
LOOK, BEN, AS THE THING, YOU WERE PART OF THE F.F. WHEN THEY WERE ON THE BEYONDER'S PLANET! YOU KNOW THAT'S WHERE THE ALIEN SYMBIOTE COSTUME CAME FROM, WHERE IT FIRST TRIED TO MELD WITH ME.
AND YOU KNOW THAT IT HATES ME BECAUSE I REJECTED IT!
NOW IT'S MELDED WITH EDDIE BROCK, WHO HATES ME ALMOST AS MUCH! WHEN THEY BECOME VENOM, THEY'RE ONE OF THE DEADLIEST FOES I'VE FACED!
I NEED HELP!
* THIS STORY TAKES PLACE BEFORE THE EVENTS IN FANTASTIC FOUR #226.-- J.S.
THEN YOU GOT IT!
I'LL GATHER THE REST O' THE TEAM TOGETHER AN' PUT 'EM ON STANDBY!

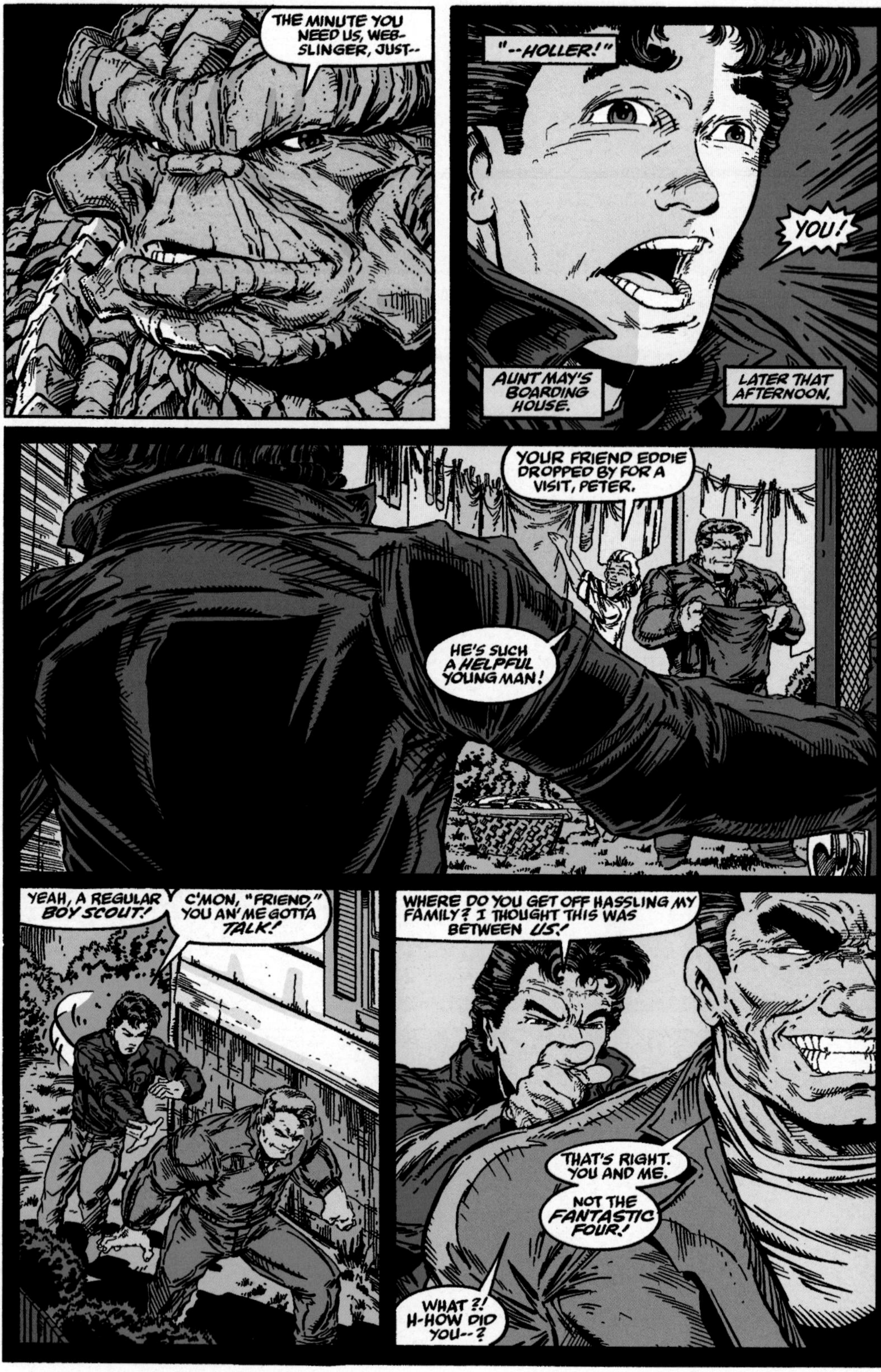
THE MINUTE YOU NEED US, WEB-SLINGER, JUST--
"--HOLLER!"
YOU!
AUNT MAY'S BOARDING HOUSE.
LATER THAT AFTERNOON.
YOUR FRIEND EDDIE DROPPED BY FOR A VISIT, PETER.
HE'S SUCH A HELPFUL YOUNG MAN!
YEAH, A REGULAR BOY SCOUT!
C'MON, "FRIEND," YOU AN' ME GOTTA TALK!
WHERE DO YOU GET OFF HASSLING MY FAMILY? I THOUGHT THIS WAS BETWEEN US!
THAT'S RIGHT. YOU AND ME.
NOT THE FANTASTIC FOUR!
WHAT?! H-HOW DID YOU--?

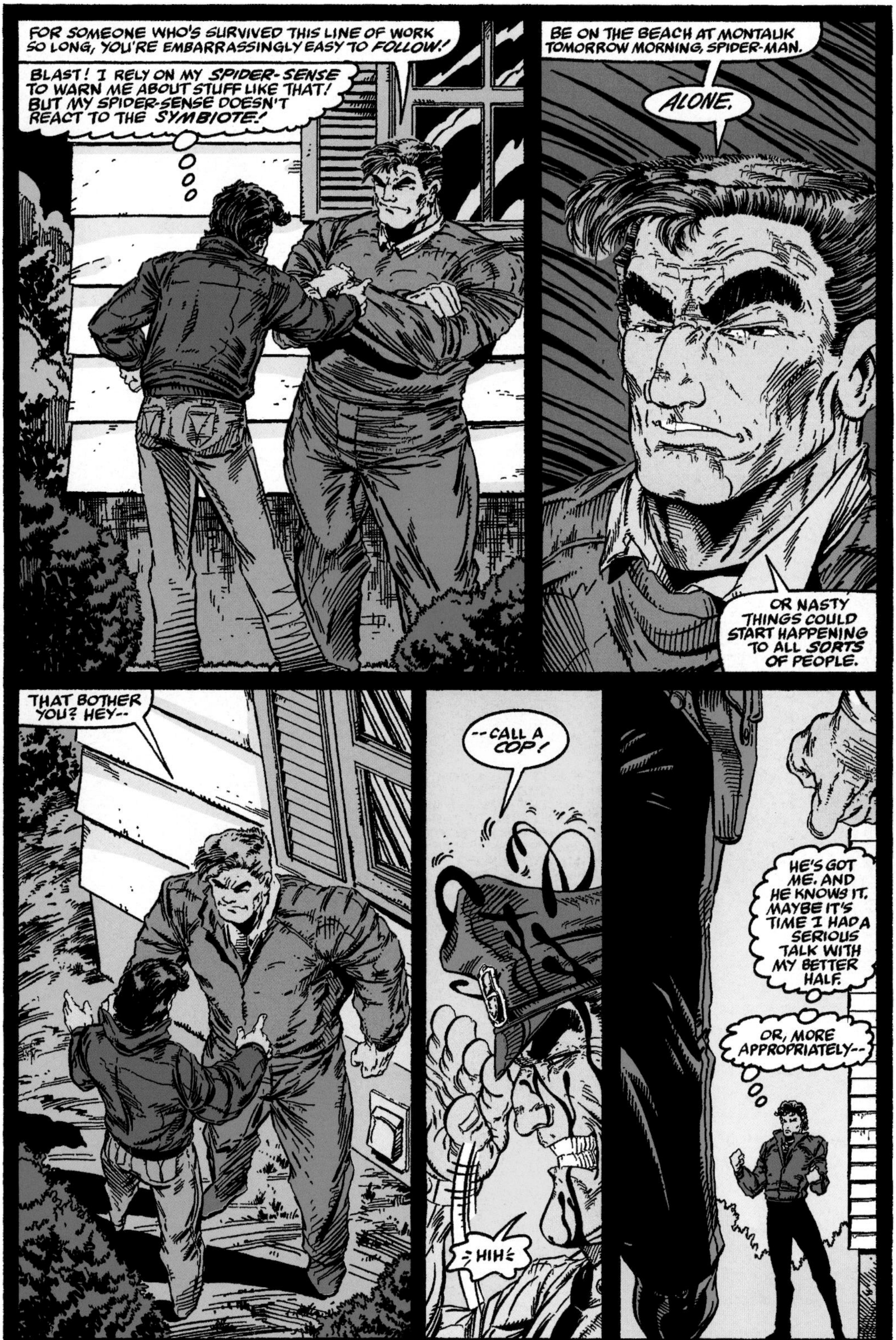
FOR SOMEONE WHO'S SURVIVED THIS LINE OF WORK SO LONG, YOU'RE EMBARRASSINGLY EASY TO FOLLOW!
BLAST! I RELY ON MY SPIDER-SENSE TO WARN ME ABOUT STUFF LIKE THAT! BUT MY SPIDER-SENSE DOESN'T REACT TO THE SYMBIOTE!
BE ON THE BEACH AT MONTAUK TOMORROW MORNING, SPIDER-MAN.
ALONE.
OR NASTY THINGS COULD START HAPPENING TO ALL SORTS OF PEOPLE.
THAT BOTHER YOU? HEY--
--CALL A COP!
HIH
HE'S GOT ME. AND HE KNOWS IT. MAYBE IT'S TIME I HAD A SERIOUS TALK WITH MY BETTER HALF.
OR, MORE APPROPRIATELY--

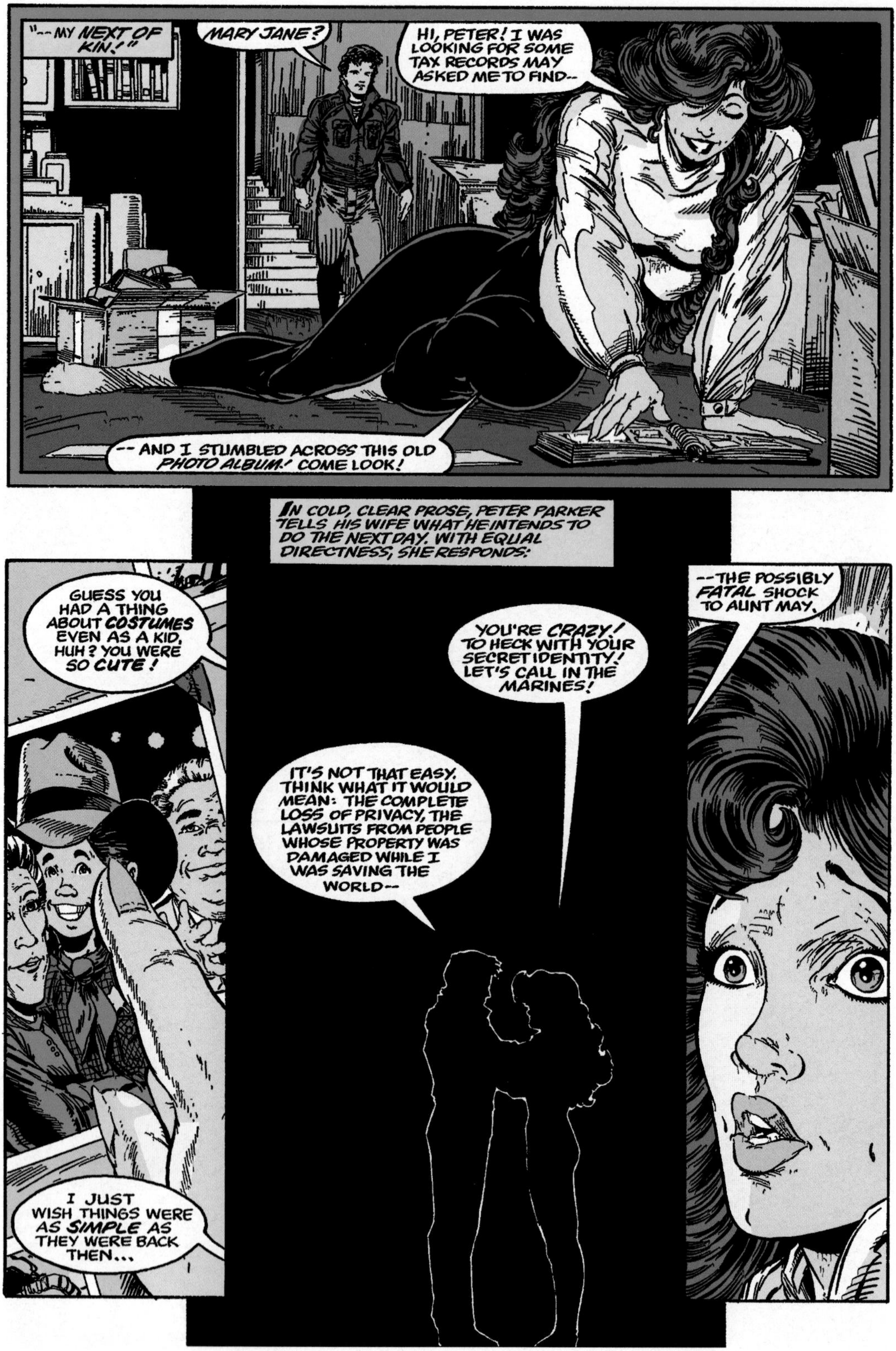
"--MY NEXT OF KIN!"
MARY JANE?
HI, PETER! I WAS LOOKING FOR SOME TAX RECORDS MAY ASKED ME TO FIND--
--AND I STUMBLED ACROSS THIS OLD PHOTO ALBUM! COME LOOK!
IN COLD, CLEAR PROSE, PETER PARKER TELLS HIS WIFE WHAT HE INTENDS TO DO THE NEXT DAY. WITH EQUAL DIRECTNESS, SHE RESPONDS:
GUESS YOU HAD A THING ABOUT COSTUMES EVEN AS A KID, HUH? YOU WERE SO CUTE!
I JUST WISH THINGS WERE AS SIMPLE AS THEY WERE BACK THEN...
YOU'RE CRAZY! TO HECK WITH YOUR SECRET IDENTITY! LET'S CALL IN THE MARINES!
IT'S NOT THAT EASY. THINK WHAT IT WOULD MEAN: THE COMPLETE LOSS OF PRIVACY, THE LAWSUITS FROM PEOPLE WHOSE PROPERTY WAS DAMAGED WHILE I WAS SAVING THE WORLD--
--THE POSSIBLY FATAL SHOCK TO AUNT MAY.

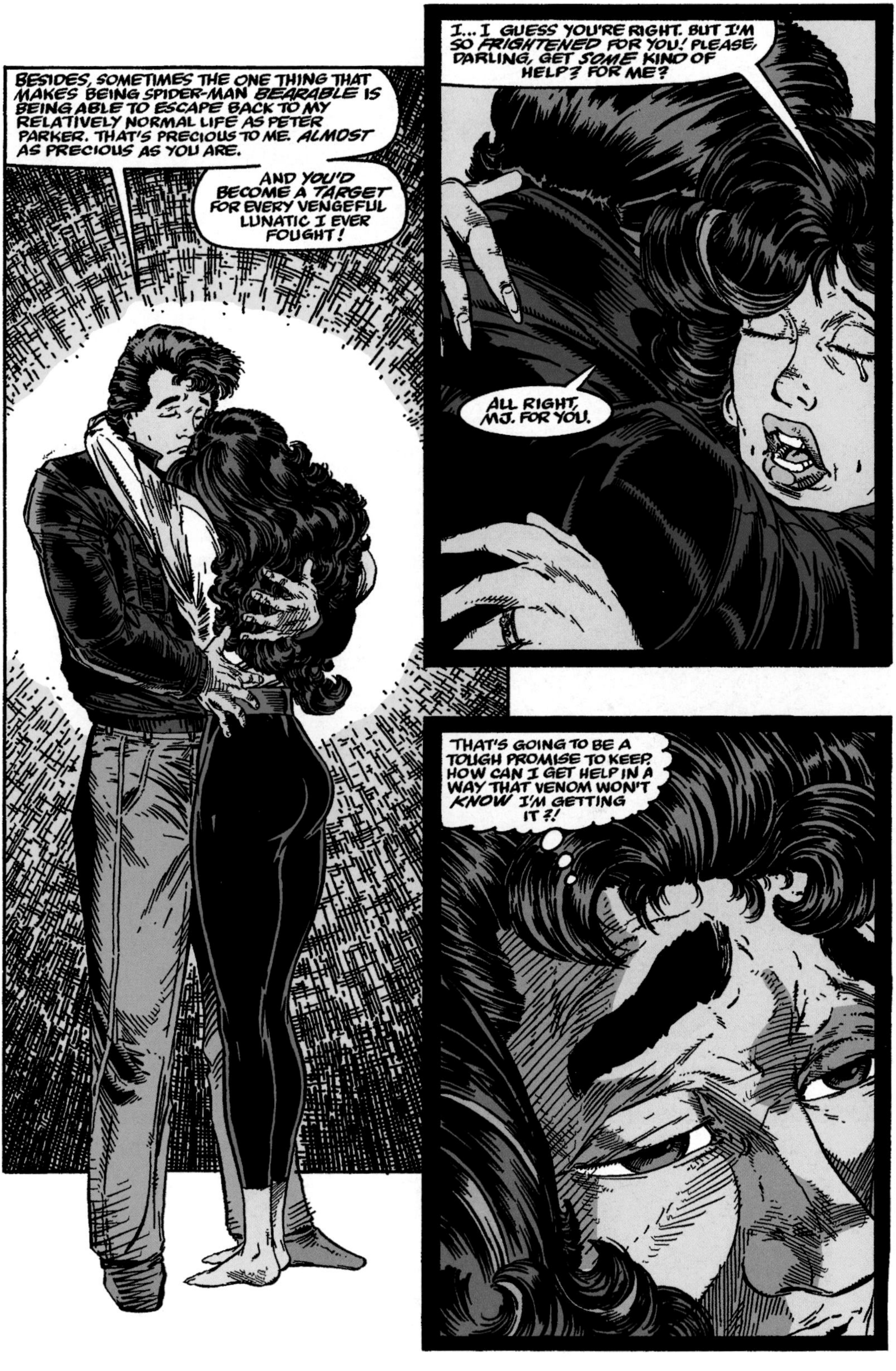
BESIDES, SOMETIMES THE ONE THING THAT MAKES BEING SPIDER-MAN BEARABLE IS BEING ABLE TO ESCAPE BACK TO MY RELATIVELY NORMAL LIFE AS PETER PARKER. THAT'S PRECIOUS TO ME. ALMOST AS PRECIOUS AS YOU ARE.
AND YOU'D BECOME A TARGET FOR EVERY VENGEFUL LUNATIC I EVER FOUGHT!
I... I GUESS YOU'RE RIGHT. BUT I'M SO FRIGHTENED FOR YOU! PLEASE, DARLING, GET SOME KIND OF HELP? FOR ME?
ALL RIGHT, MJ. FOR YOU.
THAT'S GOING TO BE A TOUGH PROMISE TO KEEP. HOW CAN I GET HELP IN A WAY THAT VENOM WON'T KNOW I'M GETTING IT?!

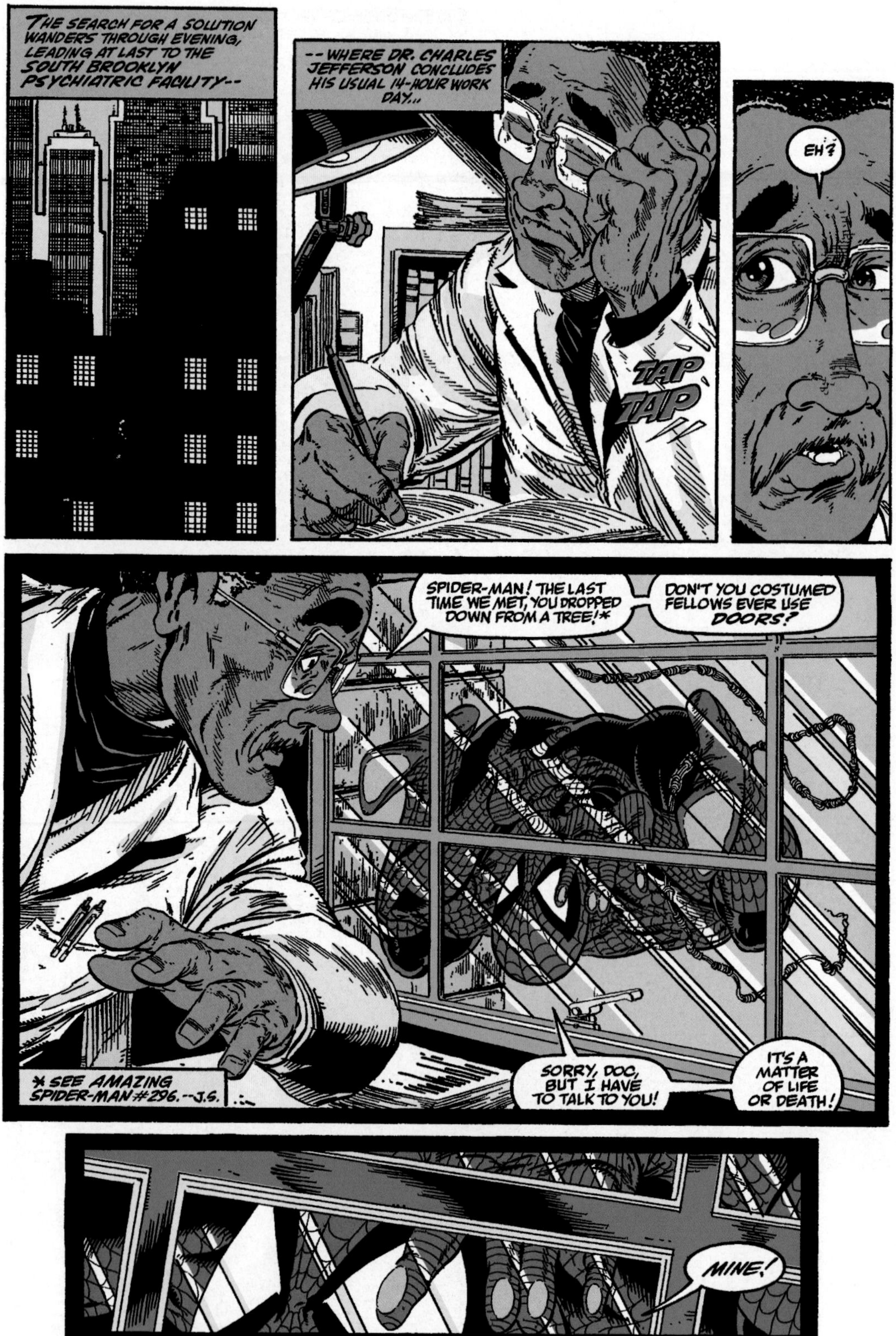
THE SEARCH FOR A SOLUTION WANDERS THROUGH EVENING, LEADING AT LAST TO THE SOUTH BROOKLYN PSYCHIATRIC FACILITY--
--WHERE DR. CHARLES JEFFERSON CONCLUDES HIS USUAL 14-HOUR WORK DAY...
TAP TAP
EH?
SPIDER-MAN! THE LAST TIME WE MET, YOU DROPPED DOWN FROM A TREE!*
DON'T YOU COSTUMED FELLOWS EVER USE DOORS?
SORRY, DOC, BUT I HAVE TO TALK TO YOU!
IT'S A MATTER OF LIFE OR DEATH!
*SEE AMAZING SPIDER-MAN #296.--J.S.
MINE!

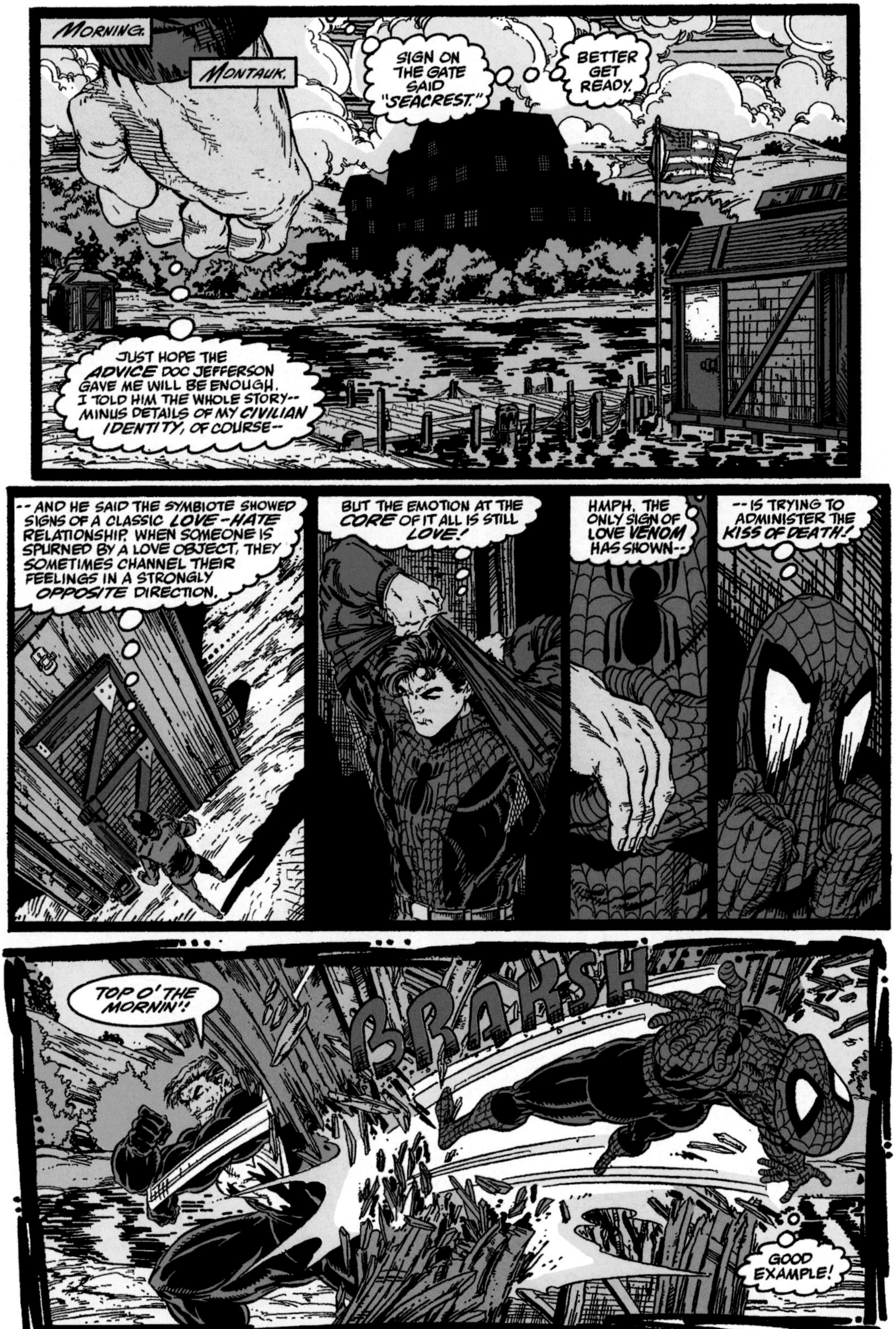
MORNING.
MONTAUK.
SIGN ON THE GATE SAID "SEACREST."
BETTER GET READY.
JUST HOPE THE ADVICE DOC JEFFERSON GAVE ME WILL BE ENOUGH. I TOLD HIM THE WHOLE STORY-- MINUS DETAILS OF MY CIVILIAN IDENTITY, OF COURSE--
--AND HE SAID THE SYMBIOTE SHOWED SIGNS OF A CLASSIC LOVE-HATE RELATIONSHIP. WHEN SOMEONE IS SPURNED BY A LOVE OBJECT, THEY SOMETIMES CHANNEL THEIR FEELINGS IN A STRONGLY OPPOSITE DIRECTION.
BUT THE EMOTION AT THE CORE OF IT ALL IS STILL LOVE!
HMPH. THE ONLY SIGN OF LOVE VENOM HAS SHOWN--
--IS TRYING TO ADMINISTER THE KISS OF DEATH!
TOP O' THE MORNIN'!
BRAKSH
GOOD EXAMPLE!

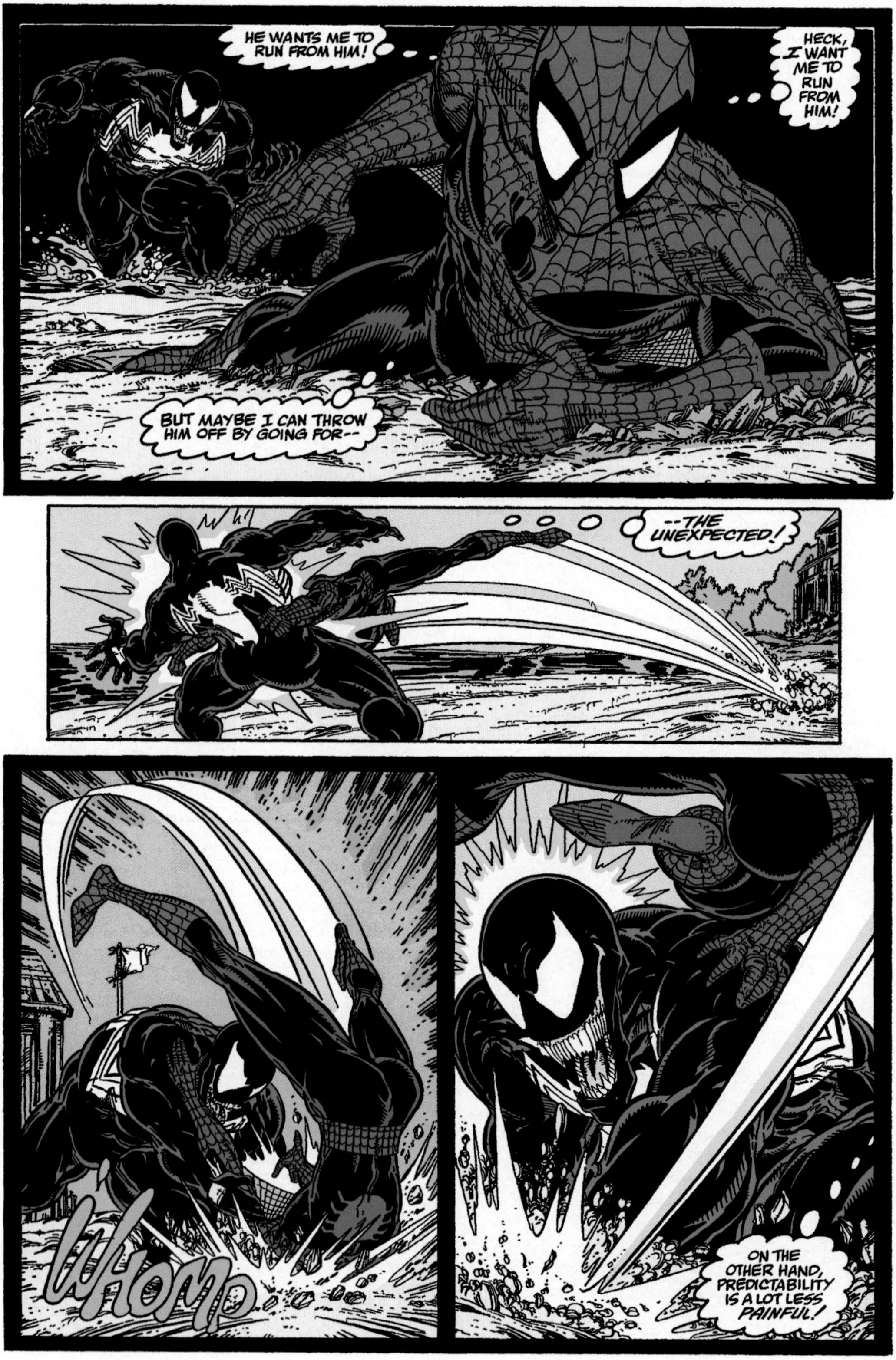
HE WANTS ME TO RUN FROM HIM!
HECK, I WANT ME TO RUN FROM HIM!
BUT MAYBE I CAN THROW HIM OFF BY GOING FOR--
--THE UNEXPECTED!
WHOMP
ON THE OTHER HAND, PREDICTABILITY IS A LOT LESS PAINFUL!

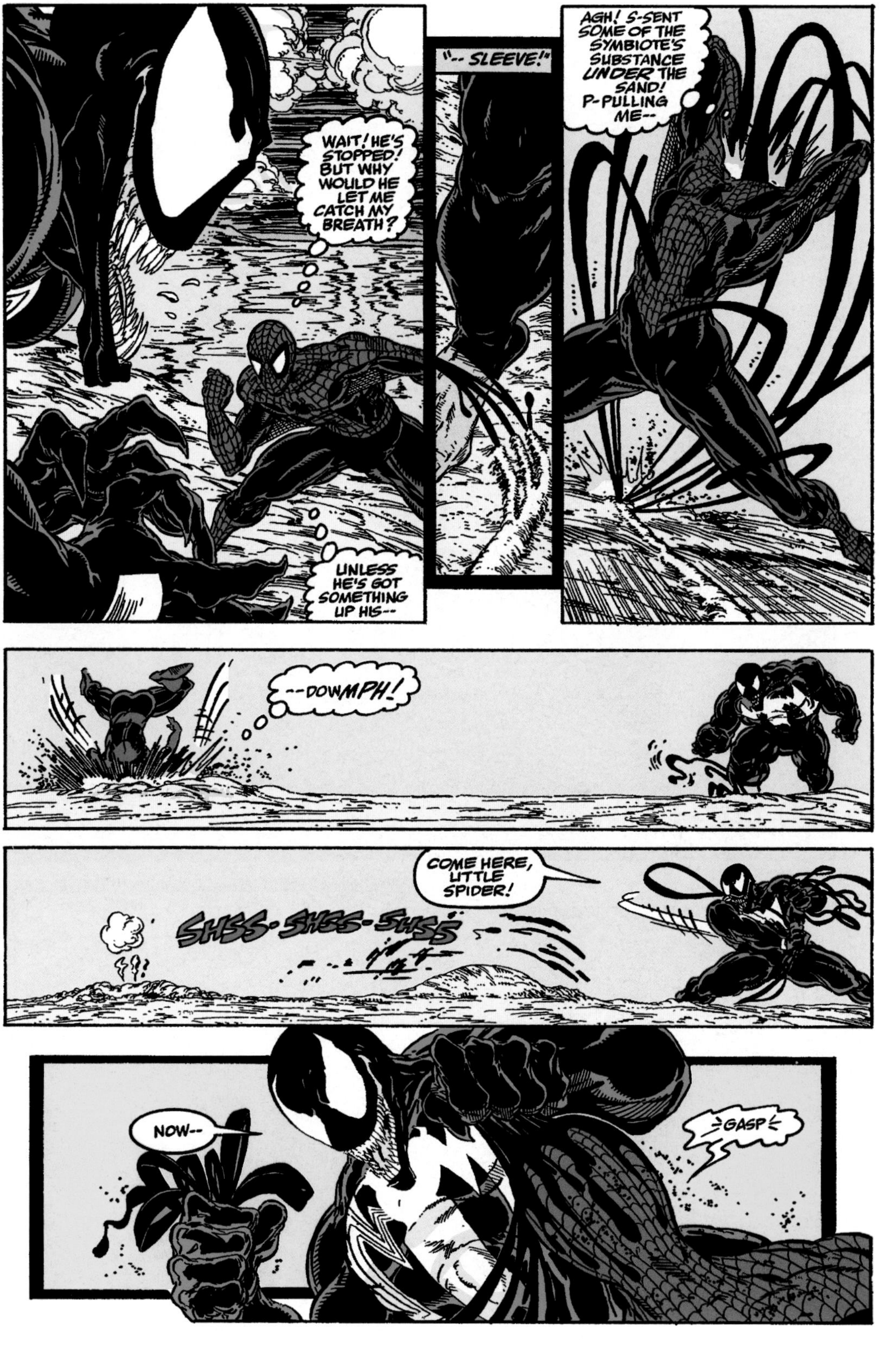
WAIT! HE'S STOPPED! BUT WHY WOULD HE LET ME CATCH MY BREATH?
UNLESS HE'S GOT SOMETHING UP HIS--
"--SLEEVE!"
AGH! S-SENT SOME OF THE SYMBIOTE'S SUBSTANCE UNDER THE SAND! P-PULLING ME--
--DOWMPH!
COME HERE, LITTLE SPIDER!
SHSS-SHSS-SHSS
NOW--
GASP

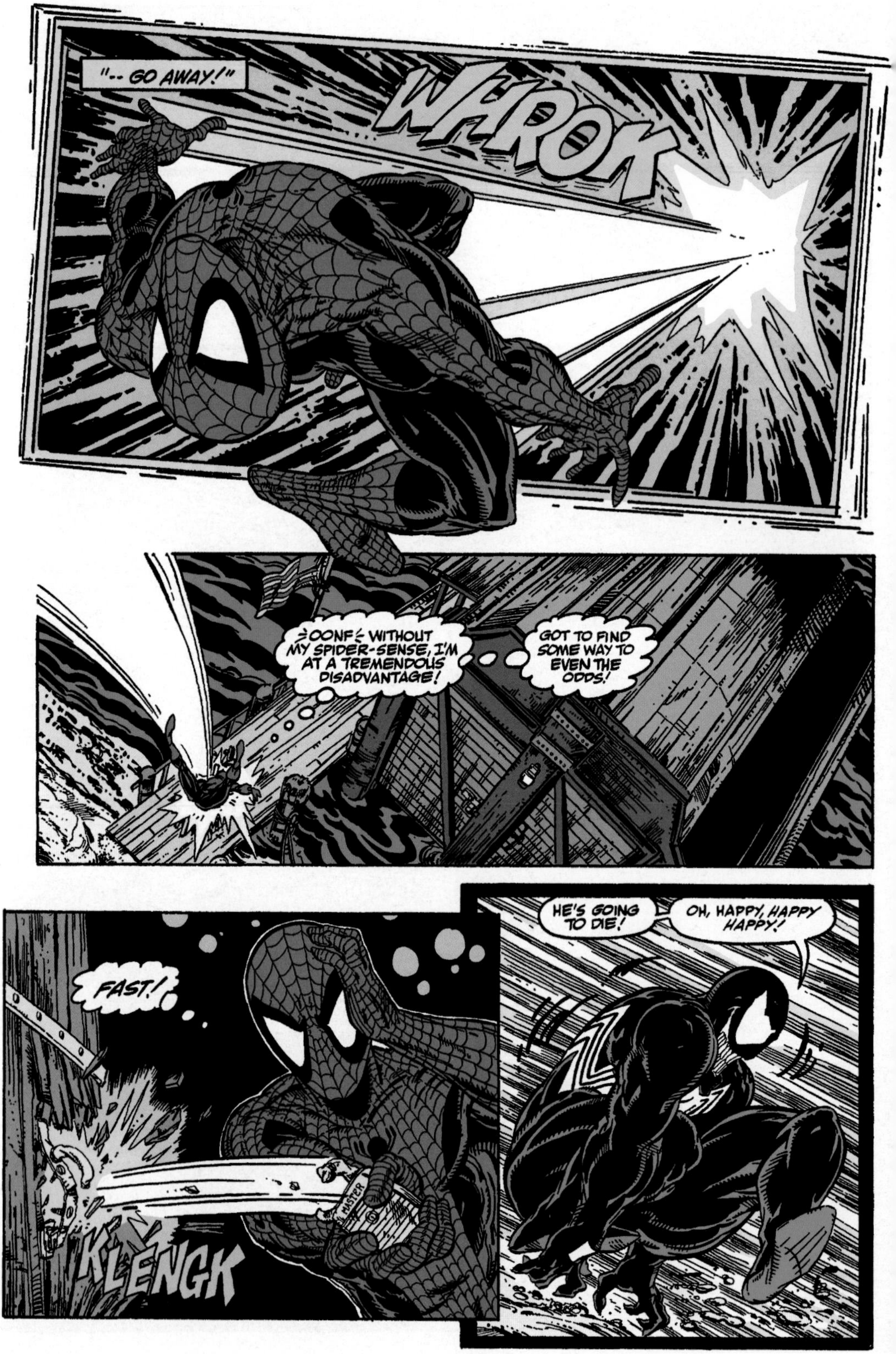
"-- GO AWAY!"
WAROK
=OONF= WITHOUT MY SPIDER-SENSE, I'M AT A TREMENDOUS DISADVANTAGE!
GOT TO FIND SOME WAY TO EVEN THE ODDS!
FAST!
KLENGK
MASTER
HE'S GOING TO DIE!
OH, HAPPY, HAPPY HAPPY!

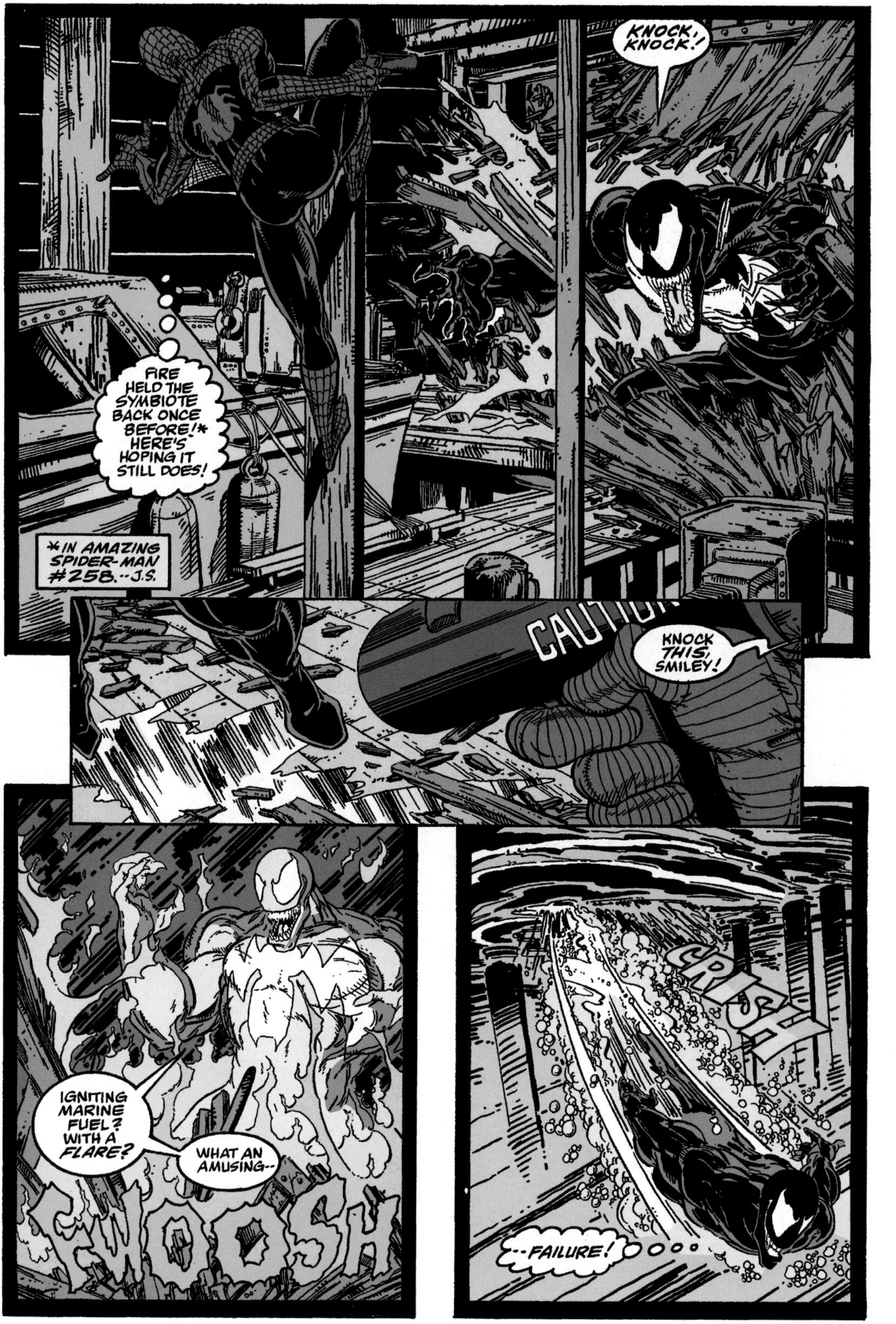
FIRE HELD THE SYMBIOTE BACK ONCE BEFORE!* HERE'S HOPING IT STILL DOES!
*IN AMAZING SPIDER-MAN #258.--J.S.
KNOCK, KNOCK!
CAUTION
KNOCK THIS, SMILEY!
IGNITING MARINE FUEL? WITH A FLARE?
WHAT AN AMUSING--
WHOOSH
CRASH
--FAILURE!

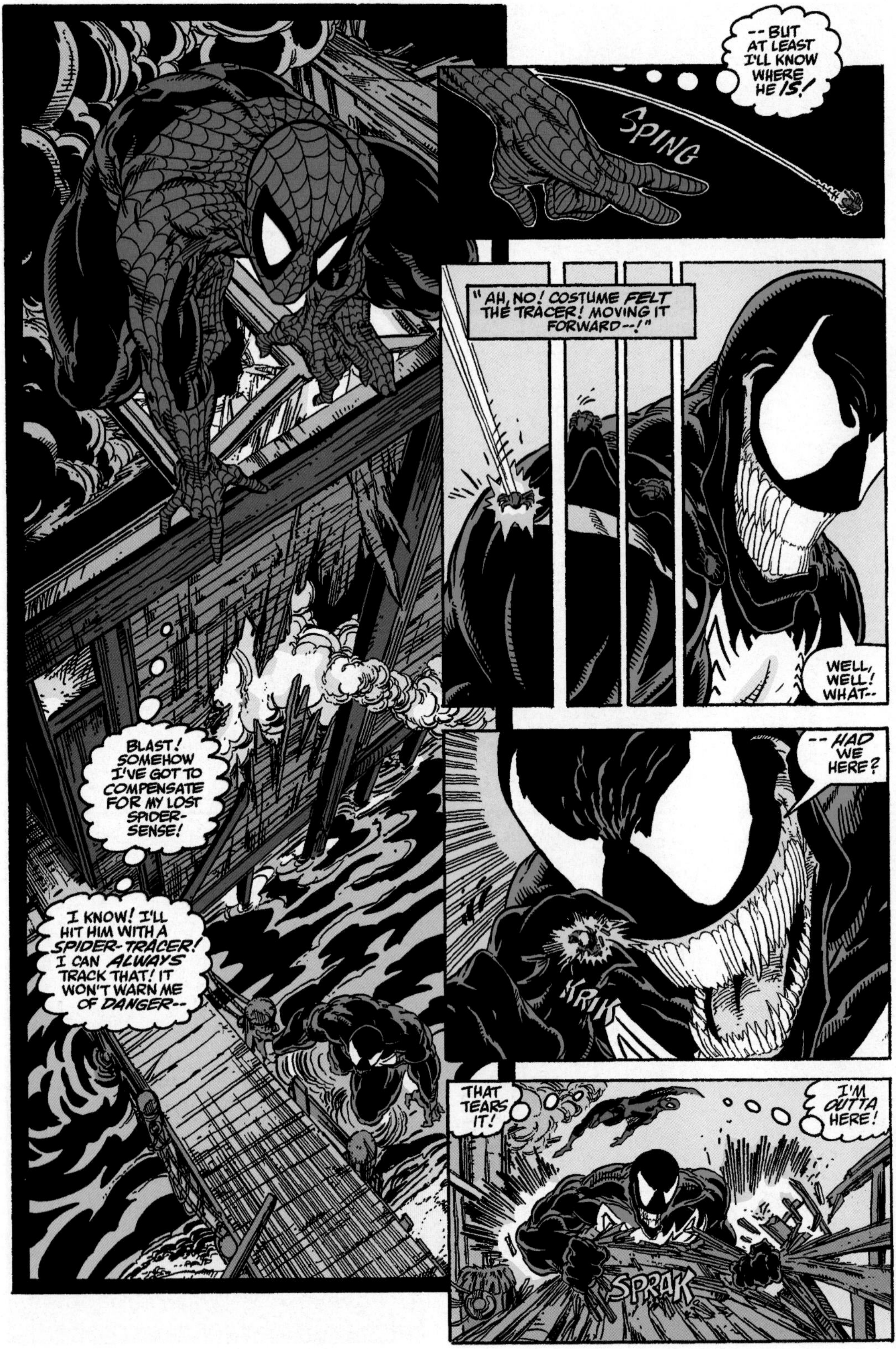

BLAST! SOMEHOW I'VE GOT TO COMPENSATE FOR MY LOST SPIDER-SENSE!
I KNOW! I'LL HIT HIM WITH A SPIDER-TRACER! I CAN ALWAYS TRACK THAT! IT WON'T WARN ME OF DANGER--
--BUT AT LEAST I'LL KNOW WHERE HE IS!
SPING
"AH, NO! COSTUME FELT THE TRACER! MOVING IT FORWARD--!"
WELL, WELL! WHAT--
--HAD WE HERE?
THAT TEARS IT!
I'M OUTTA HERE!
SPRAK

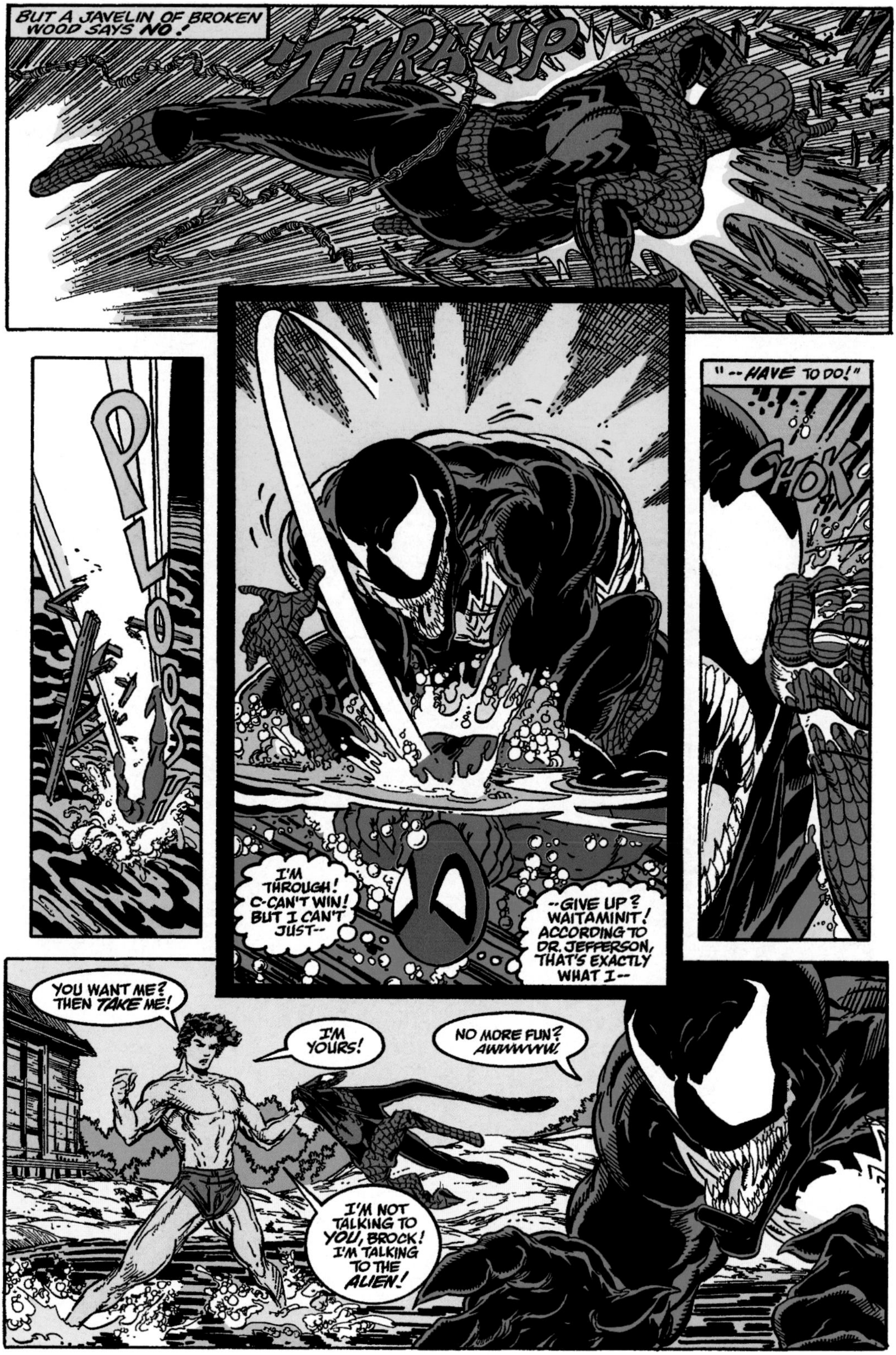
BUT A JAVELIN OF BROKEN WOOD SAYS NO!
THRAMP
PLOOOSH
I'M THROUGH! C-CAN'T WIN! BUT I CAN'T JUST--
--GIVE UP? WAITAMINIT! ACCORDING TO DR. JEFFERSON, THAT'S EXACTLY WHAT I--
"--HAVE TO DO!"
CHOK
YOU WANT ME? THEN TAKE ME!
I'M YOURS!
NO MORE FUN? AWWWWW!
I'M NOT TALKING TO YOU, BROCK! I'M TALKING TO THE ALIEN!

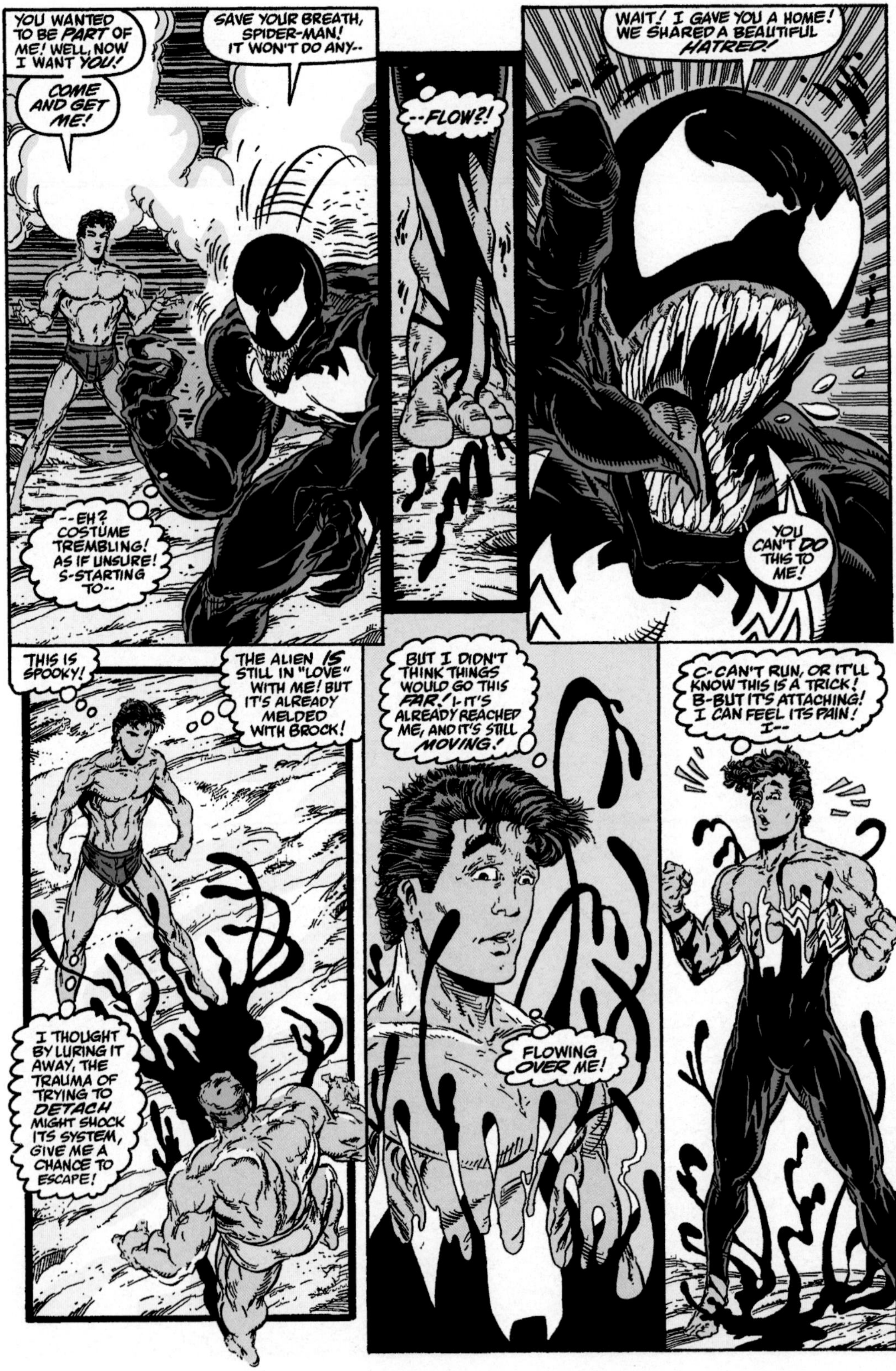
YOU WANTED TO BE PART OF ME! WELL, NOW I WANT YOU!
COME AND GET ME!
SAVE YOUR BREATH, SPIDER-MAN! IT WON'T DO ANY--
--EH? COSTUME TREMBLING! AS IF UNSURE! S-STARTING TO--
--FLOW?!
WAIT! I GAVE YOU A HOME! WE SHARED A BEAUTIFUL HATRED!
YOU CAN'T DO THIS TO ME!
THIS IS SPOOKY!
THE ALIEN IS STILL IN "LOVE" WITH ME! BUT IT'S ALREADY MELDED WITH BROCK!
I THOUGHT BY LURING IT AWAY, THE TRAUMA OF TRYING TO DETACH MIGHT SHOCK ITS SYSTEM, GIVE ME A CHANCE TO ESCAPE!
BUT I DIDN'T THINK THINGS WOULD GO THIS FAR! I-IT'S ALREADY REACHED ME, AND IT'S STILL MOVING!
FLOWING OVER ME!
C-CAN'T RUN, OR IT'LL KNOW THIS IS A TRICK! B-BUT IT'S ATTACHING! I CAN FEEL ITS PAIN! I--

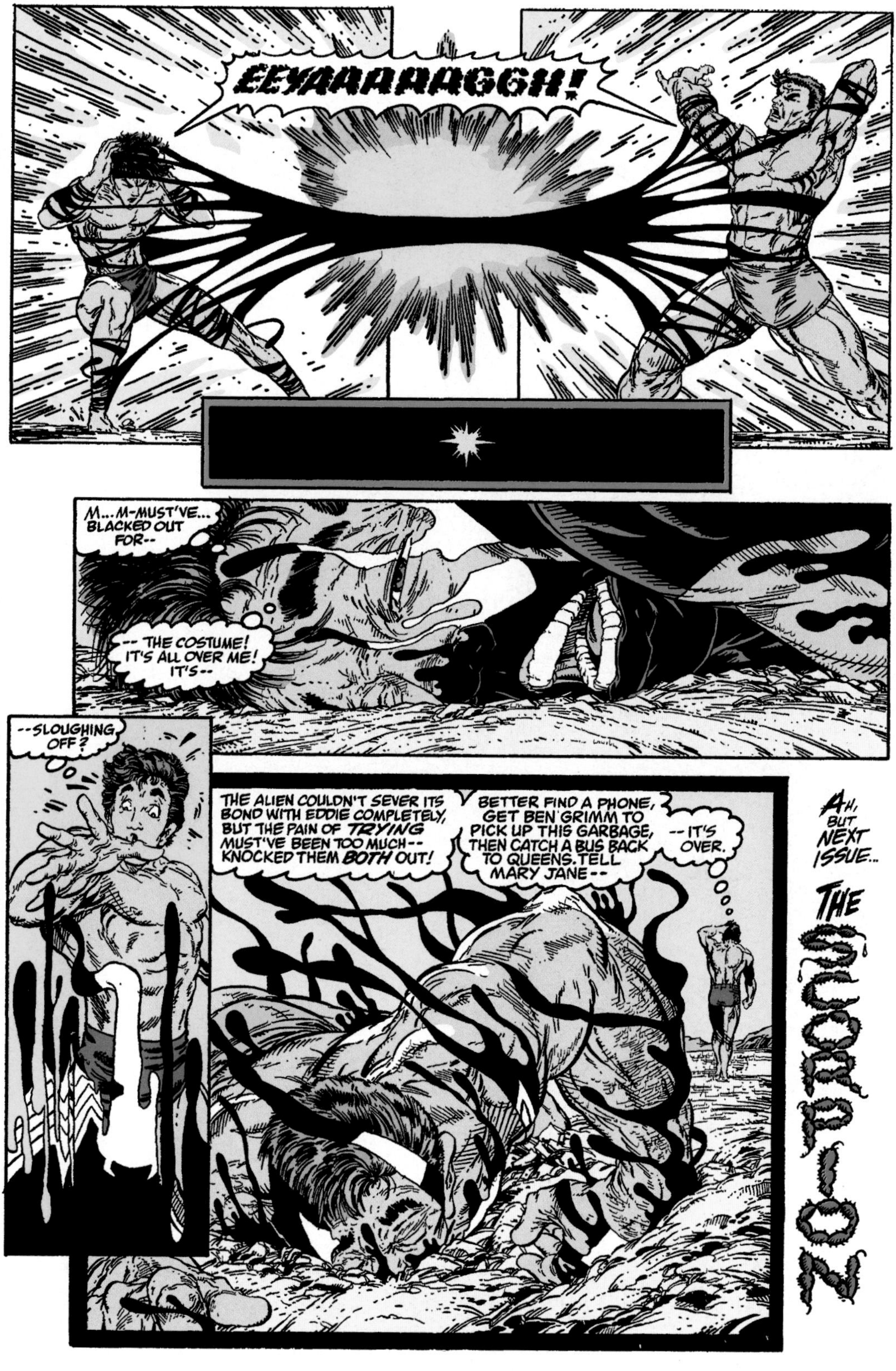
EEYAAAAAAGGH!
M... M-MUST'VE... BLACKED OUT FOR--
-- THE COSTUME! IT'S ALL OVER ME! IT'S--
--SLOUGHING OFF?
THE ALIEN COULDN'T SEVER ITS BOND WITH EDDIE COMPLETELY, BUT THE PAIN OF TRYING MUST'VE BEEN TOO MUCH-- KNOCKED THEM BOTH OUT!
BETTER FIND A PHONE, GET BEN GRIMM TO PICK UP THIS GARBAGE, THEN CATCH A BUS BACK TO QUEENS. TELL MARY JANE--
--IT'S OVER.
AH, BUT NEXT ISSUE...
THE

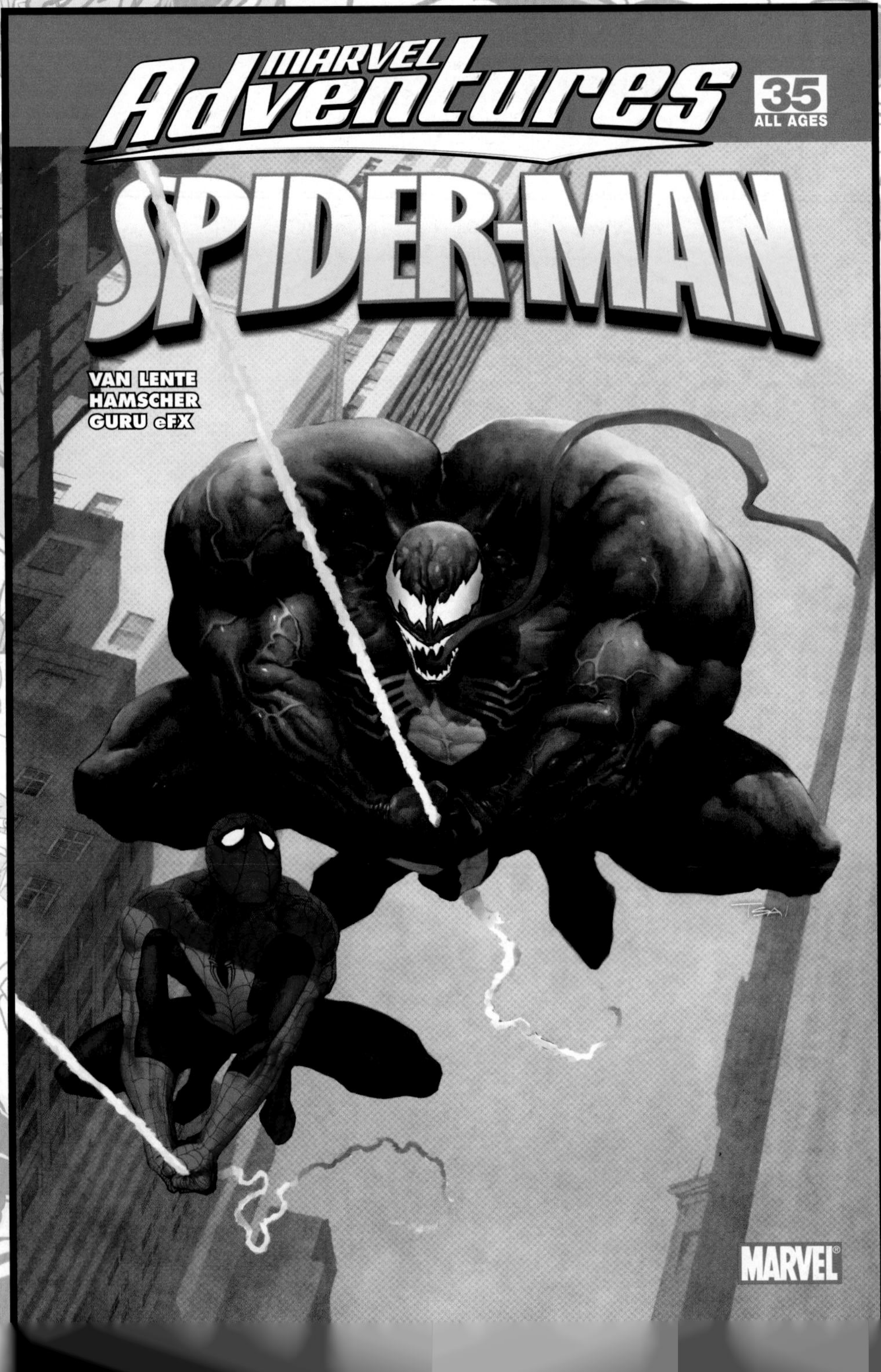
MARVEL
Adventures
35
ALL AGES
SPIDER-MAN
VAN LENTE
HAMSCHER
GURU eFX
MARVEL

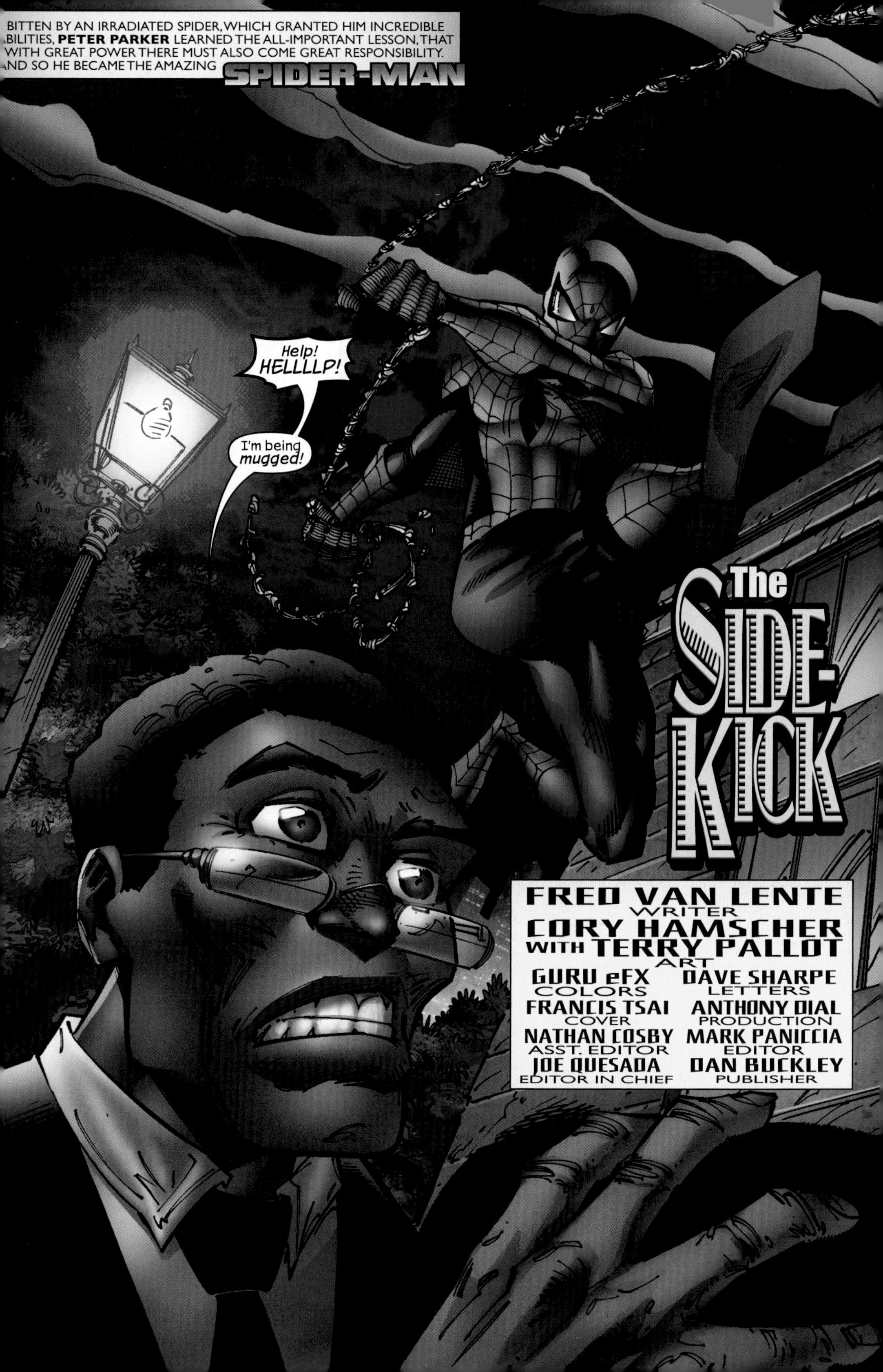
BITTEN BY AN IRRADIATED SPIDER, WHICH GRANTED HIM INCREDIBLE BILITIES, PETER PARKER LEARNED THE ALL-IMPORTANT LESSON, THAT WITH GREAT POWER THERE MUST ALSO COME GREAT RESPONSIBILITY. ND SO HE BECAME THE AMAZING SPIDER-MAN
Help! HELLLLP!
I'm being mugged!
The SIDE-KICK
FRED VAN LENTE WRITER
CORY HAMSCHER WITH TERRY PALLOT ART
GURU eFX COLORS
DAVE SHARPE LETTERS
FRANCIS TSAI COVER
ANTHONY DIAL PRODUCTION
NATHAN COSBY ASST. EDITOR
MARK PANICCIA EDITOR
JOE QUESADA EDITOR IN CHIEF
DAN BUCKLEY PUBLISHER

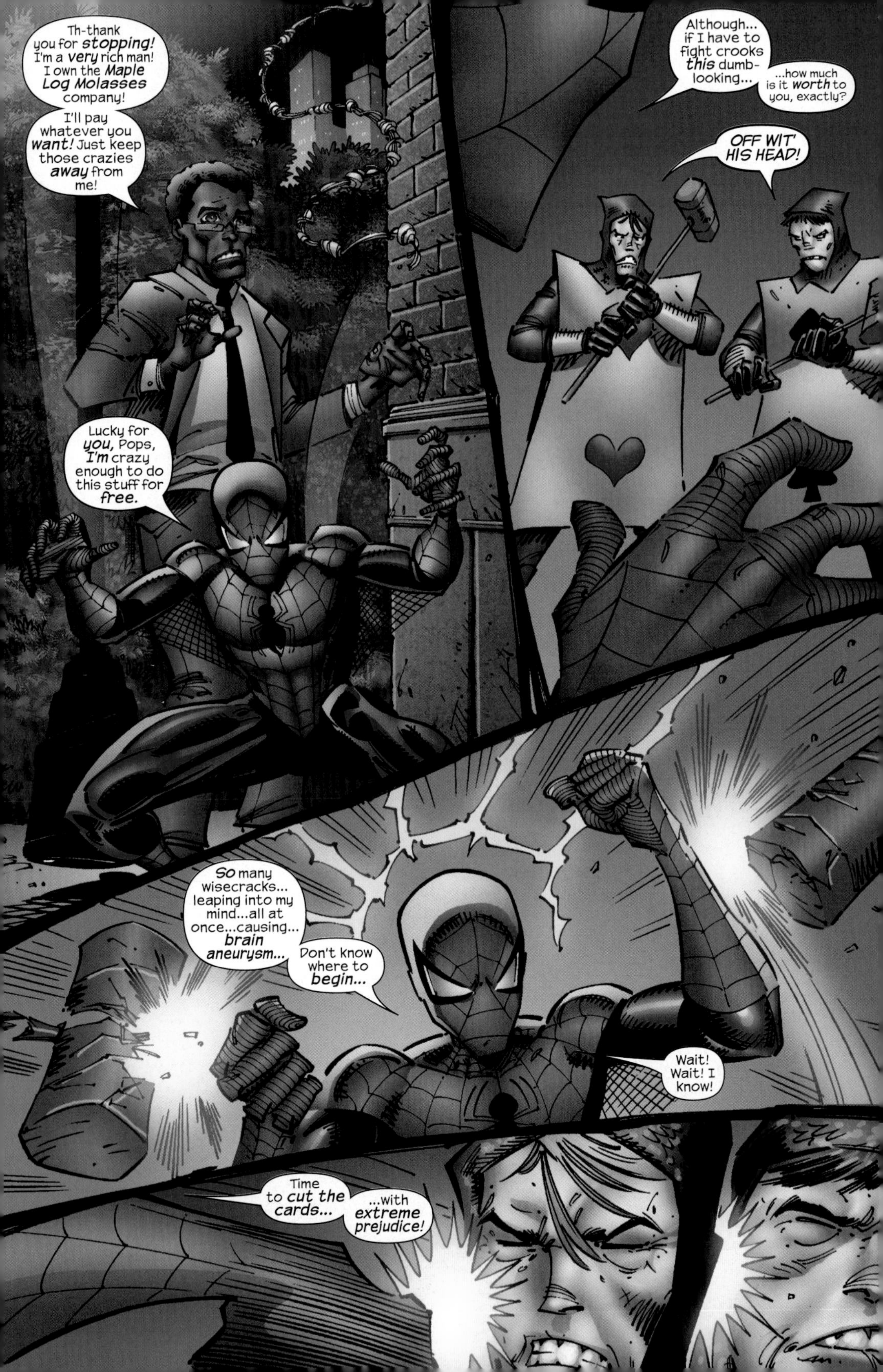
Th-thank you for stopping! I'm a very rich man! I own the Maple Log Molasses company!
I'll pay whatever you want! Just keep those crazies away from me!
Although... if I have to fight crooks this dumb-looking...
...how much is it worth to you, exactly?
OFF WIT' HIS HEAD!
Lucky for you, Pops, I'm crazy enough to do this stuff for free.
So many wisecracks... leaping into my mind...all at once...causing... brain aneurysm...
Don't know where to begin...
Wait! Wait! I know!
Time to cut the cards...
...with extreme prejudice!

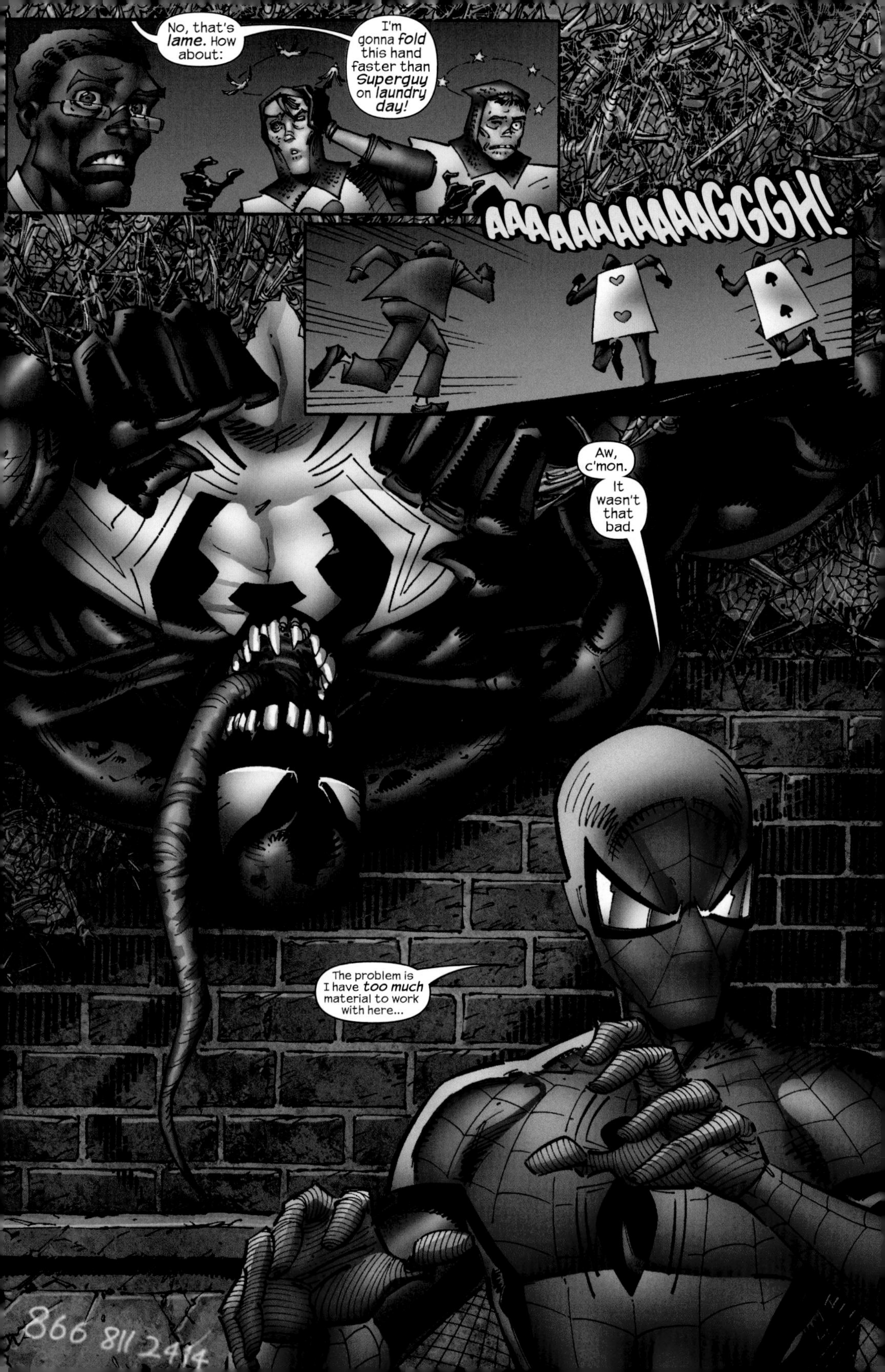
No, that's lame. How about:
I'm gonna fold this hand faster than Superguy on laundry day!
AAAAAAAAAAGGGH!
Aw, c'mon.
It wasn't that bad.
The problem is I have too much material to work with here...
866 811 2414

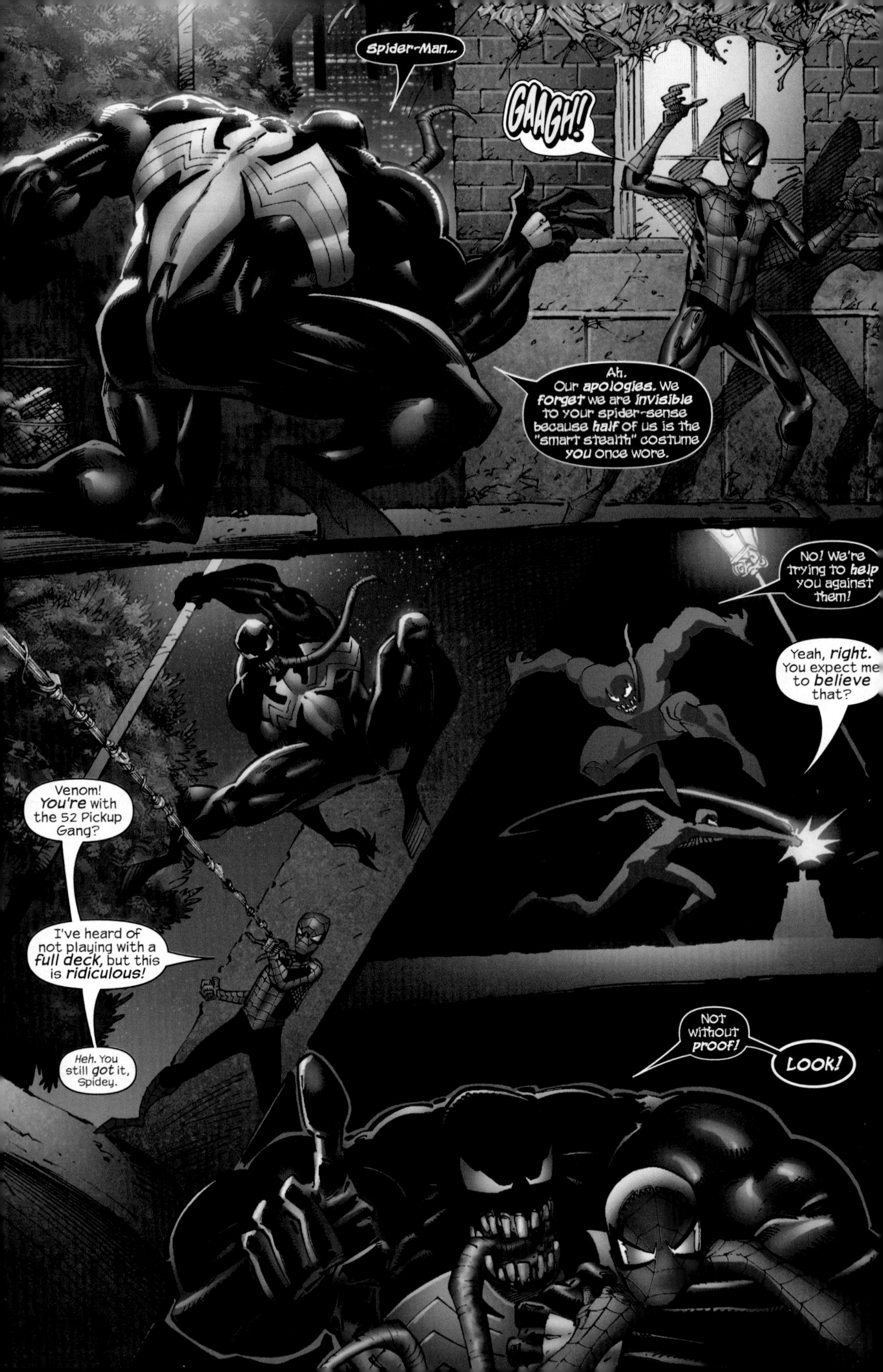
Spider-Man...
GAAGH!
Ah.
Our apologies. We forget we are invisible to your spider-sense because half of us is the "smart stealth" costume you once wore.
Venom! You're with the 52 Pickup Gang?
I've heard of not playing with a full deck, but this is ridiculous!
Heh. You still got it, Spidey.
No! We're trying to help you against them!
Yeah, right. You expect me to believe that?
Not without proof!
LOOK!

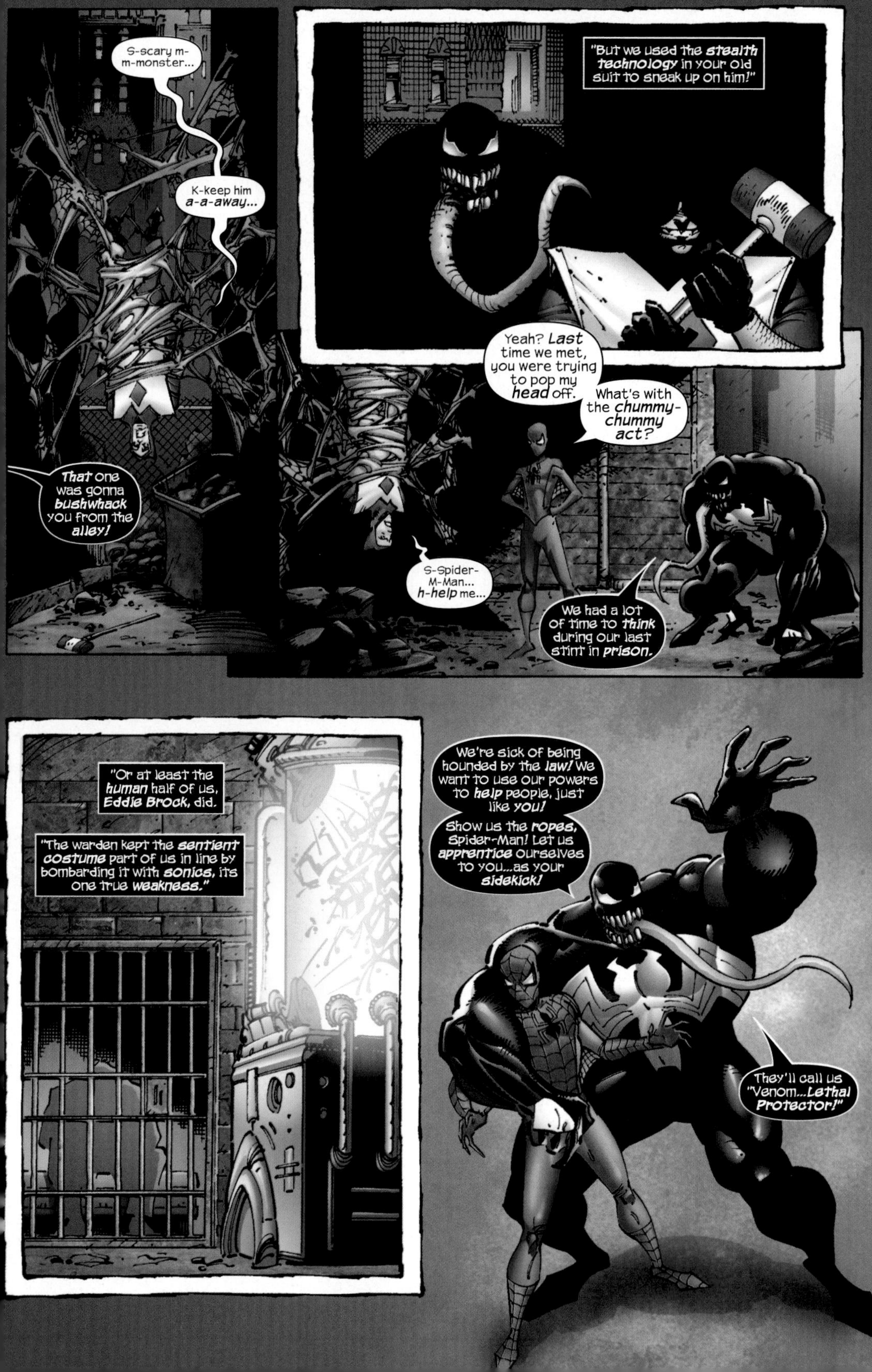
S-scary m-m-monster...
K-keep him a-a-away...
"But we used the stealth technology in your old suit to sneak up on him!"
That one was gonna bushwhack you from the alley!
Yeah? Last time we met, you were trying to pop my head off.
What's with the chummy-chummy act?
S-Spider-M-Man... h-help me...
We had a lot of time to think during our last stint in prison.
"Or at least the human half of us, Eddie Brock, did.
"The warden kept the sentient costume part of us in line by bombarding it with sonics, its one true weakness."
We're sick of being hounded by the law! We want to use our powers to help people, just like you!
Show us the ropes, Spider-Man! Let us apprentice ourselves to you...as your sidekick!
They'll call us "Venom...Lethal Protector!"

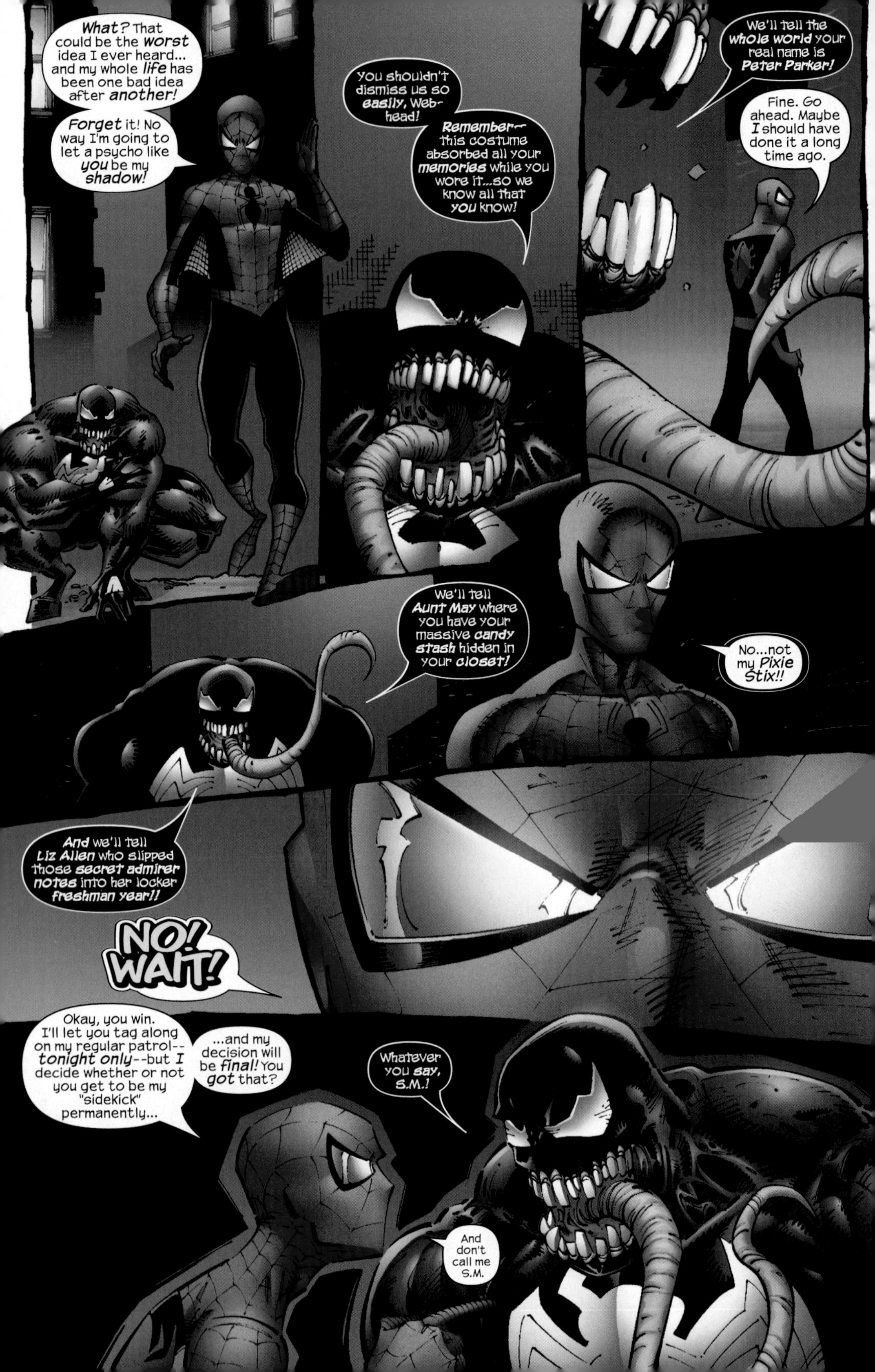
What? That could be the worst idea I ever heard... and my whole life has been one bad idea after another!
Forget it! No way I'm going to let a psycho like you be my shadow!
You shouldn't dismiss us so easily, Web-head!
Remember-- this costume absorbed all your memories while you wore it...so we know all that you know!
We'll tell the whole world your real name is Peter Parker!
Fine. Go ahead. Maybe I should have done it a long time ago.
We'll tell Aunt May where you have your massive candy stash hidden in your closet!
No...not my Pixie Stix!!
And we'll tell Liz Allen who slipped those secret admirer notes into her locker freshman year!!
NO! WAIT!
Okay, you win. I'll let you tag along on my regular patrol-- tonight only--but I decide whether or not you get to be my "sidekick" permanently...
...and my decision will be final! You got that?
Whatever you say, S.M.!
And don't call me S.M.

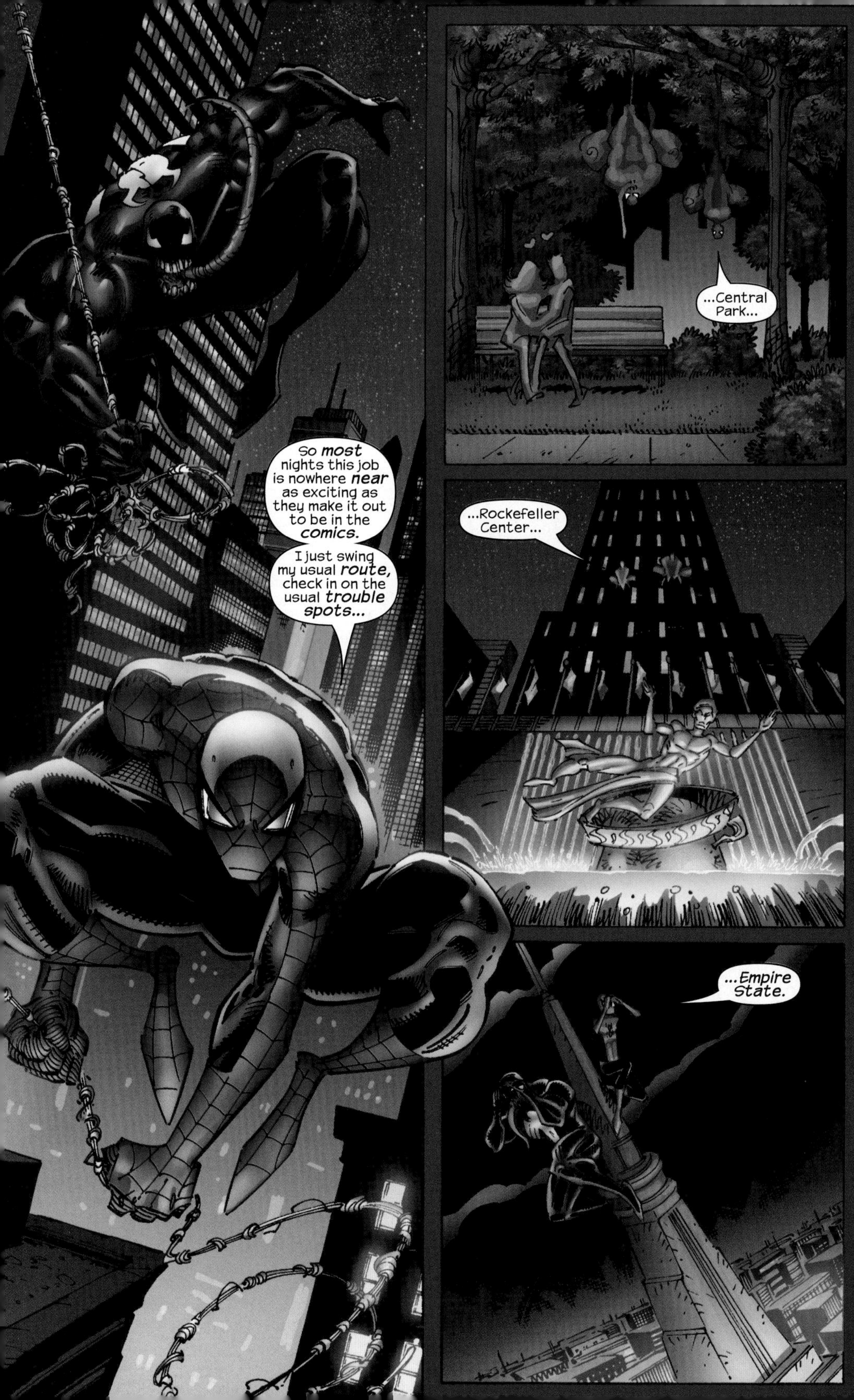

So most nights this job is nowhere near as exciting as they make it out to be in the comics.
I just swing my usual route, check in on the usual trouble spots...
...Central Park...
...Rockefeller Center...
...Empire State.

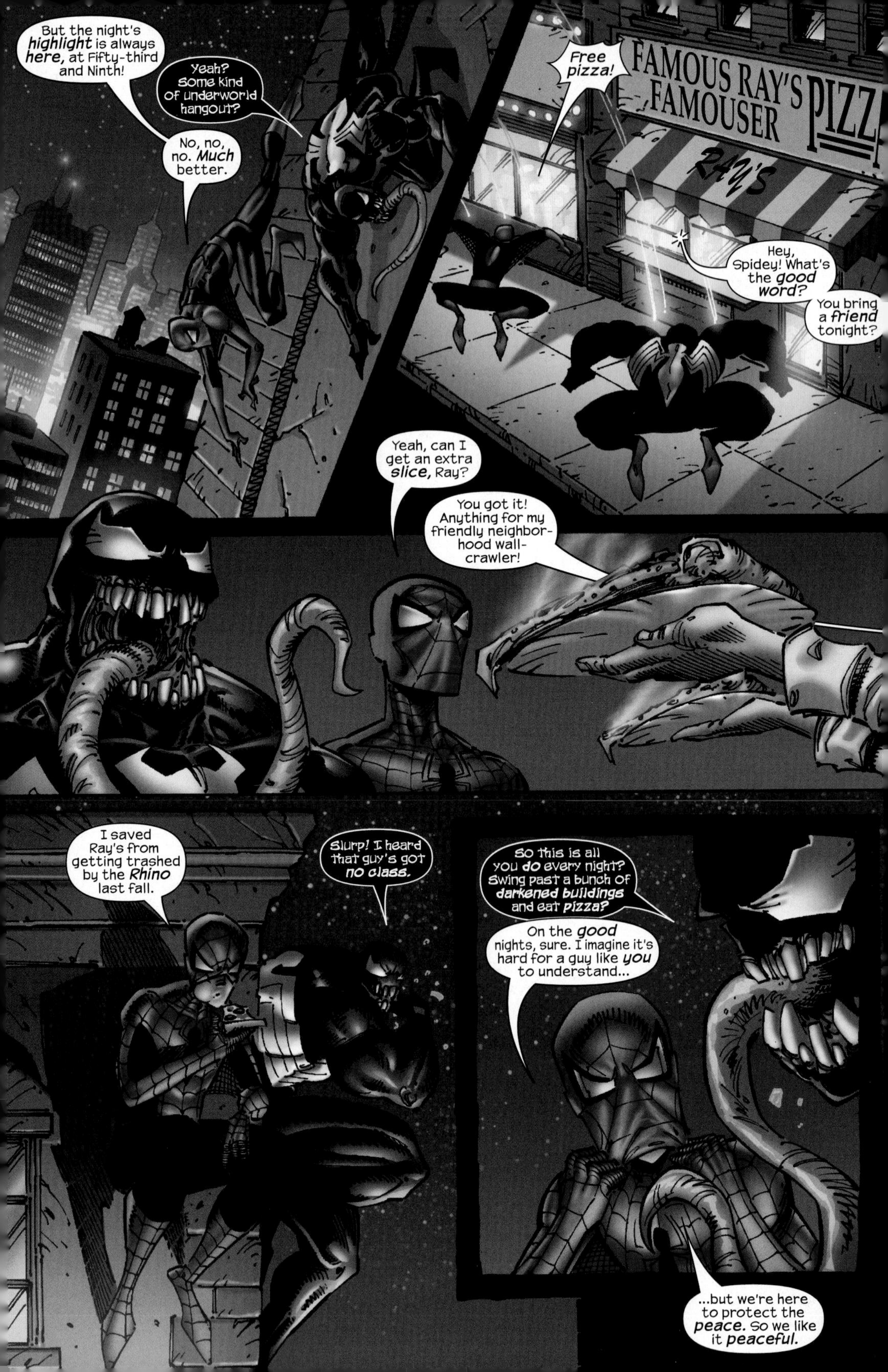

But the night's **highlight** is always **here,** at Fifty-third and Ninth!
Yeah? Some kind of underworld hangout?
No, no, no. **Much** better.
Free **pizza!**
FAMOUS RAY'S FAMOUSER PIZZ
RAY'S
Hey, Spidey! What's the **good word?**
You bring a **friend** tonight?
Yeah, can I get an extra **slice,** Ray?
You got it! Anything for my friendly neighbor-hood wall-crawler!
I saved Ray's from getting trashed by the **Rhino** last fall.
Slurp! I heard that guy's got **no class.**
So this is all you **do** every night? Swing past a bunch of **darkened buildings** and eat **pizza?**
On the **good** nights, sure. I imagine it's hard for a guy like **you** to understand...
...but we're here to protect the **peace.** So we like it **peaceful.**

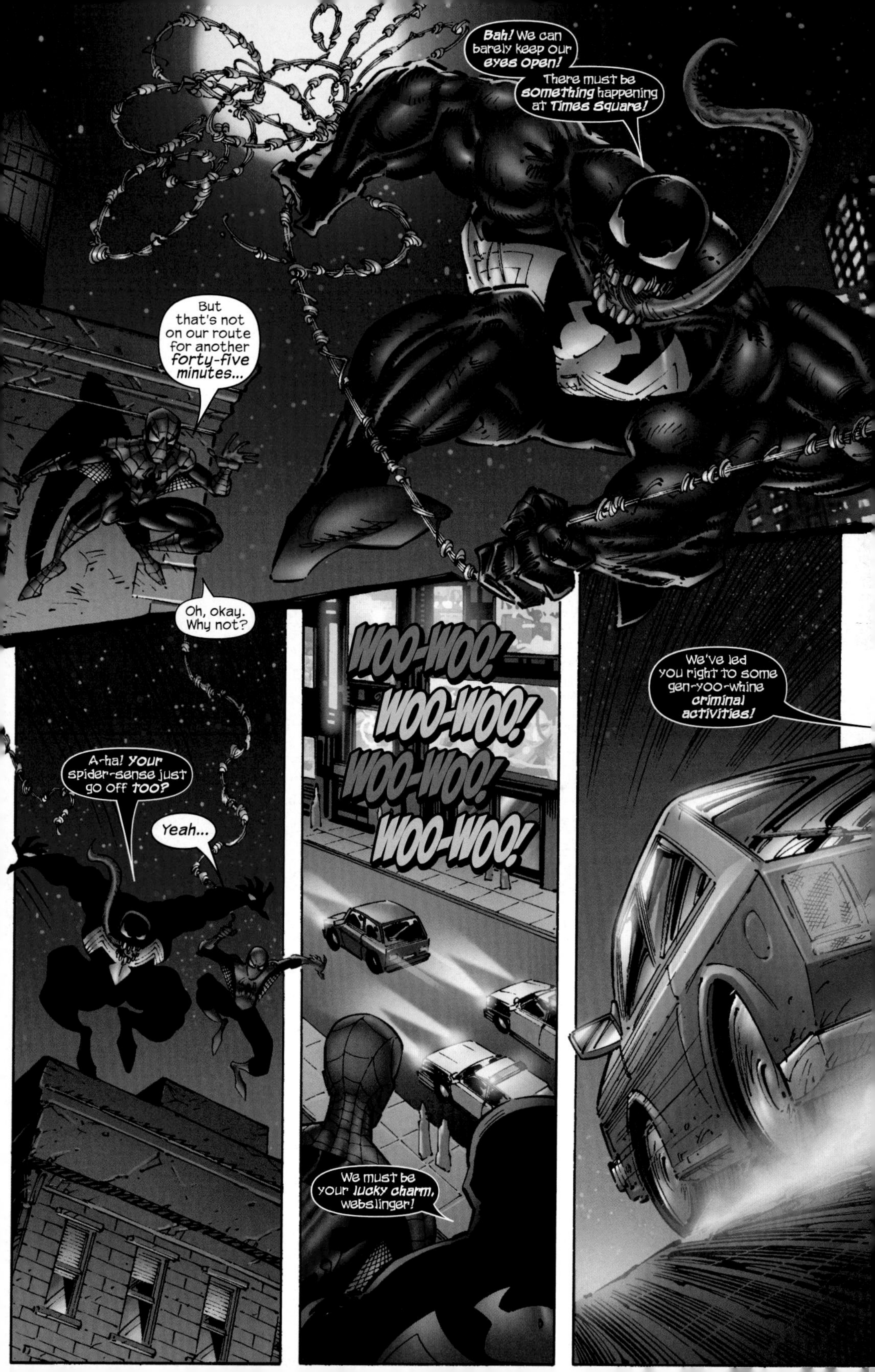

Bah! We can barely keep our eyes open!
There must be something happening at Times Square!
But that's not on our route for another forty-five minutes...
Oh, okay. Why not?
A-ha! Your spider-sense just go off too?
Yeah...
WOO-WOO! WOO-WOO! WOO-WOO! WOO-WOO!
We must be your lucky charm, webslinger!
We've led you right to some gen-yoo-whine criminal activities!

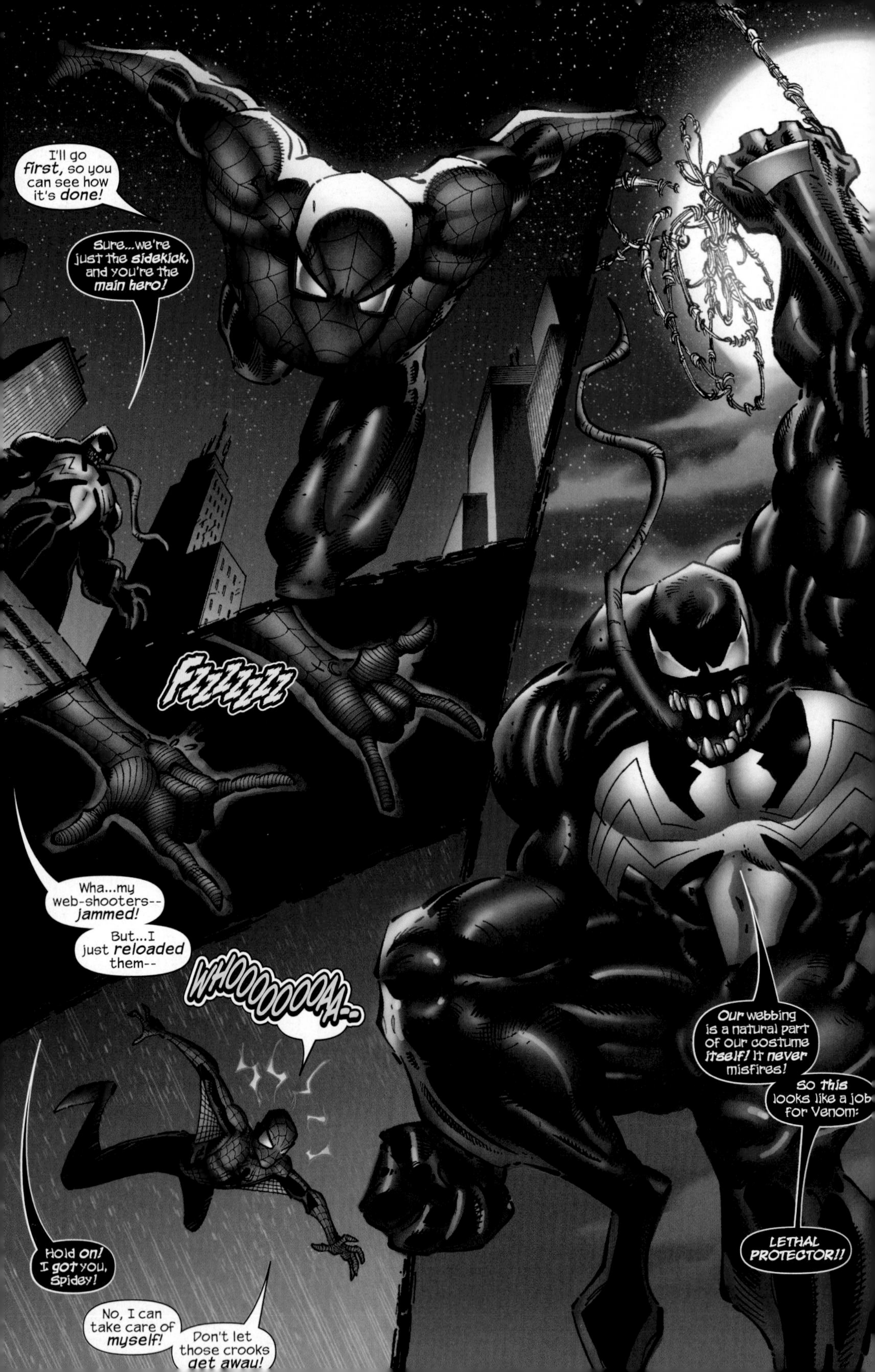
I'll go first, so you can see how it's done!
Sure...we're just the sidekick, and you're the main hero!
FZZZZZZZ
Wha...my web-shooters--jammed!
But...I just reloaded them--
WHOOOOOOOAA--
Our webbing is a natural part of our costume itself! It never misfires!
So this looks like a job for Venom:
LETHAL PROTECTOR!!
Hold on! I got you, Spidey!
No, I can take care of myself!
Don't let those crooks get away!

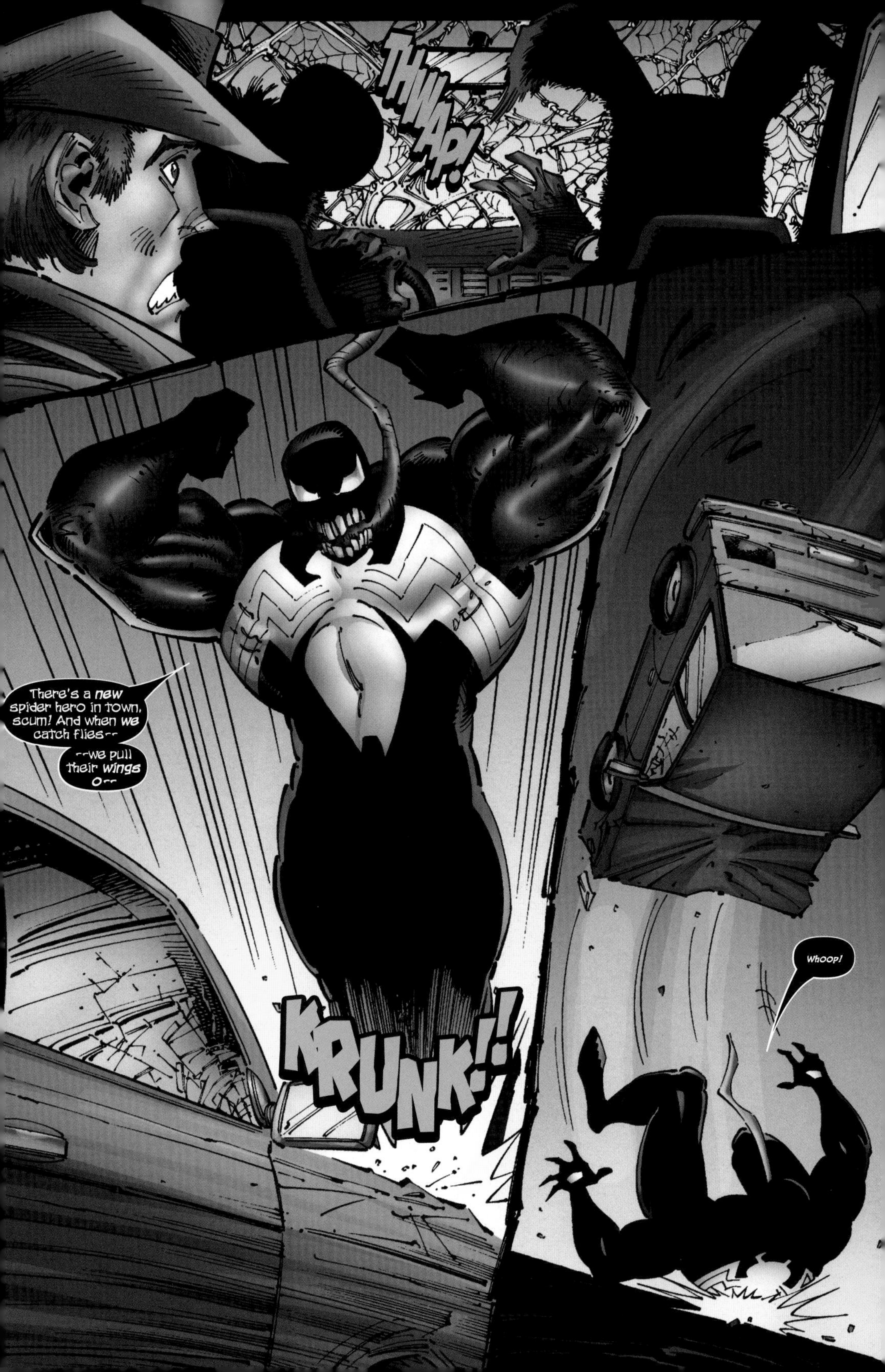
THWAP!
There's a new spider hero in town, scum! And when we catch flies--
--we pull their wings o--
KRUNK!!
Whoop!

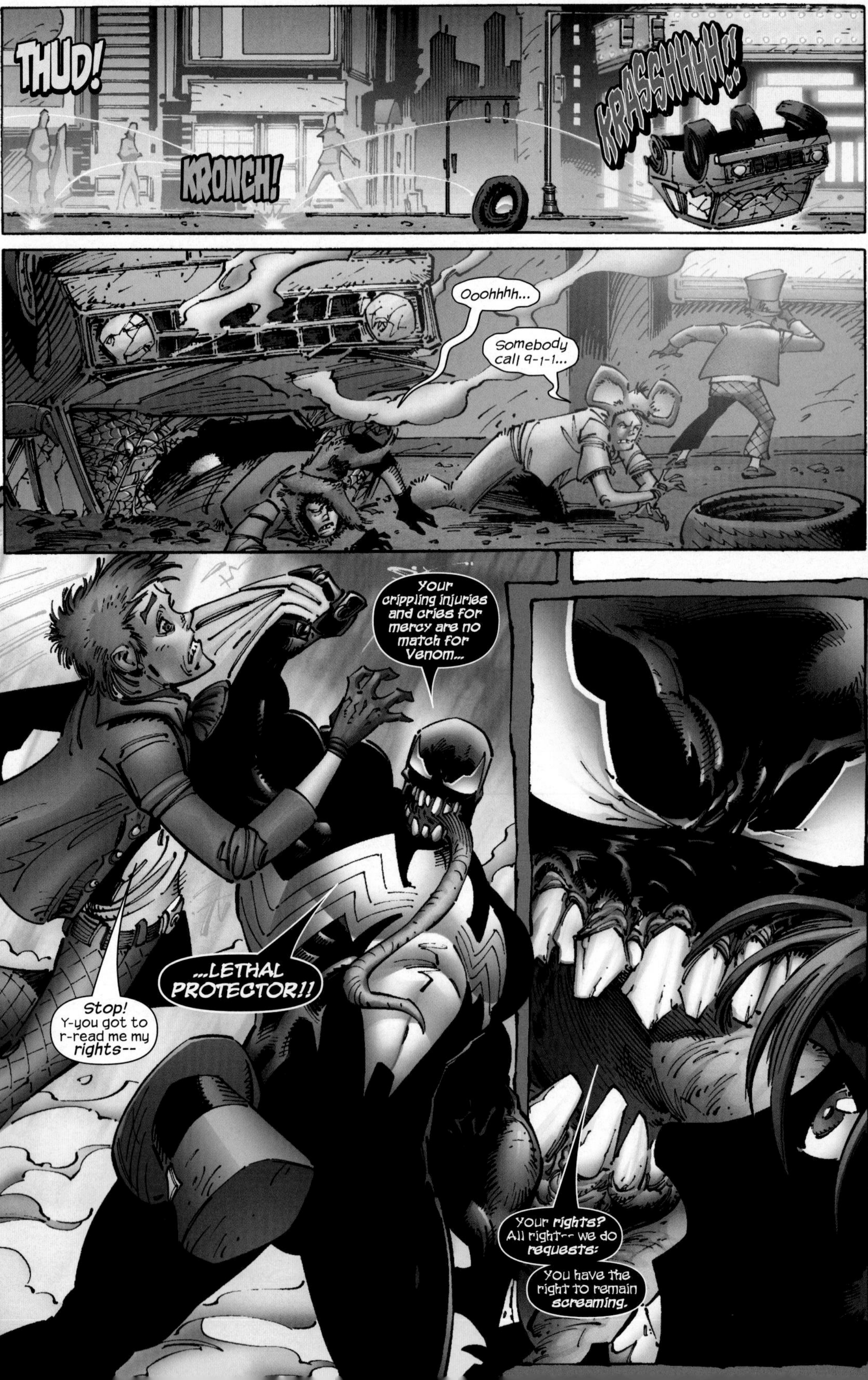
THUD!
KRONCH!
KRASSHHHH!!
Ooohhhh...
Somebody call 9-1-1...
Your crippling injuries and cries for mercy are no match for Venom...
...LETHAL PROTECTOR!!
Stop! Y-you got to r-read me my rights--
Your rights? All right-- we do requests:
You have the right to remain screaming.

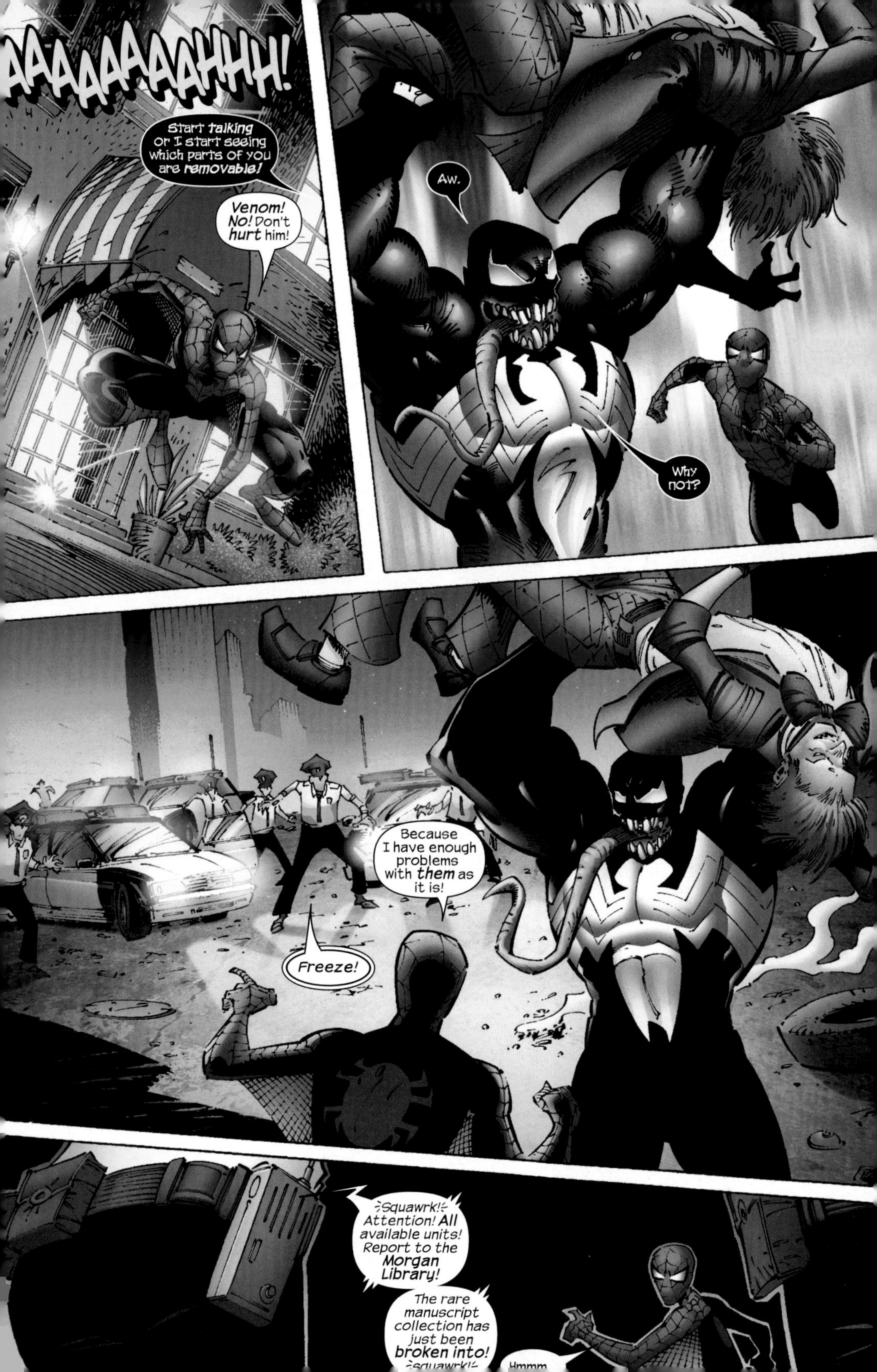
AAAAAAAAHHH!
Start talking or I start seeing which parts of you are removable!
Venom! No! Don't hurt him!
Aw.
Why not?
Because I have enough problems with them as it is!
Freeze!
-Squawrk!- Attention! All available units! Report to the Morgan Library!
The rare manuscript collection has just been broken into! -squawrk!-
Hmmm

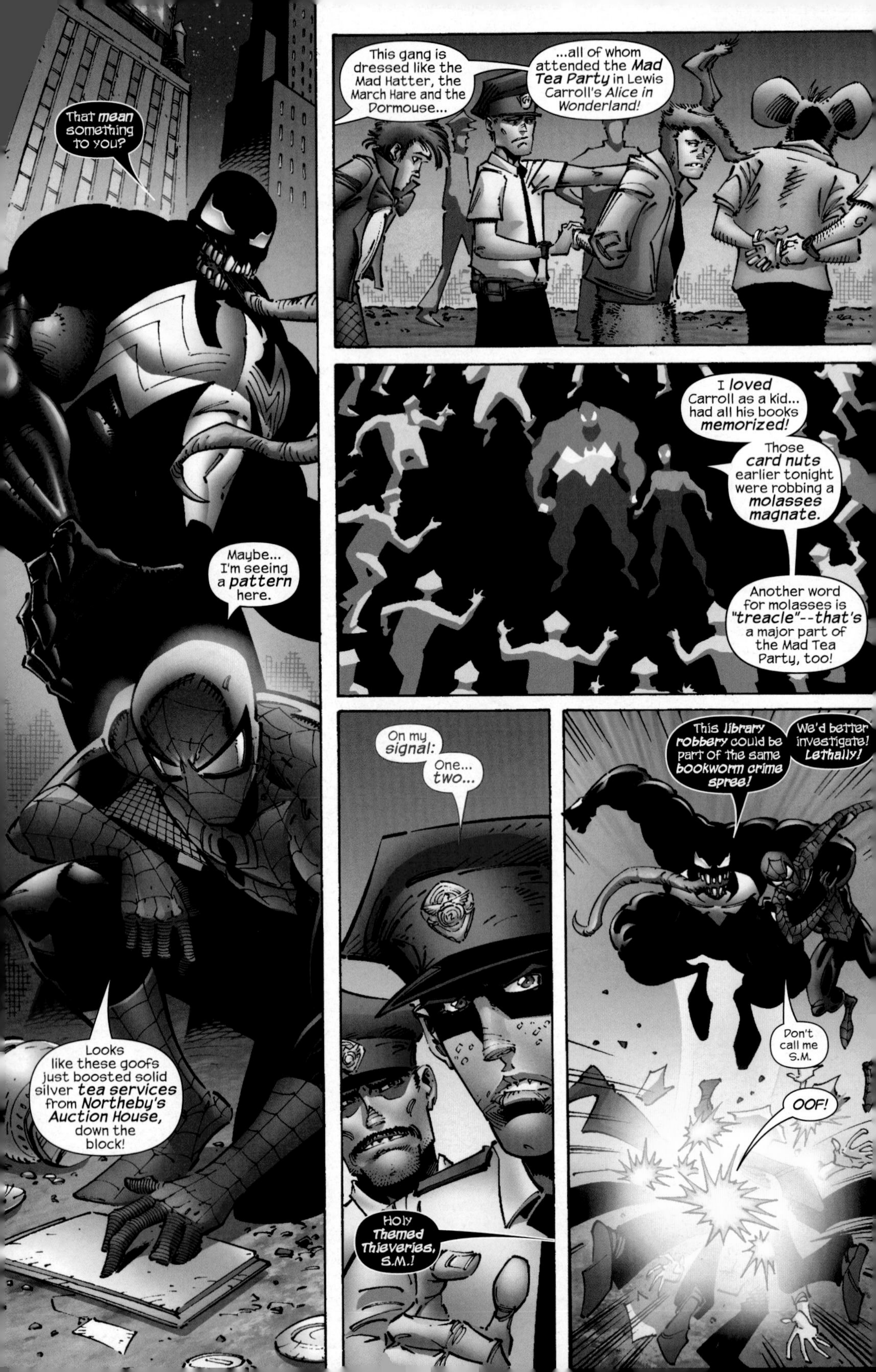

That mean something to you?
Maybe... I'm seeing a pattern here.
Looks like these goofs just boosted solid silver tea services from Northeby's Auction House, down the block!
This gang is dressed like the Mad Hatter, the March Hare and the Dormouse...
...all of whom attended the Mad Tea Party in Lewis Carroll's Alice in Wonderland!
I loved Carroll as a kid... had all his books memorized!
Those card nuts earlier tonight were robbing a molasses magnate.
Another word for molasses is "treacle"--that's a major part of the Mad Tea Party, too!
On my signal:
One... two...
Holy Themed Thieveries, S.M.!
This library robbery could be part of the same bookworm crime spree!
We'd better investigate! Lethally!
Don't call me S.M.
OOF!

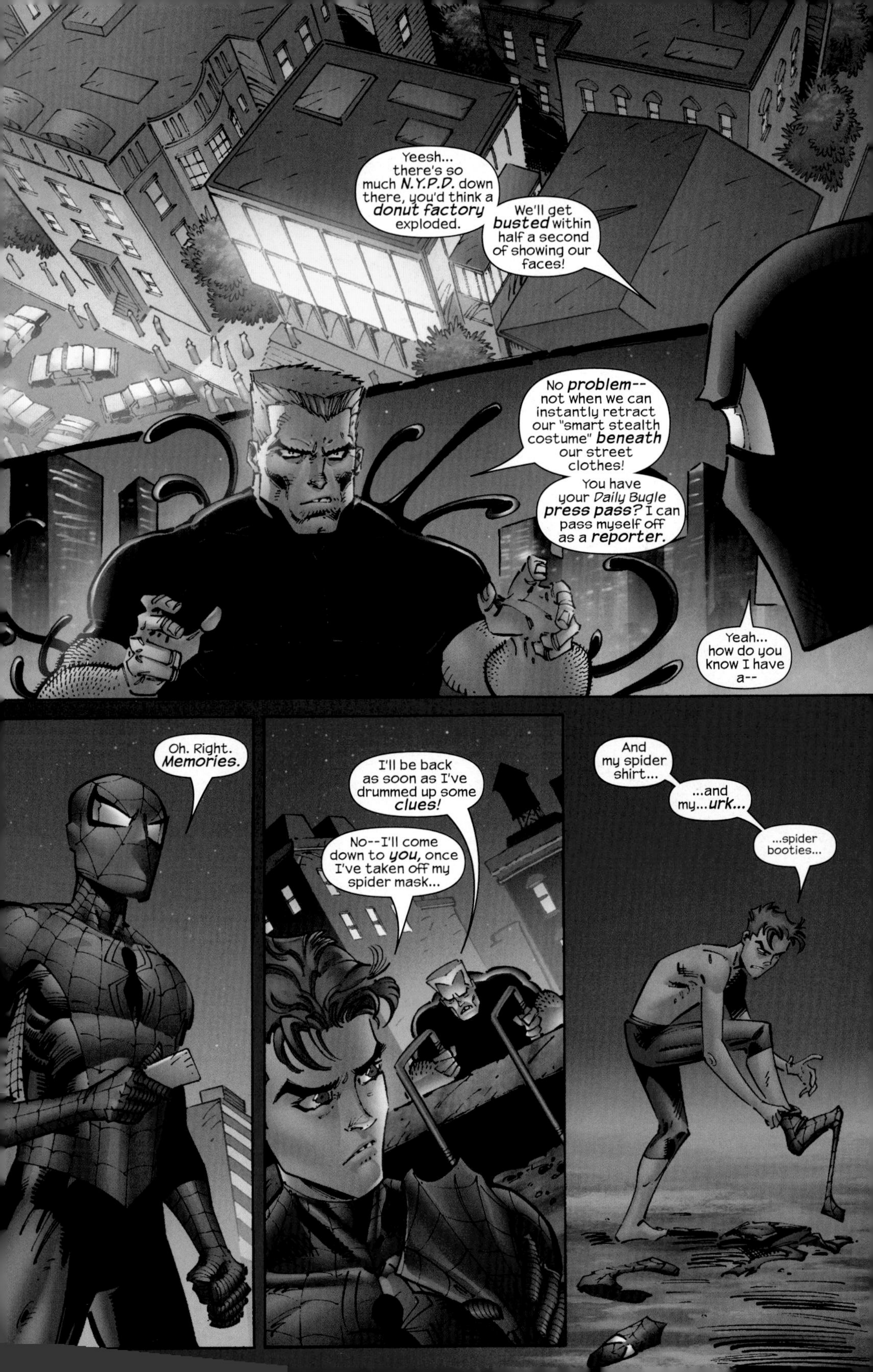
Yeesh... there's so much N.Y.P.D. down there, you'd think a donut factory exploded.
We'll get busted within half a second of showing our faces!
No problem-- not when we can instantly retract our "smart stealth costume" beneath our street clothes!
You have your Daily Bugle press pass? I can pass myself off as a reporter.
Yeah... how do you know I have a--
Oh. Right. Memories.
I'll be back as soon as I've drummed up some clues!
No--I'll come down to you, once I've taken off my spider mask...
And my spider shirt...
...and my...urk...
...spider booties...

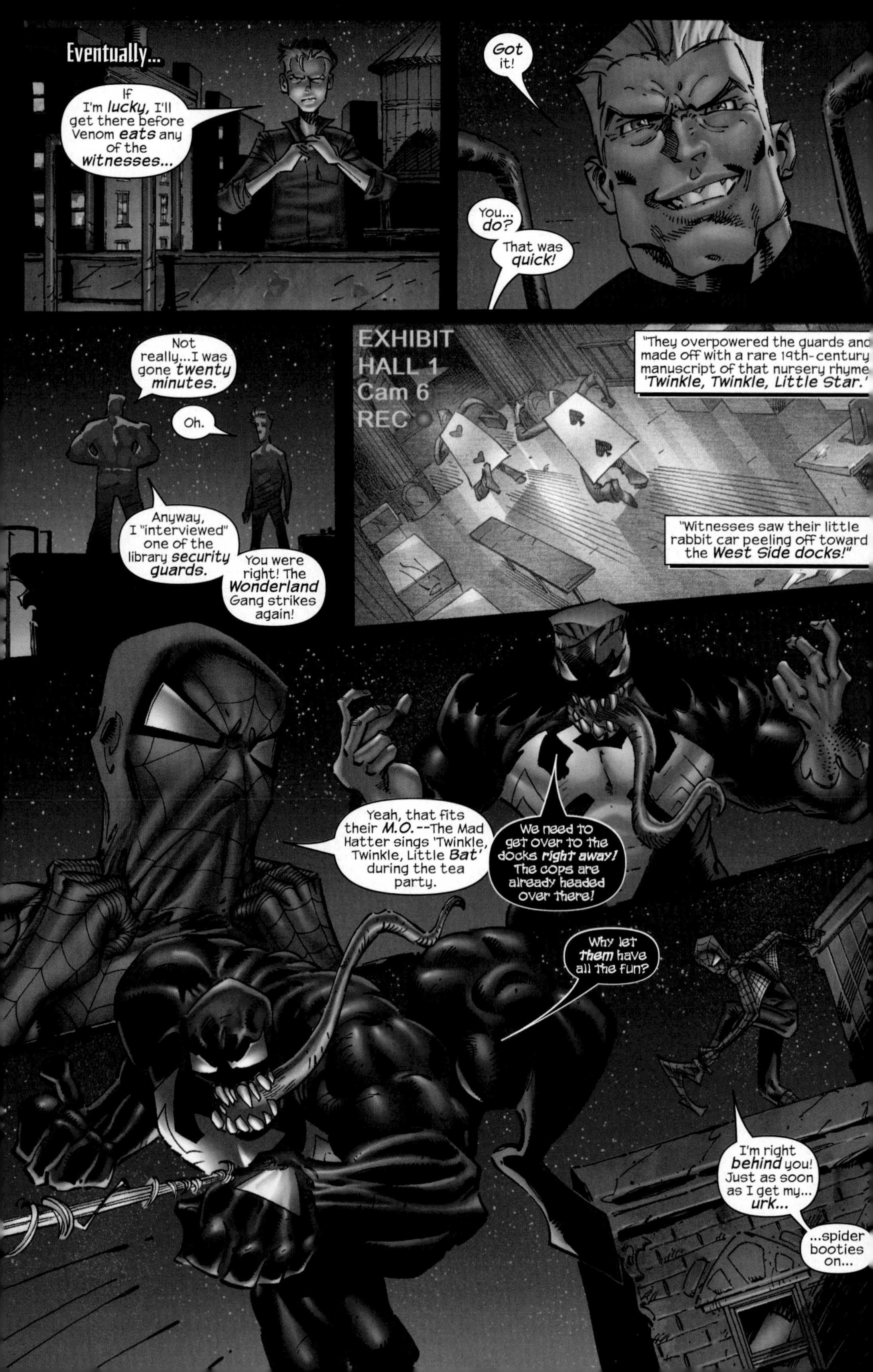

Eventually...
If I'm lucky, I'll get there before Venom eats any of the witnesses...
Got it!
You... do?
That was quick!
Not really...I was gone twenty minutes.
Oh.
Anyway, I "interviewed" one of the library security guards.
You were right! The Wonderland Gang strikes again!
EXHIBIT HALL 1 Cam 6 REC
"They overpowered the guards and made off with a rare 19th-century manuscript of that nursery rhyme 'Twinkle, Twinkle, Little Star.'
"Witnesses saw their little rabbit car peeling off toward the West Side docks!"
Yeah, that fits their M.O.--The Mad Hatter sings 'Twinkle, Twinkle, Little Bat' during the tea party.
We need to get over to the docks right away! The cops are already headed over there!
Why let them have all the fun?
I'm right behind you! Just as soon as I get my... urk...
...spider booties on...

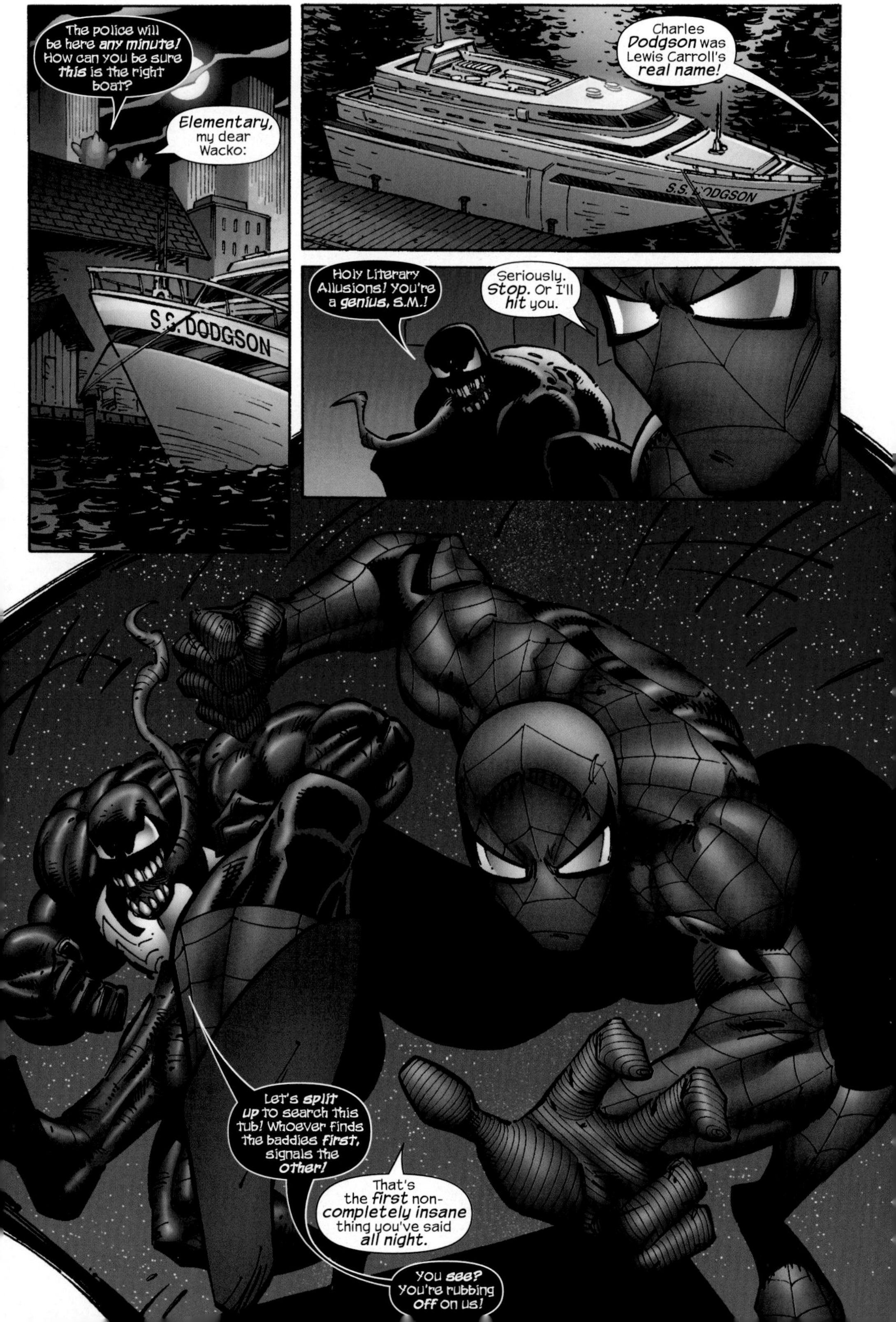
The police will be here any minute! How can you be sure this is the right boat?
Elementary, my dear Wacko:
S.S. DODGSON
Charles Dodgson was Lewis Carroll's real name!
S.S. DODGSON
Holy Literary Allusions! You're a genius, S.M.!
Seriously. Stop. Or I'll hit you.
Let's split up to search this tub! Whoever finds the baddies first, signals the other!
That's the first non-completely insane thing you've said all night.
You see? You're rubbing off on us!

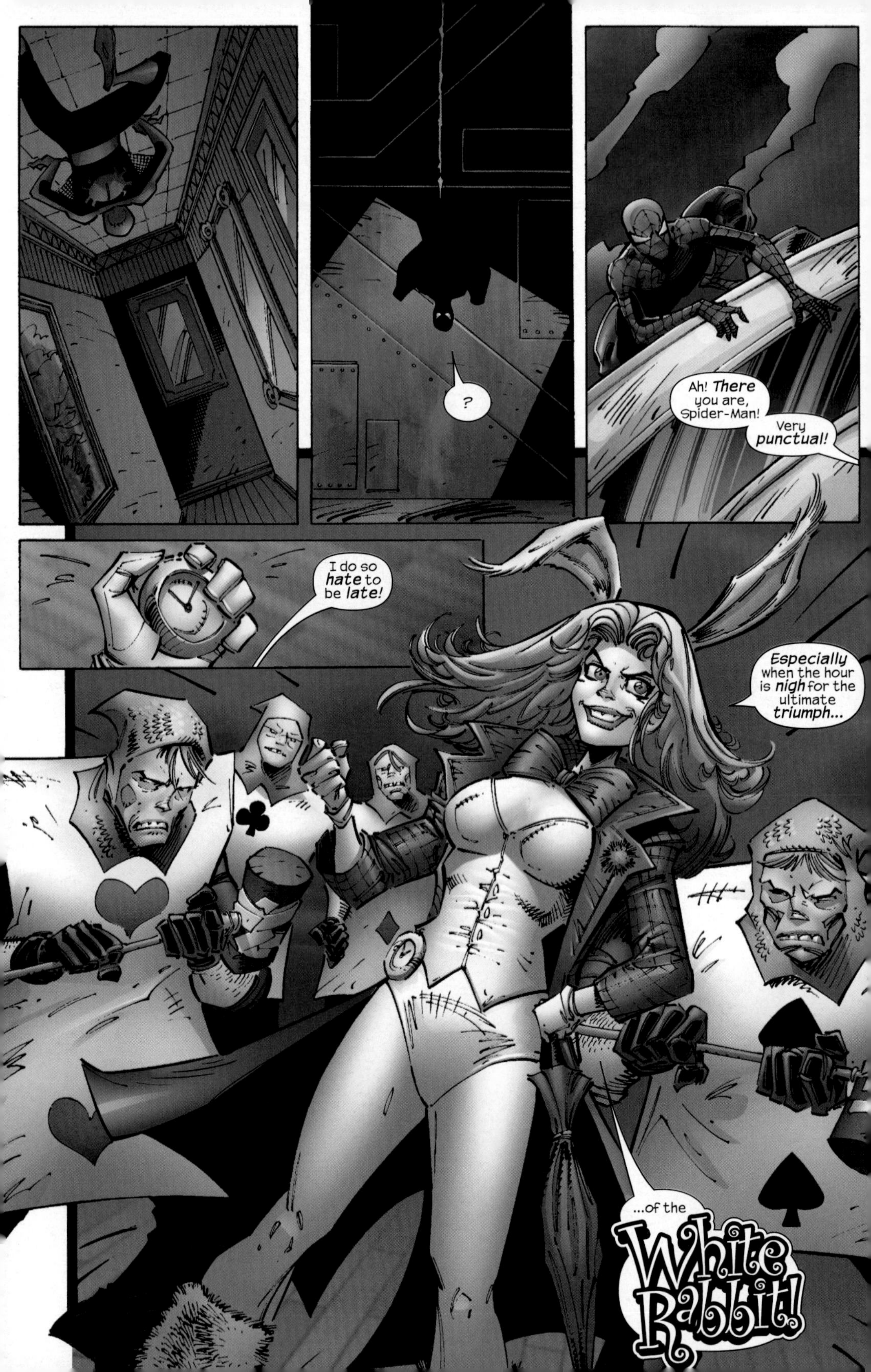
?
Ah! *There* you are, Spider-Man!
Very *punctual*!
I do so *hate* to be *late*!
Especially when the hour is *nigh* for the ultimate *triumph*...
...of the
White Rabbit!

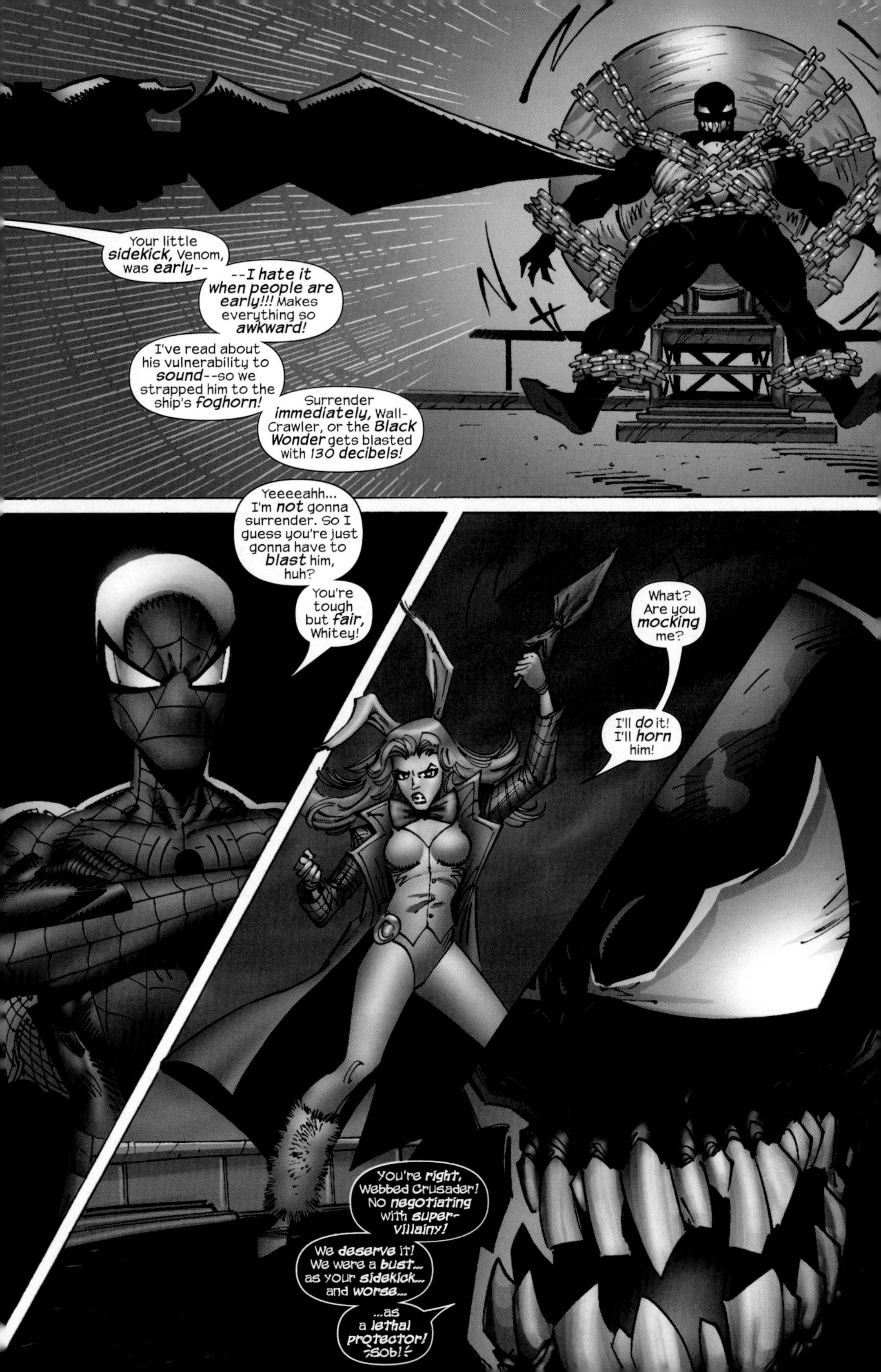

Your little sidekick, Venom, was early--
--I hate it when people are early!!! Makes everything so awkward!
I've read about his vulnerability to sound--so we strapped him to the ship's foghorn!
Surrender immediately, Wall-Crawler, or the Black Wonder gets blasted with 130 decibels!
Yeeeeahh... I'm not gonna surrender. So I guess you're just gonna have to blast him, huh?
You're tough but fair, Whitey!
What? Are you mocking me?
I'll do it! I'll horn him!
You're right, Webbed Crusader! No negotiating with super-villainy!
We deserve it! We were a bust... as your sidekick... and worse...
...as a lethal protector! ;Sob!;

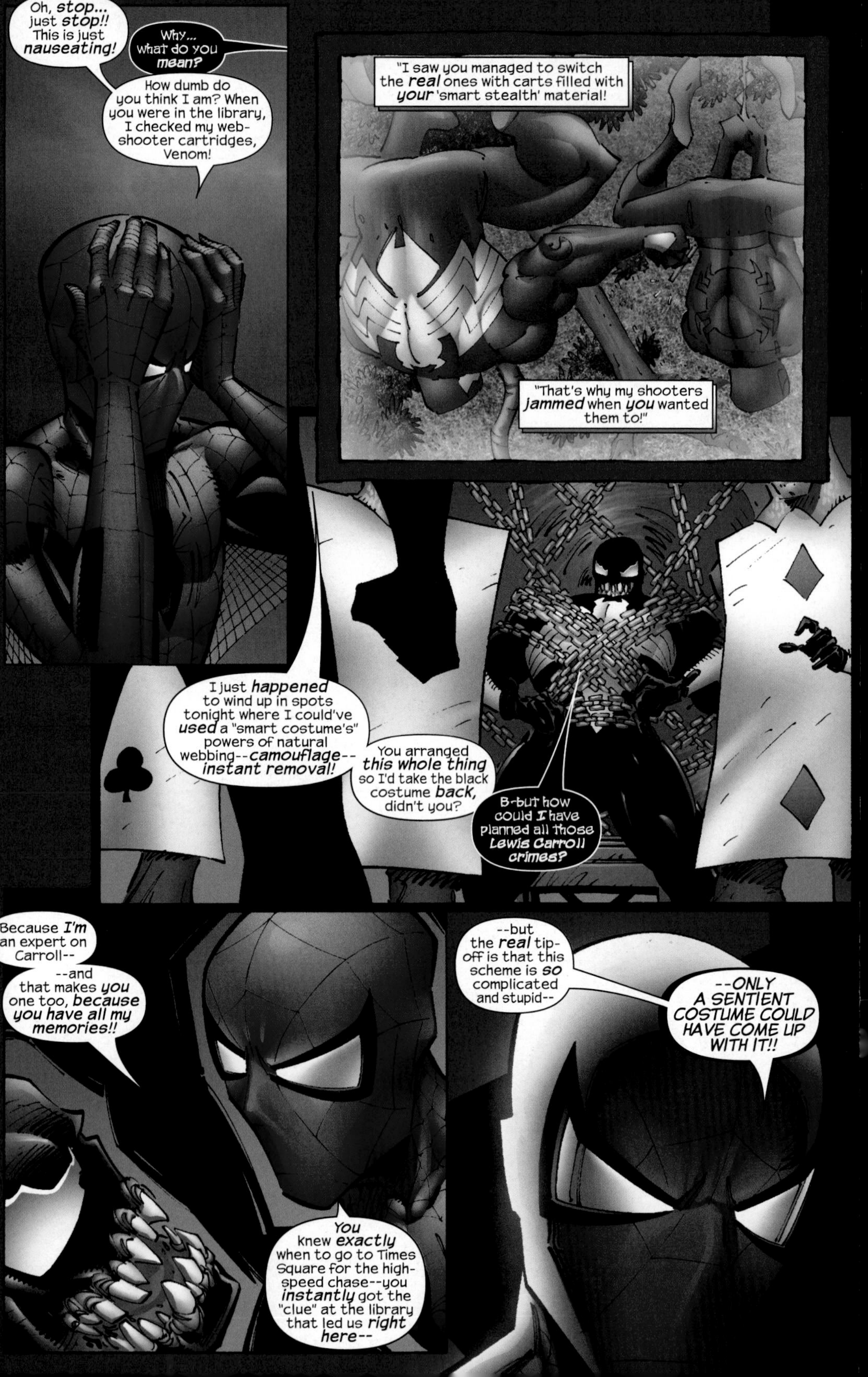
Oh, stop... just stop!! This is just nauseating!
Why... what do you mean?
How dumb do you think I am? When you were in the library, I checked my web-shooter cartridges, Venom!
"I saw you managed to switch the real ones with carts filled with your 'smart stealth' material!
"That's why my shooters jammed when you wanted them to!"
I just happened to wind up in spots tonight where I could've used a "smart costume's" powers of natural webbing--camouflage--instant removal!
You arranged this whole thing so I'd take the black costume back, didn't you?
B-but how could I have planned all those Lewis Carroll crimes?
Because I'm an expert on Carroll--
--and that makes you one too, because you have all my memories!!
You knew exactly when to go to Times Square for the high-speed chase--you instantly got the "clue" at the library that led us right here--
--but the real tip-off is that this scheme is so complicated and stupid--
--ONLY A SENTIENT COSTUME COULD HAVE COME UP WITH IT!!

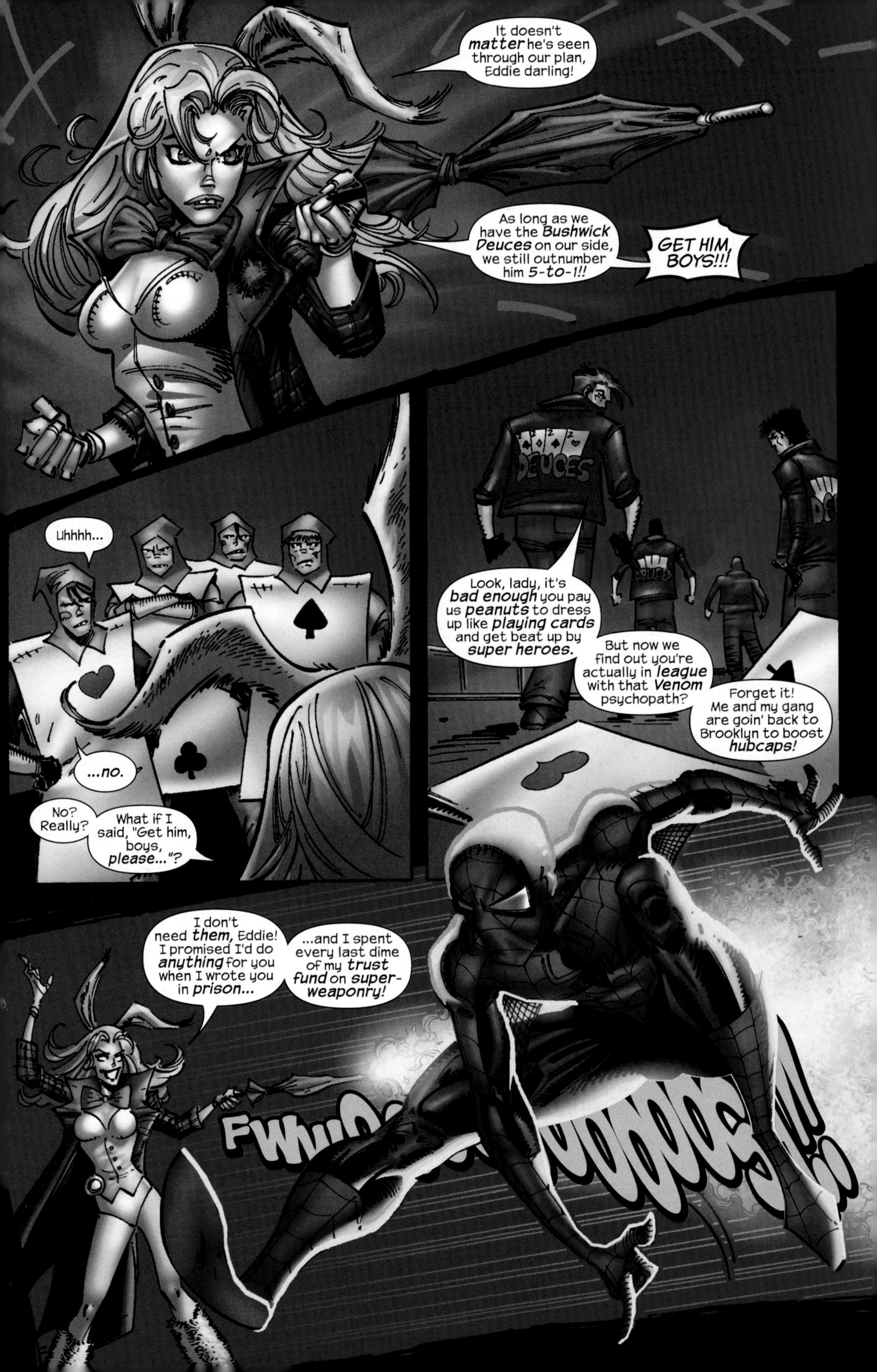

It doesn't matter he's seen through our plan, Eddie darling!
As long as we have the Bushwick Deuces on our side, we still outnumber him 5-to-1!!
GET HIM, BOYS!!!
Uhhhh...
...no.
No? Really?
What if I said, "Get him, boys, please..."?
DEUCES
Look, lady, it's bad enough you pay us peanuts to dress up like playing cards and get beat up by super heroes.
But now we find out you're actually in league with that Venom psychopath?
Forget it! Me and my gang are goin' back to Brooklyn to boost hubcaps!
I don't need them, Eddie! I promised I'd do anything for you when I wrote you in prison...
...and I spent every last dime of my trust fund on super-weaponry!

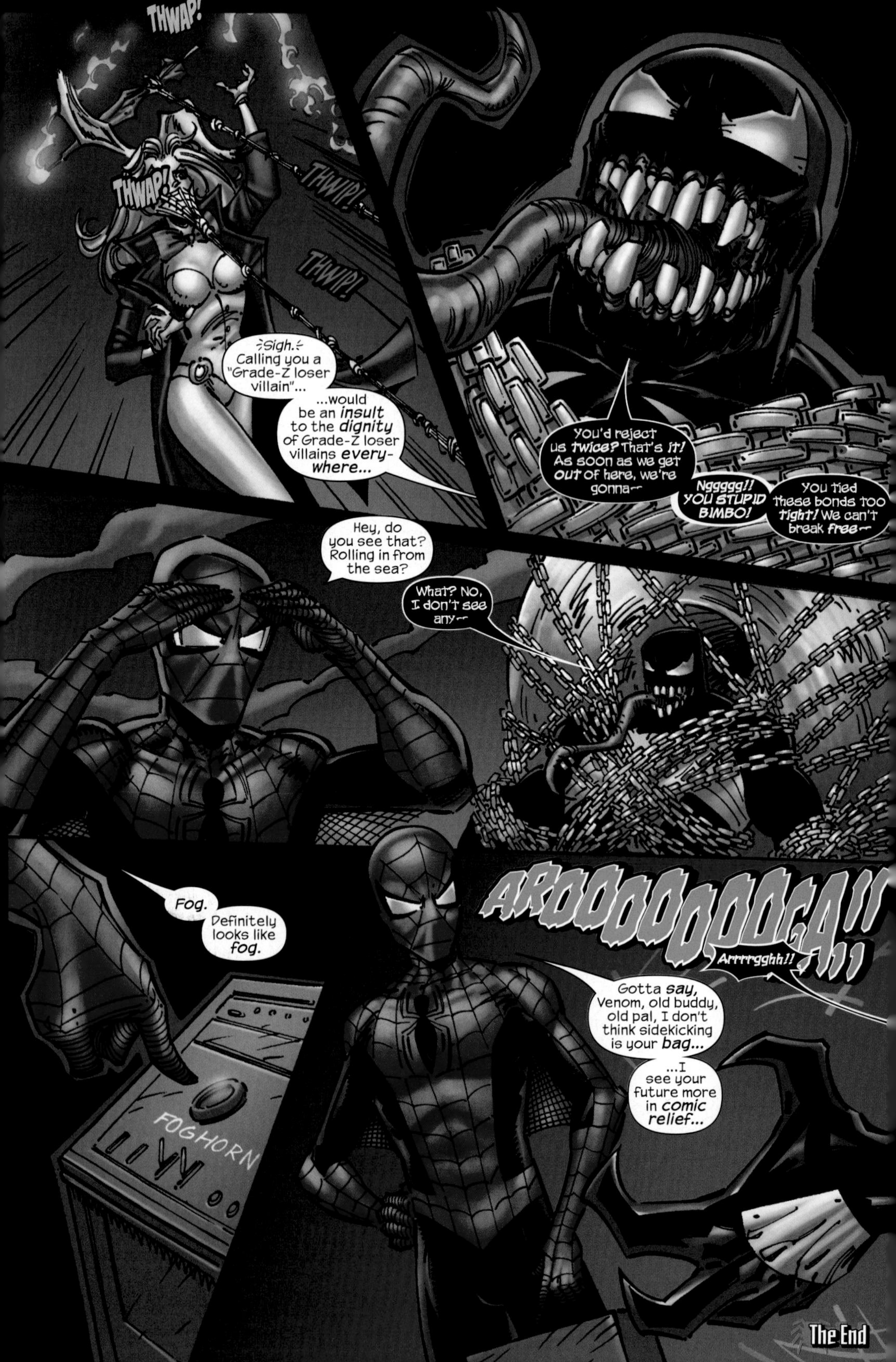
THWAP!
THWAP!
THWIP!
THWIP!
Sigh.
Calling you a "Grade-Z loser villain"...
...would be an insult to the dignity of Grade-Z loser villains every-where...
You'd reject us twice? That's it! As soon as we get out of here, we're gonna--
Nggggg!! YOU STUPID BIMBO!
You tied these bonds too tight! We can't break free--
Hey, do you see that? Rolling in from the sea?
What? No, I don't see any--
Fog.
Definitely looks like fog.
FOGHORN
AROOOOOOOOGA!!
Arrrrgghh!!
Gotta say, Venom, old buddy, old pal, I don't think sidekicking is your bag...
...I see your future more in comic relief...
The End

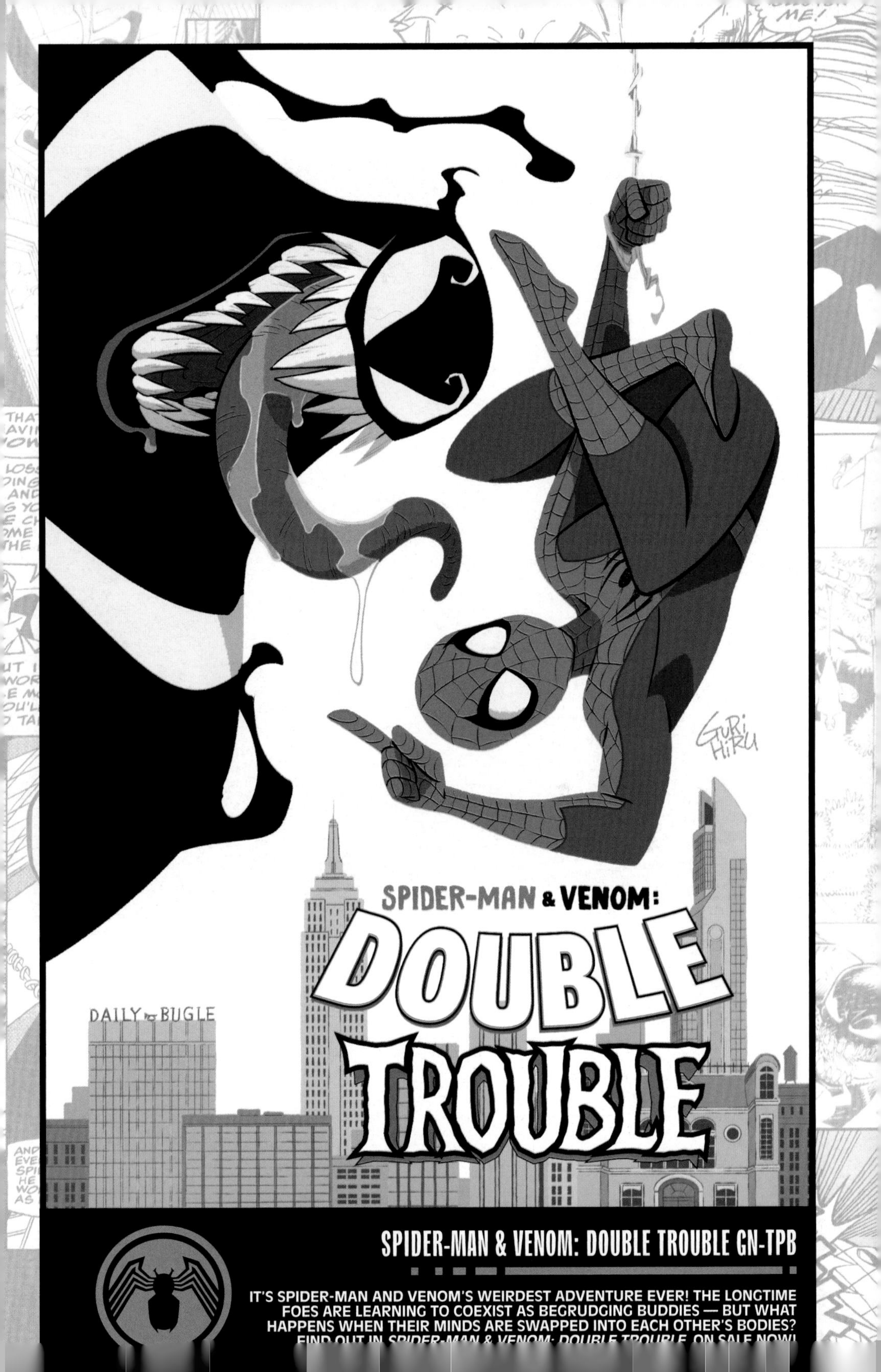

SPIDER-MAN & VENOM:
DOUBLE TROUBLE
DAILY BUGLE
GURI HIRU
SPIDER-MAN & VENOM: DOUBLE TROUBLE GN-TPB
IT'S SPIDER-MAN AND VENOM'S WEIRDEST ADVENTURE EVER! THE LONGTIME FOES ARE LEARNING TO COEXIST AS BEGRUDGING BUDDIES — BUT WHAT HAPPENS WHEN THEIR MINDS ARE SWAPPED INTO EACH OTHER'S BODIES? FIND OUT IN SPIDER-MAN & VENOM: DOUBLE TROUBLE, ON SALE NOW!

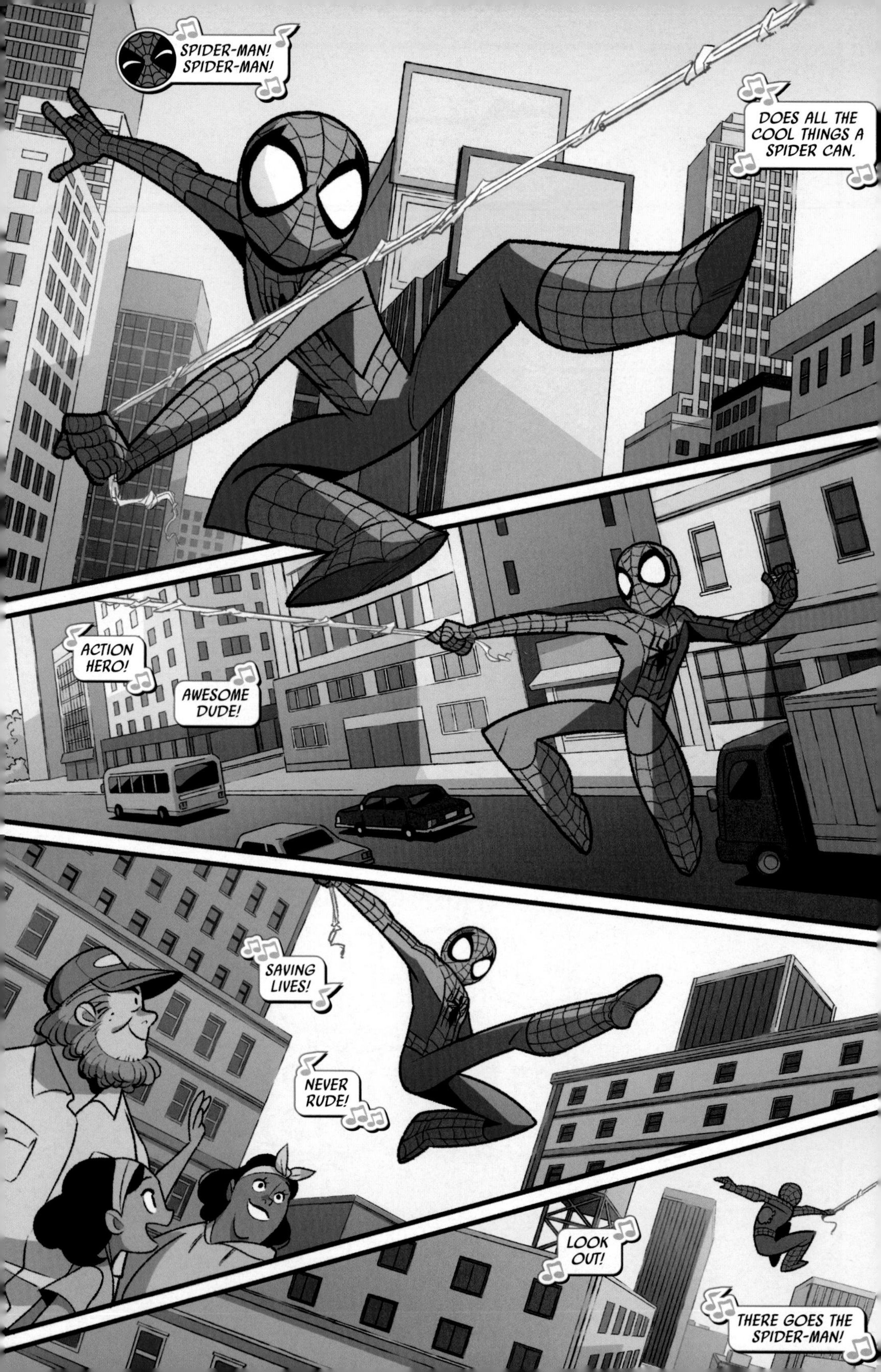
SPIDER-MAN! SPIDER-MAN!
DOES ALL THE COOL THINGS A SPIDER CAN.
ACTION HERO!
AWESOME DUDE!
SAVING LIVES!
NEVER RUDE!
LOOK OUT!
THERE GOES THE SPIDER-MAN!

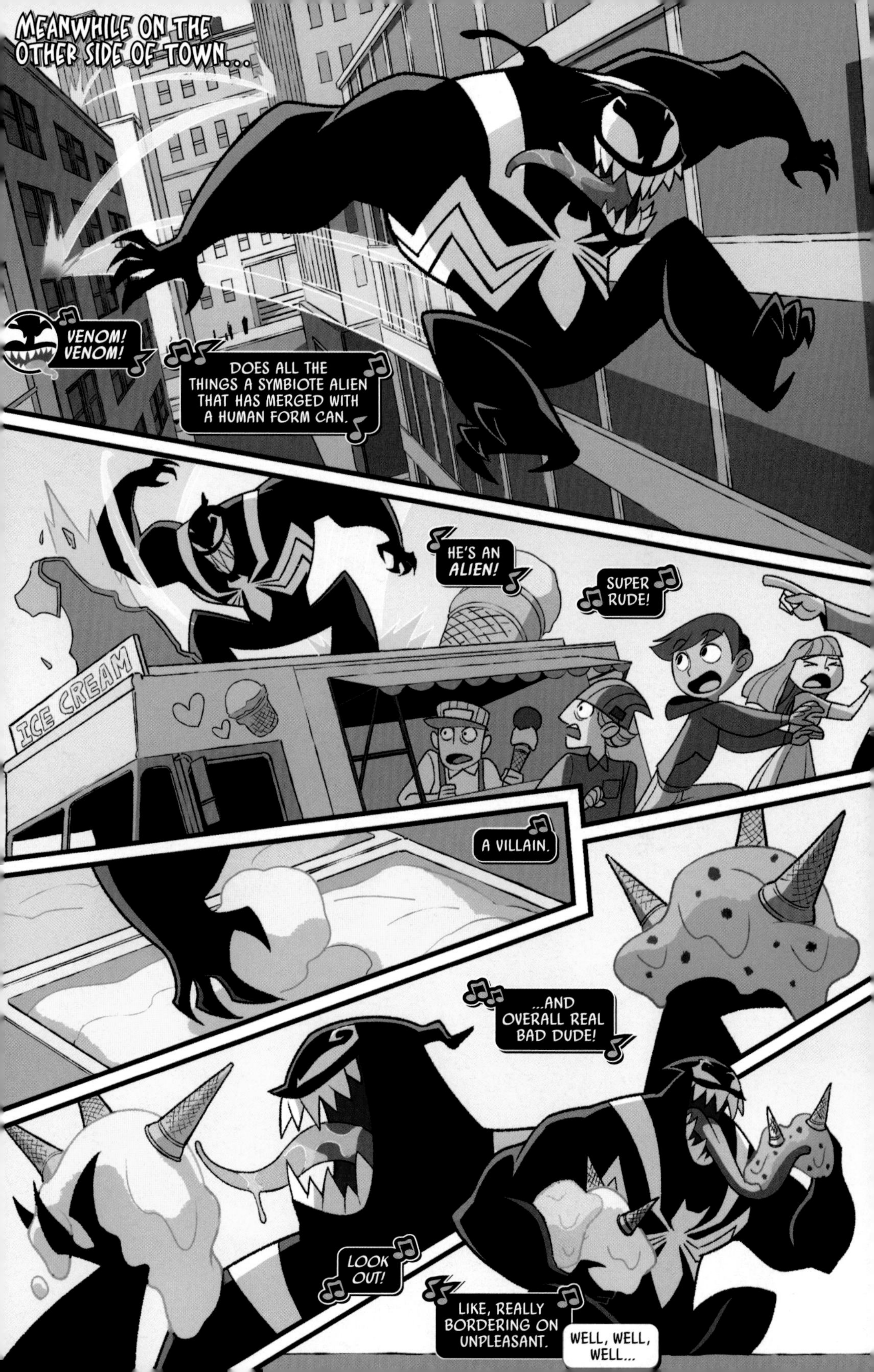
MEANWHILE ON THE OTHER SIDE OF TOWN...
VENOM! VENOM!
DOES ALL THE THINGS A SYMBIOTE ALIEN THAT HAS MERGED WITH A HUMAN FORM CAN.
HE'S AN ALIEN!
SUPER RUDE!
ICE CREAM
A VILLAIN.
...AND OVERALL REAL BAD DUDE!
LOOK OUT!
LIKE, REALLY BORDERING ON UNPLEASANT.
WELL, WELL, WELL...

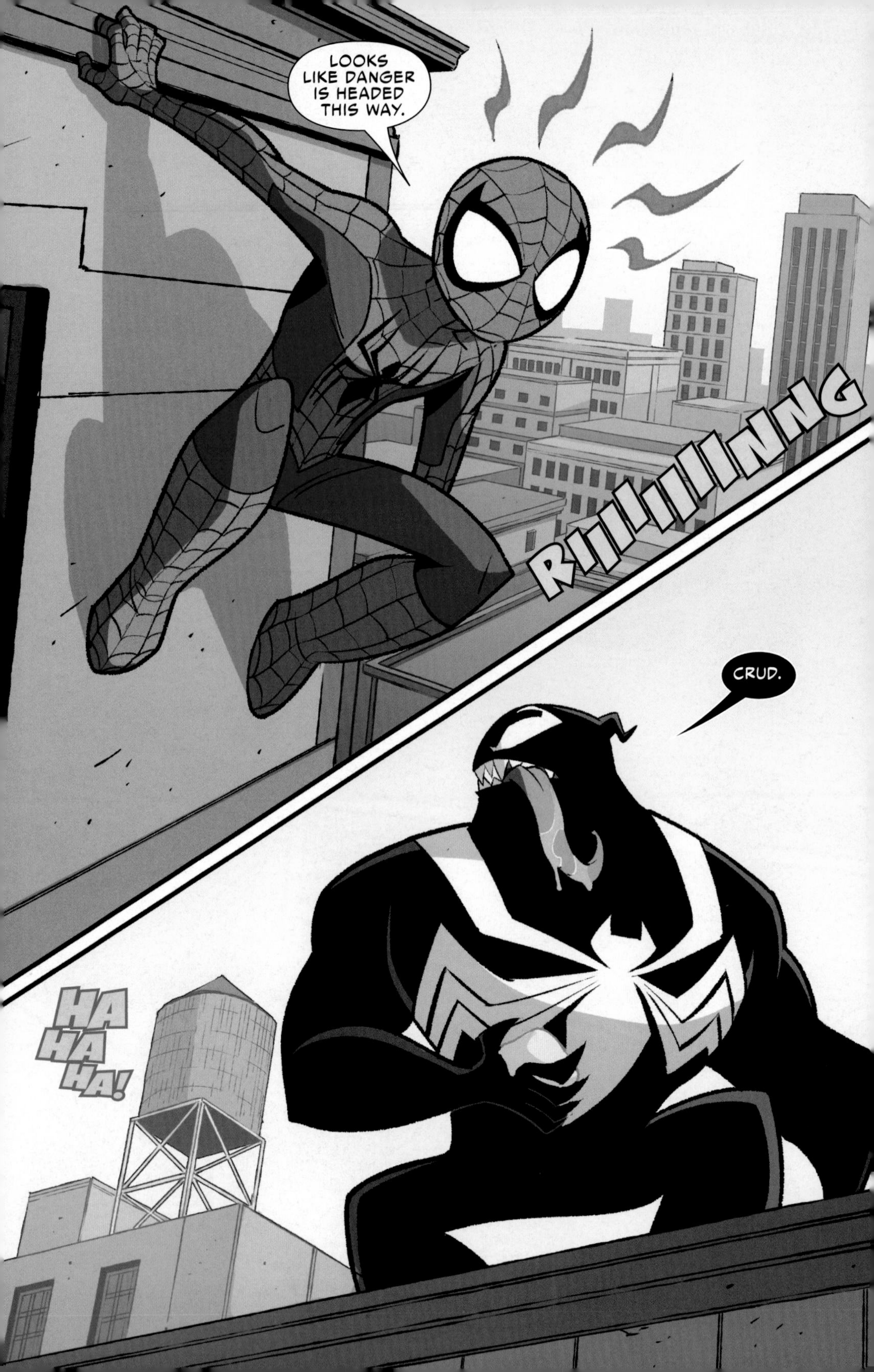
LOOKS LIKE DANGER IS HEADED THIS WAY.
RIIIIIIINNG
CRUD.
HA HA HA!

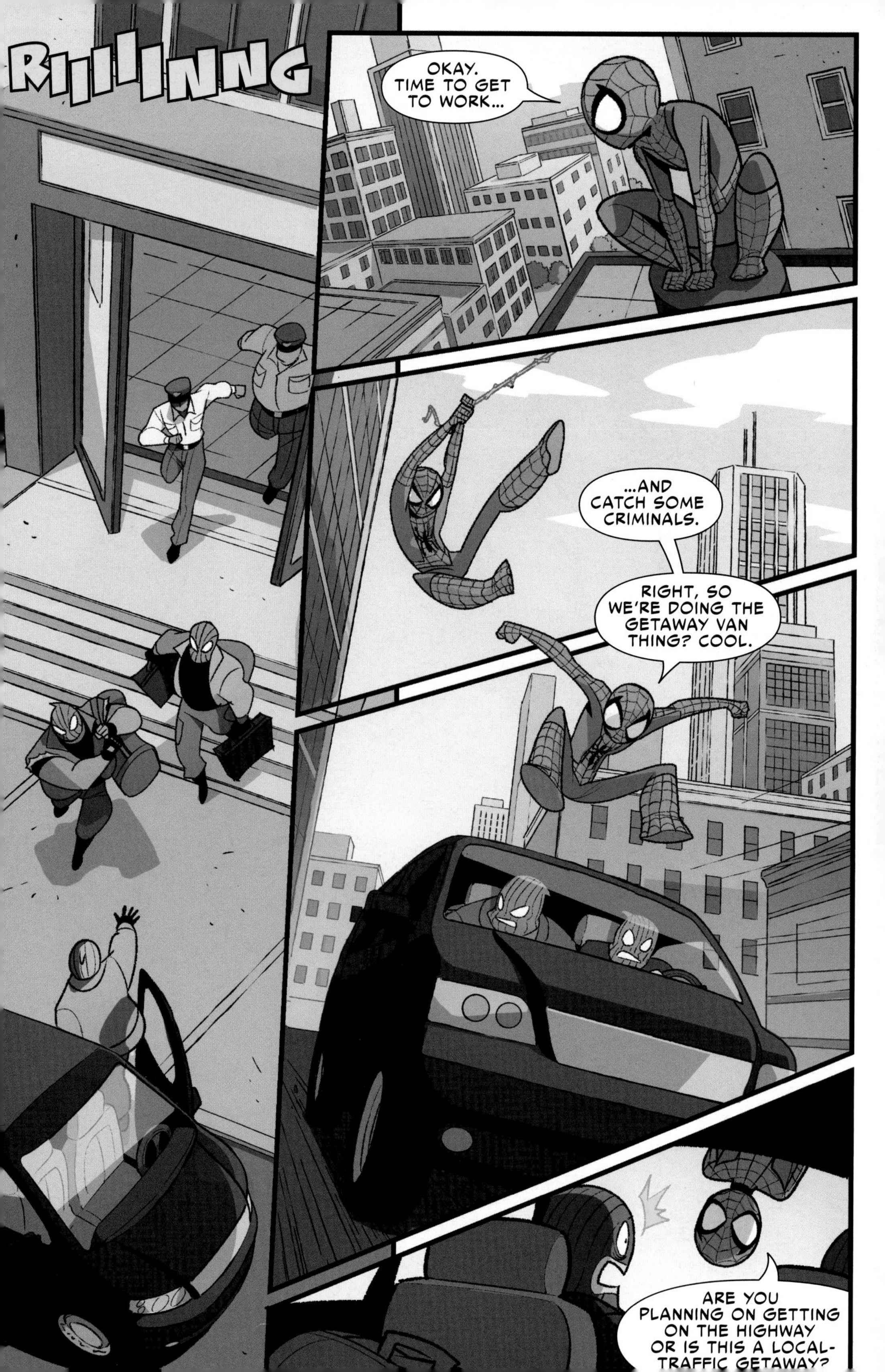
RIIIIINNG
OKAY. TIME TO GET TO WORK...
...AND CATCH SOME CRIMINALS.
RIGHT, SO WE'RE DOING THE GETAWAY VAN THING? COOL.
ARE YOU PLANNING ON GETTING ON THE HIGHWAY OR IS THIS A LOCAL-TRAFFIC GETAWAY?

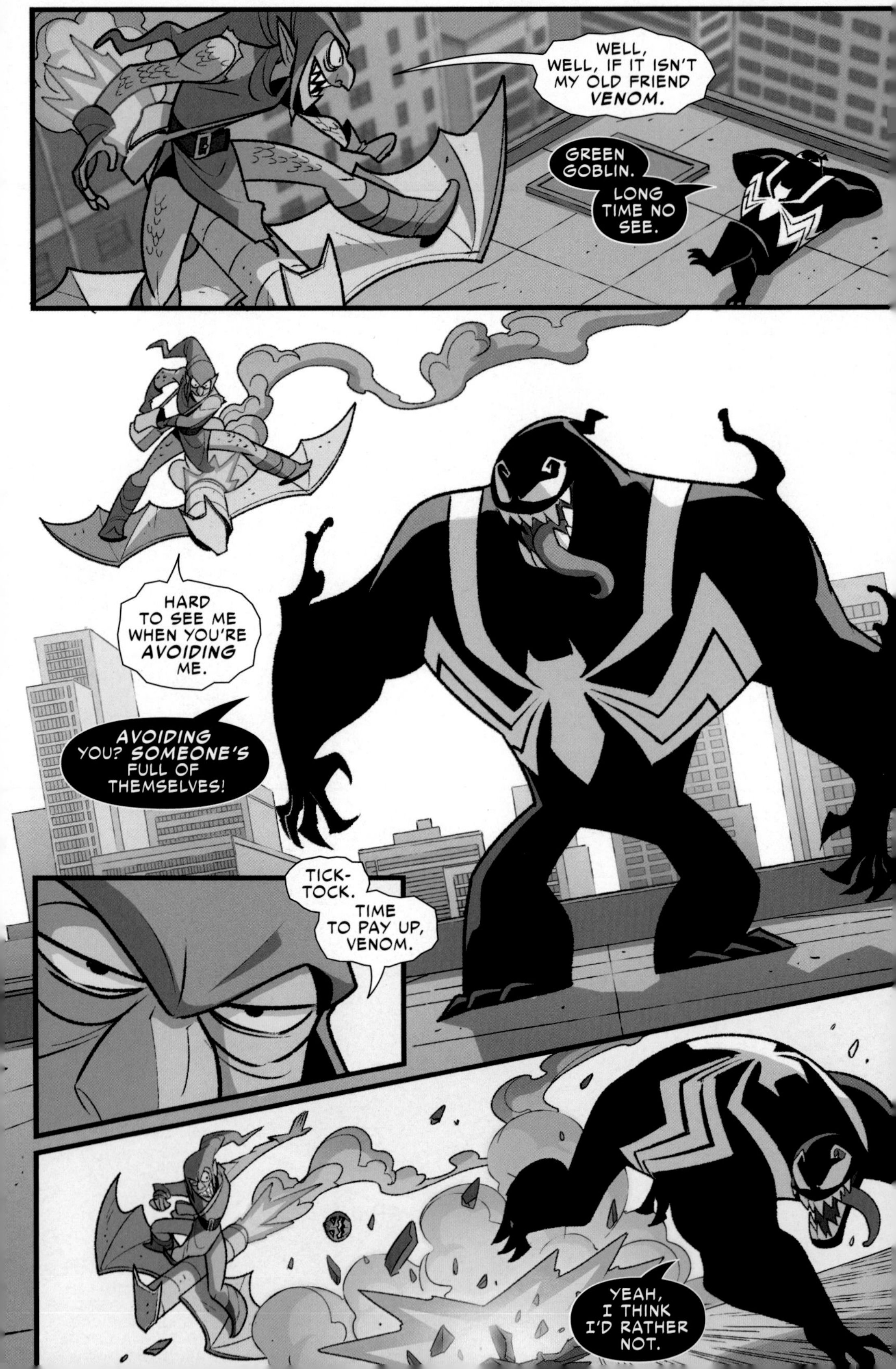
WELL, WELL, IF IT ISN'T MY OLD FRIEND VENOM.
GREEN GOBLIN.
LONG TIME NO SEE.
HARD TO SEE ME WHEN YOU'RE AVOIDING ME.
AVOIDING YOU? SOMEONE'S FULL OF THEMSELVES!
TICK-TOCK.
TIME TO PAY UP, VENOM.
YEAH, I THINK I'D RATHER NOT.

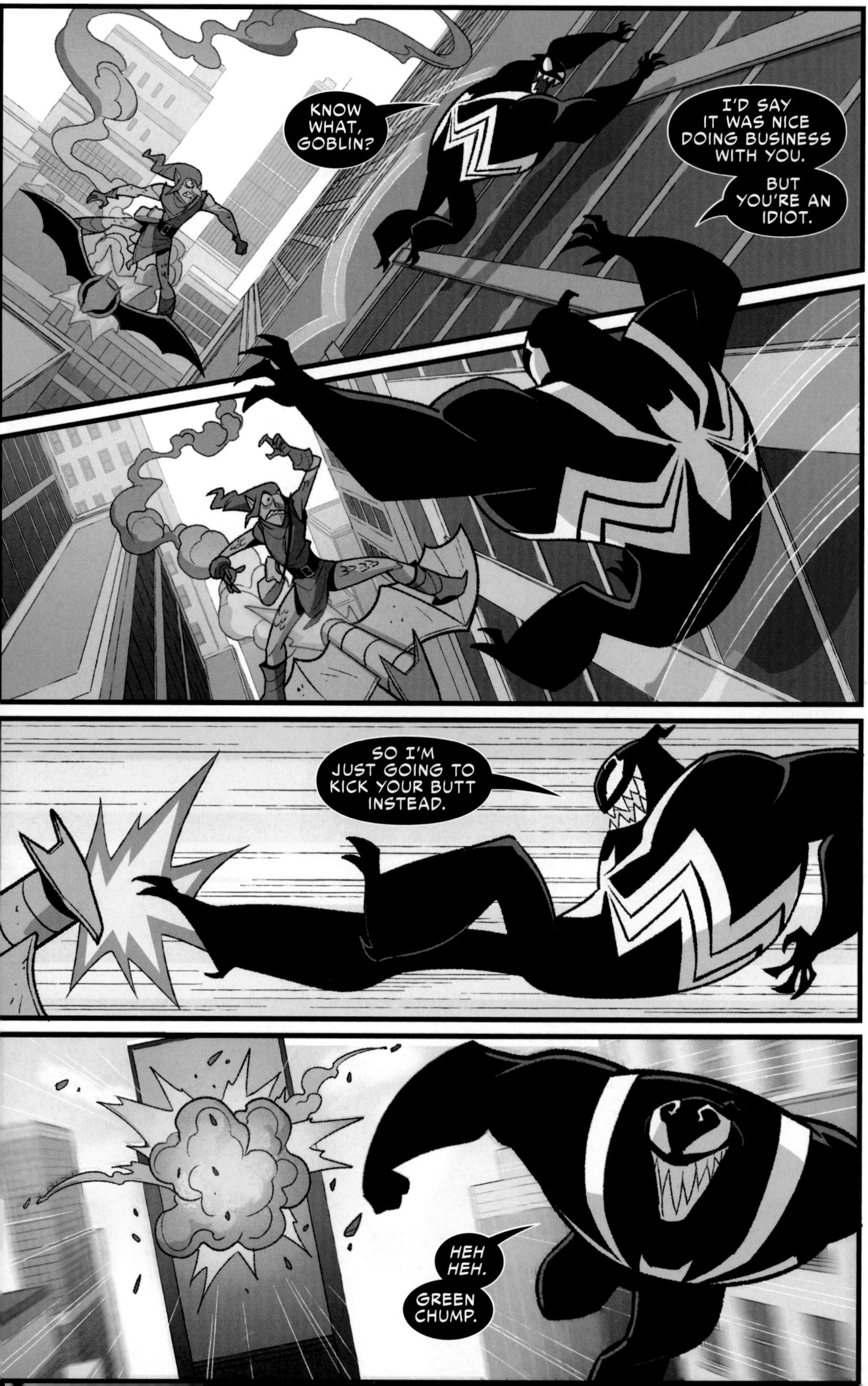
KNOW WHAT, GOBLIN?
I'D SAY IT WAS NICE DOING BUSINESS WITH YOU.
BUT YOU'RE AN IDIOT.
SO I'M JUST GOING TO KICK YOUR BUTT INSTEAD.
HEH HEH.
GREEN CHUMP.

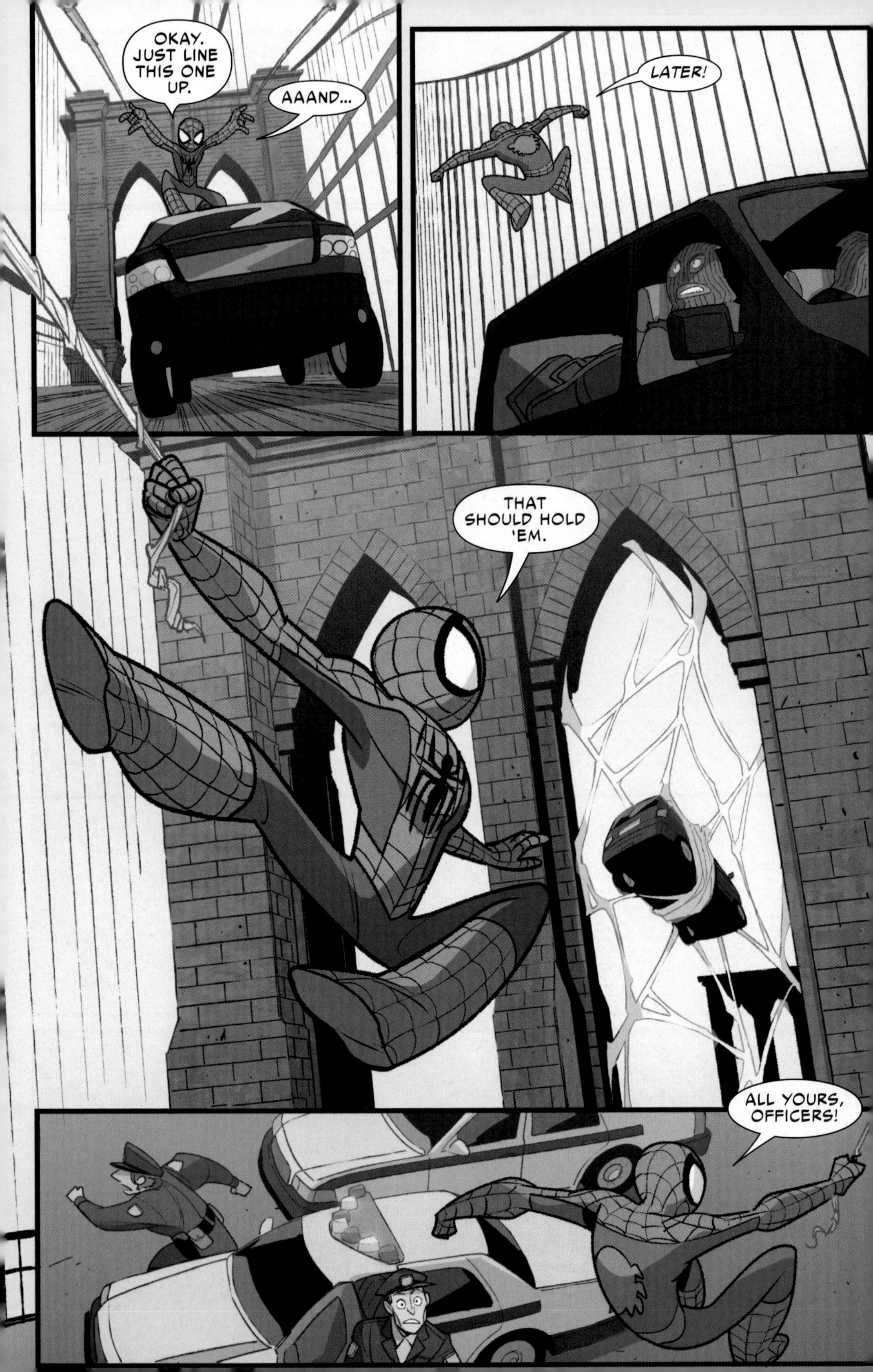
OKAY. JUST LINE THIS ONE UP.
AAAND...
LATER!
THAT SHOULD HOLD 'EM.
ALL YOURS, OFFICERS!

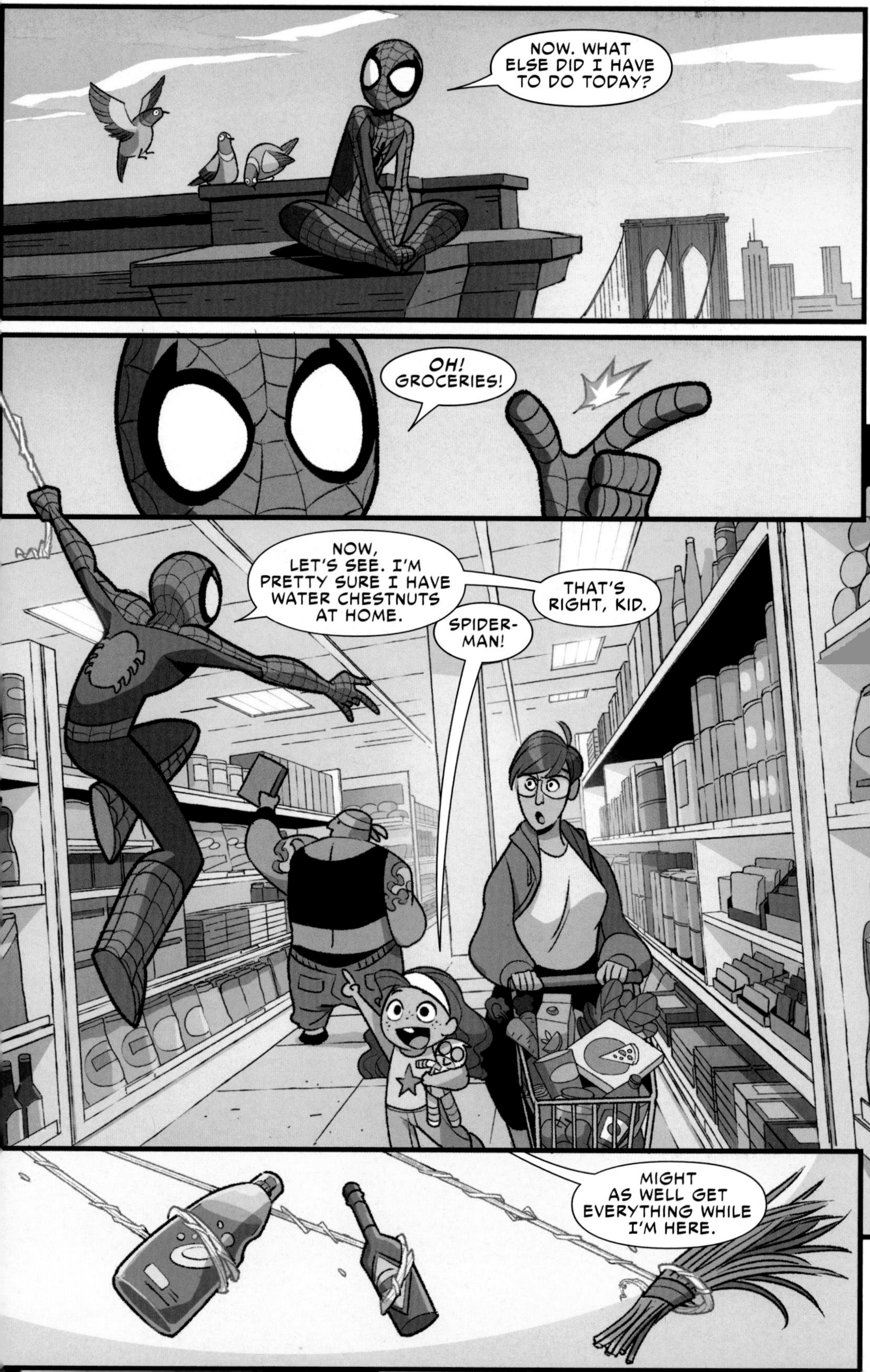
NOW. WHAT ELSE DID I HAVE TO DO TODAY?
OH! GROCERIES!
NOW, LET'S SEE. I'M PRETTY SURE I HAVE WATER CHESTNUTS AT HOME.
THAT'S RIGHT, KID.
SPIDER-MAN!
MIGHT AS WELL GET EVERYTHING WHILE I'M HERE.

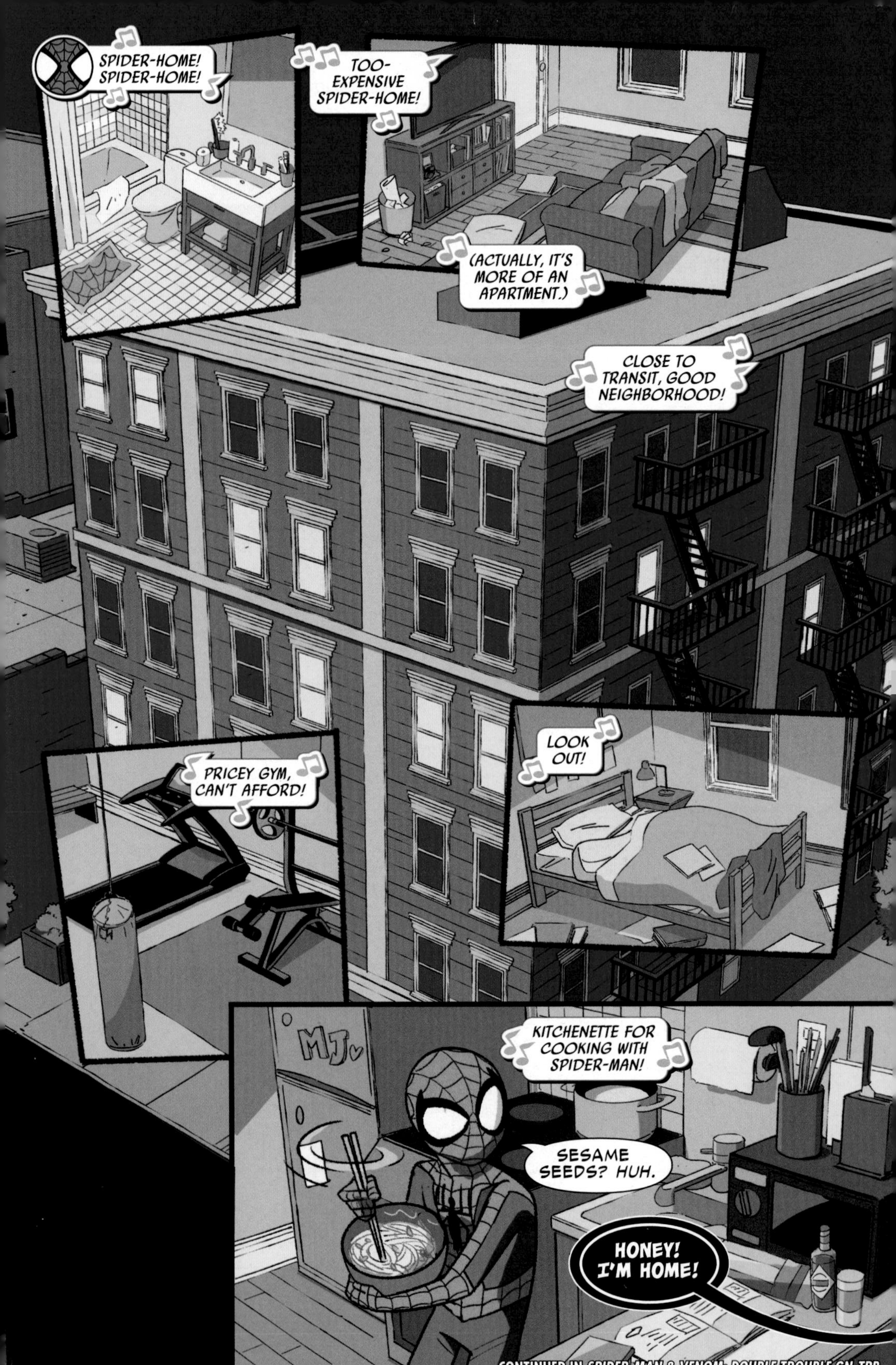
SPIDER-HOME! SPIDER-HOME!
TOO-EXPENSIVE SPIDER-HOME!
(ACTUALLY, IT'S MORE OF AN APARTMENT.)
CLOSE TO TRANSIT, GOOD NEIGHBORHOOD!
PRICEY GYM, CAN'T AFFORD!
LOOK OUT!
MJ
KITCHENETTE FOR COOKING WITH SPIDER-MAN!
SESAME SEEDS? HUH.
HONEY! I'M HOME!

CONTINUED IN *SPIDER-MAN & VENOM: DOUBLE TROUBLE GN-TPB.*